INTO THE GLOAMWOOD

Sarah G. Matthews

INTO THE GLOAMWOOD

ISBN (e-book): 979-8-9948548-0-8
ISBN (paperback): 979-8-9948548-1-5

Published by Sarah G. Matthews

www.sarahgmatthews.com

Dedicated to my family. Thank you for the imaginary adventures, epic duels with sticks, wrong turns on road trips, and shenanigans, but most of all for the love and caring that is at the heart of this book.

To ↑ Lands of Lurin
Griffin Highlands
GRIFFINS!
BEWARE! TROLLS
Gloamwood
Tree of Life
BOG SPRITES
TROLLS
TROLLS
Mt. Cauldra
Gailstone
Boar's Tusk Peninsula
(also Badlands)
Shalindale
Twin Rivers
BANDITS
Milk Road
Bristleback
Florin
Drain
BANDITS
LIONS
Mountains
Valencia
Miramar River
Lightwood
Oddment
Miritown
West Rolindale
East Rolindale
The Capital
Badlands
BEWARE UNICORNS
Midnight Bay
Crescent Coast
Windlorn Road
(maybe not real?)
N
W
E
S
The Lands of Stalt
(mostly. approximately. I tried.)
– Corrin

CHAPTER ONE

Bathilda's Request

In the dappled light of a verdant forest, there stood a fortress older than anyone could remember. Tendrils of ivy blanketed the weathered stone walls. Watchtowers sprouted crookedly from the corners; they scarcely looked steady enough to support the roosting crows and sparrows, let alone the handful of guards who idled atop them. The gate stood perpetually open, tremendous, as if the building wanted to swallow the world. The forest, in turn, seemed as if it wanted to swallow the fortress. It seemed to have *already* swallowed the lass who walked beneath its tree boughs, making her way toward those wide-open gates.

The lass, named Corrin, was a slight girl of seventeen. Years of exploring the woods had freckled her from head to toe, and her bright green eyes scanned the undergrowth alertly, though not fearfully. Her hair was red as fire, and her spindly fingers rested lightly on her satchel, which bulged with the bounty she'd gathered from the woods: medicinal herbs, berries, mushrooms... She'd spent all morning clambering up trees and poking around bushes and roots, busy as a squirrel before winter. Not that she minded—at least, she didn't mind the task itself, though she wished there weren't such a dire need for it.

Medicine kept running out awful fast, as of late. The contents of her satchel would last a few days, maybe. Maybe less. Nothing for it, though, except to keep trying, keep helping.

Corrin shook her head and kept walking.

As Corrin neared the fortress, she perked up. She might not know when the fortress had been first built or by whom, but she knew her ancestors had repurposed it at some point, like foxes claiming an abandoned badger-hole, and she knew those ivy-covered walls meant safety and familiar faces. These days, this fortress was the village of Oddment, and it was the only home she'd ever known.

A guard kept watch above the gate—an official posted specially with a few of his brethren from Stalt's capital, to assist and protect Corrin's village when need be. If need be. He didn't look so official, though, clad in piecemeal leather-and-metal armor and leaning casually against the parapet. He looked a mite too relaxed for someone who was supposed to be keeping watch, in truth. But then, she supposed she'd be relaxed too, just sitting and staring out at the woods, looking for troublesome creatures and scarcely finding any. She'd probably be bored out of her mind.

"Hello," Corrin called as she reached the gate. "Feeling alright?"

The guard straightened. "Doing just fine, miss! So far, anyway!"

"Good! Please keep it that way, sir!"

He laughed, like she'd told some kind of joke, and waved her onward.

Inside, Oddment was a maze of walls and small courtyards, with belongings and gardens cluttering the green spaces. Apartment doorways peeked out from the curtains of ivy. Corrin hurried along, stepping over firewood that had toppled out of its stack and giving passing waves to her neighbors. Ordinarily, there would be twice as many people out and about, and they'd be much more talkative. But recently, the village had been experiencing a surge in illness—more at once than Corrin had ever seen, and more persistently than a typical cold or flu. Many had fallen sick over the past several weeks, and so far, they weren't recovering, no matter what she and her teacher tried.

None dead. Yet. But the illness's persistence was most concerning. And those who caught it were gradually worsening, progressing from fatigued to wheezing to practically bedridden…

A tortoiseshell cat trotted out of the shadows, meowing, her tail held aloft like a banner pole. Corrin tried to steel her heart against the warm press of fur against her ankles and the pleading amber eyes, but the cat, whose name was Tiptoes, wouldn't let up. Corrin relented, sparing her a coo and a scratch under the chin, then moved on, her heart marginally lightened. The village cats, at least, seemed unaffected.

At last, she reached a secluded corner of Oddment and stopped at an oaken door nestled among the vines. An intricate rope crafted from vines, crow feathers, and a bell hung from a peg on the door, signifying the elder healer's status and her pledge to treat all who came knocking. Gifts from the village lay in boxes and sacks outside—a tradition to help sustain their healer, so she could in turn look after all their health. *Bathilda must've not had time to bring them in yet,* Corrin thought as she stepped around the boxes. *We've been awfully busy lately.*

Gently, she opened the door and peeked in.

Bathilda's apartment was dimly lit, with a small hearth-fire and thick shadows in the corners, and smelled of plants and earth. Herb bundles hung from the ceiling, brushing the unaware on the head. Corrin expertly evaded them and called out softly, "Hello."

Fabric rustled, and Bathilda stepped into the light. She was shorter even than Corrin, with a bun as wispy and white as dandelion seeds. Her face was riddled with wrinkles and laugh lines, a map of a life long lived, and her eyes were pale grey, as if they'd once contained color but been leeched of it. Her shoulders and arms were shrouded in a dark cloak. Bathilda was seldom without this cloak; she claimed her bones were too creaky to handle the cold, even in the temperate springtime. Her gnarled hands clutched a wood-carved staff.

No one in Oddment knew how old she was. If asked, Bathilda would just wink and say "older than dirt," her eyes twinkling with mirth. Corrin thought that was probably true. She also thought it a trivial truth, if one wanted to get real technical about it. Some dirt was young, made anew from recent decay. Bathilda was oldish, though, for sure.

Bathilda mustered up a kindly smile and beckoned Corrin over. "Hello, Corrin! Brought me a bounty, eh?"

"Yes ma'am." Corrin emptied her satchel on Bathilda's work table and separated out its contents. "Feverfew, marigold, black-cap mushrooms, blood berries—" She continued to rattle off her findings as she sorted them, and before Bathilda could ask, Corrin zipped over to the shelf and pulled out equipment for medicine-making. Corrin mumbled measurements and directions to herself as she worked. She had the formula for this blend memorized. It eased the worst of the lung congestion and seemed to slow down the illness's progression, a bit. "I was wondering," Corrin said aloud as she pounded the ingredients into a paste. "Maybe there's something in that book of pressure therapies? I haven't looked real hard at that one yet. I know it's more injury things than sickness things, so I figured it wasn't a good bet, but..."

Bathilda shuffled behind her, her staff clunking on the flagstones. "'Tis a good thought to check, but I already did. Nothing we can use right now, aside from light massage for the muscle aches."

Corrin carefully meted out doses of the paste into glass vials. Giving the wrong amount of this medicine could lead to unwanted side effects. Eventually, Corrin paused between vials to hum her acknowledgement. "And we checked all your disease dictionaries?"

"Every last one, my dear. Nothing we're trying is working. I don't know what this is, but I can't cure it through ordinary means."

"We'll figure it out," said Corrin determinedly.

Bathilda sighed. "You have too much faith in me."

"My faith is evidence-based." Corrin tried to keep her tone light and cheeky.

Bathilda shook her head and said nothing.

Corrin frowned. It was rare to see Bathilda so down. Awfully concerning. But she didn't know what to do about it, other than help with treatments as best she could. Corrin put several of the vials in her satchel. "I can do rounds," she offered. "Visit patients on the far side of the village, save you a bit of walking?" Corrin was already reaching for a soap bar and washcloth to add to the satchel. She'd wash her hands between visits. As Bathilda had taught her when she was merely eight years old, cleanliness hampered the spread of sickness. They hadn't yet identified the infection vector, but Corrin liked to think that the handwashing was helping. Whatever it was, it didn't spread as quickly as the winter sniffles, though having sick family and friends did seem to increase the risk…

Corrin's family hadn't fallen sick. Yet. She dearly hoped it would stay that way.

Bathilda's voice pulled her out of her thoughts. "Thank you, Corrin." Bathilda mustered up another smile and waved her staff. "Go on! Spare these old bones some labor."

Corrin started with Petuni's place.

Petuni was a mere ten years old, the same age as Corrin's twin brothers, and one of their best friends. She was a spirited lass, always teaming up with Frendel to coax Sam into mischief like scampering along the ramparts or running off to jump in woodland ponds. She was a curious lass, too, and prone to getting underfoot, or so some of Corrin's elders claimed.

Right now, however, Petuni was neither mischievous nor curious. She was a tiny, frail body laid up in bed, whimpering, while her father, a man named Drey, looked on anxiously.

"She's worsened again," he informed Corrin. His voice rasped. "I'm having a nightmare of a time convincing her to eat."

Corrin's heart sank. "Does she still take warm broths? And small snacks with jam?"

"She drinks the broths if—" he coughed—"if I ask her. Low on jam, but I—I could try…"

Corrin coaxed Petuni up to sitting, a hand at her back, and checked her temperature. Poor girl was burning up, to an extent that Corrin recognized as dangerous. Corrin sucked in a breath, then requested a cup of broth or water. *Dehydration's a killer,* Corrin thought grimly, *and this sickness is cooking and sweating the moisture right out of her.* While Drey fetched some broth from a cauldron in the hearth, Corrin withdrew yet another vial, this one with less medicine in it than most of the others. "This'll make the fever a bit better," she promised. "Half dose only. You don't have to take as much of this stuff as the adults."

Petuni scrunched up her nose and turned her head away.

"I'm sorry," said Corrin softly. "Bathilda and I are trying to find a cure so you can go out and play with my wayward brothers again. But for now, this is the best we have. S'better than leaving the symptoms untreated. Please, trust me."

Petuni hesitated.

"I'll ask my mum and da if we can send over some elderberry jam for you," Corrin promised. "You like jam as much as I do, don't you? On fresh-baked bread?"

Tentatively, Petuni nodded. She relaxed and accepted the vial of medicine, though her nose scrunched again at the bitter taste. Her father returned with a mug of broth, and Petuni sipped it, pausing every once in a while to cough.

Inwardly, Corrin breathed a sigh of relief. She brushed a lock of sweaty hair off the girl's forehead, then soaped up her hands and turned to Drey. "Your turn," said Corrin firmly. "Medicine and broth, and you should spend some time resting in your armchair."

Drey actually laughed, though it turned into a cough at the end. "Bathilda made a good call, taking you on as an apprentice."

"I hope so," said Corrin mildly. She washed her hands once more, just to be safe, then handed him the medicine.

Drey grimaced as he downed it, then sobered as he gazed upon Corrin. "Any progress on figuring out what in the starlands this illness is?"

Corrin frowned. "We ruled out pneumonia and several others, but we haven't been able to rule any *in,* even after scouring all our texts and comparing notes, and we're still not sure where it originated. I'm wondering if, maybe, it came from something in the woods, though. Something that jumped to us from a creature in there. First people to catch it were hunters, though not every hunter's caught it." She paused. "And I mean this in the nicest way possible, but Petuni has always been an adventurous sort. I know she loves the woods quite as much as my brothers."

"That she does, just like her mother. And like you, by my recollection."

"Not quite. I like the woods for their quietness, sir, not so much for adventures."

"Hm." Drey sat back in his armchair and peered up at her. For a second, Corrin thought he might try to argue with her; but instead, Drey asked, "You're feeling alright, though? And your family?"

"We're alright," Corrin confirmed. "So far." She shouldered her satchel and passed Drey the old quilt lying a few paces away from his chair. "Take care, Drey. And you too, Petuni."

Drey waved feebly. "Take care, Corrin. We can't be healed if the healer falls sick."

"Thank you. I'll pass that on to Bathilda, too."

Corrin took a breath, squared her shoulders, and set out for the next house.

Corrin stopped by door after door, visiting neighbor after neighbor. Each time, she took out her washcloth, soap, and canteen and scrubbed her hands outside the door. Each time, she knocked gently and called out, "Hello?" The door always opened for her, but reactions varied. Sometimes, the neighbor who greeted her was a harried and exhausted spouse; once, a fretful child. Sometimes, the sick dragged themselves to the door to admit her, for they did not live with anyone who was well. Every time, though, it was a face Corrin knew, and she greeted them with warmth and sympathy in equal measure. She tried very hard to convince some of the more stubborn ones to rest and take their medicine. *Jallen's breathing is getting worse,* she thought. *He shouldn't be trying to labor in his forge. And poor Evelyn, caring for her mum. I'm worried she'll catch it next…*

Some of them were grumpy, but some of them were kind, returning Corrin's warmth as best they could. Sweet Miriam asked after Corrin's family and apprenticeship even as she slumped in bed, sweating and wheezing something awful while Corrin checked her vitals and helped her tip medicine into her mouth.

Corrin stepped out the door and closed it softly behind her. She breathed out. The midafternoon sun beat down on the clearing in front of her, illuminating a few gardens in need of weeding and crates of supplies and tools left about, as well as two cats sunning themselves in a patch of grass. Corrin resisted the urge to sit down with the cats. How many households did she have left? She leaned against a wall of stone and ivy and started ticking them off in her head. She might be almost done. For the day, anyway. Tomorrow, she should visit some others...

A familiar child's cry yanked her out of her thoughts. "Corrin!"

Corrin startled and turned.

Her brother Sam raced toward her, practically flying across the grass and dirt. At ten years old, both he and his twin, Frendel, bore a passing resemblance to Corrin—lightweight and bony-shouldered, with pointed noses, narrow faces, and freckles as numerous as the stars. But their hair was light brown instead of red, and while Corrin had green eyes, theirs were hazel. They were also far more mischievous than Corrin had ever been, no matter what some elders claimed to the contrary.

Even so, neither would cry wolf. The look on Sam's face sent a spike of alarm through her.

He grabbed her arm, frantic. "Corrin! Corrin! Da's sick!"

Corrin's heart dropped like a stone. But she made herself say, as she had for so many others, "Okay. Take me to him, please."

Da sat in their apartment's armchair, his weather-beaten face unnaturally pale. He was a bearlike man, with hairy arms, a bushy brown beard, and shoulders so large that Corrin could probably still ride on them if she tried. But his green eyes were kindly and full of laughter. Even now, slumped and with a sheen of sweat upon his brow, he smiled up at Corrin's mum.

Corrin's mum, a short, auburn woman with clever fingers, cleverer hazel eyes, and a mind as sharp as the hunting knife at her belt, fussed over him. "If the twins hadn't fetched me," she said sternly as she swept a kerchief over his brow, "who knows what would've happened? They told me you keeled right over in front of them, you daft llama. Why didn't you come home sooner?"

Her da chuckled weakly. "I was hale and hearty until all of a sudden I wasn't. Ah, Corrin!" He beamed at her, then began to rise. He was trembling.

"Da," said Corrin severely, and pushed him back into the chair. Her fingers skated over his forehead and the insides of his wrists. His face was warm. Hands clammy. Pulse still steady, but feebler than she would've liked. His lips weren't dry, but she pushed a flask of water into his hands anyway. His breathing sounded wrong—not as clear and effortless as it should've been.

Sam hovered anxiously around Mum, who let out a slow breath and ruffled his hair. "Go, get some jam from the kitchen," she said, and he scurried off.

"Did the lad interrupt your work to make you fuss over me?" asked her da, twinkling up at Corrin. "Aren't I a lucky man, to have a family that spoils me so much."

"Da, shush." Corrin pulled out a vial full of pale green liquid. "Take this. You've got a fever."

As her da sipped the potion, shuffling footsteps and the *tap-tap-tap* of a staff crossed the threshold, and Bathilda entered with Frendel at her heels. Corrin surmised that Frendel must have gone to fetch her mentor while Sam had searched for Corrin. Bathilda gave Corrin a nod and spoke softly with Corrin's mum, asking questions about the onset of his symptoms and offering explanations as Corrin peered into her da's eyes and poked around his ears.

Bathilda had once told Corrin that a good part of healing was putting people at ease. *Can't help them if they're too scared to let you,* she'd said one day, speaking over the wailing of a scratched up five-year-old. *Comfort them, inform them, tell stories or distract them… A pliant patient is a patient more quickly healed.*

Her mum fell squarely into the needs-to-be-informed camp, much like Corrin herself. Her da, on the other hand, was happiest distracted. Jokes of the terrible da-pun variety were his favorite, but any friendly company would do, for which Corrin was thankful. Unfortunately, she was at a loss for humor. The best she could do was rehash her da's puns.

Corrin plucked a few tiny twigs and leaves out of his hair, frowning. He must have fallen into the undergrowth.

"Can't be-leaf it," said her da, shaking his head. "Knocked into the bushes by the first sprout of illness."

"Unbe-leaf-able," Corrin agreed dryly. She re-positioned the cold compress on his head.

"You'll heal me with your magic brews, will you?"

"Not magic. Medicine." Corrin kissed his forehead. As a healer, she knew better than to kiss a sick man's forehead, lest she catch the sickness herself. As her da's child, the risk was easily forgotten.

She did a couple of minor things to make sure he was comfortable—drew up the good quilt around his shoulders, made sure he kept sipping his potion, got an extra pillow to place behind his head. Her da had similar first-stage symptoms as the rest of the sick villagers, the ones she and Bathilda couldn't cure, though the onset of his fatigue had been particularly sudden. It wasn't bad yet. Maybe he'd be up and wanting to walk again after resting in his armchair a bit. It would get worse, though. If her da followed the trend, he'd be bedridden within a month.

A gnarled hand rested on Corrin's shoulder, startling her. "I'll be going back to my place," said Bathilda quietly. "Taking care of odds and ends. Got many more patients to see."

"Okay," Corrin whispered. Her chest felt tight.

"Stay well, my dear." Bathilda shuffled out the door and away, leaving Corrin alone with her worries and a slow-creeping sense of dread.

We've got to find a way to fix this, she thought. *Bathilda might—maybe there's something we missed. Please, please let there be something we missed. Otherwise, they'll…*

I can't lose them.

Once Corrin was certain her da was at ease and her mum alright with taking over again, she hurried out the door. She finished the last couple of visits she'd meant to make that day. Then, under the bruised orange light of sunset, she hastened to Bathilda's home.

"Bathilda," she called as she opened the door. "Can we talk? Please?"

Bathilda looked up from the journal she'd been writing in. Her nose was flecked with ink, the pages in front of her marked up with scribblings. She had several different vials lined up on the counter next to her and a mortar and pestle all gummed up with plant paste. *Must be noting findings,* Corrin thought. *Or calculating portions.* Whatever she was doing, Bathilda seemed to lighten just a touch when Corrin entered the apartment. "Ah," said Bathilda, setting her quill down. "Yes. I was wondering when you might be back." She gestured to the work table. "I'm mixing more medicine for the stores, if you'd like to join me."

Corrin approached the work table, but she didn't sit down at it. "We need to do more than ease the symptoms," she said. "It's been clinging too long."

Bathilda frowned. "I know, Corrin. By the spirits, I know."

"Do you think..." Corrin hesitated. "How much longer do we have to try? If we don't stop the sickness..."

Bathilda's hands stilled in the middle of mixing. Heavily, she said, "It's difficult for me to say, since every illness is slightly different, as is every person. But yes, Corrin, if we do not stop this, people will begin to die. I expect within a month or two, we may see the first deaths. In a few more... well, much of Oddment may perish come winter, including your da. I don't think I can devise a cure before then, not with the ingredients here, nor with the ingredients I'd know from a city market. I'm sorry," she added somberly. "I did warn you, you have too much faith in me."

The slow-creeping dread in Corrin's heart morphed into horror. "We can't—no, there must be something we can do. Anything. Maybe... maybe some healers in the capital know things? A consultation? We could write them. A-and I can reread all the books."

"I can write them, but there's no guarantee they'll have answers," said Bathilda grimly. "Indeed, I think the odds are rather slim. I know most of what the healers in the capital know, and then some. I wrote some of the medical texts in the capital's library, did you know?"

Corrin blinked. "No, um. You never mentioned that." Silently, she tacked on, *Never mentioned much about where you came from or what you've done at all, except in the broadest and vaguest of strokes.* This realization was strangely frustrating. Bathilda had so often nurtured Corrin's curiosity, especially in all matters of medicine, and Corrin had considered her and Bathilda close. But when it came to her life story, well... she'd never talked about it much, and had never seemed willing to.

Corrin mentally shoved this line of thought aside. It didn't matter right now. What mattered was her da, her neighbors, her home. She said, "You should write them anyway. Just to see." Corrin started pacing. "While you do that, I—I'll reread the books, and—"

Bathilda heaved herself to her feet, grabbed her staff for support, and touched Corrin's arm. "Easy, lass. There's one more thing I can think of. A last resort." Bathilda shuffled over and opened a dusty wooden chest in the corner. In all the years Corrin had known her, she'd never seen Bathilda open that chest. It was one of the few things Bathilda wouldn't answer questions about, except to say that its contents were personal and that Corrin had best get back to studying skeletal structures. Now, Bathilda withdrew a folded piece of parchment, yellowed with age. Bathilda shuffled back and placed it on the table, but she didn't unfold it just yet. Lamplight flickered across her solemn face.

Bathilda leaned on her staff and spoke. "I encountered a sickness as persistent as this one years and years ago, before you were born—before your mother was born. It was in a small village, out of the way and peaceful like this one. The village was called Gailstone."

"Was?" Corrin echoed.

"Two thirds of the people fell to the illness within a season. After the quarantine lifted, the remaining third left." Bathilda's voice rasped. "It was a plague unlike any I'd ever dealt with. And while the symptoms here are different—slower creeping, more in the lung and less in the skin—it reminds me of that plague, in the way it clings and resists treatment. I was able to save some of those poor souls in Gailstone, but not with my usual treatments. I needed a cure from the Gloamwood."

Corrin blanched.

The tales claimed that the Gloamwood was the land of Death herself, grown from her sinister powers and full of her creatures—trolls and bog sprites, lying in wait to prey on any who trespassed, and the Churikin, her chaotic helpers. Some said the ghost owls flying around the Gloamwood's edge were the spirits of the stricken, shrieking to warn people off. Others said that anyone who set foot in the forest was cursed. But Corrin didn't need to believe in Death's sickle blade or curses to fear that land. She'd heard too many rumors of bold travelers and trophy hunters who'd entered and never returned. Sane people stayed away from it. Far, far away.

Bathilda finally unfolded the parchment: once, twice, thrice, four times, until it lay flat on the table before them. "A friend made the journey with me and gave me this. An old, brave friend." She sounded terribly mournful as she said this.

It was a map.

The continent had been laid out in thin lines of ink, with winding rivers and city-marks where the people of Stalt had settled. Oddment was among those marks, nestled among the whispering forests in the middle-south. The map was rendered in great detail, though this itself didn't make it remarkable. Corrin had seen the maps Trader Amella brought, sometimes. Amella had once taken her aside and pointed out all her favorite trade routes and some of the cities she'd seen on her travels, including Stalt's capital.

But Corrin had never seen the Gloamwood marked up before, and on this map, that region was riddled with notes. The Twin Rivers snaked through it, unbroken lines weaving from west to northeast. The cartographer had added crude drawings of trolls and other beasts, and they'd written warnings in a tiny, slanting hand. *Beware troll village. Boglands, rife with sink-mud. Bridge is old, can break.* And in the heart of the Gloamwood was a drawing of a tree, labelled *the Tree of Life.*

Corrin blinked. The Tree of Life was a fixture in her people's myths and origin stories, each of which was more far-fetched than the last. Some tales claimed its fruit granted immortality. Others depicted it as a portal to the afterlife. Yet others claimed it could cure any ailment. All of them—every last one—tied it to that twilight boundary between a beating heart and eternal rest.

Corrin had stopped believing in the myths years ago. Something about seeing enough hunted rabbits, maybe. Or reading all those medical textbooks. Or perhaps helping Bathilda give end-of-life care to Old Man Tyrin. His breath had wheezed to a halt, and his eyes had glassed over. His pulse had stopped. He'd turned pale as a ghost-owl's face, and his skin had cooled until it was no warmer than damp earth. The process was ordinary, mundane, almost, and yet it had left her feeling bereft. Just like that, he was gone. He'd never again grumble at the neighborhood children or tell stories at the solstice festivals.

The cartographer couldn't have meant that mythical tree. Not literally, at least.

Bathilda jabbed that tree with her finger. The paper crackled beneath her touch. "Here lies the cure I used. This tree's fruit has healing properties beyond anything else I've seen. It accelerates all the body's repair capabilities, boosts its systems to fix things and fend off sicknesses it ordinarily never could."

Wait, thought Corrin. *Bathilda* ***used*** *that tree's fruit?*

Immortality was implausible. Even Bathilda couldn't stop herself from aging; surely she had grown more wizened in the past decade, at least a little. But medicinal properties in a plant—compounds that bolstered the body's ability to heal, or that warded off certain kinds of sickness—that, Corrin had seen many a time before, and that, she could believe. Particularly if Bathilda herself said it worked.

"I remember them. They were small and round, the size of crabapples but not half as hard. Bright purple." She gazed upon Corrin and said, "You wanted to do something? Anything? Here it is. You must seek out this fruit and bring back as much as you can carry. Stuff your satchel with them, then put more in a pack."

"You want me to go," said Corrin bleakly. She pointed to the Gloamwood. "In there."

"Yes," said Bathilda firmly. "This needs a healer's eyes and a healer's courage, my dear—and a healer's urgency. It will take you at least a month to reach this fruit, and another month to return. Maybe longer. The timing is tight, even if you depart now. If all else fails, we need to have this cure in time."

Corrin gulped. "A soldier's strength and sword skills would do far better than me, by my reckoning."

Bathilda scoffed. "If you can convince one of Stalt's finest to go, I'll eat my cloak."

"What do you mean?" asked Corrin, bewildered. Surely the guards would do it. It was their job to face danger and protect people, wasn't it? That's what they'd signed up for. Corrin had never signed up for anything like that. "It's their job to handle the perilous stuff. They'd be braver than I am, I would think."

"Corrin, my dear, you greatly underestimate yourself. And you greatly overestimate them!"

"Well, it doesn't hurt to ask. I'll try." She picked up the map. "I'll show them this, if you're alright with it."

Corrin could swear Bathilda hesitated, her pale grey eyes flicking between the map and the dusty old chest. But in a blink, her shoulders sagged, and she waved Corrin off. "Alright, lass, give those fools in the guards' tower a try."

Corrin nodded decisively. "They've got to see. I'll convince them." She folded the map, stowed it in her satchel, and strode determinedly out the door. If she made sure they understood that this was Oddment's best chance, that they needed to fight to fix this sickness just like they would fight to protect the village's borders from beasts…

Someone had to go. *Someone* had to help save Oddment. And she thought, surely, that those who'd trained for conflict and crisis would have the best chance.

Bathilda's pale, knowing eyes tracked Corrin down the path. "Luck to you," she called after her. "Would be splendid if I end up eating my cloak!"

CHAPTER TWO

A Bit of Madness

Corrin made her way to one of the four corner towers that rose from the walls of Oddment, where the guards sent from the capital usually liked to stay. The current guard had moved here, oh, about a year ago. They changed in and out, usually switching in a fresh six or seven every couple of years. Corrin knocked, and when a voice called out to invite her inside, she peeked cautiously into the circular room.

The two guards inside were playing a game of Battle Dragon. The board with its little wooden figurines and chips was laid out on a rickety table. The guards had only their leathers on, no metal greaves or breastplates or any other pieces of armor. They greeted her with lazy waves and an invitation to join the game. "Want to pull up a chair?" asked the first, a bearded fellow with a beer belly and a tremendous mustache. He grinned at her. "Watch me crush my pal over here?"

"No thank you," said Corrin politely, while internally, she despaired. If she recalled correctly, this guard's name was Vern. She did not think him the most adept of guards, nor the most wise. Last spring, he'd taken a tremendously foolish dare out of boredom and perhaps too much drink: he'd agreed to stand with an apple on his head and be shot at, with the expectation that the arrow would just barely miss him and pierce the fruit. His companion had mis-aimed a truly impressive amount and hit him instead, and he had (understandably) screamed like a dying creature. His companion had told the tale while Vern quailed in a chair, flinching as Corrin applied numbing salves, removed the arrow, and cleansed and sewed up the wound. Vern had whimpered and squirmed as she worked, though she'd tried to be gentle. She'd felt awful for him at the time, but a mite incredulous, too.

Corrin mentally pulled herself together. *He's still a guard,* she told herself firmly. *He still went through military training, and he can still fight better than I can, if he has to. And that other one hasn't agreed to be shot at on a dare, far as I know.*

She took a deep breath and said, "I need you to do a favor for Oddment."

Both guards frowned. "What kind of favor, lass?" asked Vern.

Corrin explained it all carefully, trying to convey the importance of the quest. The persistence of the sickness. The timeline. The urgent need for a cure. The potential solution that Bathilda had presented. She laid the map on the table and explained where it had come from. "No one who's been lost in the Gloamwood had a map like this to guide them," she concluded. "Not that I've heard, at least. So please. Help us."

The guards balked.

Vern nervously scratched his beard. "That's—well. Our job is to guard this little patch of Stalt. We make sure no bandits or wild beasts make it into your village. The Gloamwood, you see, it's just not in our job description."

The second guard, a short, wiry man with a perpetual scowl, piped up. "How do you even know this fruit will fix things? What if it only fixes one kind of plague?"

Corrin thought she'd told them, but she tried again. "Bathilda said the mechanism of healing—"

Vern raised a finger and cut her off. "Even if the old healer lady is right," he said, as if there were any doubt to this—as if Bathilda weren't a brilliant medical expert but instead delusional, or misguided, or simply not very smart—"the Gloamwood is too much of a risk. No, we'd likely lose our lives, and all for some wild fairytale hope. Best we can do is hope the ill recover, and if need be, set up a quaranti—"

The other soldier elbowed him, cutting him off. "Corrin, isn't it?"

Corrin nodded numbly.

"Alright then. Corrin, go home. Mix your poultices, we'll man the keep, and no one goes into that spirits-forsaken place. We'll send a message to the capital about this town's predicament."

Corrin's throat went tight, and something inside her felt stung. She'd been dismissed. Worse, the wisdom of her mentor had been dismissed, and by the same fool who'd let himself be shot for a game! A pressure built in her chest, a horrible, boiling-over feeling, like she wanted to yell at them. But the guards were already turning away from her, and she had no idea what words to use. She'd never been a yeller, anyway; if reasonable words didn't work, making more noise felt futile. They weren't listening. They wouldn't help, and that was the end of it.

Blast it all, she thought, *Bathilda was right. Of course she was.*

Corrin turned to leave. Just as she drew the door shut behind her, she heard the *thump* of a hand swatting the back of someone's head. The second soldier said, "A quarantine won't help if everyone knows about it and runs all across the realm before we can set it up!"

Corrin retreated to one of her thinking spots. She scaled one of the ivy-covered walls of Oddment, her spindly fingers expertly gripping the vines, and sat with her legs dangling over the edge of the parapet. As twilight descended upon the village, her thoughts churned.

Corrin's and Bathilda's treatments couldn't stop this illness. Their best hope lay in lands that even the guards wouldn't brave. As it stood, the plague would creep in and take everyone, one by one—her da, her neighbors… The phantom of grief pressed in on Corrin, almost like a physical pain. She couldn't let them succumb to this illness. She couldn't bear it.

She had to fix this. But she needed help.

Surely there was someone bolder than both her and the soldiers. Someone well-traveled. Someone who knew their way around fearsome beasts and bandits and other troubles that could pounce on the unwary traveler. Most importantly—and most unlikely—someone who was willing to enter the Gloamwood. But where in Oddment could she find such a person? Where, among the peaceful farmers, quiet hunters, the young, the ancient, and all those laid low by sickness?

It hit her like a lightning strike: *Trader Amella.*

Trader Amella wasn't a soldier or mercenary by trade, but she was the most well-traveled person in Oddment, the most raucous at festivals, and the loudest teller of tales. She claimed to have faced bandits and won all manner of bar fights. She always came back to Oddment with a pack full of rarities from across the land: spices, maps, seashells, silk, fine jewelry, and sometimes a griffin feather or the scale of a sea serpent. She had just returned this past week, in fact. If Corrin knocked on her door, surely she would answer.

Corrin had mixed feelings about Amella. She liked Amella's friendliness and the way she brought stories and high spirits to a crowd. But Amella was also loud and intimidating, and she had a way of talking people into spending more than they meant to. Corrin never dared bargain with her. Sometimes, though she would never say this out loud, she also thought Amella a bit mad.

Then again, a bit of madness might be what she needed.

Like Bathilda, Trader Amella lived in one of the quieter corners of Oddment, out near the edge of the village. Unlike Bathilda, it wasn't because it was a peaceful place to treat patients or peruse medical texts. Amella preferred her apartment because it gave her easy access to the exit gate and the main road.

Amella's donkey, Oatmuncher, drowsed outside Amella's home. He was a grey, round-bellied creature with a fuzzy coat and droopy eyes. He didn't mind much of anything, it seemed. He would tolerate kids playing with his tail and cats winding around his ankles. Sometimes, if he was feeling particularly awake and someone patted him just right, he'd bob his head, as if to say, *Yes, that's the spot, please carry on.*

Corrin petted his nose. He twitched an ear and blinked, but otherwise didn't stir.

Corrin stepped past him and stopped on Amella's doorstep. The door had a boar's tusk mounted on it. It was a fearsome tusk, spanning the length of Corrin's forearm and curving wickedly to a point. It hadn't been there before Amella's most recent trip.

Did she win that in a bar fight, or did she hunt the boar herself? Corrin wondered.

She mentally chided herself for getting distracted, then tapped the door with her knuckles.

No response.

She gulped, then tapped harder. *Rap-rap-rap-rat-a-TAT—*

Hinges creaked, and the door swung inward. Daylight threw Trader Amella into sharp relief. She was a tall woman with nut-brown skin and hair shorn close to the scalp. She wore a doublet, a thick, leathery one designed to take blows, and one she claimed had saved her from a knife swipe more than once. Even at home, she kept a one-handed sword and a hunting dagger belted at her waist.

Her doublet was loose at her neck and her bracers absent from her wrists, and she peered down at Corrin with curious brown eyes. A heartbeat later, a grin split her face, sudden and bright as a sunbeam breaking through clouds. "I'll be starred, it's our resident mini-healer!" said Amella. "I don't think I've ever seen you stop at my home. What's brought you to my doorstep?" With a spark of mischief, she asked, "You aren't here to tell me I'm on my deathbed, are you? Sick as an infected frog and had no idea?"

Alas, Amella's humor was lost on Corrin, mired as she was in anxiety. "I, um. I have a favor to ask."

Amella's eyebrows rose, and her grin dropped. "Well, then. Ask."

Corrin gulped. "Can you, uh, I mean, I need you to, please, go-to-the-Gloamwoodandretrieveacureforme?"

"You want me to what now? No, wait," said Amella before Corrin could try again, "you should come inside and sit down for this. Seems like your favor is going to get complicated."

Amella had a crackling fire in her hearth and woven rugs full of geometric patterns. Her walls and shelves were full to bursting with goods and trinkets. She and Corrin sat around her table, the map spread between them and bottles of ale at hand. Amella got through a third of her bottle, but Corrin's remained untouched; she was too busy talking, explaining all that Bathilda had told her and how the guards wouldn't help. How Amella could help. How Corrin knew she could.

"You would have this map," said Corrin. "You wouldn't be wandering blind, and that's more than—"

"—more than most can say, yes." Amella's eyes reflected the firelight. Her expression was unreadable. "The Gloamwood... by the Churikin, what a thing to ask."

Corrin's hope flickered like a candle in the wind.

Amella took a draught of ale. Corrin waited, scarcely breathing. "All right," said Amella at last. "I'll go."

Corrin opened her mouth to sing her praises and shower her in gratitude.

"*If* you go with me."

The praises died on her tongue.

"Drink your ale, kiddo, you're looking pale as a ghost-owl's face. And hear me out. I'm not going into that forsaken place by myself, no way in stars. Not even for a cause as noble as yours. But with you? We've got a better chance. It's a blessing to have a healer on the road, raises our odds of survival a good bit, and you're a healer if I've ever seen one. Aye," she said, before Corrin could correct her—she was still an apprentice, still learning—"you are, you're good. Besides, you'll know best what this fruit is supposed to look like. So we'll go together." With steel in her eye and fire in her voice, Amella asked, "You in?"

Corrin sipped from her bottle. The ale was sweet and heavy, and it settled warm in her stomach. It would've settled nicer if her insides weren't tying themselves in knots, but alas.

Thing was, Corrin knew her answer. Alone, Corrin would surely end up a snack for a beast. But with Amella, she might—no, she *would* have a chance. A chance for Oddment, for Da... Corrin had to take it, even if the prospect of going left her shaking in her boots.

"I'm in. Th-thank you."

A warm smile split Amella's face. "I'm glad you asked me. You're not the only one who cares about the people here, you know. This village has been good to me." Amella stood and clapped her on the shoulder. "Let's leave at first light tomorrow, before everyone gets sicker and those guards get a quarantine in place."

Corrin told Bathilda first.

Bathilda beamed at her. "Clever, clever lass! You've made a wise choice. Amella will be a good travel companion for you, better than those dufts in the guards' tower."

Corrin's heart pounded with anxiety and anticipation. She went over to help Bathilda mix medicine, but Bathilda pushed her away from the table. "No, you've done your work. You must pack and prepare, and get some rest tonight. You have a long road ahead of you. Oddment is counting on you to return swiftly."

Alive, Corrin mentally added. *Don't die, that's what she's saying. Great. Will do, I hope.*

"Be careful on the road, my dear. Hunt and gather when you can. And when you get to the Gloamwood, watch out for the bog sprites, the riddle beasts, the sink mud, the wyrms, and most of all, the trolls." And then, much to Corrin's surprise, Bathilda embraced her. Her mentor's arms felt thin and fragile as dried twigs, but their hold was tight.

Fondness kindled in Corrin's heart, and she hugged Bathilda back.

"Stay safe," said Bathilda. "I will await your return."

Corrin did not tell her mum and da that she was going to the Gloamwood, specifically. No need, she reasoned, to cause them more distress than was necessary. But she did tell them that she would be leaving to retrieve medicinal ingredients far to the north. Her parents were about as chuffed as one might expect to hear their child was wandering so far afield, which was to say, not chuffed at all.

After his initial protests—"must you go, really?"—her da hid his worry behind a hair-ruffle and a request for souvenirs. Corrin played along. She said she'd bring him back a seashell, or maybe even a book.

Her mum, though, was such a... well, a mum, which was both maddening and comforting in a way Corrin would never admit.

"Why couldn't they send someone else?" asked her mum, as she heaped hard-tack and travel biscuits onto Corrin's sleeping pallet. Corrin attempted to add fresh bread and a jar of elderberry jam to the pile. Her mum whisked that away, convinced that it would spoil on the road and take up needless space, which was ridiculous. Corrin would eat it well before then.

"What's so far north that you can't find in the forests here, anyway?" Her mum aggressively re-folded all of Corrin's spare tunics and pants and placed them in a pile on her floor. She added Corrin's festival vest and tasseled skirt, which were made to flare and twirl in a dance—and which Corrin knew she'd put back the moment her mother turned away. She'd have no use for festival wear on the road.

"How does Bathilda know this cure is worth anything?" Her mum yanked open Corrin's medicine drawer, likely with every intention of sorting through which parts of it to pack, only to stop and frown in befuddlement. Corrin had at least a dozen jars of poultices, as many bandages as clothes, bundles of dried ingredients, a pestle and mortar, and other such tools. No mortal mum could be expected to pick what to pack, not even Corrin's, unless they had a healer's knowledge.

Corrin slid the drawer shut. "I'll handle that, Mum. And I told you, Bathilda's used it before. A long time ago, but she did. It's our best chance of healing everyone, including Da."

And just like that, her mum fell silent. No more *whys* or *whats* or *hows*.

"I'll be back as soon as I can, Mum. I promise. I'll finish packing, and you see to Da, okay? Make sure he drinks his fluids."

Her mum's hug was fiercer than Bathilda's.

Corrin didn't have a chance to tell her brothers until late that night. While she'd been out, they'd left to visit Petuni. Sam in particular had a soft spot for her, and if Frendel didn't pull Sam into schemes himself, Petuni swayed him. When the door creaked open and the twins entered, their worry was palpable. Frendel's brow was furrowed, and Sam's shoulders hunched. *They're as worried about her as I am,* thought Corrin sadly. *Maybe even more so.*

Corrin greeted them with sympathy and a hug, which they bore far more willingly than they usually would. Then she told them that she'd be leaving for the north to retrieve a cure—though, as with her parents, she obscured some details.

Frendel took it well. His expression cleared, and he told her to be fast and to beat up anything that stood in her way. Then he squirmed out of her embrace and charged off to do who knew what.

Sam, though... Sam was quiet. At least, he was until he found her later, when she was trying to pack and mourning the fact that she couldn't simply take her entire medicine cabinet.

"You're leaving tomorrow?" he asked tentatively.

"Yes."

"Is it going to be dangerous?"

"You needn't worry," Corrin said, and hoped her little brother wouldn't see through her. He was perceptive. He might have already figured out the secret of adulthood, which was that adults did all the things that they told children not to do, like lie to make people feel better. "I'll have Trader Amella with me."

"You'll come back, and cure Da and Petuni?"

"Sure will," Corrin said, and hoped she wasn't lying this time. She reached out and ruffled Sam's hair. "Just look after Mum and Frendel while I'm gone. Especially Frendel." She leaned in conspiratorially. "Don't tell him I said this, but I think you're the more sensible sibling. Less likely to get into trouble." She paused. "Which isn't saying much, in truth."

Sam smiled crookedly.

"Go pull Frendel out of whatever mud pit he's jumped into, will you? I need to finish packing."

"Wait!" Sam dug around in his pockets and withdrew something in his clenched fist. He held it out to Corrin and uncurled his fingers, revealing... a rock. It was a nice rock, granted, smooth and rounded with ribbons of quartz decorating its surface, but it was otherwise unremarkable, of no more use than the pebbles Corrin kicked around on the dirt paths. "This is my lucky rock. You can have it. But don't lose it."

Corrin couldn't bring herself to turn him down. "That's very kind of you." She plucked the rock from his hand and put it in her pouch. "I'll take good care of it."

"Okay, good. If you take care of the luck, it will take care of you too."

"O...kay. Thanks."

"Welcome." And with that, he gave her one last, tight hug, then fled.

Corrin rose before the sun, when the land was cast in twilight and orange scarcely tinged the horizon. She crept past the sleeping twins and her da. She embraced her mum, who was awake, and they traded "love you"s at the door. Corrin clung to her mum longer than she would normally, and she slowed down as she crossed the threshold. And when her mum shut the door gently behind her, she had to fight the urge to turn back.

Corrin stepped softly along the paths of Oddment. Tiptoes wound around her ankles and mewed. Corrin regretted that she couldn't spare the little cat any tidbits, but she gave her a chin scratch and a murmur of affection. Tiptoes trotted off with perked ears and her tail-tip curving like a fisher's hook.

"Bye," Corrin whispered after the cat's retreating paw-steps.

Amella waited for her at the western gate. Oatmuncher was with her, laden with saddlebags. He looked ready to fall asleep on his hooves. Then again, he always looked ready to fall asleep on his hooves.

Amella clapped Corrin on the shoulder and grinned. "All right, kiddo," she said. "We're off." She set off, in great long strides that ate up the path before them, with Oatmuncher shambling after her. Corrin nearly had to jog to keep up.

Strangely, they were headed dead west, and the Gloamwood—according to Corrin's map—was dead north. "Where are we going?" she asked.

"Miritown. I have some merchant friends there who sail up along the coast. It'll be faster and safer to tag along with one of them, then go east from the peninsula, than it would be to try walking across the badlands. Trust me on this." Amella clapped Corrin on the back this time, firm enough to make her stumble forward. "Keep the pace as best you can. We've a long road ahead of us."

CHAPTER THREE

Miritown

They climbed hills and traversed woody patches, forded streams and crossed stretches of prairie. Amella chattered endlessly, pointing out how that crumbly-looking dwelling had once been an outpost; or how she liked to camp in that nice hollow on her way back; or how she'd first journeyed along this path coming from Miritown, when she was fourteen and even smaller than Corrin. She told stories, too—about a bear that had nearly decided to eat her, a tangle with a bandit, and a time she saw a firebird.

"There was this wildfire," said Amella as she gave Oatmuncher's lead rope a tug. "Devoured the land and chased me straight on to the river, it did. And wildfires are where you see firebirds. Beautiful hawks. Their feathers are this blazing red with oranges and yellows that catch the light of the flames, so they look like fire themselves—and what they do is, they fly close to the flames and pick off the panicked rodents and rabbits. Savage, brilliant opportunists, they are." Her eyes glinted with admiration. "You ever seen a wildfire yourself, Corrin?"

"No ma'am," said Corrin, and privately thought she could live without ever seeing one.

"Oy, stop making me feel old." Before Corrin could stutter an apology, she grinned and said, "Kidding, but really, no need to be formal with me. Anyway, wildfires. They're beautiful, dangerous things. But let me tell you, they're not the most dangerous thing. At least you'll see a wildfire coming. You won't see the firebird waiting to pluck you off just when your luck's taken a turn for the worse, and your attention is elsewhere." She pointed a finger at Corrin's face. "Tip for the road—when you're most scared is when you most need to keep your head on your shoulders."

"So when I'm panicking is when I need to not panic, is what you're saying."

"I'm not saying it's easy. I'm not saying your heart won't quicken and hammer at your ribcage like it's trying to break out, or that your hands won't tremble, or that every bone in your body won't be screaming at you to flail and run. I'm saying that despite that, you should try to keep your wits about you. 'Tis a skill, and a hard-earned one at that." And out of nowhere, Amella drew her sword and yelled, "*HARR!*"

Corrin jolted and backpedaled frantically. Her boot caught on a rock, or a clod of dirt, or perhaps nothing but thin air—either way, she fell backward with a shout, arms pinwheeling.

Amella towered over her. She sheathed her sword and chortled. "First step will be not tripping over yourself when you run."

Oatmuncher stood calmly behind his master. He bore the expression of an animal who had seen too much of Amella's nonsense to be startled by it. Or perhaps he had no survival instincts, and he'd happily stand in place and munch on grass while someone advanced on him with an axe. Hard to tell with him.

"Maybe if I do that a few more times, I'll train the stumbling out of you." Her eyes gained a mischievous glint. Very concerning.

"Please don't."

They continued on until nightfall. Corrin's legs grew weary, and her stomach ached. But Amella showed no signs of needing rest, and Corrin did not ask. She told herself it was because the sooner they reached Miritown, the sooner she would reach her goal. But in truth, that fall of hers had stung what little pride she had, and she didn't want it stung more.

When the sky turned dark, Amella stopped to set up camp. "I am famished," she said as the two of them gathered wood. "Starving," she insisted as Corrin pointed out that the greycaps were edible, unlike the blackcaps; and that herb over there would aid with digestion; and that one next to it did nothing medically, but was sweet and made potions less foul, so it would work nicely with their stew. "Amazing," said Amella as, at long last, Corrin hoisted Amella's stewpot off the embers. "Smells good enough to be food of the stars."

"Stars don't eat," said Corrin, bewildered.

"Aah, never heard that figure of speech, have you? You all say food of the spirits. The Miritown folks say food of the stars."

"Yes, and neither of them make any sense. The dead don't eat, either."

Amella laughed. "In Miritown, they also call one side of a sailboat 'starboard,' even though it has no stars. You travel enough, you'll hear odd idioms aplenty."

They ate their stew in companionable silence while Oatmuncher grazed behind them. Then Amella volunteered for first watch, and Corrin didn't argue. *Rest! Sweet rest!*

But when she'd rolled out her blanket and swaddled herself in its folds, she couldn't sleep. The rustle of wind in the trees and meadow grass sounded like beasts creeping up on her. The call of a ghost owl nearly made her jump out of her skin; Corrin twisted, and the sight of its moon-white face peering out from the branches sent a chill down her spine.

Willing her heart to calm, she told herself firmly, *It's only a bird. And even if it* ***were*** *a wayward spirit like those old tales say, that doesn't mean it'll hurt me, right? 'Course not.* Corrin lay back down and tried to settle, watching Amella, who in turn watched the flames die down to embers.

When Amella turned and caught sight of Corrin, she chuckled. "You're an anxious one, aren't you? Relax, my startle-prone friend. I've watched nights for years, and we have the valiant Oatmuncher to whisk us away."

Oatmuncher snored.

"Sleep," Amella insisted.

Corrin thought it would be impossible, and she closed her eyes believing she would spend the night staring intently at the backs of her eyelids, dull and dark though they were. But the weariness of a long day's travel weighted her bones, and her worries faded into nothingness.

Amella shook Corrin awake when light had just begun to tinge the horizon, then flopped down on the ground and started snoring without so much as a goodnight. Corrin gave herself a minute to boggle at how easily Amella fell asleep, then turned her attention to the dying embers of their campfire and the sunrise as it seeped across the sky. When the blazing ball of light cleared the skyline, Corrin woke Amella.

They walked until the sun passed overhead and broke briefly for a lunch of hard bread and dried meats. Soon after, they started seeing faces on the road—another merchant, whom Amella gave a wolf's smile; a caravan of performers, who waved and played merry lute chords as they passed; a party of guards on horseback, who grumbled to each other about something or other involving "back in my day" and "lousy new recruits." And then, as Corrin and Amella crested the biggest hill yet, Corrin saw something stranger even than Oddment.

The road ahead of them snaked down a sloping meadow, which ran alongside a ribbon of glimmering river. Beyond that meadow, the river spilled into an expanse of blue that stretched as far left and as far right as Corrin could see, and all the way out to the horizon—and there it met the sky, a lighter expanse of blue.

So this is the sea, she thought.

Supposedly, the sea flowed all the way over the edge of the celestial turtle's shell, which was what the elders said carried the world. A curved turtle's shell, they reasoned, would explain the unevenness of the ground and the way the horizon shifted as one travelled—the world couldn't be flat, so it must rest on something curved. And the owner of the curved thing must be a patient, steady being, to bear a burden so great.

They had never agreed on where all the water went when it spilled over. Corrin had once hypothesized to Frendel and Sam that the sea dispersed into the sky and rained back onto them. Maybe it rose like regular water did when it boiled, in great tendrils of steam under the heat of the sun.

But the sea was not the strange thing, vast and mysterious though it was. No; after Corrin's moment of awe passed, she noticed the truly strange thing—the town on the shoreline.

Despite its peculiarities, Oddment's maze of walls formed a normal square-ish structure, which once upon a time would have made for a sensible fortress. The buildings ahead were not like that. They clustered along the seashore and the riverbanks, a wobbly crescent of wooden structures. They all had angles and curves in odd places, as if they were meant to be something else. Poles stuck out, lopsided, with tattered flags flapping in the wind. The only conventional-looking building was the keep, a stone tower that rose out of the ground a smidge further inland and loomed over everything else. The keep looked so out of place that Corrin felt the urge to hold her thumb up in front of her eye and block it from view.

"Miritown," said Amella happily. "Weirdest, most beautiful town you'll ever see."

Corrin's gaze slid away from the bizarreness before her and shifted to Amella—to the crinkles at the corners of her eyes and the contentment on her face. Amella looked sideways at Corrin, and the contented expression shifted, turning thoughtful. "Y'know," Amella said, "this is a pretty short jaunt from Oddment. Couple of days. You and your family ever come here? See the sights, shop around the market?"

"No ma'am. Uh. I mean. No, Amella."

Amella tilted her head. "Why not?"

Corrin blinked, bemused by the question. "Why would we? We've no family here, nor business."

Amella stared just as bemusedly back. "Don't you ever just want to wander? See new sights, meet new people?"

"Um. Not really. Two days' travel seems awfully far just to see things when we already have such lovely forests at home, and I'm happy enough with the people I already know. Besides," Corrin added defensively, feeling very much like she was being judged, "I have my healer's apprenticeship with Bathilda. I've always got more to help with and learn. Supplies to gather, medicines to prepare, patients to treat, books from Bathilda's library to read and reread... Making sure I know all two hundred and six bones and the different kinds of joints and all the organs and soft stuff in between, and learning about what can ail them and how to treat them. And I've been apprenticing since I was seven. So—so that keeps me occupied," she concluded awkwardly. "And, um. I guess—well, that's the only reason why I'm out here now. Because I need to be, to be able to help them heal."

Amella was quiet for an agonizingly long time. "Huh," she said at last. "It's hard for me to imagine *not* wanting to wander. I was born and raised on the road, with questers-turned-merchants for parents. We'd travel the lands together, and they'd do all kinds of daring things. Retrieving difficult-to-find materials, hunting down beasts, you name it. Every day was new. Made life more fun. Full of adventures." She frowned. "I don't think it's healthy, to not have far-flung adventures. Limits your view of the world."

Corrin stared doubtfully up at Amella. "Well, limiting far-flung adventures limits risk of injury and peril, too. M'not so sure they're *good* for health, on the balance."

"They're worth it," said Amella stoutly. "In any case, we're on an adventure now, so we might as well make the best of it." Before Corrin could even think of a reply, Amella continued. "Like here. Miritown has an interesting history. It's said the first people who sailed here were nomadic traders and pirates. But one day, a crew's ship was hauled ashore for barnacle scraping, and lo and behold, it was in too poor shape to put back in the water. Seemed a shame to waste it, so they made a house out of it, buttressed it up and filled it with creature comforts. Turned it into a rest stop for other people and did booming business. And another crew did that, and another. And so, Miritown was born. Now, it's tradition that when a ship's grown old and unreliable for sailing, she's pulled ashore and repurposed as a home. Or a bar." Amella grinned. "Lots of good bars in Miritown, bars and inns. Miritown as a people appreciate their mead." Amella clapped Corrin on the back. "Let me show you my favorite of the lot!"

The air in Miritown reeked of fish and perfumes, and dirt footpaths squiggled between the ship-houses. People bustled along everywhere, forming a cacophony of brightly colored fabrics and glinting ornaments and chatter in sharp, fast voices. Many of them wore skirts and wraps around their legs, which made Corrin wonder if there was a festival; that was the only time folks wore skirts back home. But perhaps folks just dressed differently here. Others wore piecemeal leather-and-metal armor, and some dressed in simple vests and pants, which didn't look festival-ish at all. Most everyone had a dagger, axe, or small sword belted at their waist.

Corrin drew close to Amella. In truth, she couldn't see what was so beautiful about Miritown. She preferred Oddment with its relative quiet and surrounding forests, where she could retreat to gather herbs or hunt rabbits.

They reached an open square at the join between the river and the ocean, where merchants and peddlers of all kinds had set up their shops—small tents, wooden counters, or sometimes simply a blanket with a jumble of wares, laid out on the ground. Amella picked her way through the horde. She gave a bearded, scowling man a jaunty wave, and she winked at a woman with tasseled clothes and jars of fruit preserves for sale. Oatmuncher shambled after her. They made it to the other side and stopped in front of a massive barge-house.

Rickety wooden steps led up to a door that stood ajar. The sign hanging above it read *The Cuddly Bear,* and it had a painting of a snarling bear beneath the text. Corrin could not imagine what kind of madman would cuddle a bear, much less a snarling one.

It was the sort of idea that would make the twins snicker. Frendel would insist on going inside if he were here, and Corrin would refuse. And then he would call her a boring grown-up, which, to him, was the worst conceivable insult. But in her opinion, it wasn't such a terrible thing to be. Boring grown-ups lived safer, better-fed lives.

At least in theory.

Amella pushed some coins into Corrin's hand. "Get yourself a drink and a warm meal, and rest those weary feet of yours for a while," she said. "I'm going to go look around town for some friends of mine. At least a few of 'em go north every month or two." And before Corrin could protest that her feet weren't tired and she'd like to stick with the person who could swing a sword, thanks, Amella had vanished into the crowd, leaving Corrin in front of *The Cuddly Bear.*

Laughter and shouts spilled out from the doorway, raucous and loud.

Corrin took a deep breath and stepped inside.

The ship-house was dimly lit but warm, and the air was so thick with scents that she could scarcely breathe it—freshly brewed mead and seared fish-meat and stewed vegetables and the reek of sweat and travel grime. People clustered around tables, swigging from tankards, devouring plates of food, holding arm-wrestling matches, or passing each other coins. Possibly making bets on the people in the arm-wrestling matches.

There was a counter at the back, where more people sat on stools. A broad-shouldered lady with a scarf over her hair bustled behind it. She had the scowl of someone who'd exhausted all reserves of patience and would actually, literally kick out the next person who troubled her. She was also the person providing the food and drink.

Corrin picked her way through the crowd, much as Tiptoes would pick her way through treacherous terrain, and took a seat at the counter. It was a seat surrounded by other empty seats, and she waited for a few minutes while the barkeep handled customers at the far end. A man with sun-bronzed forearms paid five copper pieces for a piping bowl of stew. When the barkeep turned to Corrin, she put exactly that much coinage on the table and asked for the same.

"Right on," said the barkeep, and gave Corrin her stew.

"Thank you, ma'am."

The barkeep's nose wrinkled. "M'name's Ida, lass. Nobody uses ma'am or sir around here."

"Thank you, Ida."

Ida chuckled. It was a low, wry sound, coarse but not unpleasant. "Nobody's polite around here, either. Where're you from? And eat this while it's warm," she admonished, tapping the bowl with her forefinger, "because wherever you're from, they aren't feeding you enough. Put some meat on those bones and blood in your skin."

Corrin refrained from pointing out that she couldn't answer Ida's question and eat at the same time, and she obligingly gulped down her stew. The savoriness of tender-cooked meat and vegetables burst across her tongue. Warmth settled in her stomach and spread all throughout her bones until her toes curled with pleasure. Ida grinned —the first grin Corrin had seen from her. It was hearty and genuine, much like the food she sold.

Then someone sat next to Corrin and said, "Tankard of mead, darkest brew you have, and a bowl of your sea bream stew."

"Right on," said Ida, just as she had with Corrin, but her expression was oddly rigid. She plonked a frothing mug of dark liquid in front of the stranger, and she accepted her coin without comment.

Corrin peered at the stranger. Like Corrin, she wore a cloak, but unlike Corrin, her cloak was fine and unpatched. She'd drawn her hood over her head. Corrin could see bits and pieces of the stranger's face sticking out: a nose that looked like it'd been broken at least once, and brown hair spilling out from beneath the hood. Her shoulders were thinner than Da's but broader than Corrin's. She didn't seem like the sort Corrin would want to cross swords with—not that she wanted to cross swords with anyone, really.

The mystery person took a swig from her mead and caught Corrin looking. "Who are you and what aren't you spitting out?" With the stranger turned fully toward her, Corrin could finally see her face. She had a strong jaw and brown eyes that glinted with light from the hearth-fire.

Corrin gulped. "I'm just a traveler. Sorry, didn't mean to stare."

"Traveler, eh? What're you traveling for?"

Corrin swallowed another spoonful of stew, considering, and at last, decided on the truth: "I'm searching for a fruit in the Gloamwood." It wouldn't matter if a stranger thought her foolhardy, surely. Perhaps if she thought her foolhardy enough, she'd tire of talking to her and leave her be.

Ida, who had been ladling stew into a bowl, stopped short.

The woman's glass *plinked* against the counter. "A slip of a lass like you, venturing into the Gloamwood?"

"Are you mad?" Ida hissed. "That place is a death sentence."

"Hah! Don't discourage her. I'd love to see how she does against the trolls."

Ida set the bowl of stew in front of the stranger. Liquid sloshed over the edge and spilled onto the countertop. "Because it's not your bloody neck on the line, is it?" She turned to Corrin and said forcefully, "Don't go wandering in there, lass. It's not worth your life."

"Really?" mused the stranger. "Because I've heard legends about that fruit. Said to cure any ailment, even grant immortality to the one who keeps eating it." She stirred her stew, unperturbed by the spillage. "Immortality is an infinity of lifetimes. That's worth risking a single life an infinity of times over, if you ask me. But that's assuming it exists, and assuming you can get to it. What drove you to try?"

Corrin hesitated, unsure of how much to say. She'd come from a plagued village, and she didn't want to alarm them into sending her back. But she herself felt hale and hearty, and there had been no quarantine when she'd left—probably still none, yet. It would probably be alright to be honest with them, wouldn't it?

She ventured to tell the truth. "Half my village is sick, including my da, and they won't get better."

Ida frowned. "I'm sorry to hear that, I really am. But the traders 'round here have all sorts of tonics. Could be one of them would help."

Corrin shook her head. "We've tried tincture of feverfew, marigold, ginseng, child's daisies, concoctions derived from the works of Telmir, the pressure-point therapies of Yelt, poultice of the pneumonia fern, warm beds, clean blankets, cool rags on the head, mint to cleanse the throat, and all sorts of vitality brews. We've read and reread dozens of medical texts, and it was no good. I mean no offense, but I don't think your traders will have anything we haven't tried."

Ida blinked. "By the turtle's back," she said. "I don't recognize half of those."

The stranger spoke. "So you're desperate, is what you're saying."

"Yes."

"Nothing like desperation to drive a person." The stranger leaned toward her and propped her elbow on the counter. Corrin leaned back until she felt her bar stool threaten to tip. "All right. Tell me, how are you getting to the Gloamwood? You traveling alone? You have a plan for finding your way through?"

Behind the stranger, Ida tensed.

Corrin took a slow breath and said, "I'm traveling with a friend, a brave one who knows her way around a sword. She will find another friend, who will take me north on a boat. And then—and then my friend and I will head for the Gloamwood on foot."

Ida had a stricken look, and Corrin felt a strong impulse to reassure her—kind of like what she felt with her mum, sometimes.

"I have a map from someone who's been there, so I won't be going in blind."

Said map was tucked safely in her vest's inner pocket. She hadn't wanted to cram it in her pouch, or in her pack with the rest of her supplies. The old paper seemed too fragile for that.

Ida didn't look reassured.

"Interesting," said the stranger. "Very interesting. What's your name, little healer?"

"Corrin."

The stranger stuck out her hand. It was large and riddled with scars, rougher than the fine cloth she wore. "I go by King." She grinned, revealing a mouthful of straight teeth. Corrin's own were crooked and large in the front—*cute as a rabbit's,* her mum had once said, but Corrin knew a mum's bias when she heard it. "Just a nickname, but one I use more than my birth name. I'm not claiming to be the oh-so-esteemed king, sitting fat and protected in their castle." Those last words were barbed with scorn.

Few saw the king. Most everyone understood that they existed, and that the king was the one who sent out guards to protect the cities in their domain and sent the tax collectors out at autumn's end. (A cunning move on the king's part, Corrin thought, to collect taxes when folks were enjoying the fruits of their harvest and would feel the sting the least.) Beyond that, they interfered little, and most didn't think much of them. Plenty liked it that way. Plenty others thought them a lazy layabout. The king didn't arrest people for saying so—Corrin had once seen her neighbor in public, screaming it to anyone who'd listen, and all the guards had done was tell him to stop disturbing the peace and get himself a brandy—so Corrin suspected they were a decent sort. Her elders said that tyrants were terrible at taking criticism…

Ah, the stranger King's hand was still waiting for a response.

Tentatively, Corrin reached out. King's fingers dwarfed hers, and her skin was bumpy with callouses. She had a crushing grip. "Well met," said Corrin. Privately, she willed this King to let her have her circulation back.

"You don't sound so certain about that." King withdrew. She looked amused. "But Corrin, this is a fortuitous meeting. I can go in your stead, if you like. My price is but a portion of the spoils, and, of course, the map, so I might navigate."

For a heartbeat, Corrin considered saying yes. This King who was not king looked like she knew her way around heavy weaponry and had made it through a lifetime of fights alive, which made her suited for a perilous quest such as this one. Certainly more suited than Corrin. She could wait here, safe with her head secure on her shoulders, and let someone stronger than her confront the wilderness of monsters and sink-mud.

But she knew so little about this King. What kind of stranger would volunteer to go into the Gloamwood, alone, without repayment in coin? Even Amella wouldn't have chosen to accompany her if their home's fate hadn't rested on their shoulders. Besides, there was something about King—the way she carried herself, the way she looked at her… It was hard to pin down why, but for some reason, King made her uneasy. It wasn't just her, either. King seemed to make *Ida* uneasy, too. Corrin hadn't missed the way Ida tensed when King arrived, nor how on edge she seemed now. Something wasn't quite right about that.

She would have to say no, then. Politely.

"That's all right, ma'am," said Corrin, forgetting that no one said 'ma'am' in Miritown. "If you're a king, you're a king to some people who value your life."

King's brow quirked. "An interesting notion."

"What are you king of, then?"

"Of my people. As you said."

"Who are your people?"

"Oh, a few sellswords, some traders, hunters and travelers…"

"That's a lot of people," noted Corrin.

"Yes. But not a realm's worth, eh?"

Corrin scraped the bottom of her bowl. "True. You didn't mention healers or farmers. Or smithies, or weavers, or fishers…"

"OY, CORRIN!"

Corrin jumped. Her bowl skittered to the edge of the counter, where Ida caught it with a deft hand and a scowl.

Amella made her way through the crowd, but where Corrin had tiptoed, she sauntered; where Corrin had squirmed past, she plowed through. She clapped Corrin's shoulder with a heavy hand and grinned down at her. "I found our ride. Looks like you got your food, eh?" She turned to Ida, who, to Corrin's surprise, lit up in recognition. "Thanks for taking care of my companion, Ida. I'd stop for a bowlful myself, if I wasn't in a rush."

"Glad to." Ida set down the bowl and wiped her hands on a cleaning rag. "You watch out for each other, you hear? She told me where she's going, and I don't like it."

Amella sobered. "She also tell you why?"

"Yes, and I still don't like it."

"Aye, well. Not much to be done about that. We'll come back this-a-way for a good, long drink afterward, though."

"You do that."

"Of course." Amella smiled in response, more gently this time, then glanced at King, who had observed the exchange with interest. Amella's brow creased, and the hand on Corrin's shoulder tightened its grip. She tugged Corrin away from the counter. "Alright, then, off we go."

And with that, she chivvied Corrin out the door. She grabbed Oatmuncher, who'd been left tied by his lead rope to a docking post, and led the way across the square, then down a side street. It got quieter. There were still people about, but not as many as in the square. Corrin could hear the *clack clack* of Oatmuncher's hooves on cobblestone.

"You were talking to that stranger at the bar, right?" Amella said. "Hard to tell from a ways off, but it looked like it when I walked in."

"Right. Just a little."

"Find out anything interesting about her?"

"She calls herself King. She said she leads some mercenaries and traders, and other such people. Maybe like a guild?"

"Hm. Maybe." Amella fell quiet for a moment. Oatmuncher's footsteps *clacked* on cobblestone. At last, she said, "Word of advice: be careful who you trust. You can meet some dodgy folks at a trading port. And if you ask me, anyone who calls themself 'king' without being a king is suspect."

"Okay."

They walked in companionable silence for a spell. The road sloped downward. Corrin could see slivers of the ocean through the gaps between the ship-buildings—glimmering hints of blue too dark to be the sky, carved in irregular shapes by prows and ship-cabin roofs.

Corrin asked, "Where are we going, anyway?"

"The port. I told you we'd be sailing north, didn't I?"

The port was larger than Corrin had imagined. The shoreline had no buildings to obscure the sea, and over a dozen piers jutted out into the water, splaying like fingers where the river met the ocean. Ships of all sizes bobbed at the ends of the piers: barges, flat and sail-less; fishing dinghies, which might have carried two people and a net and little else; grand ships with multiple masts and painted sides, bobbing on the waves; and even a guardship, a midsize sailing boat with the realm's insignia (a crimson feather crossed with a sword).

Sailors with sun-bronzed arms and ruddy faces tramped up and down the port, hefting crates, hauling nets, rolling barrels, and unloading and prepping ships. There was less chatter here, more barked commands to *move it* and *haul that ashore, mate, we don't have all evening.*

Amella strode confidently past them all, until she stopped in front of a small, rickety-looking sailboat. It had a steering wheel and a flat-looking cabin in the back. Two rolls of fabric were lashed to a single mast. Traces of blue paint clung to one side. The paint might have been part of an insignia, once, before wind and saltwater had worn it away.

The sailboat bobbed forlornly on the waves. It didn't look like the sort of boat that could weather the kinds of sea monsters and typhoons described in seafaring stories. It looked like the mildest ocean squall could break it apart.

A grim-faced man with a shabby tunic leaned on the railing, watching them. A walking plank extended from the deck to the shore, inviting them to board.

Corrin asked, "Can you swim?"

"Nope," said Amella cheerfully. "Can *you* swim?"

The answer was yes. Corrin attributed this to her brothers. They kept doing foolish things like running off into the woods and jumping into ponds and streams, which was even more foolish when they hadn't yet learned to keep their heads above water. Like when Frendel had cannonballed into the middle of Catfisher Pond from Lookout Rock. He'd been helpless as a kitten with his head bobbing in and out of sight... Corrin had gone tearing into the water after him, and she'd forgotten that she couldn't swim either. On instinct, she'd kicked her feet and held air in her lungs, even as cold seeped into her skin and her clothes weighed her down. She had lost her boots, but she didn't realize this until she and Frendel were safe on land, sodden and dripping, and stones and twigs dug into the soles of her feet hard enough to hurt.

She'd been thirteen. Frendel had been six.

Corrin hadn't liked it and wouldn't have put a toe in water again, but her brothers had decided that almost drowning was a splendid adventure and made a habit of trying to hide in the pond. And then Corrin would have to go in after them. She grew accustomed to splash wars and water tussles, and to paddling after her wayward siblings.

"Yes," she said, "I can swim."

Amella looked impressed. "That's an odd skill even for someone who lives in Oddment."

"What's that supposed to mean?"

"Means you're lucky. If you fall in the ocean, your chance of living is twenty percent instead of zero." Amella wagged a finger in front of Corrin's face. "Don't go thinking the ocean is like some woodsy pond. If you're close to shore, powerful currents can pull you under and dash you against the rocks. If you're far from shore, then you're a starred sight farther out than most humans can swim, even those who know how."

Corrin shuddered.

"Don't look so worried. You're in good hands. Let me introduce you to my friend."

And so, Amella coaxed Corrin onto the boat. There was no need to coax Oatmuncher; he didn't so much as twitch an ear at the creak of wood beneath his hooves or the water churning below. Corrin, on the other hand, felt uneasy with the timbers creaking under her boots, and the deck rocking back and forth, and even with Amella's friend offering a soft hello and a handshake.

The man's hand was cold as a dead fish. His limbs were bony and rail-thin. "Well met," he said. Perhaps it was Corrin's imagination, but he sounded sorrowful, as if he secretly knew she'd be subject to some terrible doom. Which, depending on what Amella had told him about her quest, might not be too far from the mark. "I'm Turner. Amella told me what you're after."

A cat peered at them from atop the railing. It was enormous, probably twice the size of Tiptoes, with long grey fur and black stripes. Its eyes were round and yellow as ripe squash, its ears pointed and keen, and its paws broad, good for balancing. Turner caught where Corrin was looking and smiled faintly. "That's Dragon. He's an excellent ratter—you won't find any pests on my ship."

Dragon swished his tail and lifted his nose.

"Well met, Dragon," said Corrin.

"He'll like you, I'm sure. He can tell you're the sort who pays proper respect to cats." Turner cleared his throat. "But back to business. I'll take you as far as Boar's Tusk Peninsula, but no farther. I'm not setting foot in the Gloamwood. Couldn't get me into that forest if you paid me a king's ransom."

"That's alright," said Corrin, "I wouldn't go in there either, if I had a choice."

"You always have a choice, miss."

"My other choice is so bad I'm not sure it counts."

"Well then. You have my condolences."

"Enough of your dread and gloom, Turner," said Amella. "We haven't even set out yet. When are we shoving off, anyway?"

"Sunrise tomorrow. I'm prepping my ship, getting my supplies loaded, finding my last few shiphands... You might want to find an inn for the night." He said this as if he meant, *You might want to write your wills and hand off your worldly possessions.* Or perhaps Corrin was just imagining that he said it like that. Or maybe it wasn't his voice at all, but hers—a quiet, insidious one in the back of her mind, whispering that she'd fail and end up a troll's meal.

Wouldn't even make a meal, said the voice that was decidedly not Turner's. He didn't seem the mean sort, after all. *More like a snack. They'd gnaw your bones clean as an appetizer and use your femurs as toothpicks.*

Doesn't matter, Corrin told herself firmly. *I have Amella. She'll eat* ***them*** *for breakfast. Or challenge them to an arm-wrestling match and win.*

Amella's cheerful reply to Turner pulled Corrin out of her thoughts. "Will do. Alright, you've met Corrin and we have our schedule, so we'll get going. Good day, old friend."

They stayed at an inn near the port, a place called *The Selkie's Song*. The floorboards were rickety and the innkeeper surly, but the sleeping pallet was firm and the walls thick in a way that reminded Corrin of Oddment. It made her feel safe. It also helped that it faced a main street, so Corrin could peer through the little round window and watch passersby. Somewhere, someone strummed a lute and sang about a woman and her fish lover. Apparently that was something people did here—sat outside and played music at night. Amella said it was called "busking." Thus far, Corrin liked the buskers.

A guard walked by the window and noticed her watching. He saluted. Corrin saluted back—it seemed the polite thing to do, like returning a hello or a wave—and he moved on, smiling beneath his mustache.

"Oy, to bed with you," Amella chided. She was stretched out on her sleeping pallet with her arms tucked behind her head. "We're getting up with the sun."

"I get up with the sun anyway," said Corrin, but she obligingly laid down on her pallet. "I'm used to it."

Amella rolled onto her side to face her. Her eyes reflected the light of the lamp between them. "Huh. I didn't know that. I always sleep in, if I've nowhere to go."

"How do you sleep through the birdsong?"

"How do you not? You've lived there your whole life. Aren't you used to it?"

"I got used to waking up early for chores. And early mornings are nice. Peaceful, I think."

"Hm... I suppose." Amella frowned in thought. "When I was your age, I liked the middle of the day best. All the hustle and bustle of everyone going about their business. Always preferred the cities, too, especially after my ma—well." She shrugged her free shoulder. "Mind you, I like having Oddment to get back to after a long journey. Good place to rest. Oatmuncher likes it too."

"How can you tell?" Oatmuncher—in Corrin's recollection, at least—had never seemed to care much where he was.

"Just can. He's my travel partner. It's hard to explain."

Cheers floated in through the window. The busker had finished her song. She started another, one so slow and soft that Corrin couldn't hear what it was about.

"Lullaby," Amella murmured. "One of my favorites."

But the lullaby did not lull Corrin; she still couldn't settle down and sleep for the life of her. So she asked one of the many questions bouncing around her head. "Um. You said Turner's an old friend? How old?"

Amella chuckled lowly. "Very old. I've had decades of adventures with that man, Corrin. Back when I... well, when I started traveling alone, I was, oh, four or five years older than you. 'Round then, I took a job as a shiphand." Her voice was layered with a mix of emotions that Corrin wasn't quite sure how to parse. She sounded a touch nostalgic, maybe. Maybe even sad. Not what Corrin expected at all. "I didn't know anyone on that ship and didn't have much experience as a shiphand, but I needed some coin and some time to think about what to do, so I was stuck swabbing the decks. Turner was a sailor on that crew, toiling for the captain. He showed me the ropes, literally. Was always patient, that man, though quiet and perpetually woebegone. He was a good listener, too." She paused, then added softly, "I don't want to get into it, but I needed a good listening friend and didn't even know it. Meant a lot, then, that he offered me his ear."

The last notes of the lullaby petered out. Corrin waited with bated breath, wondering what in the lands had burdened Amella and what she would say next.

Amella rolled over and stared at the ceiling. "Anyway. He welcomed my tales, and I welcomed his sailing skills and kindness. And when I found out he was trying to save up for his own ship, I offered to help him out. Suggested we go adventuring together, land and sea. Since he taught me what he knew about ships, I'd share what I knew about the sword. We'd train up. Then we could go questing for good coin." Her tone turned fond. "He'd claim he wasn't the daring sort, but mark me, he agreed in a heartbeat. And he stuck to it. Hunted beasts and ventured into strange caves right along with me, helping me acquire rare and precious resources. Then I'd do most of the bargaining and trading to get us our rewards. Took us years, but we got Turner his ship."

Corrin frowned. "That one we're about to ride?" Privately, she still thought it looked old and feeble and inspired little confidence.

"Aye, that's the one! She's a fixer-upper, and she's aged, but she's got good bones, that ship. Or so Turner tells me. He'd know better than I." She paused, then continued. "'Course, once he had his ship, he wanted to spend more time on the sea, transporting goods, while I'd rekindled my love of traveling the land." Corrin couldn't see Amella's grin, but she could hear it in her voice as she added, "Mind you, I still talk Turner into the odd adventure. And Turner transports me and my trading goods at a madly generous discount. I've had to talk the man out of doing it for free!" She chuckled. "He's a soft heart and a brilliant sailor. Trust me on this, Corrin: we're in good hands."

Corrin's anxiety didn't simply vanish, but Amelia's sincerity moved her, gave her hope that maybe Amella was right and she needn't worry so much about the creaky looks of the ship. Another melody drifted through the window, and Corrin let it carry her away.

Corrin slept restlessly and woke at a light touch to her shoulder. She and Amella gathered their things and crept out to the dock. Turner's ship awaited them, sails unfurled. Shiphands scurried across the deck, hauling ropes and crates and other gear. Turner himself had his arms full. "Put your beast of burden in the cargo hold, will you?" he said, and jerked his head to indicate the center of the ship.

Corrin followed Amella and Oatmuncher down a ramp and into a dark, cavernous space that smelled of salt, grains, and metals. Barrels and crates were stacked in pyramids, threatening to scrape the low ceiling. They found a box stall in the corner with a thin carpeting of straw.

Amella cinched Oatmuncher into the harness and patted his shaggy neck. "You'll be fine here, old friend," Amella assured him.

Oatmuncher blinked, then dipped his head and nibbled on the straw.

Amella guided Corrin back out and led her in a roundabout way around the ship, making sure Corrin knew its layout, winding around the bustling shiphands. Amella pointed out the ship's sails, the crow's nest, and the raised deck with the steering wheel in the back, as well as the captain's quarters beneath it. Corrin couldn't help but stare at the ropes that stretched like lute strings between the sails and the mast; at the wheel that spun gently in the wind, giving the illusion that it had a mind of its own; and, in the cabin entryway, at the shelf full of shells, old scrolls, jewelry, and bits of pottery with unfamiliar designs. It seemed Turner liked to collect keepsakes.

"Turner won't mind if you look at them," said Amella. "He'd probably be tickled if you asked for stories, in fact. But handle with care, and always put them back in place."

Then Amella directed Corrin to the crew's quarters, belowdecks in the front of the boat. They reached a row of bunk beds. Corrin shrugged off her backpack and dropped it on a bed in the corner. The bed was narrow, but it was long as her bed back home and comfortable enough.

"Alright, I'm headed outside to lend my hands," said Amella. "You're welcome to come, or to stay and get settled. Just don't get underfoot, alright, kiddo?"

She left Corrin sitting on the bed, blinking in the light of an oil lamp.

It smelled fishy. *Fish oil,* Corrin realized. *Probably the easiest oil to get, for someone who spends a lot of time in sea ports.*

Corrin pulled out her map and unfolded it across her knees. Miritown was far south of Boar's Tusk Peninsula. The sea was unmarked, except for an enormous fish the cartographer had doodled in the corner. Corrin dearly hoped it meant, "Plenty of fish to eat!" and not, "There's a giant fish-beast lurking in the ocean, ready to swallow you whole!"

A winding road snaked parallel to their northward course. It connected dot after dot in the realm of Stalt—Valencia, a settlement said to bloom with a rainbow of flowers in the spring; Druin, a mining town in the Bristleback Mountains (her neighbor Jallen had once told her he'd like to visit that one, someday); and small villages, scattered across plains and hills in the realm's heartlands. Crude drawings lurked along the path. Bears. Bandits. Mountain lions. And unicorns—horse-like beasts with skewering horns sprouting from their heads, fearsome and dangerous in all stories told. Corrin mentally thanked Amella for steering her toward the sea instead...

...but northeast of Boar's Tusk Peninsula, she'd have to contend with griffins in the highlands. Great winged lion-eagle beasts, they were, said to pluck unwary travelers off the ground like hawks hunting rabbits. They seldom ventured into the heartlands of Stalt, what with all the guards and folks who had crossbows and fire. If she stayed south of the plains, she could avoid those lands and journey through Mount Cauldra instead. However, the cartographer had drawn an ink dragon slumbering in the depths of Mount Cauldra, and it was awfully detailed...

Risk a dragon's fire or risk getting skewered by talons and beaks? What a choice to make...

...And beyond, in the outskirts of the Gloamwood, glowered a troll's face. She had no choice there. She couldn't avoid those lands, not if she wanted to get to the Gloamwood's heart...

The map also warned of bog sprites and sinking mud, and—

Corrin tore her eyes away. She folded the map into a minuscule square and tucked it in her vest, so snug and flat that she could almost pretend it wasn't there. She wasn't the best at pretending, though. Sam and Frendel had more of a knack for it. She couldn't forget the paths laid out before her, nor that she had no idea if she was going to get past all those beasts alive and back again. Bathilda was mad, asking this of her. And Amella, insisting that Corrin come along, that Corrin could do this.

She'd have to hope she was lucky, and Amella as mighty as her tales suggested.

Corrin took out the rock Sam had given her and weighed it in her palm, eyeing the ribbons of pink quartz critically. She wondered, what did it mean to take care of one's luck, anyway? Having control over luck undermined the whole concept of luck, didn't it? Wasn't the point of luck that it was chance and circumstance beyond anyone's control? Sounded like a load of nonsense to her, it did, this controlling-the-uncontrollable business.

The door creaked open. "Hey, kiddo, we're shipping off."

Corrin started. Amella leaned against the doorframe, waiting for a response. Corrin mumbled an "alright" and stowed her rock away, then followed Amella outside. The shiphands had stopped hauling crates and started checking rope knots and such. One of them had shimmied up to the basket-y thing atop the mast. Another two stood ready near the base of the sail.

Turner stood at the wheel, his back to the rest of the ship, his shoulders squared.

"CAST OFF!"

The shiphands untied the boat; the boat shifted; the sails billowed; and, with the creaking of old timbers, the ship drifted away from the dock.

And just like that, they were off.

CHAPTER FOUR

Interlude: The Encampment

Beyond the borders of Miritown, deep in the woods and beneath the shadow of the Bristleback Mountains, twenty tents were pitched, a dozen campfires blazed, and a force of forty-odd people lurked. And they were odd, certainly, though not in the ways of Oddment. They had no insignia, no banner, and no armor, and they wore jewelry over tattered jerkins. Some of them were silent and lean, others rowdy. Some were young, others less so. None were old. All carried swords and axes at their belts, and they all had a hard look about them. Perhaps it was the scars they wore like badges of honor. Perhaps it was just the way they carried themselves, or something about the way they sized each other up, like they were plotting to murder each other in their sleep.

Some of them roasted meat and drank from pilfered bottles. Others sharpened daggers or lazed about, prodding the campfires for the pleasure of watching them burn. A few hid away in their tents.

In one of the tents, a brother and sister played a game of Wyrms and Trolls.

The siblings could almost have been each other's reflections. They were both lean, with pointed faces and blonde hair pale as ash, and their eyes had the same shape, the same cool grey irises. They wore a hodgepodge of fine cloth and leathery overclothes worn thin. However, the sister was slightly shorter, and the brother had a pack at his knees, while the sister had a battered leather case strapped to her back. The game board and the little figurines they used were masterfully crafted, but dented and scratched from careless handling.

The brother grinned as he skipped his wyrm over two of his sister's trolls. He plucked them off the board. "Sucks to be you, sis."

The sister retorted, "Kiss a cactus, Limerick."

"Our boss calls you Verse, and that's the best comeback you can come up with?"

In response, Verse picked up her troll and used it to knock over a wyrm. Limerick's grin dropped. Verse felt a surge of vicious satisfaction as she eyed the board. The wyrm with the gem in its nose was trapped in a corner. "You were saying?"

"Kiss a cactus, Verse."

"Funnily enough, there's a legend about one up in—"

The tent flap was yanked aside, and Verse cut herself off.

The Bandit King ducked inside and strode over to the board. She scanned it, her hands clasped behind her back and her gaze roving over the arrangement of pieces, calculating. After a moment's pause, her lips curved in a self-satisfied smirk. "Limerick, move that wyrm back along the diagonal. Attack her flank and seize her leader."

Limerick cackled. Verse scowled. It was straight-up cheating, getting help from the boss.

"Don't sulk, Verse," said the Bandit King. "We're bandits. We thrive by refusing to play fair."

Verse schooled her face into a neutral expression. "Yes, Boss."

The Bandit King crouched down and eyed the board appreciatively. "I might borrow this."

"No one's stopping you," said Verse.

"Hm… I might like to play you instead."

"I'm not enough of a challenge."

The Bandit King smiled. "I'll crush the both of you together, then."

"Sure, if you want."

The Bandit King settled at the table but made no move to set up the board.

Verse scooted her chair to give her boss more room. The Bandit King's whims were a small price to pay, Verse reasoned, for not having to live her old life as a starving bard. She remembered those days with bitterness: traveling with her brother from tavern to tavern, singing side by side and surviving by lousy tippers. Trying to, anyway. It hadn't been enough. So she and her brother had come up with a new double act. Verse strummed her lute and wove stories through song, while Limerick slipped through the crowds, picking the pockets of distracted clientele. It'd worked, for a time. Usually. As long as he didn't get caught, they'd get to eat and sleep in comfort that night. If he did get caught, well… it could end with a fight, or getting thrown out of the tavern, or worse.

That very misfortune had led them to the King—or, perhaps, the King to them.

On a particularly unlucky night, their audience had run Verse and Limerick out of the tavern and formed a mob, bent on chasing them down. But the Bandit King had been among the people in the tavern, and she, apparently, had found Verse and Limerick worth salvaging. Something about their willingness to steal, and their skill with sleight of hand. Something about the supposed kernels of truth embedded in the stories Verse sang, too. And so, the Bandit King and her followers had swooped in and knifed the lot of the crowd before they could harm Verse or her brother. King had been a vision of power and competence, a panther in a den of jackals. She'd cut down the drunkards like a farmer reaping wheat.

And then she'd come up to Verse and Limerick and held out her hand. Verse recalled her offer clear as day: *if you follow me, you can do better than skulking in corners and stealing scraps.*

Verse had looked to Limerick, who had in turn looked to Verse and given her a small, tentative nod. If Verse was alright with it, he was, too.

So Verse had said yes. And now, here they were.

With Verse's lute kept out of sheer, stupid sentiment, its strings old and untended to, and with a boss ready to destroy them at Wyrms and Trolls.

"How was your trip into Miritown?" asked Limerick. "Steal anything interesting? See anything worth plundering? Anyone get caught by the guards?"

"That's what I've come to see you about." The Bandit King leaned forward, her eyes glinting. *Ah,* Verse thought. *She's found something valuable.* Which probably meant someone, somewhere, was going to get knifed. Verse would probably have to do some of the knifing. She'd felt squeamish about it her first few times, but now, she merely felt resigned to it. More work. Price of a comfortable life, for her and her brother. "I met a traveling healer. Interesting character. You remember that story you once sang about the Tree of Life, Verse? The fruit of immortality?"

Verse blinked. "Yes?"

"She's after it."

"Sounds like she's mad."

"No, she was a timid sort. The kind who'd ordinarily hide or run away at the first sign of trouble, I'd wager." The Bandit King picked up one of the lesser wyrms and weighed it in the palm of her hand. "But she's desperate. Her village is incurably ill. And she said she had a map. Dead convinced it will lead her to the fruit. And if it truly exists —if it's like your tale once told—imagine, seizing immortality! Having infinite time, amassing infinite power and influence!" The Bandit King's eyes gleamed with greed. "I offered to take it off her hands, but she unwisely declined." The Bandit King placed the wyrm in the center of the board. Had they been playing a game, it would have been swapped out for a greater piece. "Makes her an interesting target."

"You didn't take her captive?"

"No. No opportunity. The tavern was too crowded, and she went off with her friend." The Bandit King toppled the wyrm with one finger. "But by my spy's word, they've left port to sail north this morning. We'll rally the pirates and ex-sailors among us and follow at nightfall."

Verse did not argue. She did not say that this reward was uncertain at best, or remind her boss of how a good tale was distorted with every retelling. She didn't ask about the spy, or when the Bandit King had placed the spy or where, because the King had about as much trust as a thrice-bitten fox and controlled information like misers controlled coins. She didn't point out all the trouble they were about to go through, with no gold at the end of it. They'd have to steal a ship, a good one with provisions. They'd have to evade the guards. Miritown was crawling with those cursed armor-heads.

The Bandit King had probably figured out a plan already. Her plans hadn't failed them yet.

Verse bit her tongue and nodded. "Alright. What do you want us to do?"

CHAPTER FIVE

Sailing Through the Storm

Dragon was an apt name for the cat, Corrin discovered, because the fluffy, cuddly-looking beast had a dragon's confidence and a dragon's ferocity. He would leap onto the ship rails and march along, sea spray in his whiskers and a breeze buffeting his tail. He would deign to let the humans pet him, sometimes, but he would lash out with his claws if anyone disturbed his slumber. And he liked to steal and hoard random objects, like coins and clam shells, in a secret corner of the cargo hold.

Corrin found that secret corner in short order—because after they set off, she took to hiding there herself. It was the only place she could get away from the people.

At first, the people weren't a problem. A couple of the shiphands didn't much care for her—one of them, a wiry fellow named Ricker, grumbled about greenhorns bringing bad luck, and another just seemed gruff and disagreeable in general, inclined to think everyone else was in the way—but the rest were friendly enough. Chevira, a lean, ebony-skinned woman with an easy smile and beautiful tattoos snaking around her arms, taught her how to tie a sailor's knot and estimate the water's depth. Vinny, a freckly bearded guy with a beer gut and deft hands, taught Corrin how to make sailors' bread, which was like regular bread but denser and saltier.

Turner, melancholy though he was, made for a brilliant bard. He told all sorts of stories around the dinner table—legends picked up from across the land and passed down through generations—and made them sound mysterious and haunting. He would gaze at them all over his bowl of gruel, his rail-thin face solemn and shadowed, and tell them how no one knew what happened to the sea-beast, or that rumor had it the girl who had drowned still haunted the lookout point on Boar's Tusk Peninsula... that he might have even seen her one night, drifting along the cliff face...

(Corrin reminded herself each night, before she went to bed, that she didn't believe in ghosts. Each night, ghosts—and beasts, bandits, and odder things like carnivorous squirrels and monstrous plants—crept into her dreams anyway.)

Amella, meanwhile, was the life and spirit of the ship. When Turner was somber, she was boisterous; while his tales were melancholy and haunting, hers blazed with triumph and elicited raucous laughter.

Unfortunately, she was also the one who drove Corrin to hide.

Amella hadn't forgotten her idea to condition the jumpiness out of Corrin. She would sneak up just when Corrin's focus had narrowed to a knot that needed tightening, or to the hypnotic rise and fall of the waves. Corrin wouldn't notice the sneaky-soft footsteps or the rustle of clothes behind her until—

"*HARR!*"

Corrin would jump. Badly. It was a reflex she couldn't seem to turn off. She would ask Amella, politely, to please not do that.

Amella would roar with laughter, then clap Corrin on the shoulder like they'd just shared a joke.

Some of the shiphands (including Chevira and Vinny, who had seemed so nice at first) decided this looked like great fun and took up the game as well. By day two, Corrin had dropped a mug, broken a plate, tripped over a pile of rope, and nearly pitched over the side of the boat. Any time she ventured out onto the deck, she felt like a mouse trapped in a barrel full of cats.

Hence, the cargo hold.

Dragon seemed to understand. He tolerated her hiding in his secret cargo corner, and he even let her scratch his ears. His purr rumbled so deeply that it sounded like the noise of a beast ten times his size.

Corrin sat cross-legged with her back pressed against the rocking hull of the ship, her fingertips buried in warm fur, her eyes closed and her mind drifting to Oddment—to Bathilda, her mum and da, Sam and Frendel, and Tiptoes and the neighbors. To the vines crawling along the crumbling walls, and to solstice celebrations and stories told around the town bonfire. She wondered how they were doing. Had Bathilda kept the sick ones stable? Had others fallen ill? Did they have enough healthy hands to fetch food, repair things, administer care and do all the other minutiae that needed doing? Had they been placed under quarantine?

On the fourth day, Turner discovered her. He came around a stack of boxes, somber-faced as always, with a dead fish swinging from his hand. "Dragon," he called, "I brought you some—merciful Churikin!"

"Hi," said Corrin awkwardly, and kept scratching Dragon's ears. Dragon's eyes narrowed contentedly. "Um. You have a very nice cat, sir."

Turner blinked. "I, well. Yes. Best cat in the land, I'd say."

"Are you going to give him the fish?"

Turner countered her question with another. "Are you going to hide in that corner all day?"

"This is a lovely corner. I just might."

His lips quirked. "You need to eat at some point, child."

"I'm seventeen."

"That's still a child to me. I've lived nigh six decades and had a lifetime's worth of travel." Turner knelt and placed the fish under Dragon's nose. It smelled like saltwater and pungent oils. Dragon dipped his head and sank his teeth into the fish, still purring. He even ate like a dragon, or how Corrin imagined a dragon would, tearing off chunks and gulping them whole. "You can't hide from them forever, you know. Might want to consider telling them off… or retaliating, perhaps."

"They're twice my size."

"Aye," agreed Turner solemnly. "Or they're Amella. And still, you need to stand up to them." He frowned. "She's not a cruel-spirited sort, you know. She'd stick up for me back in the day—got in a brawl on my behalf and everything! But she doesn't always realize when she says something insensitive or takes a joke too far. I can have a word with her, but she won't believe she needs to stop unless *you* tell her. Firmly."

Privately, Corrin thought that her odds of getting through to Amella were about as good as her beating Amella in an arm-wrestling match. Outwardly, she just shrugged and tickled the nape of Dragon's neck. He ignored her utterly.

Turner's expression turned contemplative. "I have an idea. Wait there." And before Corrin could say a word, he vanished behind a stack of cargo.

The rasp of shifting boxes filled the hold, and something heavy thumped on the floorboards. Turner swore. At last, he popped back into view, dust in his beard and two swords in his hands. Their blades had gone dull, and one of them had a dent in the middle, as if some drunkard had tried to use it as a hammer. "Practice blades," said Turner, waving them emphatically.

Corrin pressed her back against the wall. Terrible blade safety, that was, waving them around like that. And here she'd thought Turner a sensible sort.

"Blunt as farming shovels, don't you worry." He held one out—the undented one—like he expected her to stand and take it.

Corrin eyed the blade dubiously. "Beg your pardon, but are you telling me to threaten Amella with this?"

"Oh no. No no no. I've just noticed you don't carry any weapons except for that dagger, and I thought handling something bigger might... well, all I know is, back when I learned the sword, it helped me. Made me more confident."

"Much appreciated, sir, but I'm no good with heavy weaponry."

"It's Turner," he said. "Please call me Turner. And I'm not asking you to carry a mace. Trust me, child, if you're deft with a dagger, you can learn to be deft with a sword. We could have an hour of practice a day. It'd give us both a break from the doldrums, if you're willing to learn." He knelt and offered the weapon hilt-first. The hilt was thin and wrapped in worn leather. Looked like a comfortable grip.

Dragon meandered over and sniffed the blade curiously. He flicked his tail, eyes narrowing, then turned his nose up and went back to his meal. His scorn was obvious. A hunk of metal couldn't compete with fresh fish.

"Alright," said Corrin, and grabbed the hilt. The leather was warm from being held. She wanted to use two hands, but there wasn't room to grip it that way, so she used her right. The weight felt awkward. Lighter than she'd expected, but nowhere near as nimble as her dagger. "But I'm warning you, I won't be able handle it worth beans."

Turner's eyes took on a glint she'd never seen in them before. It made him look vibrant and alive; he scarcely resembled the solemn rail of a person who chilled her bones at the dinner table. "I'd bloody well think not," he said. "You think anyone's born knowing how to swing a blade?"

So it began. Turner would find her each morning in the cargo hold, and they'd make a space among the crates and barrels. He would lecture her on the importance of stance: of spreading her feet for stability, of angling her body so she wasn't such an easy target. He'd have her practice how to move and shift her weight, how to stab—*don't telegraph like that, go straight in, be swift*—how to parry—*with the base of your blade, not the tip, you have more power at the base*—and how to counterstrike.

Dragon, who couldn't nap through the din of clashing metal, would find a viewing spot on a crate or bin and watch them with wide yellow eyes. He must've thought them mad. If Corrin were a cat, that's what she would have thought. Here they were, waving these metal sticks around and making a racket when they could be napping or eating.

Corrin grew used to the weight of the blunt blade and the routine of blocked strikes and aching muscles, and she even started to look forward to practice. It got her up and doing something. It made her forget her homesickness. It pulled her away when she was staring at the notes on her map, wondering how soon she might encounter each of the mortal threats its author warned about. Sometimes, when Turner wasn't there and the homesickness and worry crept up on her, she would pick up the practice sword and run through exercises on her own. She'd stab imaginary bandits through their middles.

Ha! Take that, hypothetical threats.

'Course, they'd probably be the ones running her through if they ever clashed for real.

Turner didn't talk about their practice at supper, so Corrin didn't either. But the others noticed her scarcity abovedecks, and one night, Amella commented on it.

"Nearly a fortnight at sea and you're still pale as a rabbit's underbelly," said Amella. She heaped a second helping of gruel into Corrin's bowl before Corrin could say, *No thank you*. Corrin stared forlornly at the morass of brown sludge and chunks. It hadn't driven anyone to the railing or the bunk beds yet, so she didn't have an excuse not to eat it. "Been hiding from the sun on purpose? It's scorched most of us dark and spotted. Look here." She bared her forearm. It was bronzer than Corrin remembered, with dark flecks. Amella curled her hand into a fist, and her muscles shifted and bulged.

"Nice arm," said Corrin.

"Thanks, kiddo. But seriously. Pale as a rabbit's underbelly. It's not good for you to avoid the sun. Where've you been hiding?"

Corrin shrugged. "With Dragon."

"He's better company than us, eh?"

"Yes, he is."

She didn't realize the weight of what she had let slip past her lips, or how sharp her voice was, until she saw Amella's smile flicker out like a candle flame in a storm. Corrin blinked. She opened her mouth to apologize, to reassure Amella that she hadn't meant it.

But the problem was, she had meant it. The darned cat was better company than a bunch of prankster shipmates who kept spooking her. The lot of them, with the exception of Turner, bugged her so much that she'd retreated to the ship's underbelly.

And from the look on Amella's face, the vitriol in Corrin's voice had rung too true to take back. She looked as if Corrin had grown a tail or horns, or perhaps sprouted fangs.

Corrin closed her mouth and said nothing.

Chevira cleared her throat and forced a smile. "Hey, I think cabin fever's gotten to us. We'll be landing soon enough, won't we? Be able to shake off the sour moods when—"

"What's up with you?" asked Amella, speaking over Chevira. "You're the one who asked me to come on this mad quest to chase a miracle cure in a place where sane people don't go. And I have. I've stuck with you and planned our route and everything." Her fist hit the table. Dishes rattled. Gruel sloshed over the side of Corrin's bowl. "How in the name of Death's scythe does that make me bad company, kid? Where's your gratitude?"

Corrin bristled. "Maybe if you'd stop jumping me and startling the life out of me, I'd have room for it."

"That was all in good fun! Honing reflexes!"

"Troll dung."

"What is your—"

"It's good fun for you but not for me, alright? But you won't listen." Corrin gripped the handle of her mead mug until her knuckles turned white. The sounds around her grew faint and indistinct, muffled by the pounding of her own blood in her eardrums. "You know what, I'll fight you to make you stop. I will. You wait there and I'll get the weapons."

Amella said something, possibly in protest. Corrin didn't know. She didn't care—she was already up and across the cabin. She went out the door, and across the deck, and then down the steps and into the shadowed cargo hold. She knew where Turner kept the practice swords by feel and by heart, and she grabbed them instinctively, the good one in her right hand and the dented one in her left. She headed back abovedeck. Everything had gone dark—the water opaque as the brownest ale, the sky grey and dense with clouds. The ship rocked and bobbed.

Amella waited on the deck with her arms crossed. Her face was masked by shadow. Corrin couldn't tell if she was furious, incredulous, or simply disbelieving.

The ship hands and Turner had clustered behind her. Far behind her. Their backs were up against the cabin.

Corrin held out the dented sword. "Take it."

"You're serious."

Corrin waited.

Amella stepped forward and grabbed the sword by the hilt. She inspected the edge. She murmured something that might've been an oath or a prayer. "Balance on this is terrible. But whatever. Better than using the real thing." She shifted her stance, angling her body to minimize the target area. Corrin copied her. "You sure you want to do this?"

CLANG.

Corrin's sword pressed fruitlessly against Amella's; she'd blocked Corrin's opening jab in a blur of silvery steel. Her dark eyes narrowed. "Fine." *CLANG.* Corrin barely blocked her parrying strike, and her arm quivered as she held it off. "Have it—" *CLANG.* Another strike, another block. "—your—" *CLANG.* The impact rattled Corrin's bones. "—way!" *CLANG.* Corrin stumbled back, barely avoiding getting swiped, and made a desperate lunge for Amella's knee.

Parry. Jab. Amella traced a phantom cut across Corrin's stomach, one that would have sliced her open like a fish at the market, had the blade been sharp. Corrin stumbled back, tried to knock it away—but a rap on her knuckles, flat and direct, forced her sword hand open. Corrin's weapon clattered against the deck.

Cold metal touched her collarbone.

"Match is mine," said Amella. She wasn't smiling.

Corrin felt drained. And damp. The atmosphere felt thick with humidity and strangely still and weighty, like it was holding its breath.

"Alright, Corrin, I heard you. You're sick of the reflex training. You're so Churikin-cursed sick of it you're willing to pick a fight, which for you is a novel thing." She paused. She still wasn't smiling. Corrin couldn't tell if Amella was angry or not, which was unnerving, because usually Amella wore her feelings like a second skin. "Where'd you find those, anyway? Leftovers in the cargo hold? Been practicing with them?"

Corrin hesitated.

"Come on. You have my ear now. Make use of it."

"I, uh. Turner lent them to me. He's been helping me learn how to use them."

"I'll be starred." Amella turned a critical eye to Turner, who watched them both with his hands in his pockets, solemn as ever. "Secret sword-fighting lessons and nobody told me?"

Turner offered a half-hearted shrug and the ghost of a smile.

Chevira elbowed Vinny with a grin, and Vinny passed her something between half-concealed hands, scowling. A couple of the shiphands muttered to each other. Amella opened her mouth to say something else.

In that moment, the weather went mad. Wind ripped across the deck, nearly knocking Corrin off her feet. Thunder pealed. The clouds boiled and tore open. Rain came down in vision-blurring sheets and pounded the deck. Corrin staggered, startled and soaked through, water sloshing in her boots.

In Oddment, there was a sensible gradient between dampness, drizzle, and downpour. It seemed the sea had no gradient.

"Chevira!" yelled Turner. "Ricker! Get the sails!"

Chevira and Ricker, the standoffish sailor who'd grumbled about Corrin at the start of the voyage, scrambled up the mast.

"Amella, Corrin, go inside! The rest of you, oilskins! We'll keep 'er steady!"

The remaining shiphands leaped into action: Vinny and the gruff, blonde-bearded shiphand who didn't like anybody. (Bruin was his name. At least, Corrin thought so. Hard to remember because he only spoke in scowls.)

Amella glanced back at Corrin, who stared back at her, storm water collecting in her boots. Amella grinned, but it was a bit off, crooked and half-hearted. "Nothing like a cooling soak after a bout, eh? C'mon, now, you don't want to catch your death." She turned and disappeared into the Turner's cabin.

Corrin picked up her sword and trudged, socks squelching, through the door.

Corrin sat on a cushioned bench in the captain's quarters with her arms wrapped around her knees. The ship rocked and heaved. The ceiling creaked with the impact of Turner's boots as he stomped abovedecks. A puddle sloshed around Chevira and Ricker, who sat side by side on the bench across from her and shivered. They'd brought in the sails alright ("reefing," they called it), but they'd gotten soaked to the bone, their hair plastered to their skulls and their tunics bloated and dripping. Bruin and Vinny were still outside; Vinny had ducked in briefly, clad in a heavy-looking oilskin, but only to let them know he and Bruin would stay outside to help Turner. Then he'd ducked back out again.

Dragon wasn't with them. He was probably curled up somewhere in the cargo hold. Perhaps he'd found Oatmuncher. The cat didn't spend much time in Oatmuncher's stall, but Corrin had once seen him perched on Oatmuncher's back, sniffing the donkey's withers while Oatmuncher stood placidly. She hoped they weren't frightened.

Thunder roared. Her heart stuttered.

"Shouldn't they come in?" Corrin asked, and jabbed her finger at the ceiling.

Amella shook her head. "Nah. Turner's trying to guide the ship through to the other side of the storm, and Bruin and Vinny are helping at the oars. Turner'll have tied himself to the wheel post."

"That's lunacy."

"It's our best chance of not capsizing, kid."

"You… you think there's a good chance of that?"

Amella made an aborted motion with her hand, as if she'd been about to reach out to her but thought better of it. "We'll be fine. It's just a squall; he's seen 'em before. Heck, I reckon most people on this ship have." She raised her voice. "Hey, show of hands—who here's weathered a sea squall?"

Every hand other than Corrin's went up—thick and slender, gnarled and not, but all calloused from handling ropes, anchors, and oars; or, in Amella's case, mostly from handling swords and goods. Ricker looked unamused. Chevira mustered a reassuring smile for Corrin.

"There you go."

Conversation lulled. The rain beat a frenetic rhythm abovedeck. The ship heaved and rocked, and Corrin's stomach heaved with it. She breathed deeply through her nose, willing the gruel in her belly to stay in there, and stared at her boots. She contemplated shedding them and peeling her socks off. They were cold and drenched and stuck uncomfortably to her feet.

"Kiddo—I mean, Corrin. Can I ask you something?"

Corrin nodded.

"Why'd you come at me with a practice sword? You could've just yelled at me."

Corrin wrapped her arms around her middle and considered the question. In truth, she hadn't thought it through—all she remembered was the frustration, building up like pressurized steam until all of a sudden it burst out of her—but— "You didn't stop when I asked. I don't think you would've stopped if I yelled, either. They're the same thing, except one's louder." The ship gave a particularly nasty heave, and her stomach flipped. She breathed in slowly, then out, willing the nausea to subside. "Hard to ignore a piece of metal swinging at your face, though."

"...I see."

At last, Corrin looked up.

Amella had her hands clasped in her lap and her gaze downcast. "I didn't mean to make you feel like that. Like you had to draw a weapon to be heard. I'm sorry I did."

Corrin scuffed her boot against the floor planks. "S'okay. Just please, don't do it anymore."

"'Course not." Amella hesitated; then, soft and a smidge uncertain, she asked, "So we're alright?"

"We're alright."

They lapsed into silence. Corrin still felt cold and nauseated and generally uncomfortable as the storm raged above them. The atmosphere felt thick and awkward, like it was waiting for something, like it needed more words to fill it.

Corrin peeked at Amella from the corner of her eye. Amella was slouched over, her expression distant, like her thoughts were a horizon away. Corrin thought of what Turner had said about Amella: how she'd stuck up for him. How she wasn't a mean sort, really. Tentatively, Corrin said, "Turner told me you got in a brawl for him, way back when."

Amella sighed. "You can ask me straight, you know. Not that it's much of a tale, that one."

"Um. Okay." The cold, damp socks were bothering Corrin too much, so she shed her boots and socks. Amella watched her with a sort of lopsided, wry smile, and she straightened slightly as Corrin asked, "If you don't mind telling me, what happened? Why'd you end up in a brawl? What'd they do to Turner?"

"Said a few insulting words. Doesn't matter what they said, really, just matters that it was mean enough that even I noticed." Amella frowned. "Mind you, I was more hot-tempered at that point in my life. Felt angrier about a lot of things, in general. Part of me just wanted an *excuse* to fight. So it wasn't the most selfless thing I did, getting into that brawl. I won," she added, in the most uncharacteristically brief and dismissive recounting that Corrin had ever heard from her. "Didn't take too long. Came out of that fight a lot better off than the other guy, and they did leave Turner alone afterward. So there's that."

Corrin didn't know what to say. "That's... good? I think?" As Amella's face showed a touch of amusement, Corrin ventured to ask, "Why were you angrier, though?"

Her smile slipped away. "Ah."

"M'sorry," said Corrin quickly, feeling that she may have ventured too far, "you don't have to if you don't—"

"I lost my ma."

Corrin's mouth snapped shut.

Amella clasped her hands in her lap. Her mouth was a firm line, her eyes glassy. "I was a few years older than you. Ventured with my parents into the heart of the griffin highlands to gather some valuable goods. We'd done this sort of thing before, gotten through fine and had grand triumphs to tell. But we had a seriously unlucky run-in. They, uh. My parents protected me. But my ma, well, we think an infection got into one of her battle wounds, and before we could make it to a healer..." Amella shook her head. "Anyway. That's why I was short-tempered for a while. Mad at the griffins, mad at Death, mad at myself."

"I..." Corrin's heart twisted painfully in her chest. "I'm so sorry."

"You needn't be," said Amella gently. "It was decades ago. I'm alright now. Came to terms with it. And to this day, I believe the adventures I got to have with my parents were worth it." She took a breath, and steel entered her voice. "Still. If I can spare you that kind of pain—if I can make sure we don't lose your da, or mum, or any of the other kind people of Oddment before their time—Corrin, I swear by my sword, I'll do everything I can to help you."

"O-oh." Corrin blinked furiously. "Well, um. I really appreciate it. And I'll—I'll do my best." Her voice strengthened. "I swear by my salves."

At that, Amella smiled, warm and genuine. "I'm counting on it."

It seemed to take an eternity, but the thunder lulled and the ship steadied, and the pounding rain turned gentle as a lullaby. Corrin lay on a spare cot in the captain's cabin and drifted in and out of slumber, until at last, Amella shook her awake and told her there was something she had to see. "It's the most beautiful sight you'll ever lay eyes on," she said. "Worth getting up for, trust me."

It was a double rainbow, twin rings of light encircling the sun. The colors shifted before Corrin's eyes like a mirage.

Her da had once told her that light turned rainbow when it moved through water, sometimes. Depended on the angle. And that was why rainbows appeared after rain, when the air was full of droplets that hadn't managed to fall.

Corrin shared this tidbit with Amella, who seemed both amused and intrigued. "Never thought about what makes a rainbow, honestly," she said, resting her forearms on the railing. "I just listened to the stories about sky fairies and the sun ghost who painted it to ease the rain ghost's gloom. I always thought of 'em as a sign of fortune and happiness. Like, you've weathered a storm, and now you get to see something amazing for it."

The days flew by after that. Turner and Amella tutored Corrin in turns, now, keeping her scampering across the decks half the day—or sometimes the cargo hold, if they got too much in the shiphands' way. Corrin's feet grew quicker and her arm stronger with the weight of tempered steel. She watched sunsets and sunrises and tickled Dragon under his chin. She helped Amella mind Oatmuncher, who seemed bored but otherwise alright.

One day, after they'd hauled a bundle of hay to Oatmuncher and left him nibbling happily, Corrin asked Amella which path they should take to reach the Gloamwood after reaching shore. The cartographer hadn't left any recommendations, and everywhere looked perilous to Corrin.

"I vote we head east," said Amella. The two of them were huddled over a table crafted from a barrel, tucked in a corner of the crew's sleeping chambers. She traced a path across the yellowish parchment with her finger, across fields and copses and through the mountain with the inked-in dragon. "I've had a few too many close shaves with griffins—not just the one from my youth. Deadly creatures. They'll dive-bomb you out of nowhere and try to seize you from behind, like a falcon snatching a rabbit. Can't say I've ever met a dragon, but at least the stories say it sleeps."

Corrin hoped the stories were right. She had a sneaking suspicion that if the dragon was awake, they'd all end up spit-roasted.

At last, Turner announced they'd reach the peninsula by tomorrow's sunset.

"See that spur out there?" he asked, pointing over the wheel.

Corrin followed his finger. Most of the shore was a smudge on the horizon; they'd stayed just well enough in sight of it to make it easy to keep their bearings. But up ahead, where Turner was pointing, a part of the shoreline arced into the sea—a grey and green thing sticking out and curving across their path, as if to catch them.

"That's Boar's Tusk Peninsula."

The passage of time, which Corrin had all but forgotten about, crashed in on her.

She'd been at sea for, what, a few weeks? How long would it take her to find the fruit? How long to get back? Assuming she avoided the griffins, the dragon, the sink-mud, the trolls, and whatever other unmarked dangers awaited her, and made it back to Oddment at all…

Corrin's feet itched for land while her heart dreaded leaving Turner's ship.

CHAPTER SIX

A Leap of Faith

The next morning, Corrin watched the sunrise, as she had taken to doing out here. It was a lovely one, a spectrum of light pinks and dandelion yellows seeping up from the horizon and highlighting the underbellies of clouds. It was a good sign for the weather, too; Turner had informed her that brilliant oranges and reds foretold a sea squall, while softer hues promised gentle breezes and clear skies.

A black and brown smudge stained the horizon, though. Strange, there hadn't been anything there yesterday… She couldn't for the life of her tell what the smudge was, but it looked like it was getting bigger.

She left the railing and scaled the rope net that stretched from the deck to the crow's nest. It was a ways higher than any of the walls in Oddment, and it had taken some convincing from both Vinny and Chevira to get her to climb up the first time. But it was also much easier climbing, with a better view. Corrin popped up through the gap in the nest's floor.

Chevira was already up there, gazing northeast toward the peninsula. She didn't notice Corrin until Corrin was at her elbow, saying a soft hello and tugging on the sleeve of her tunic.

"There's something south of us," Corrin told her.

"That so?" Chevira shaded her eyes with one hand and peered intently. "Huh. Would ya look at that—I think it might be another ship."

"You have the spyglass?"

Chevira grinned and pulled out a tube with curved lenses at either end—one bigger, one smaller—and more lenses and prisms inside. Corrin was seventy percent sure she'd seen Amella peddle something like it, once upon a time. Chevira handed the spyglass to Corrin. It was cool and heavy in her hands. "Why don't you take a look for us?"

Corrin pressed the spyglass to her eye. It turned her view of the world into a narrow but detailed window. She shifted the window around until she could see a timber prow cutting through the waves and a deck crawling with people. Two masts with billowing sails rose from the deck, and a flag fluttered at the top. She focused on the flag. It was black, with a white dragon painted on. She relayed all of this to Chevira.

Chevira swore vehemently and grabbed the spyglass.

"I don't believe it," she said, and shoved the spyglass in her belt pouch. "Feckin' bandits are tailing us."

Corrin's stomach dropped.

"Tell Turner, now. Sooner we get to port, the safer we'll be."

Corrin scrambled down like Death herself was chasing after her and hurried to the back of the boat, where Turner had his hand on the ship's wheel and a profoundly serene look about him. She took a deep breath and said, "'Scuse me, but we have sea-faring bandits closing in on us."

His serenity vanished. A grave expression took its place. He told her, "Get Vinny and Bruin on the sails. Warn Amella. We'll pick up as much wind as we can. Tell me, lass, did you see oars?"

"No sir."

"Alright. Alright, that's good." But he did not look reassured.

Corrin found Amella asleep in her bunk. She shook her awake, or awake-ish, anyway; Amella's eyes cracked open, but she grumbled incoherently and shoved her face into her pillow.

"Bandits," Corrin hissed, and shook her more vigorously. "Sailing after us."

Amella sprang out of bed so fast that Corrin stumbled back, her arms pinwheeling. Oaths flew from Amella's lips, in between which she said, "Stay out of sight." She grabbed her sword from beneath her bunk and thundered out to the deck. Her doublet lay forgotten in a heap.

Corrin grabbed the doublet and, finding it heavy and awkward to carry, put it on. It was loose around her shoulders and middle, and the sleeves dangled past her fingertips.

The ruckus woke Bruin and Ricker, who'd been half-buried in blankets in their bunks—and once Corrin told them what was going on, they, too, rushed outside. Ricker muttered something about the bad luck of greenhorns on the way out. Corrin elected to ignore him.

Corrin raced back across the boat, ducked into the galley kitchen, and found Vinny kneading dough, whistling. She tugged on his arm. "'Scuse me, but Turner needs you out at the sails."

"What now? Ah, lassie, sails can wait 'til I'm done with this batch of bread."

"But bandits are tailing us."

His smile slipped away quick as soapy water, and he hastened past her, his fingers still dusted white and a chef's apron fluttering around his legs. The dough sat forlornly on its kneading board, a pale lump of sticky, wet flour and salt that was sure to dry out.

Corrin threw a moist towel over it. She fiddled with the sleeves of Amella's doublet, thinking, unsure of what to do. Then she went back outside.

Vinny and Bruin clambered about the sails, tightening a rope here, changing the angle there, making them massive. Ricker was nowhere to be found—checking the cargo, perhaps, or getting a weapon. A single human figure stood at the top of the crow's nest—looked like Chevira. Amella stood at the aft, her tunic billowing in the wind and her sword at her hip, her hands gripping the rail and her eyes on the bandit ship.

Corrin could tell it was a ship without the spyglass, now, if she squinted and shielded her eyes from the sun. She unfastened the doublet and pushed it into Amella's arms.

Amella looked down at her in surprise. "Oy, I thought I told you to stay out of sight."

"I will." But she didn't move. The pirate ship wasn't anywhere near them yet. Now that she was out here, watching it grow little faster than a plant, she couldn't sustain a proper sense of panic. This was the slowest-approaching, most well-foreseen doom she'd ever dealt with. Even sickness didn't advertise how terrible it would be until it had already hit—and with sickness, at least she could mix poultices and administer medicines as soon as she saw it.

With these bandits, they couldn't do anything, except angle their sails as best they could and twiddle their thumbs. It was almost boring. Would've been, if it weren't so dread-inducing.

"Maddening, isn't it?" said Amella.

"Huh?"

She pointed to the ship. "Can't do anything about them, they're out of reach. Our ship isn't equipped with long-range weaponry." She paused. "Could be Turner's got some crossbows buried around here somewhere. And maybe some swords with edges on 'em. Why don't you take a look, tell me what you can find."

Corrin scurried off to the cargo hold, grabbing an oil lamp off its hook on the way in, and wended through the barrels and crates, searching for the gleam of metal or the curve of spring-ready wood. She cast her lamplight in corners and poked her nose beneath crates. For her troubles, she found the following:

A case of beer bottles, half of them empty. A good drink could numb them before they got pummeled with cannon fire or pierced through with arrows, but otherwise, not useful.

Dried and salted fish. Corrin could practically feel Dragon's stare from the shadows as she closed that one.

A barrel that held nothing. Corrin reckoned if she stepped inside and curled up, she could hide in it. Yup, no one would find her, and then… and then, she might end up trapped on a ship with a bunch of bandits for who knew how long. *So much for that idea.*

Dust bunnies.

Flour. It drifted into her nose. She sneezed.

Blunted swords. *Why all the blunted swords?* she wondered. *Who had a use for all these blunted swords?*

Grain. *Perhaps I should give some to Oatmuncher. Poor donkey, stuck down here with no idea what's going on…* But the thought had scarcely occurred to her when something else caught Corrin's eye.

A bow. Not a crossbow, a traditional longbow. It was tall as Corrin, with thick wood, and had a quiver and a handful of arrows to go with it. Such a bow would take fearsome arm strength and skill to draw, unlike a crossbow, which would be easier to use. But it was better than nothing. Corrin grabbed the bow and quiver and slung it over her back. Maybe Amella knew how to shoot one, or perhaps Turner had bow talents heretofore not bragged about…

Dragon's stash. But Corrin scarcely had a chance to look at it. Dragon stepped out of the shadows as if conjured, his pupils dilated and flashing an eerie green as they caught the lamplight. He padded in front of his treasure hoard and sat down with his tail curled over his paws. His ears faced forward, but his eyes narrowed in warning. His tail-tip twitched. His meaning was clear.

"Easy," said Corrin, "your trinkets wouldn't do me any good right now anyway." She walked away, hoping for better weapons—a sword that was actually sharpened, a crossbow that almost anyone could use

—come on, Turner, give us something to work with…

Warmth and fluff wended around her ankles. Dragon seemed keen to stay close to her as she kept searching.

She chanced upon a scuffed scabbard and belt, half-buried in a barrel full of farm tools. It looked quite as battered as the other practice swords, as did the worn hilt that stuck out of it. Corrin set her lamp on the nearest crate and drew the blade. The steel glinted in the light. It was cold to the touch. She pressed the pad of her thumb against the edge, expecting a dull pressure—but pain lanced through her skin, and her thumb came away red.

She sucked on the wound and inspected it. Terrible medicine practice, that was. Bathilda would've whacked her across the shins with her staff for not practicing wound hygiene. Fortunately, the cut was tiny. Nothing to worry about. Corrin glanced down at Dragon, who pressed against her boot and stared up at her, whiskers twitching. For once, he didn't much resemble his namesake. "S'all right," she reassured him, and buckled the sword around her waist. "Your claws could've done worse."

Corrin searched for more weaponry, but to no avail. She trudged back up the steps with the bow at her back and the short sword at her hip.

Dragon followed her.

She walked over to Amella and offered up the bow. "Sorry it's not a crossbow. I looked, but couldn't find anything else."

Amella inspected the quiver and twanged the bowstring. It hummed. She frowned. "I'm arse with a bow—and honestly, I'm not sure any of us can handle this one well. Feels like it requires a titan's arm. But it's good to know we have it." She slung it over her back.

Corrin drew the shortsword. "I also found this. If, um, anyone could use it."

"You should hang on to that," she said. The seriousness in her voice filled Corrin with foreboding.

Hours passed. Dragon paced abovedecks, and so did Corrin. Vinny and Bruin kept minding the sails, and Chevira stayed up in the crow's nest. Corrin, in her restless wanderings, stumbled across Ricker in the captain's office. It was a small, cramped space, tucked in the back beyond the sitting room with the benches. A lantern on the desk cast light on the papers, ink bottles, and quills that cluttered the desktop. A rickety bookshelf groaned under the weight of dozens of scrolls and leather-bound books.

Ricker looked through the desk drawers, mumbling to himself.

"Ricker?" Corrin asked.

He nearly jumped out of his skin. "Churikin's hands, girl, make a bit of noise while you walk."

"You looking for something in here?"

Ricker drummed his fingertips on the narrow desk. "I could ask you the same question. Turner tell you to fetch him something?"

Corrin shook her head. "I was just wandering. But you were digging through his drawers." *Twitchy,* she thought, eyeing the way his weight shifted and his hands fidgeted. *Definitely twitchy, like he's up to mischief. The twins are better at feigning innocence than he is.*

Ricker scowled. "Nothing for you to worry about. Just wanted to check his maps." He shouldered past her and out the door. "Mind you keep your greenhorn luck out of the captain's cabin."

And now Corrin was the one scowling. By her reckoning, he ought to have forgotten his superstitions. How could someone be cooped up on the same ship with another person for weeks, with no harm done to them (alright, aside from a bit of rain), and still think that person was a curse? Besides, she didn't like that he was poking around in Turner's desk, rummaging through his things. Seemed like the sort of thing a thief would do.

Full of donkey manure, that one.

She approached the desk.

There were, in fact, two maps laid atop it. One of them was for the current area. Another was for the southern waters that they'd left behind.

Corrin narrowed her eyes, but she left the desk without further inspection. She closed the door behind her and went to grab her pack.

Outside, Ricker had joined Amella at the rail. Chevira was with them. She must have clambered down from the crow's nest. She'd gotten herself an axe, a smallish one that had a wickedly curved edge, and stuck it in her belt, and a short bow was propped against the rail next to her. Ricker only had a dagger. Amella had set the bow aside, though the quiver remained on her back, and held the spyglass to her eye. The sea breeze carried her curses to Corrin's ear.

"—dragon dung, mangy jackals—"

"What?" asked Corrin.

Amella jumped. "Fricking—ah, to heck with it. Just look." She shoved the spyglass in Corrin's face.

Corrin took it and examined the prow of the ship.

It was close enough to make out faces, now, with the help of the spyglass. There were dozens of them—plump and thin, hairy and smooth, most grimy, many scarred. None that she recognized, until she spotted the person standing at the prow.

A dark cloak of fine cloth billowed out from her shoulders. Her hood was back, unlike when Corrin had first met her, so she could see the mass of brown hair spilling from her scalp like a wild beast's. One eye squinted against the sun; the other hid behind a spyglass that was pointed right at her. She recognized the once-broken nose, the powerful shape of her face, the scarring on the hand that held the spyglass...

King lowered her spyglass and grinned.

She had five people with crossbrows by her side, aiming, ready to shoot the moment her ship drew near enough.

Trolls' breath, thought Corrin vehemently.

"That's the woman from the tavern, isn't it?" said Amella. "By Death's scythe, what did you say to her?"

Corrin thought back to that afternoon in *The Cuddly Bear.* She'd said that she was going to the Gloamwood, in search of the legendary fruit. That she was traveling with a friend, and that she'd be traveling north with a friend of a friend by boat, and then on foot afterward. And that she had a map. Which King had offered to take off her hands.

Either King was after the map, or she'd chosen them as a target for jollies. Those were the only two motivations Corrin could think of, and one seemed far more likely than the other.

Amella was still waiting for an answer, so, cringing internally, Corrin relayed what she'd told King. Amella did not look happy. Nope. Definitely not happy. Probably wanted to wring Corrin's neck a bit. But all she said was, "No point crying over it now. We'll handle it. Prepare to jump ship, if need be."

The bandit's vessel gained fast on them, but they, in turn, gained fast on the Boar's Tusk Peninsula. Corrin could see where the rocky shore shifted to grass and shrubbery, and where huts dotted the land near the base. There was a watchtower, too, a great stone keep with a pointed roof that jutted proudly up from the cliffside. Turner kept to the wheel and tilted it with every shift of the wind. The sails of Turner's ship swelled with a lively breeze, and Corrin grew hopeful. The tip of the peninsula curved toward them. Maybe they'd actually make it to shore, and they could run for the guards who tended the tower—

Rrrip thunk.

Corrin started.

A crossbow bolt hit the deck near Turner's feet, quivering. He jumped away from it and swore. One of the sails had a hole in it, and it sagged.

The ship erupted with noise—Amella shouting orders, Bruin and Vinny scrambling down the mast with panicked yells, the *twang* of a bowstring as someone fired a retaliating shot, the beat of pounding footsteps, and the *thunk thunk thunk* of more bolts hitting the deck. Turner stayed at the wheel, his lips pressed in a pale line and his gaze set grimly on the tip of the peninsula. *Brave of him,* thought Corrin as she sprinted for the crew cabin. A bolt missed her by mere paces; her heart stuttered. *Brave and nuts.* She tore open the door and yanked it shut behind her. All noise became muffled, except for the pounding of blood in her ears.

A scream pierced the doorway. Corrin couldn't tell who it was, but it sounded like they'd been shot.

She opened the door a crack, letting the cacophony in again, and peered through the narrow opening.

Bruin staggered toward the cabin, a bolt sticking out of his shoulder and Vinny and Ricker at his elbows. The three of them swore and shouted. The King's boat loomed large before them, aimed to collide. Amella crouched at the stern and kept peeping up over the rail to fire potshots with the longbow. Chevira crouched beside her, providing backup fire (and more accurate fire, truth be told) with the short bow. Bruin was ten paces away—five—Corrin opened the door wider and tugged him inside, then snapped it shut—and Bruin collapsed onto the bunk.

"You're a healer, right?" said Vinny urgently.

Corrin nodded. She reached for Bruin's shoulder. He didn't protest as her fingers skimmed the fabric, the projectile, and the bloody spot where the bolt had punched through skin and sinew. Distantly, she warned him that this might hurt a bit. Listening to her own voice was like hearing someone else speak; the words were automatic. She'd given the same warning all the time back in Oddment—relocating joints, stitching up knife wounds (clumsy, some people were, and not careful in the kitchen), and once, under Bathilda's watchful eye, pulling an arrow out of that poor, foolish guard.

Bruin, being Bruin, responded by scowling at her. His jaw clenched and knotted, and his good hand gripped the edge of the mattress.

She pressed down, feeling the bone at the joint and 'round the back. It felt like it was where it should be—the shoulder blade had the right shape, the socket and ball felt aligned—though she could only tell so much through a layer of muscle. Hopefully it wasn't fractured. Hopefully the bolt had confined its damage to flesh. It seemed at an angle where that was likely.

She'd never dealt with a crossbow bolt before, but it would be the same principle, in theory, as treating an arrow wound. She'd need to remove the foreign object, which in this case meant yanking it out the way it had come in. Avoid leaving bits of it in the entry wound, if she could. Cleanse the area and stitch it up right quick, to minimize blood loss, and bind it tight.

Corrin grimaced. "This'll hurt like a troll bite, m'sorry."

No one said anything. Bruin nodded.

She put a wadded bandage between Bruin's teeth, then turned him so his back was facing her. One hand on the bolt, one hand to hold him steady. She yanked. Bruin screamed, but the bandage muffled it. The bolt came out clean—in a healer's manner of speaking, anyway. The hand's breadth that had gone in was coated in blood, but it was whole. She handed the bloody bolt off to Vinny, who looked a mite squeamish but took it without comment.

Blood welled up in the puncture wound. Not fast enough to be an artery, she didn't think. At least, she hoped not.

"Bolt's out. I'm going to cleanse you and stitch you up, alright?"

Bruin made a noise like a dying coyote around the bandage, but he nodded.

Corrin pulled out her cleansing solution—bit of whiskey, bit more of lavender—and washed the wound. Bruin didn't wince. The sting must've seemed like nothing after having the bolt pulled. She got the needle and thread next and sutured the wound, biting her lip in concentration. The process was remarkably like sewing fabric. Not that she'd ever tell a patient that. Bathilda had warned her that it might scare them. They liked to think their bodies were being treated with more care than cloth.

Corrin tied a knot at the end, pulled the bandage out of Bruin's teeth, and wiped her hands on it. She applied honey to the area she'd stitched up, to seal the sickness out. Then she wrapped a fresh bandage over it. She used the old one to bind the corresponding arm in a sling, tying it snug against Bruin's ribcage. "Done." She felt strangely calm. "You can't use the shoulder for a few weeks, at least, then only for light work a few more. Might be weak for longer. Don't try to move it yet; you'll mess up the healing process."

"Thanks," said Bruin. His voice was tight with pain. "But there're bandits about to board us, so your advice ain't all that realistic."

Thud. The boat juddered.

Corrin jumped.

"Troll bites," swore Vinny. "I'd bet one of my arms that's them boarding us." Bruin scowled—Corrin supposed he wasn't in the mood for arm jokes, what with having a bolt yanked out of his shoulder and his skin stitched up and no painkillers for any of it—but Vinny just offered a wry smile. His hand drifted to the dagger at his belt, and he took a step toward the door. "They'll come in here eventually, and then we'll be trapped. I say we meet 'em out there. Give ourselves a chance to choose—death by bandits skewering us or death by water in the lungs?"

"Not funny," said Bruin through gritted teeth.

"Nope, not at all," Corrin agreed, but made to follow Vinny all the same. Amella's instructions echoed in the back of her mind: *prepare to jump ship, if need be.*

"Stop," hissed Ricker.

She stopped.

At some point during the gallows humor, Ricker had sidled closer to Bruin and drawn his dagger. Said dagger was now pressed to Bruin's neck, the edge threatening to slice the jugular. One of the few regions of the human body where even Bathilda couldn't undo the damage.

Troll bites, Corrin swore internally.

"Give me the map," said Ricker.

Corrin swallowed. "What map?"

"The one with the Gloamwood."

Double troll bites. Corrin asked, "Why do you want it?"

"Not me." His expression could have been carved from stone. "The Bandit King."

The what—oh. No-good backstabbing scumbag who called herself King, chasing after them with a ship full of bandits. Bandit King. Of course.

And Ricker was working for this Bandit King, apparently. Ricker had been rummaging around the captain's desk, so maybe he had thought she'd handed the map off to Turner—or maybe he was just looking for extra baubles to steal. But how'd he end up on the ship with them? By chance? Or had the Bandit King sent out her people to pose as ship-hands, to tell her of any boats sailing north, and to watch for a redhead named Corrin?

Terrible luck, either way.

"Give me the map, you accursed girl."

Corrin considered the likelihood of getting them all out alive if she did as he said. Not high, she guessed. She'd buy them maybe another hour and then they'd all end up tied to rocks, hurled overboard, and sunk to the bottom of the ocean, if they didn't get cut up like butcher meat instead. Either way, she couldn't trust the word of a bandit farther than she could throw him.

The map was tucked safely in her inner pocket, as always.

"Sir," she said, her voice shaking, "I left it with Turner."

Her attention wavered to Bruin. His breaths were shallow, and he held very still. Except for the hand on the hilt of his dagger.

Good ol' Bruin. Good, prickly, stabby Bruin.

"Don't lie to me," said Ricker.

"I'm not lying. He felt real worried about me going to the Gloamwood, so he asked to borrow it. Wanted to take a look and see if there was anything he could advise me on, like maybe how to get past the trolls." It sounded plausible even to her ears. She was making a ploy worthy of her twin brothers.

She'd very much like to live to tell them about this.

"You didn't have a chance to look through his desk properly, right? I reckon he's got it in the back of a drawer somewhere."

Ricker looked like maybe, just maybe, he believed her. The dagger wavered, then shifted a finger's breadth farther away from Bruin's neck.

Bruin struck—his dagger flashed—Ricker yelled—Bruin scrambled back as Ricker doubled over—Vinny moved in, his expression hard—

Corrin bolted for the door and burst out onto the deck.

The Bandit King's ship was flush against their own. It was thrice as long and twice as wide, with a sharper-cut prow and sails that loomed ominously over them. Gang planks stretched between the ships, narrow and wobbly, and bandits swarmed across them like ants. Amella stood square in front of one, her sword a blur, her feet planted. Turner fought beside her, holding up another plank with a flurry of stabs and parries—but there was a third, unguarded, and bandits' feet were already hitting the deck.

Two bandits grabbed Chevira and hauled her to the aft. The rest looped around to surround Amella and Turner.

Corrin backed toward the far side of the boat, heart pounding—she couldn't do anything; she could've practiced the sword for fifty years and this swarm would still overwhelm her—

The Bandit King stepped aboard. She looked around, assessing, as if she was seeing a ship on the market and deciding whether or not it was worth buying. She caught Corrin staring at her and grinned. It put Corrin in mind of one of the water beasts Turner had told a tale about —*a shark,* he'd called it, *with over a hundred dagger-teeth and a smile that promised death…*

"Fine day for sailing, isn't it, Corrin?"

Behind the Bandit King, her subordinates brought Amella and Turner to their knees and bound their hands. A group of them headed for the cabin. Another group descended into the cargo hold.

Corrin took another step back.

The Bandit King held out a hand. "The map."

Corrin's pack bumped the railing.

"There's nowhere for you to go." Her voice was smooth and honeyed. "We outnumber and outarm you, and your friends are already bound." She stalked toward Corrin. "I'd be sorry to run you all through with a sword. You're a bright lass. You could give up the map and tell me everything you know, and I'd let all of you walk free."

"She's lying," shouted Amella, quite unnecessarily. Corrin had figured as much. "Get out of here!"

The Bandit King pulled out a dagger and twirled it. "Don't be ridiculous. She can't."

Corrin turned and peered over the railing. The sea churned beneath them, blue as a sapphire and unknowably deep. It wasn't a woodland pond, nor the river that flowed lazily through the forest. This water could hide a beast the size of a ship, or several, or several hundred. Perhaps it did. She wouldn't find out, if she was lucky.

The shore was close. Steep and jagged with rocks, but close.

The deck creaked with the Bandit King's footsteps. "Word of advice, little healer, don't turn your back to someone with a—"

Corrin leaped overboard.

The Bandit King shouted something, maybe a curse, she didn't know, because the whoosh of rushing air swept her voice away. Corrin's heart jumped up her throat. She hit the water feet first, and it may well have been solid, with the way it rattled her bones and her joints and forced the air out of her lungs. Spray stung her face. Before she could draw breath, her head was submerged in a shock of cold. The air was temperate, but beneath the surface, the sea was frigid.

Salt burned her eyes, and she screwed them shut. The sea pressed in on her. Corrin fought to get back to the surface, but her pack was saturated with water, dragging her down, down…

…she shrugged it off and kicked viciously, trying to go back up, or in a direction she hoped was up, toward the light she'd seen just before she'd closed her eyes…

The pressure lessened. Her head broke through the surface. Corrin spluttered and gasped. Nothing but sea in front of her. She turned around. A wall of curving timber, with an insignia weathered beyond all recognition, loomed over her. Turner's boat. She tilted her head up, and back, and met the gaze of the Bandit King.

The Bandit King's mouth moved. She might've sputtered something, which Corrin couldn't hear because her ears were full of water, but it didn't matter when the Bandit King's face spoke so plainly for her. Gobsmacked, she was, might well have had her belt stolen or the rug yanked out from under her feet. The expression didn't suit her at all. Corrin almost laughed.

And then she recalled that the Bandit King had a legion of underlings and a ship ready to plow her over, and the urge to laugh vanished, replaced by the more sensible urge to kick off the ship and paddle for shore as fast as her piddly hands and feet could take her—before the Bandit King ran her over or, worse, found a lackey who could swim and sent them in after her.

Distantly, she heard shouting and a ruckus, and Turner's ship started moving again—but its damaged sail couldn't catch the wind properly, and Corrin had fear and adrenaline zinging through her veins, spurring her on. She angled for the sheltered spot in the curve of the peninsula's tip, where the water looked quiet and rocky outcroppings broke through the waves.

She passed one outcropping, and another, and clung to a third for a moment to catch her breath. Her hands were stiff and clumsy, but they still worked. She glanced back.

The ship had stopped.

They're steering clear of the rocks, Corrin realized. *They can't get the ship through.* Elated, she kicked off the outcropping and paddled onward, farther into the rocks.

Unseen currents tugged at her, but mercifully no more than that (Turner had told horror stories of riptides and shattered ships and people). She followed the currents in zigzags and swirls, letting them carry her while she kept her head above water. She willed herself to keep moving, to push past the exhaustion and the tingling in her limbs, the cold numbness seeping into her—until, at last, she had her hands on the jagged cliff face and waves sloshing against her back. She ducked her head between her hands and felt her way along. She found where the rock face grew sandy and less steep, and, with gritted teeth, she hauled herself ashore.

Her soaked clothes weighed heavily on her limbs. Her legs trembled. Cold numbed her skin and made her bones ache. A slope peppered with long grass and sea roses stretched up in front of her, rolling and rustling gently. Her vision kept going in and out of focus, blotching and fuzzing, and she felt unsteady on her feet—but there was a great grey stony thing a ways up the slope, and she figured if she got to the great grey stony thing, she'd be safe.

Corrin's lungs heaved, and her heart hammered with exertion. She stopped halfway up. Forcing herself to start walking again was torture, but as she trudged onward, the great grey stony thing gained detail.

Ah. The tower.

People trickled out of the tower, blurry faces and blobs of metal and leather. Voices drifted down, rough and urgent. Corrin threw her hand up and waved. Two of them broke off from the rest of the group and clambered down toward her. A hand rested on her shoulder (*heavy*). Someone knelt down in front of her—someone twice her size and clad in piecemeal armor, but with kind hazel eyes and a worried downturn to his lips. He had a beard as patchy and brown as a molting deer's fur.

"Are you alright?" he asked. "What happened?"

In answer, Corrin turned and pointed out to sea. The ships were still just beyond the rocks. "Bandits."

"Bandits," he echoed, and stared out at the ships. "You escaped from the bandits." A pause. His tone grew incredulous. "You escaped by *swimming.*"

"That'd be why I'm wet," said Corrin. Bit slow on the uptake, he was. It amused her probably more than it should have.

"Your lips are turning *blue.*"

She blinked. *Blue. How odd.* "M'not deprived of air." Her mind churned, sluggish, and gradually, comprehension dawned on her. A tiny voice in her head (reminiscent of Bathilda's) screeched warnings of lives extinguished by cold, but the voice and alarm that came with it both felt far away, like they weren't hers. She didn't feel like she was dying. Didn't even hurt. Just felt like she wanted to sleep. "Blood flow problems. Hypothermia. Throw me by a fire 'n' pour hot soup in my stomach to fix me up." She pointed sternly at the ships. "Friends need help first."

The kind-faced guard gripped her shoulder harder and turned to his companion, who seemed old as the speaker did young. He had iron grey hair and a beard cut short, and stone grey eyes to match. He didn't have as many wrinkles as Bathilda, but they were there, sharp lines etched in his face as if with a chisel. "Ragnor, sir," said the kind-faced one, "we need to get her back—"

"Do so. The rest of us will fight."

"Yes sir." Thick arms slid beneath Corrin's shoulders and knees. The guard scooped her up, just as easily as her da used to when she was small. He jogged toward the tower, and Corrin was bounced and jostled in his grip.

Everything after that was a blur. There was a door opening and banging shut, and stairs, maybe, and the crackling of the fire. Something orange-red flitted in the corner of her eye. The guard kept saying words she didn't quite catch, except for phrases here and there —"hot soup," he promised, "blankets, come on—"

"Blood flow," said Corrin blearily. "Specially in th' hands and feet."

She felt arms unwrapping, a sinking sensation, blankets draping over her. A hand at her back. Warm liquid at her lips, which Corrin drank obediently. She felt a tugging at her feet, and then a lightness, air on her toes and the squelchy slap of something wet hitting the floor. A finger tapped her cheek, and she realized the guard was saying something… "—sleep—" he said urgently, "don't fall—"

Sleep sounded like a splendid idea, particularly if she was so tired that she was falling over.

That's not right, I'm lying down, aren't I… can't fall if I'm lying down…

She closed her eyes, and in a breath, she'd succumbed to slumber.

CHAPTER SEVEN

Friend Lost, Friend Made

Corrin awoke with a start and an eyeful of stone ceiling. For a second, she thought the Bandit King had caught her and thrown her in a dungeon. Then she realized that this place smelled like stewed meat, whereas the dungeons she'd heard stories about all reeked of waste and decay. Torches and a hearth-fire illuminated the room, too bright and warm for a doomed person's cell. Windows dotted the walls, showing strips of night sky. Corrin was in a bed—the only bed in this room.

A man sat in a wooden chair, his hands clasped in his lap and his head bowed. He was huge, but something about him put her in mind of a young deer. Maybe it was the color of his hair or the patchy beard…

And then she remembered his hand on her shoulder, his arms carrying her, his worried voice making promises and telling her not to fall.

Corrin sat upright. It took more effort than it should have. She had blankets heaped on top of her, and her tunic and trousers were mercifully dry, as if someone had wrung her clothes out by the fire and returned them freshly warmed. And yet, she still felt cold and weak. "'Scuse me," she said, "sir, um, mister guardsperson, whatever your name is, could you wake up? Sir?… Uh… SIR?"

He jolted upright. Caught sight of her. Blinked. And then he smiled, delighted and relieved. "Thank the gods you're awake," he said, and oh dear, his voice was trembling with emotion. Seemed like a bit of an overreaction, considering all she'd done was nod off for… er…

"How long was I unconscious?"

"A half-day and—" The guard glanced out the window. "—a half night, by my reckoning."

Oh.

"Your *lips* were *blue*."

"Insufficient circulation can turn the skin blue," Corrin explained, hoping that he could find reassurance in understanding. She checked her fingertips. They were pink. "Cold can cause blood flow to concentrate around the vital organs and retreat from the extremities. It happens a lot, especially in winter when folks go out to look for food or get wood and don't bundle up properly." She flexed her hands. They were stiff, but responsive. "Bathilda says it's a real good excuse to drink mead, whiskey, or other fiery brews." Corrin wiggled her toes experimentally. "'Course, right after she says that, she tells me to make an herbal remedy instead."

"I knew that. Er, some of it." The guard rubbed the back of his neck sheepishly. "But you didn't look well at all, and—anyway, are you feeling better, miss…?"

"Corrin." She swung her legs over the side of her bed. Her toes touched cold flagstone, and she shivered. "Thank you for hauling me up here, sir. What's your name?"

"Tenno." He smiled. "Well met."

"Likewise. Are the other soldiers out rescuing my friends?"

"Yes. I think. They've been a while. I'm not sure what's taking them so long, actually…"

"Did they know they'd be fighting bandits?"

Tenno's brow wrinkled in confusion. "Ragnor said—yes, my commanding officer knows, at any rate. Ragnor recognized the insignia. We all assumed there'd be a platoon of thugs. My squad's taken a ship loaded with crossbows and cannons." Tenno leaned forward. "Was our estimate right?"

"How much is a platoon?"

"Forty or so."

Corrin sifted through her memories, trying to recall the size of the ship and the number of bandits that had swarmed across the gang planks. Too big, too many. "Maybe. I just remember there were a lot, and they were all wielding daggers or axes or what have you. Their leader called herself the Bandit King. She's after my map." Tenno's eyebrows shot up in a silent question, but Corrin barely noticed; she had just remembered that said map had been on her person, and paper wasn't half as waterproof as human skin. She reached in her vest's inner pocket—maybe, just maybe, the leather had protected it—

Her fingertips found a square of paper. She eased it out and, with great trepidation, pried it open. Pried, because the edges had gotten stuck together.

Internally, she swore.

The inked words had blurred into illegible blotches. Rivers had swelled into lakes, paths into swathes of grey, mountains into indistinct lumpy patches. Corrin could recognize what these things once were only because she had stared at this map so many a time, and even so, she couldn't remember every twist and turn. She couldn't recall whether this one splotch warned of bog sprites or trolls, or if that other one had been a bridge or a mud pit. And the Tree of Life was gone. A black smudge engulfed the heart of the Gloamwood, like an unfathomable black lake.

Corrin felt a tide of panic rising within her—and she recalled, unbidden, Amella's words about panic and needing to keep her head.

Amella. Her throat tightened. What had happened to her friend?

Firmly, she told herself, *Don't think about that. Don't panic. Stop panicking. Think, what would Amella do, if she were well and with me? What would she say I should do, right now?*

Corrin took a deep breath.

First, she splayed the map flat on her bed. If it was laid out in the open air, maybe some of the ink splotches would miraculously regain definition. (She was fooling herself. That wasn't how ink worked. But it couldn't hurt. Couldn't get worse, right?)

Next, she asked, "Can I borrow a quill and piece of parchment?"

"Of course." Tenno disappeared down a staircase. He returned with a half-empty bottle of ink, a fresh roll of parchment, and a quill. The quill was of a kind Corrin had never seen before—longer than a crow's pinion or even a hawk's, with a spectrum of crimson and orange that glinted like embers. But it did its job all the same.

Corrin scrawled down everything that she could remember. The result had more blank spaces and maybe-this-maybe-thats than she would've liked, but it was still better than nothing. Technically. If she tilted her head and squinted, she could almost convince herself her spotty memory hadn't mixed up the Tree of Life with a troll's den.

"Why would a bandit be after a map?" asked Tenno. "How'd she even know you had it?"

Oh right, thought Corrin, *poor man must be awfully confused.* Aloud, she said, "My guess is she wants the same thing I'm after: the thing my map is, or was, good for. See, my map had details for the Gloamwood.

It told me where to find a fruit in there—one that's supposed to cure illnesses that regular medicine won't. I'm after the fruit to save my da and others in my village. It's, um, the cartographer labelled the source after that old Tree of Life tale."

Corrin thought back to before the Bandit King chased her on the water, before Corrin had known better than to trade words with her—back to their conversation in Miritown. "I met the Bandit King in a bar. Didn't have a clue who she was, so when she asked where I was headed, I told her about my map and what I was after. She offered to take my map and do my quest for me."

"That's, uh. That's suspicious."

She smiled wryly. "You're telling me, eh? Good thing I said no." She tucked away her sheet of scribbles. "She might be one of those superstitious types—she might think this fruit's like in the stories and can help her live forever. She brought up those immortality tales, back in the bar. Seemed interested in the idea. Or," she added, shrugging, "it might be she just wants the fruit to sell for a fortune. I dunno. Didn't ask her. Wasn't like I had much room for curiosity, what with the mortal terror and wanting to save my neck."

Tenno's brow furrowed. "To reiterate: you met the Bandit King in the bar, but you didn't know who she was. You told her you have a map of the Gloamwood. And you intended to follow this map into the Gloamwood's heart, the most dangerous place in all the land, in search of a miracle cure from old legends? And the Bandit King has decided she wants your map and the cure, so she's after you?"

Corrin didn't miss the way he said *intended,* like he thought she couldn't—or wouldn't—go anymore. She'd been leaning on Amella, true, and even if she still could—even if Amella had made it out—she hadn't bet on bandits coming after them. She was scared. But she was scared of what she stood to lose more. "I'm still going. If I don't do this, I'll lose my da. I'll lose my neighbors, and I'll lose my home."

"It's hard to lose the ones you love," said Tenno gently, "but sometimes there's nothing you can do about it." He looked old all of a sudden, his face weary and shadowed.

"But if I find this fruit—"

"You could lose your own life."

Corrin curled her hands into fists. "I know. But it's worth the risk."

Tenno closed his eyes as if in pain. He breathed in, slowly, and out again. "You can't be more than fourteen—"

"*Seventeen.*"

His eyebrows shot up, but a heartbeat later, his look of surprise turned to one of consternation. "My apologies. Seventeen, then. At your age, I'd just started basic training. I didn't have any real duties, not even the simplest of watch-keeping shifts, until I turned nineteen. You have so much life ahead of you." He took another one of those slow breaths. "I'm sorry about your da and your home. I really am. But I think—I think given the choice, he'd rather see you alive than him. Parents are like that."

Corrin's eyes burned, full of saltwater even though she'd long since left the sea. "But I'm making the choice, and I want to save him. And not just him—the rest of my village, too. This fruit's our last chance."

Tenno looked troubled. "But why send you? Why not someone older?" In the silence, Corrin heard the unspoken question: *why someone so small and unprepared for danger?*

Corrin rubbed at her eyes until they cleared. "It wasn't just me. I have a friend, a strong one, who was traveling with me." She paused, then added, "The military—"

"—never sends soldiers beyond the borders of Stalt." Tenno rubbed a hand over his face. "Dragon's fire, Corrin, I wish the king would send a legion of our finest to search that forest in your stead. But it would risk too many lives. We don't have people to spare on ghosts of chances. We have to be around to bring criminals to justice, drive beasts from populated areas, rescue people from accidents, and, ah, sometimes break up street fights." Tenno sighed. "Surprised me, actually, how much of our job involves pulling apart two people who've had too much to drink."

"Well there you go," said Corrin wearily. "Soldiers won't take this quest."

Tenno clasped his hands in his lap. "I'll ask Ragnor if it's possible to make an exception," he said. "I can't promise anything, mind you, but I will see what I can do."

"Thank you." Corrin swung her feet back on the bed and slumped back against the pillows.

"Would you like some stew?" asked Tenno kindly.

Corrin shook her head, her eyes closed, though both her ma and Bathilda would've scolded her for turning it down (both of them were convinced she needed to eat more). Her stomach felt like it had some room, sure, but she didn't feel hungry, and she was tired…

Tenno said, "Alright."

He tugged the blankets out from under her feet and drew them up to her chin. Corrin nestled beneath the covers and drifted between waking and sleeping. She heard the *crackle-hiss* of a dying hearth-fire and the soft *thunk*s of footsteps on flagstone as Tenno moved about. She dreamed of the crackle of lightning and a hissing cat, and the footsteps of the Bandit King as she strode toward Corrin, dagger gleaming, cloak billowing, teeth bared—

"*SCREE!*"

Corrin jolted awake.

Something heavy clattered against stone. She blinked. A chair lay upended by the hearth-fire, and Tenno lay sprawled on the flagstones, cursing. Before Corrin had time to wonder what had happened, he sprang to his feet and ran to the window, where a bird shuffled on the sill.

Corrin almost mistook the bird for a hawk. It was the same size as one, with a similar shape to the head, and tucked in the window as it was, she couldn't well make out its colors. But then Tenno brought it into the torchlight, and its feathers glimmered like flames. It had beady dark eyes, which it used to peer curiously at Corrin, and its talons grasped Tenno's forearm confidently. It had a scroll tied to its leg.

Tenno lowered his arm to Corrin's bedpost, and the bird shuffled onto it. Corrin shuffled back, unnerved by the wicked curve of its beak and talons. The bird shuffled after her, chirping, but stopped when Tenno snapped his fingers. "Give it here," he said sternly.

The bird *scree'd* and stuck out the leg with the scroll.

"One of our firebirds," Tenno explained as he freed it from its burden. The bird chirruped. Tenno murmured a command, and the bird fluttered to his shoulder, where it roosted and fluffed out its feathers happily. "This one's named T—" He broke off. His cheeks flushed. "Just call her Junior."

Junior pinned Corrin under her beady stare. Corrin brought her blankets to her chin. "You train firebirds?"

"When we're lucky enough to have them, yes. They're rare and often prefer wilderness, but they can relay messages from ship to tower, they can hunt, they can help with fire rescues..." Tenno tickled Junior fondly under the beak. Junior closed her eyes blissfully. "They're clever creatures, and quite useful. This'd be an update from Ragnor, I think." He unrolled the scroll and skimmed it. His face fell. Corrin's heart sank.

"What does it say?"

"Corrin, you should rest, we can discuss this in the morning—"

"Can I please see the scroll?"

Tenno took a slow breath. "Technically, I shouldn't let you read military correspondence." He said this, but his hand offered the message. Corrin plucked it from his fingers and read the note someone had penned in a neat, economical hand:

Tenno—

Merchant ship without functional sail. Only passengers left a cat and a donkey. Merchants' whereabouts unknown. Bandit ship escaped.

Dropped merchant ship's anchor. Will patrol harbor, then head to shore. ETA before sunrise.

Take shift on watch tower. Hope your charge is well.

-Ragnor

Corrin wordlessly handed the scroll back to Tenno. Amella, Turner, Bruin, Chevira, Vinny—all missing, either captured or thrown overboard (*almost surely overboard,* whispered the most pessimistic corner of her mind, *and they can't swim*). Ricker a traitor. Oatmuncher and Dragon the only known survivors. And what were they supposed to do without their owners?

Actually, Dragon, being Dragon, could probably handle himself fine…

She swiped at her eyes.

"We'll do everything we can to track them down," Tenno said. "I swear by my sword and armor. Please, get some rest."

Corrin thought for sure she wouldn't be able to. But a breath and a heartbeat later, she was asleep.

Footsteps thudded against flagstone. Voices murmured urgently, gradually dragging Corrin out of the fog of slumber, until at last, she opened her eyes.

The sun had risen, and its light passed through the windows in buttery beams. A half-dozen soldiers clustered in the center of the room. They were all clad in piecemeal armor: chunks of steel hammered into leather vests and greaves, imperial insignias painted seemingly wherever—on shoulders and helmets, sometimes on breastplates, in one case on a woman's glove. They kept their voices low, unaware that Corrin had awoken.

A lump of grey fur pressed against Corrin's side—a large, stripey lump, whose ears twitched when she shifted. Dragon. His eyes cracked open, twin slits of yellow and black. He reached up and rested a paw on her stomach, as if he were telling her to stay put.

Corrin lay still and listened.

"—patrol up the coast, down, northeastern border—"

"—take messenger birds—"

"—need someone here to keep watch—"

"—send to Stalt for backup—"

"—notify Miritown—"

"—supplies?"

Tenno was among them, close to her bedside and with his back turned to her. His voice rumbled gently, for the most part lost among the others, but sometimes Corrin caught snatches from him about contacting the king (not-bandit), and a couple mentions of her name. She shifted, lifting her head a smidge, trying to hear better—

"She's awake."

The speaker was a man with grey hair and a roadmap of lines and scars on his face. He was a head shorter than Tenno, maybe the shortest one there (discounting Corrin), but something about the way he held himself made him seem tall. Or maybe it was the way everyone fell silent when he spoke, or the way people looked to him. His eyes were as gray as his hair, with irises like stones. He seemed familiar. Had she seen him somewhere before?

The man strode over to her bedside and rested his hand on the bedpost. His pinky was crooked, as if it had been broken and hadn't healed properly. He'd probably injured it in the field and gotten the splinting wrong. Hands and fingers were tricky pieces of anatomy, intricate and hard to set right unless you knew exactly what you were doing.

"Well met, Corrin," said the man. "I am Ragnor, military general, northern division."

She had a hazy memory of his name and his face. Yesterday. He'd been there yesterday.

"Well met," Corrin said, even though she wasn't sure if it was true yet. He wasn't smiling. The lines in his face didn't look like laugh lines. He did not seem unkind, but he looked to be all steel and sternness, while Tenno was soft and gentle-humored.

"Tenno's informed me of your situation. We're discussing what to do right now. Current plan is to notify Their Majesty of the Bandit King's movements, alert Miritown, and request an increased military presence in all the realm's northern cities. We'll deploy scouter birds to try to pin down her location." Ragnor's face could have been carved from stone. "We won't let outlaws threaten our people."

Corrin swallowed. "Okay. Thank you, sir."

Ragnor inclined his head.

"Did Tenno also tell you about my quest, sir?"

"He did."

"Then is there any chance you could—I mean—could you spare some soldiers to help me navigate the Gloamwood?" But even as she spoke, she took in Ragnor's expression, inscrutable, unchanging, and she knew instinctively that this request was a lost cause.

"No," said Ragnor. "I can't ask my soldiers to risk their lives for a fragile hope."

Corrin watched her own fingers curl on the bedcovers, and her throat tightened. At this point, that fragile hope was all she had.

"I also request that you stay here. From what I understand, you're a target."

Under less dire circumstances, Corrin would have been grateful for the chance to stay safe in this tower, with a crackling fire and Tenno making her stew. Stone walls were preferable to forests full of monsters, or roads with bandits at her heels. But her da was getting sicker a boat's ride away, and she'd left Bathilda alone to slow Oddment's plague. And she'd sworn, she'd *promised* Amella that she'd do her best. So as it was…

Corrin said firmly, "I have something I need to do, sir."

Ragnor remained impassive. "Rumors of this 'Bandit King' haunt whispers in taverns and the shadows at the edge of town. Little is known about her for certain, but they say she knifed her way to power and has inspired followers into awe and terror, and she keeps outmaneuvering us. She's a killer. This killer is after you."

Behind him, Tenno paled.

"After my map," Corrin corrected, even as her blood ran cold and her spine tingled with fear. "Which is ruined."

Ragnor's eyebrows rose, a movement so minute she almost missed it. "Does she know it's ruined? And do you realize, Corrin, that in the absence of a map, your memory is the greatest substitute?"

Well gee, sir, if I hadn't realized it before, I've sure realized it now. Her thoughts churned. Every word he spoke seemed to make the stone walls more comforting, the beams of sunlight more ominous. But she couldn't get detained here. She had to convince him to let her go, before his words sapped the last of her resolve. So she said, "If you spread rumors that you're holding the map here, she'll forget about me. She'll be lured to this tower like a fly into a honey trap. I'd best be out of the way when that happens, right?"

"Interesting strategy, but a risky one."

"Riskier than using me as bait?"

His eyebrows rose further. "Yes. If you were bait, you'd be the most well-protected bait I've ever met."

Corrin pictured a squadron of soldiers crouched around a worm. She imagined the worm trapped in a jar, with dirt and leaves and nowhere to go. That was all right for a worm, but it wouldn't do for her. "Will you force me to stay?"

Ragnor remained stoic. "No, I will not. We want to protect you, not imprison you."

"Then I appreciate your hospitality, sir, but I must be going."

The guards left, presumably to hold further counsel, disperse to their lookout posts, or do whatever else they did around here. The exception was Tenno, who made her stew and tea and hovered over her while she took inventory. She'd lost her pack, and her spare clothes, food, and medicine supplies with it. She still had her boots, her hunting dagger, and the "lucky" rock Sam had given her. (*Some luck this brought me,* she thought wryly as she weighed the rock in her palm. *I've been chased down at sea by bandits, and my map's soaked through.*) She also still had the sword, the one she'd dredged up in Turner's cargo hold. Tenno had laid it out by the hearth to dry for her. He'd even sharpened it; he told her as much when she checked the edge, looking for signs of rust or dullness.

"Are you trained to use that?" he asked as Corrin buckled it to her waist.

"Barely."

He frowned. "Are you sure you want to—"

"Where's Oatmuncher?"

"...Sorry?"

"The donkey. He belonged to my friend Amella."

"Ah. Oatmuncher is in the stables with our cows and horses."

Dragon, who had taken over Corrin's spot on the bed, watched the two of them through narrowed eyes. Corrin leaned over and gave him an ear-scratch. He purred at her, but his tail-tip twitched, a sign of thinning patience. He was probably feeling stressed, what with all the fighting abovedeck and getting dragged to a new place by people he didn't recognize. Corrin let him be and turned back to Tenno. "Could Oatmuncher stay with you? He's good for carrying supplies on well-traveled roads, but I'm not so sure about wilderness. 'Sides, he's Amella's. If you find her, I think she'd like him back. If—if not, then I think... I think she'd rather he be somewhere safe."

"Well, yes, we can take care of him, but—"

"Thank you." Corrin counted up her coins. They weren't much. Certainly not enough to replace the supplies she'd lost. She grimaced. "M'sorry to ask this, but do you have spare rations and medical supplies? And maybe a slingshot for hunting? Lost my flint block, too. I could pay in labor," she added earnestly, "polish the weapons, scrub the pots, that sort of thing. I just can't stay for long. I might have to repay you after."

"Corrin, no, you don't have to do that. I'll make sure you have what you need."

Tenno went upstairs. Corrin occupied herself with lying back on the bed and trying not to dread setting out, until at last, he returned with a bulging pack. It was larger than Corrin's old one, made for someone of Tenno's size, but it fit well enough. The leather was worn and supple from years of use. She inspected the contents. Tenno had filled the pack with dates, dried meats, hard biscuits, a canteen, a slingshot, and a stack of bandages and cleansing salve, among other supplies. "This is fantastic," she said. "Thank you." She tucked everything back inside.

"Of course. I couldn't just let you go running off with nothing."

"Still, it's awfully kind of you." Corrin shouldered the pack. "Alright. I'm ready now, so I'd best be going."

Tenno shifted from foot to foot, looking peculiarly anxious.

"Fortune and spirits be with you. Hopefully I'll come back through here."

Silence. More fidgeting. He opened his mouth, then closed it, as if he were about to say something but thought better of it.

Corrin cleared her throat awkwardly. When Tenno still failed to answer, she mustered up a weak smile and turned to leave. Much as she'd rather go with a proper goodbye, she couldn't dally here forever, waiting for Tenno to untie his tongue. Though she couldn't for the life of her imagine why it was tied in the first place...

"Oh for the love of stars," he burst out, "wait there a moment, please!"

He bolted up the stairs before she could protest. Corrin watched him go, bewildered.

Thumps and clangs echoed down through the door he'd left ajar. It sounded like the cacophony of someone running into every inanimate object and slamming every drawer imaginable. Tenno returned in a hail of thundering footsteps and muffled swears. He wore a pack too, one even larger than hers and stuffed fit to burst, but he bore it like it weighed nothing. He also had Junior, perched on his head like a giant, feathery ornament. Junior preened. Those talons must've been poking Tenno's scalp something awful, but he didn't so much as grimace.

"I'm accompanying you," he announced.

What? "But I thought Ragnor said—"

"I know what he said." Tenno smiled. It was a crooked smile, showing more teeth on one side than the other, but it was sincere and warm and large enough to reach his eyes. "Listen. I entered this profession to help people—to protect, and to aid those who need it most. Right now, that's you. I think Ragnor will understand. He joined the military for the same reasons I did, and I've, er, left him a note. But if he doesn't… Well, then helping you is still more important.

"So I'll go with you into the Gloamwood, and I'll stick with you until we're back out. Then we'll see about finding you a ride back to Oddment. Alright?" He paused. His smile dropped. "I'm sorry I can't give you more of an escort than just me, but…"

You wonderful, giant tender-heart of a human being, Corrin thought, and something loosened in her chest. She felt lighter. She didn't have to go on alone, after all. "That's a heckuva lot better than what I thought I was going to get. Thank you so much."

"Of course." He laid a hand on her shoulder. The weight reminded Corrin of Amella, of her camaraderie and steadfast bravery, and she felt a pain in her heart and a prickling in her eyes. But before the tears could spill, Tenno spoke again. "Alright, then. Let's get going."

CHAPTER EIGHT

Interlude: The Bandit King

Far away, deep in a network of tunnels, the Bandit King smiled.

When that girl had escaped into the rocks, King had commanded her people to seize the prisoners, turn her vessel around, and hasten for the secluded Leviathan's Maw. (Her name for it. She felt that any place so grandly hidden, and grand enough to hide one such as herself, ought to have a grand name.) It was a cave that yawned open in the shadowy part of an inlet. It was craggy, narrow, and difficult to spot unless you knew precisely where to look. A ship could sail all the way through to the opening at the north end, but the bandits didn't bring their vessel that far.

Partway through, they'd brought the ship to moor by a pebbly shore and set up a camp among stalagmites thicker than a man's waist. Lanterns formed a semicircle, and in that semicircle, the Bandit King and her forces stretched their legs. They still felt the sea-sway of the rocking ship and the compactness of the ship's hold—large though it was, her people were many.

The Bandit King felt satisfied. It was the most interesting day she'd had in a long, long time.

Her target could swim! Who would have thought? How inconvenient. How resourceful. And the girl had the resolve to jump, too. It was the kind of desperate thing the King herself might have done, back when she was a mere street urchin with a rusty dagger and quick, hungry hands: jumped into deadly waters and guarded her own life above all else, letting other fools take the fall. Well. If the Bandit King could swim.

But it wasn't like her target—this Corrin—was a younger her. Not really. Unlike the Bandit King, the girl probably had scruples, probably felt guilty about leaving her companions behind. She'd seemed the type to have scruples, at least, back when the King had talked to her in Miritown. How fortunate. King could use that. It would be a more interesting chase than she'd had in a while, but a quickly resolved one.

The Bandit King flashed a command in hand signals. A ripple went through the crowd as her people repeated the signal to each other. Everyone stilled. All was silent, except for the drip-drip-drip of moisture off a stalactite.

"Bring forth the prisoners," she ordered.

Her followers shoved them to the fore: five of them, arms and feet bound in rope. A woman with brown skin, short-shorn hair, and a fierce glower: the berserk fighter among them, the healer girl's friend. A willow branch of a man with hints of grey in his beard: the hidden snake, the one with a surprisingly swift blade—or so the King's subordinates had reported. A scowling, blonde man with a bandaged shoulder. A man with a paunchy stomach—a mark of comfort, of a soft life, of weakness. How pathetic. And lastly, a smaller, wiry woman. She and the berserker probably had ancestry in the far northern lands, like Ricker—the lands where the sun beat furiously and desert stretched from horizon to horizon.

Her guards grabbed the scruffs of the prisoners' necks and forced them all to kneel before her. The Bandit King took a moment to amuse herself with the sight of them there, forced to pay her tribute. Then she commanded, "Rise."

The prisoners were dragged to their feet.

"I trust you all understand the position you're in. I can't let you go because you'd scurry off to your feeble king and report where you last saw me, and they'd send out their forces. That would cause me no end of annoyance. But I haven't run you through yet. Obviously, if I haven't run you through, then there's something more you can give me—something that can, perhaps, save your lives."

She strode forward and stopped in front of the thin willow branch of a man. "Your name?"

"Turner." The man gave it readily. Perhaps he thought there was no value in withholding a name. In this case, he'd be right. Smart man.

"Turner. A fine name. Implies a certain flexibility. You were the captain of the ship?"

He nodded gravely.

The Bandit King's smile broadened. "Thought so. I know a leader when I see one. It's in the way the other prisoners look to you."

Turner said nothing.

He wasn't won over by honeyed words, she could tell. That was fine. In truth, the Bandit King would have been disappointed if he was. An easily flattered captive made for a weaker one, a less intriguing challenge. So the Bandit King changed tactics. She rested a hand on the pommel of her sword and got to the point: "Tell me what route the healer girl is taking."

Turner's gaze flickered to the Bandit King's weapon, but still, he said nothing.

The Bandit King drew her blade and rested the tip ever-so-delicately on Turner's collarbone. "You were the one charting the course."

Still, he said nothing.

A voice snapped, "He was charting the *water* course, you lily-livered monster."

The Bandit King turned.

The berserker—named Amella, was she?—glared back at her. "Leave him alone."

"Why?"

It was a simple question, and yet, Amella's brow furrowed and beaded with sweat.

The Bandit King felt a glimmer of satisfaction at this. It was gratifying to see how her mere word could induce stress, once her targets were beaten and under her power. She'd never be the weak one. Not anymore. She gripped her dagger firmly, a cool smile curving her lips as she awaited Amella's answer.

Amella swallowed and spoke. "Because he's a bystander. He won't know. You ought to be interrogating me." Her expression hardened. It was a look that the Bandit King had seen only rarely, on certain targets when they knew they were cornered and had resolved to fall fighting. "Not like I'll just spill anything you want, of course. I hate your guts too much for that."

"Hate my guts," the Bandit King echoed, amused.

"You fired on our ship, took us prisoner, looted our cargo, threatened to kill us, are probably aiming to kill us, and you're hiding behind your lackeys while they dirty their hands, you starlands-forsaken jackal."

The Bandit King's amusement died. She pressed the edge of her blade lightly against Turner's skin. "I don't hide. Hold your tongue."

And Amella did, even as her eyes blazed.

"Now. Tell me the route she's taking. The healer girl—Corrin."

Silence.

"Speak, or this one dies."

Still no response.

The Bandit King narrowed her eyes and pressed more insistently. Blood beaded around the steel. It wasn't much—yet.

Amella's eyes grew round. She burst out, "She'll be angling northeast, through the griffin highlands, and back south through the Gloamwood."

The Bandit King weighed her words. They had tripped over themselves on their way out of her, marked with the clumsiness of fear and hastily given. *Too quick. Too easy.* "You'd think a merchant would know how to lie better." She held the blade steady. A fingernail's breadth deeper would hit an artery. Necks were fragile things, so she needed to take care—before she'd solidified her power among the bandits, her own neck was nearly cut open thrice, no, four times—

King squashed that train of thought. It was irrelevant. All that mattered was, this *captive's* neck was fragile, and she didn't want to end her *captive's* life. Not yet. Not while he could still be used.

Amella asked, "Why do you think I was lying?"

"You told me yourself—you said you wouldn't spill anything I wanted. This is your chance to change your mind. Tell me the truth, and I won't decapitate him. Stay silent, and I will. Lie, and you're next."

"Fine. Just stop."

The Bandit King waited. One heartbeat. Two. Three. Perhaps she should—

"I told her to head straight east."

Ah. This was the truth. The Bandit King knew because it came with the sagging of Amella's shoulders, the dousing of her voice's fire, the cracking of something in her expression. The words had rasped out of her this time, as if the Bandit King had reached in and pulled them out in her clenched fist.

East. Toward Mount Cauldra, then. Interesting advice. The Bandit King had heard dark stories about that mountain, the sort woven around a campfire late at night and told in shadowy corners of bars. But then, she'd also heard that the mountain's monster slept. "Good," she said, and took her sword away from Turner's neck. The man's breathing, which had gone shallow, deepened so that his chest heaved like a bellows.

The Bandit King would let Turner live, for now. She was a person of her word. (Which was rich, one of her subordinates had once said, coming from a bandit. That subordinate hadn't lasted for long.) But she couldn't let these prisoners think she was soft. She'd need to make an example out of someone.

There. The one with the flabby stomach.

He'll do.

CHAPTER NINE

Moving Onward

Corrin couldn't remember the name of the village she and Tenno were leaving behind. She couldn't even remember if it was marked on the map. But she caught glimpses as she passed through—of people carrying basketfuls of fish, some stopping to look curiously back at her, and cats and chickens scurrying about—and she tasted the sea-salted air. She formed an impression of the place, an image of wooden huts and lives meandering on. It seemed nice. If she'd had time, she might've stayed to get to know the village properly.

But alas, she didn't.

She led the way up a hill, following a faded dirt path dead east. At the crest, she turned and looked back to reassure herself that Tenno was still following her. For such a big person, he had quiet footsteps.

He strode up the path with Junior perched loyally on his shoulder. Behind him lay the rolling slope, the stone tower, and the huts that were scattered across an expanse of meadow-grass and sea roses. Corrin imagined the villagers enjoying the evening on their porches, kids scrambling around as kids were wont to do, and folks pausing just to appreciate the view of the ocean. She could still see it from here —a vast, unending blue that went on and on until it met another, lighter unending blue.

Tenno drew level with her and stopped. "Lovely place, isn't it?"

"Yes." Corrin took in one last, salt-seasoned breath, then turned around and kept walking. As Tenno fell in step beside her, she asked, "What's its name?"

"Boar's Tusk Peninsula."

"I meant the village."

"It doesn't have one. We just call this place the peninsula."

"Oh. Okay."

"..."

"Did you grow up on the peninsula?" Corrin asked, mostly to fill the silence. She'd grown unaccustomed to silence, traveling with Amella. Amella's love of storytelling meant that Corrin had gotten used to chatter, to a friendly voice that filled the space between them with tales of grand exploits, jokes, and random bits of advice. Even on the ship, it seemed there was always someone chattering or the bustle of shiphands adjusting the ropes and sails—or, in those moments she'd stolen in the cargo hold, Dragon purring away, his rumble as mighty as a wild beast's.

Tenno, however, was proving quiet, and paired with Corrin's own propensity for quiet, it was just... a whole lot of quiet. Awkward quiet. She could hear her own footsteps, muffled though they were by the dirt, and the breeze rustling the meadow-grass.

"No, actually, I grew up in a mountain settlement called Druin. Known for its miners and metalworkers. And, uh, for folks growing up short. Somehow I didn't, though, ahahah..." Tenno scratched the back of his neck. "I thought I'd be a smith for a while, follow in my parents' footsteps, you know. But, uh, I decided I wanted to help protect people, so I applied to the military instead. Moved to the capital, finished basic, then got stationed out here. Been here for... oh... a few years, now."

"What made you decide? That you wanted to protect people, I mean."

Tenno's face fell. "Oh, no, you don't want to hear that story." It sounded like he meant, *Oh no, I don't want to tell that story.*

Corrin blinked. Curiosity gnawed at her, but it was the kind she knew she should ignore. Like when she wondered what a person's heart looked like as it beat, or their lungs as they breathed, or any part of them that oughtn't be poked at or opened up because it would hurt them if she did that. "Alright. Well, um, you know why I'm out here, but I became a healer's apprentice when I was seven. Had an accident with some pointy rocks, and Bathilda—I mean, my mentor—stitched me up. When I found out you could fix people like that, and not just cloth or metalwork, it seemed like the most amazing thing."

Tenno's mouth quirked. "So you went through an excruciatingly painful procedure, and it won you over?"

"It wasn't that bad," said Corrin defensively. "She used a local numbing agent, so I didn't feel much except tingles and some weird tugs. It was interesting."

"Interesting," He was holding back laughter, now; she could hear it in his voice. "Has anyone ever told you that you're just a little odd?"

"No, but someone once told me I'm very odd. They were being a hypocrite, though. I guess when home is a place called Oddment... well, it's right there in the name, isn't it?"

He actually did laugh at that. He had a nice laugh, warm and deep.

They lapsed into silence, but this time, it was a comfortable one.

Time passed in dollops, with great long stretches of walking broken up by little moments.

At Tenno's signal, Junior took flight and circled overhead, a blaze of crimson against a backdrop of cottony clouds and blue skies. She'd wheel out so far and so high that she turned into a speck, nigh impossible to spot. "She's a smart bird," said Tenno. His voice was warm with pride, like her da's was when Corrin overheard him talking about her with a neighbor. "If she sees anything amiss, she'll notify me."

Corrin watched Junior circle diligently overhead. "My friend Amella told me about firebirds once," she said thoughtfully. "About the wild ones who wait and watch for the creatures scrambling away from wildfires, then pick them off when they're least expecting it. Makes sense that they'd be real good at spotting trouble, if they're sharp-eyed enough to do that."

"Amella?" echoed Tenno. "What's she like?"

It was an innocent question, clearly an attempt to make friendly conversation; Tenno smiled slightly, his brows raised inquiringly. Even so, Corrin felt a pang of loss and guilt. She'd left Amella behind. Amella had told her to, and it wasn't like there was much else Corrin could do, but it still bothered her. "Amella's the strong friend who was traveling with me," she said quietly. "A trader who lives half in Oddment and half on the road. She's a fantastic swordsperson, and brave, and strong, and maybe a bit mad, and—and she's the reason I made it to shore. Yelled at me to abandon ship, even though she couldn't follow."

Tenno's smile slipped away, replaced by a look of somber understanding. He looked, maybe, like he expected Corrin to continue. Or, at least, was giving Corrin the chance, in case she wanted to.

So Corrin told him about her. How she brought high spirits to gatherings and meals with her tales of far-flung adventures, the sorts that only a madperson would dive into—and how, even then, she wouldn't brave the Gloamwood unless Corrin went with her. How she and her friend Turner had taught Corrin swordsmanship while at sea. Just a smidgeon, a couple weeks' worth, maybe, but still. How she knew so much about so many places. The treasures she brought back from her travels. The times she'd called Corrin over and showed her souvenirs, even though Corrin wasn't carrying coin for shopping. The boar's tusk on her door.

Tenno listened patiently, only very occasionally making an encouraging noise for Corrin to continue.

And so she did, until her voice grew tired and petered out. She hadn't talked so much since... she didn't even know. She wasn't usually a talker.

A moment of quiet stretched between them. At last, Tenno said softly, "Amella sounds incredible."

"She is. Or at least, she—if she didn't make it—"

"We can hope for the best," said Tenno gently, "and cope with the worst if we have to."

Corrin was grateful to him for listening, and grateful to him for not speaking promises or platitudes. They would ring too false to be believed.

As they passed a tree, Tenno asked Corrin to wait. He stripped the tree of its two lowest branches—snapped them off with his bare hands, he did. The branches looked thick around as her wrist. They were splintery at the bases where they'd snapped and leafy and green at the end, but they were straight in the middle.

The tree would be fine, or so Corrin hoped. It had branches left aplenty and a trunk thicker than Tenno's waist.

Tenno unsheathed his hunting knife and set to work. With swift flicks of his knife, he sliced off all the leafy bits and un-splintered the bases, and he cut the wavering ends down until they were sturdy and blunt. He left bark covering the middle, though. It reminded Corrin of the sticks her da had whittled for her and her brothers to play with, back when she was a kid.

Tenno handed her one of the makeshift staffs with a kindly smile. It was lighter than she expected. Had a bit of spring to it. "Thought you might like a walking stick."

"Thank you very much." Corrin tried it out and found she quite liked it. "I think I understand why Bathilda is so attached to hers now.

This is nice."

"Bathilda... You've mentioned her a couple of times. She's your mentor, right?"

"Yep." Corrin once again found herself chattering, telling him all about Bathilda and her books and all the fascinating things Corrin had learned from her. Tenno seemed quite surprised by Bathilda's books, said it was unusual for a single person in a small village to have a stockpile of old tomes. But it wasn't unheard of, if the person was very scholarly (which Corrin promptly asserted that Bathilda was), and he understood how valuable books could be.

Tenno told her about the capital's library. The quiet halls, the maze of towering shelves. He told her about some of his favorites, ones he'd perused by lamplight on dark-shrouded evenings after training—not often, but sometimes. Histories, fables, essays on strategy.

Corrin took her turn listening, letting him reminisce as they strode on, and on, and on.

They passed a farming family's fields and a copse with a small pond and what looked like a ghost owl's nest. The pond had pale lilies. It also had newts and salamanders scurrying along the shore, and if Corrin were back home, she would've been catching the blue ones to bring back to Bathilda. They secreted a slime that, if brewed with the right herbs, could help alleviate nausea.

As it was, Corrin pointed the salamanders out to Tenno and explained how they could be used and why they worked (or so she and Bathilda had theorized) and what other things were needed for the tonic, and how it could lose its potency if you over-boiled it or under-boiled it or didn't give the ingredients sufficient time to react. She also did this for the fever-flowers that peeked out from behind a tree root, and then for a patch of gout-grass, and for anything else she could find that looked helpful.

"It's a pity we can't take it all with us," Corrin said, thinking longingly of spacious satchels and shelves brimming with all the tools and ingredients she could want.

Tenno just looked bemused.

The sky turned dusky orange, and then purplish, and Tenno said they should make camp.

"Camp" consisted of a cheery fire and blankets laid out, and a dinner of jerky and dense biscuits. Junior glided down to them and winged around the flames, making them flicker. She looked like a flame herself, with how her feathers caught the firelight. Eventually, Tenno called her off, and Junior found a nearby tree to roost in.

Corrin watched the ash and charcoal build up. Her mind drifted—back to Amella and Turner, who'd defended the ship so fiercely; to Amella, yelling for her to run; to Bruin—grumpy Bruin, brave Bruin, who'd forced himself to sit still while she threaded his flesh back together; to Chevira, with her easy smile and her eagerness to show her how to tie a ship's knot, and how that smile vanished when she was afraid; to Vinny, who'd shown her how to make sailor's bread.

She hadn't known them for long, except for Amella. Even so, she wished that she could believe they were alright. She wished that, at least, she could know what happened after she jumped ship. She probably wouldn't like knowing for certain what the Bandit King had done with them, but she didn't like not knowing, either. As long as she didn't know, she could imagine any number of horrors: bound to rocks and drowned; decapitated; stabbed through; kept alive but bound somewhere dark, with too little to eat…

A dreadful weight settled in her chest. If she hadn't asked Amella to help her, Amella would've been hale and hearty, probably planning her next trip through the realm. It would've been a good trip, too, full of rare treasures, honeyed ale, raucous laughter, and pouches of coins. Turner wouldn't have gotten involved either, or any of those shiphands, and they'd've had years of salty sea air and billowing sails ahead of them.

Or, what if she hadn't talked about the map in that tavern? If she'd only thought to tell the dodgy stranger a lie? If she'd only kept her mouth shut?

What if she hadn't abandoned them? What if she'd stayed and at least tried to help, tried to get them out of the peril she'd gotten them into?

I would've been dead in a heartbeat, Corrin told herself firmly. *Amella wanted me to escape. She **told** me to.*

Something hard prodded her knee. Corrin started.

Tenno sat a few paces away from her, holding his walking stick like a spear. "Sorry," he said, "but are you all right?"

Corrin considered this. Her chest felt heavy. Her heart couldn't be giving out, could it? The medical texts had said a heart failure would come with a sharp pain or a squeezing, constricted feeling, though. And heart failure scarcely ever afflicted the young and healthy; it struck the elderly and weak, those who were worn down or whose organs had to work too hard to sustain them. No, she decided, she just felt sad, and she hadn't any medicine for sadness.

"Yes," she said. "Just thinking."

Tenno *hmmm*'d. It was a soft, thoughtful sound. "If you'd like to think about something different, I have an idea. Why don't we practice with the sword? You show me what you've learned so far, and I'll show you what I learned from the military. Considering where we're headed, I'd really, *really* feel better if I could see you handle a weapon."

Corrin considered the swords belted at their waists. Specifically, how sharp and pointy they were, and how easy it would be to slice a finger or slash an artery. She placed a protective hand on the hilt. "Won't we cut ourselves to mincemeat with these?"

"Huh? Oh, goodness no, we won't spar with those. You'd do form and footwork drills with the blade, but for sparring practice, we'd use these." Tenno tapped the ground with his walking stick. "They won't match a real weapon's weight, but if I pare them down, they'll at least match the length. If you could hand me yours—thanks—now give me just a minute…"

In a trice, Tenno modified their sticks. He even shaved a bit off the sides to give them a blade-like shape. He then set them aside, though, and told her to take a battle stance with her real weapon. Corrin complied, taking the position Amella and Turner had drilled into her. Feet facing forward. Angled torso. Blade-tip up, ready to defend (according to Turner) or stab the neck (according to Amella).

Tenno circled her. "You want to make sure you're stable—keep your feet a bit farther apart—yes, good. Good angle. Definitely important to keep as much of yourself behind the sword as possible, don't want to make yourself a bigger target…" He stopped and stood off to one side. "Alright. Show me a lunge—again, don't pitch forward like that, move your feet, shift your center—good—okay, let's see a swing—overhead—across—diagonal—block—block again—block and stab, in succession—watch your balance—better, again—again—good. Now, switch hands."

"But I'm right-handed."

"The military requires us to learn with both in case we injure one. I hope that doesn't happen to you, but it's better to know. Trust me."

She switched. The blade felt newly foreign in Corrin's left hand.

"Okay. Firm your grip. Combat stance—keep the tip higher—okay, overhead swing—uh, okay, try that again, make that less wobbly—

again—"

He kept Corrin at it until her arm burned and sweat coated her skin. Her grip grew slippery. On the last swing, the sword slid dangerously in her grasp, threatening to escape it.

"Alright, *HALT.*"

Corrin let her shoulders sag and her sword dangle. Her heart hammered in her chest, and she felt tired and quivery, like she'd just sprinted across a glade.

"My basic instructor would've bellowed himself hoarse at me if I dropped my guard like that." Tenno didn't sound like he was going to yell, though. If anything, he seemed amused. "Seeing as he was nuts and you're not in the military, I'll be nice and suggest you take a break instead. Remember, though, if you do end up under threat, it's important to keep your weapon ready until you know you're safe."

Corrin gratefully sat down. She noticed that it seemed darker than before. Actually, *much* darker than before.

Plum twilight had faded to an inky black. She could scarcely pick out the shapes of the trees in the darkness. Their campfire had burned down to ash and embers, and Junior had settled down within inches of the orange glow; the firebird slumbered with her head tucked under her wing, her feathers puffing with each breath in. If Corrin tilted her chin back and looked up, she could see that the stars had come out, twinkling and uncountably numerous. The moon was bright and round as a winterberry.

Tenno must have drilled her for an hour, at least. No wonder she was so tired.

A massive hand popped into view, proffering a canteen. "Don't forget to hydrate."

"I'm the healer; aren't I supposed to be telling you that?" But her wheezy breath took the punch out of her jest, and she drank greedily.

Tenno sat beside her and waited for her to finish. When she did, he took the canteen for himself and swigged it. "We used to do this every morning in training," he said as he screwed the canteen's cap back on. He spoke with fondness, and the corners of his mouth stretched into a grin. "Right after we finished our warm-up lap around the city, and right before we broke for breakfast."

Corrin wondered if it was a military madness thing—looking back on grueling training rituals, aches, pain, and misery, and thinking, *Ah, what lovely times*. Then again, she couldn't picture any of the guards back in Oddment reminiscing fondly about laps and drills, so maybe this peculiarity was specific to Tenno.

"We did combat practice, rescue training, and study of the king's law after that. Everyone would be falling asleep at the tables by the time we got to the law. Which, ahah, wasn't such a good thing..." Tenno scratched the back of his neck. "But I couldn't blame us, especially not in the beginning. That kind of intensity takes some getting used to."

They fell quiet. Corrin watched the gentle puffs of Junior's feathers and the rise and fall of her chest. The firebird cooed in her sleep and nestled her head deeper beneath her wing. It was adorable. It made her think of the kittens who were born in the spring back in Oddment. They'd totter around, all fluffy and bushy-tailed and curious, and then all of a sudden flop over, curl up, and tuck their faces under their paws because they were so dreadfully bushed.

"I was going to suggest sparring, but I think I overdid the drills with you. You kept up pretty well, though, considering you've never been to basic. Did you like to run around a lot when you were younger?"

Corrin let out an amused huff. "Not so much liked as had to. I keep having to chase my little brothers around, to get them out of mischief or into the house for dinner."

"You have brothers?"

"Two of 'em, both about seven years younger than me. They're twins."

"Aaw." Tenno's eyes twinkled. "What are their names?"

"Frendel and Sam." Tenno scooted closer and wrapped his arms around his knees, and Corrin elaborated, her fingers curling absentmindedly around the rock in her belt pouch. She described what they looked like and how they scrambled all over the village and the woodlands. How they always ended up in trees and ponds and rivers, or atop the village walls, and how they'd goad her on to chase them. How the two of them were thick as thieves. How, that one time, they'd convinced her that there were fairies hiding out in a copse of trees, and the three of them spent the whole day looking—and Corrin still didn't know if they'd tricked her on purpose or if they'd believed their own words...

...How they'd all conspired to bribe their mum with good behavior and then picked three basketfuls of elderberries, in hopes of having sweet jam for dinner (and how her mother had laughed at them, her voice bursting and bright as a bluejay's call). Her da had liked that idea and decided to try it himself. He'd given her mum fresh-hunted meat and honey, theatrically offered with his knee on the ground, and they had all cooked together that night…

…Corrin's eyes were growing heavy…

…distantly, she heard a gentle goodnight and felt the warmth of a blanket that was thicker than any she'd packed…

…and she sank into a deep slumber, one that Tenno wouldn't interrupt until dawn.

Days passed in a rhythm of tired legs and aching arms. Tenno insisted Corrin learn to fight with her left, and he sparred her with his bearlike strength and inescapable reach. Days also passed in a chorus of birdsong and rustles in the underbrush that made Corrin start; in meals of dried, hard-to-chew food, mixed with fresh-picked herbs and berries and the rare sling-shotted rabbit; and in regular visits from Junior, who would alight on Tenno's shoulder to nibble his earlobe and ply him for treats and head scratches (successfully, every time; this bird was more spoiled and greedy than Tiptoes). Corrin could feel her limbs growing wiry and see the freckles blooming on her skin. Her forearms kept getting more of them, like new constellations, until the flecks were more densely clustered than the stars at night.

The road winnowed away, turning from a clear-cut strip of dirt into a vague indentation in the grass.

"I've never been out this far east," said Tenno quietly. "I don't think there are other settlements out here. Maybe the odd hermit or two, but nothing really… not like a village." He paused, then added, "I've heard things about the mountain out this way—Mount Cauldra, right? Bards say that a dragon slumbers inside of it. Then the Gloamwood's beyond it. And any farther north would take us to the griffin highlands. People don't want to live close to any of those, you know?"

Corrin knew. She almost wished for the bliss of ignorance. Almost. "The dragon was on my map."

"Well. That's… that's unfortunate."

"I'm hoping it's hibernating."

Tenno's parries and strikes had Corrin dancing backward until her back was up against a tree. Knobs and rough bits of bark dug into her back. Her tunic was stuck to her skin. Tenno wasn't even breathing hard, though the bridge of his nose glistened with sweat. His every movement was swift and neat, and all the while, he smiled encouragingly, as if to say, *come on, strike me, you can do it!*—even though Corrin hadn't once, not since she'd met him, even though his

stick kept jabbing for her gut, and he was always, always out of reach
—

—she knocked his weapon to the side, and for a heartbeat, she saw his hand, right there within stabbing reach—

"You've severed my fingers," said Tenno in a faux dramatic voice. He dropped his stick. "Woe is me, I have been defeated!"

A laugh burbled out of her.

"Really, though, good work. If you get someone's hand, you cripple them. 'Course, I usually wear a wrist and hand guard for exactly this reason. But most people don't own wrist and hand guards. If you get a bit quicker on the draw, more efficient with your blocks and strikes, and a bit better at spotting your openings, you'll become a force to be reckoned with." He retrieved his stick, but instead of settling into a battle stance, he strode over and clapped her on the shoulder, beaming. "I am so proud of you."

In that moment, Corrin quite forgot that she'd rather be safe back home; that she liked a sensible, boring life; that she wouldn't have ventured anywhere near this far if she hadn't been desperate. A warmth blossomed in her chest, a giddy, triumphant feeling, and she beamed back at him.

Corrin and Tenno crested a hill. They'd reached a stretch of open terrain after spending the last few days in woodlands, and it was refreshing, having all this open space and a hearty breeze to steal the sweat from their brows. There was no sign of a road anymore; they navigated instead by the moss and sun and constellations at night. The stars looked much as they had above Oddment—a comforting constant in the face of an unfamiliar landscape.

Tenno shaded his eyes with one hand and squinted. "Hm. We're probably just a day's walk away from the mountain. It actually looks like less than that, but I think that's just because it's enormous."

Mount Cauldra loomed ahead of them, a great, jagged thing erupting from the ground and piercing the clouds. If Corrin shaded her eyes and squinted, like Tenno did, it looked like a fang; and the land around it was the gum, swollen and inflamed with hills.

Corrin considered the mountain, the land around the mountain, and how ominous it all looked, and she re-evaluated her plans. "Maybe we should angle south and skirt the mountain. Might save us time, not having to climb all that jagged terrain… or, well, maybe not, maybe it'd take longer, but at least it'd be safer…"

Tenno bit his lip. "Won't that take us into the badlands, though?"

Corrin frowned. Amella had said to avoid the badlands, but she couldn't recall why, exactly, they went by that name. Tentatively, she asked, "Remind me what's bad in the badlands again?"

"Giant wolves, boars, unicorns, wyrms. I've heard and read more horror stories about that place than I can count."

"Wyrms as in giant tunneling snakes?"

"Yes—actually, a couple of my friends had a pretty fierce debate about whether they're more closely related to snakes or to dragons, by ancestry. They never decided, and I've no idea. But I guess, since they look an awful lot like snakes—"

"Except big enough to swallow us whole."

"Yes, except big enough to swallow us whole. Anyway, I guess you can think of them as the giant tunneling snakes. Just don't forget the scaly crests and the forked whip on the ends of their tails." Tenno frowned in thought. "I read in the capital's library that once, there was a tribe that used to hunt them as a ritual and collect their teeth to use as daggers. I think that ritual contributed to that tribe's dying out. But, of course, it's not like most historians are willing to go and investigate the badlands, so we don't know for sure." He cleared his throat. "In any case, I'd rather chance the giant man-devouring beast that's hopefully sleeping, as opposed to the giant man-devouring beasts, plural, that are almost certainly active."

Corrin gulped. "Okay. Giant death mountain it is."

If it weren't for Tenno and his militantly steady pace, Corrin would have subconsciously dragged her feet. As it was, Tenno covered ground in massive strides while she scrambled to keep up. They hastened down the hill, into a copse of trees and out again, and up another hill. And then Corrin caught a blur of crimson out of the corner of her eye. She tensed instinctively and turned to look.

"*SCREE.*"

Junior cannonballed onto Tenno's shoulder. He staggered with the impact.

"What's the matter?" Tenno asked, bewildered, as Junior rapped the side of his temple. Corrin winced. No blood was drawn, but that beak looked awfully pointy and uncomfortable. Tenno merely frowned and pressed, "You saw trouble?"

Junior bobbed her head in a way that looked suspiciously like a nod. Corrin started to wonder just how clever this bird was. Corrin had known that Junior was smart enough to deliver messages, charm her owner for treats, and obey certain commands, like *fly* and *fetch*. She'd also noticed that Tenno talked to Junior almost as if she were a person, but Corrin had always thought it was the same as her talking to Tiptoes. Mere habit, with no expectation that the creature would understand—at least, not beyond tonal inflections of pleasure or displeasure.

"Was it trolls?"

Junior ruffled her wing feathers and shook her head side to side.

"Bandits?"

More head-bobbing.

"Ahead of us?"

Nod-nod.

"North or south?"

Junior's wings snapped out, expansive. One of them pointed north. One of them pointed south. She shuffled her feet on Tenno's shoulder. She seemed anxious.

"A pincer movement." Tenno frowned. "How in the starlands did they move so fast? Junior, are they closing in on us? Do they know where we are?"

Junior folded her wings back in, then shifted them up and down in what Corrin could only describe as a shrug. A bird-shrug. Impressive that Junior knew what a shrug meant, but also utterly unhelpful. If the bandits already knew where they were, versus if they were just lying in wait, there would be no point in trying to sneak by them or changing course—because the bandits would pursue them no matter what they did. But if they didn't know Corrin's and Tenno's position…

Tenno turned to Corrin and asked quietly, "Do you want to turn back?"

Corrin's sensible side screamed at her to say yes, *for the love of the spirits turn back, save your neck,* but—"I can't. My family and village are counting on me."

"Honestly, I thought you might say that. But it doesn't hurt to ask."

"Do *you* want to turn back?"

"I will go as far as you go."

She felt great gratitude and greater fear. It wasn't just her life she was risking.

"Listen," said Tenno softly, "if we move quickly and quietly, we might be able to sneak past them. Junior indicated that they're covering the north and south, which are dangerous lands to begin with, so a detour would be as risky as going forward… but perhaps, if we go dead through the middle—"

"—we won't end up actually dead?"

"Yes. Good optimism. Keep it up."

They resumed their pace from before, but Tenno took care to make his footsteps soft, and Corrin followed suit. Every rustle, twitter, and *chuk-chuk* around them sounded amplified, and all the greenery looked brighter, as if the danger had sharpened her senses. They kept to sheltered ground as much as they could: the shadowed sides of hills, thick copses of trees, and patches of long grass that stretched tall as wheat. Junior stayed on Tenno's shoulder, now. He'd commanded her to stay with him. Otherwise, there was too great a risk of the bandits spotting her flying overhead; she was flaming red, while the lands were green and the sky was blue.

A fox darting out of a bush made Corrin start. She kept tensing and listening to the chatter of squirrels in the trees. She took a deep breath and reminded herself that the squirrels were a good thing. If there were a bunch of bandits tramping around the area, the animals probably would've scampered into hiding. Even so, her heart rabbited.

"Almost there," Tenno whispered.

So they were. They had to tilt their chins back and stare up, up at the sky to see the top of the mountain, now. Corrin could pick out scrubby bushes around its base, craggy boulders, and a shadowy patch that looked like it might be a cave entrance. If so, it couldn't possibly be the one the dragon used—it was too small.

Tentatively, the two of them started across the narrow strip of open, rocky terrain that lay between them and the mountain.

And that was when the Bandit King stepped out from behind a boulder. She grinned like a wolf. Or like a dragon, maybe. "Found you," she called out. "You can't escape into the water now, little fish."

Death's scythe, Corrin thought fervently, and rested a hand on the hilt of her sword. The training Tenno had given her, which had seemed so intense at the time, now felt woefully inadequate. She looked to Tenno, silently asking, what should she do? What should they do?

He caught her looking out of the corner of his eye, and his lips moved soundlessly: *Retreat.*

Corrin took a half-step backward, preparing to duck back into the wood—

The Bandit King raised her hand with her fingers bunched in a signal, and behind her, three people shuffled out. The first two were bandits, dressed in doublets (of fine quality, presumably stolen) and wielding daggers. But Corrin scarcely noticed them, except for the way they grasped the arms of the person between them, and the way they kept their daggers to her neck—because the third person, with her head bowed and her hands bound, with her tunic worn and her face gaunter than Corrin remembered, was Amella.

Corrin froze mid-step, like a night creature caught in lamplight. Her heart skittered. Her friend was alive. The Bandit King had her friend. Her friend was okay. She might not be okay for long.

"That's right," said the Bandit King, triumphant. "Resist, and your friend dies in a heartbeat. All it would take is the press of a blade. The longer you cooperate, the longer you live." The Bandit King strode toward her. Ashore, with firm soil and stone beneath her, she moved like one of those panthers that lurked in the thicker parts of the wood.

Corrin had seen a panther once, when she and her da had been hunting for rabbits and wildfowl and stayed out later than they should have. She hadn't spotted it until it was almost too late—a dark shape in the undergrowth, fur black as coal, eyes gleaming, moving with a languid fluidity that was so like the cats in the village, yet so much more ominous. Her da had drawn his axe, and the panther had retreated. He'd then sworn under his breath, and he and several of the other villagers had gone out that night to chase the panther away, deeper into the woodland from whence it came. Unfortunately, she doubted some wood-axes and rattle drums would scare off the monster prowling toward her now.

The Bandit King stretched out her hand. "The map, Corrin."

Troll toenails and dragon spit and pants on fire, Corrin thought, with great feeling. Wordlessly, she pulled out the map, the indecipherable, blotchy piece of parchment that now looked like some kind of abstract art, and dropped it into the Bandit King's waiting palm. Her unreliable, sketched-from-memory copy remained hidden in her pocket. "It got soaked when I jumped off the ship," she explained, as the Bandit King eyed it with distaste.

The Bandit King pried the map open anyway. Evidently Corrin's word wasn't enough, or perhaps the Bandit King just didn't want to believe her. The more the Bandit King stared at the map, the more her brow creased and her eyes flashed with anger. "Useless," she said at last, and ripped the blotchy mess into shreds. She had an air of forced calm about her. "So you ruined the map. I suppose I can see why that happened. Unfortunately for you, it leaves you little to bargain with." The Bandit King twirled her dagger in her hand. "Should I get rid of you? And your friends? I still have a couple of the others with us to use as bargaining chips. I usually don't bother to keep bargaining chips, you know. They're more trouble than they're worth."

Next to Corrin, Tenno had a white-knuckled grip on his weapon. Junior perched on his shoulder, eyeing the bandits beadily.

The Bandit King signaled again, and more bandits came out, marching three more prisoners between them. Bruin was tight-lipped and pale, and his shoulder was still bound. *His bandage needs to be changed,* Corrin thought, eyeing the dirt that had collected on it. *It's going to get infected.* Chevira was visibly frightened, her eyes wide, her lips pressed together. And Turner had gone from thin to skeletal. Turner gazed upon her with the most mournful expression, like he could already envision the eulogies at her funeral. Corrin imagined it would go something like, *Here lies Corrin, who blathered to the worst possible person at a bar. She walked for miles, jumped off a ship, and studied the sword for weeks, but she was killed mid-quest anyway. So were her companions. She will soon be joined by half her village. At least she tried.*

Vinny was conspicuously absent. Corrin's throat closed. If he wasn't here when the others were, then the Bandit King must have...

"If you don't have anything else to offer me, we're done here." Her hand started to form another signal, one that looked like a slashing blade.

"WAIT!"

The Bandit King paused.

"I remember the way." It was a half-lie. She sort of did. She sort of didn't. The sketch in her vest was a testament to all she did, and didn't, remember. Her heart hammered like it was threatening to burst out of her. *Let her believe me. Let her buy my half-truth.* "I must've looked at that map a hundred times, deciding which way to go and worrying about what was ahead. I've got a path memorized." Corrin tapped the side of her head. "There's a map in here. I'll give you access, but only so long as you spare my friends."

The Bandit King narrowed her eyes. "Hm. If that's true... Friend singular."

"No, all my friends. You hurt even one of them, I'll decide I'd rather die than help you." It was a bluff, and a terrible one at that. She could hear her own voice quaver. She would very much like to live.

"You lie." She sounded amused. "A bold move, but your fear betrays you."

"It's not a lie." Which was, of course, also a bald-faced lie, but this one might've come out a smidge more convincing. Corrin hoped. "I could—I could misdirect you later. If I decide I hate you enough. You spare my friends, all of them, and I'll—I'll be grateful. I'll help you with everything I have. And—and I'll think clearer too, knowing they're alive. It's important for me to think clearly, if I'm supposed to be guiding you."

"Is that so?"

"Yes."

"I should keep your friends alive so you don't go mad with grief. So you can still be useful, and not a wailing wreck."

"Yes."

"Sounds plausible." The Bandit King withdrew a small warhorn from her pouch, a fine, gold-decorated instrument, and placed the narrow end against her lips. She blew, and a single, pure note rang out across the land. She held up a hand and signaled, *Wait.* So Corrin waited. Bushes rustled. Shapes flickered at the corners of her vision. One by one, the other bandits gathered, dirt-smudged and ragged, blade-wielding and wild-haired. They looked to their King questioningly. Corrin counted ten, twenty, thirty-four in total, including the Bandit King herself.

"All right then. This is what you're going to do: you and that scruffy-faced guardsman are going to hold your hands behind your back and let my people tie them. You'll come with us quietly. Corrin, you'll guide us through the mountain and to the depths of the Gloamwood, where you'll identify the fruit for us. No tricks with that silver tongue of yours, little one." The Bandit King grinned, and she balanced her dagger by the hilt on the back of her hand without looking at it. Clearly her parents had never warned her about playing with sharp, pointy things. "You don't want to anger the person with the giant knife."

CHAPTER TEN

Beneath the Mountain

The moment the Bandit King's lackeys came close, Junior launched off Tenno's shoulder as if shot from a cannon. An archer drew her weapon and tracked the crimson frenzy of wing-flaps and feathers, an arrow nocked, bowstring tautening. But Tenno let out an alarmed yell that made the archer hesitate mid-draw. Just for a heartbeat. It was the heartbeat Junior needed to get out of range. Convenient timing, that was...

Corrin dared to hope, *Maybe she's going to find help.*

Then again, Tenno looked distraught as he watched Junior fly away, and his eyes had a worrying glassiness about them. Doubt prickled at Corrin. Perhaps Junior was abandoning them. Perhaps Junior was just a spoiled, ungrateful bird, externally a firebird but internally a chicken. Or perhaps she was a realist, and she knew an irredeemable situation when she saw one.

Probably a realist, thought Corrin glumly. *She can't save our necks, so she might as well save hers—that's probably what she's thinking.*

"Hold still," grumbled a bandit from behind her, and bound her wrists together.

Corrin tried to flex her hands. The rope pressed in so hard that her bones felt it. This was going to be terrible for her circulation, she could tell. Not terrible enough to permanently damage her hands (she hoped), but still.

The Bandit King took Corrin lightly by the elbow and steered her to the front, where she could lead. Corrin tried to catch Amella's eye as she passed, but for some reason, Amella kept staring at her boots. That seemed wrong. Since when had Amella ever been afraid to look someone in the eye?

The Bandit King's people gathered behind her, and the other prisoners—Tenno, Amella, Turner, Chevira, and Bruin—were jostled into the middle of the horde. "Lead on, little one," said the Bandit King, watching her intently. The hairs on the back of Corrin's neck rose. "If you were telling the truth about your memory, then you'll know the best way to move forward from here." When Corrin hesitated, the Bandit King raised an eyebrow and prompted her again. "I'm not a patient person. Where's this so-called map in your mind?"

Corrin gulped. She made herself take a shaky step forward, then another, until she was standing at the shadowy cave mouth she'd spotted earlier. It was a craggy entrance, high and narrow, like a giant had taken an axe to the rock and cleaved it. It was dark and descended steeply, so she couldn't see more than a few feet in and couldn't gauge how far it went. She could swear the map had said something about tunnels, though. And the dragon was said to sleep underground. Could be that this was a shortcut.

Or it could be that the darkness and the twisty turns in this tunnel would throw her captors off, present her with some kind of opportunity. It was risky, and it might not work, but…

"We've got to go in here. The fastest way through is to travel underneath the mountain."

The Bandit King *hmmm'd.*

They went inside.

A water droplet hit the back of Corrin's neck, making her start. She forced herself to calm down. Runoff from a stalactite, that's all it was, not dragon drool or an impossible indoor storm. The air was cool and damp, and it condensed in odd places, dribbling off the ceiling and trickling through patches of floor. She could see this because some of the Bandit King's lackeys held torches and lanterns aloft. Firelight quivered on the walls, illuminating patches of the path around them—a ribbon of quartz here, a stalagmite there. Once, she saw a peculiar rodent with a hard, blunt-tipped nose, no eyes, and paws ending in solitary nails like pickaxes. It looked almost like a mole, but not quite right. The moles Corrin had seen had multiple claws and softer noses.

They also chanced upon a colony of black creatures with leathery wings. Their eyes gleamed like glass-brushed beads in the torchlight. They dropped from the ceiling and swarmed overhead, flapping furiously. They made faces like they were screaming, but no sound came out, at least none that Corrin could hear.

"Bats," said the Bandit King, amused. "Have you never seen one?"

Corrin shook her head silently.

The tunnel continued on an incline. It widened as they went deeper, until ten people could stand side by side if they wanted. It was here that the Bandit King called for her horde to halt and set up camp.

Lanterns were set about, beddings unrolled, and finely woven rugs spread on the ground. All around them, bandits settled down on cushions and rugs and pulled biscuits and tough meats out of their packs. One of them took out playing cards, another a bottle of ale. The lot of them chewed and chattered noisily, like they were normal folks and not hardened practitioners of murder, theft, and coercion. It was a bizarre sight. But then, what did Corrin expect? Spontaneous knife fights? Devouring of live kittens?

Rough hands brought Corrin into a cluster with her bound companions, and they were left to sit and wait on the stony floor. Corrin wriggled around so she could see her friends. Turner sat cross-legged and stared off into the distance. Chevira sat still as stone, and her expression seemed permanently carved with fear. Bruin grimaced as he shifted his shoulder. He badly needed a bandage change, and perhaps a cleansing, but Corrin didn't like her odds of convincing the Bandit King to let her do that. Tenno took in their surroundings pensively, his brow furrowed, but he offered her a forced smile when he noticed her looking at him.

"We'll be alright," he said kindly. Corrin, in turn, kindly didn't tell him she knew he was lying through his teeth. He hadn't a clue how this would end. He couldn't possibly.

Amella still seemed to have trouble meeting Corrin's eyes, and that worried her.

"You alright?" asked Amella, looking somewhere around Corrin's midriff. Her voice was hoarse, as if it had rusted with disuse.

"I'm alright," said Corrin, and mustered a reassuring smile. "Glad to see you're alive."

"...Yeah."

An uneasy quiet fell between them, and Corrin felt an overwhelming urge to break it, by any means possible. So she said, "The big guy I was traveling with is Tenno. He's a guard. He offered to come with me out here against orders." Corrin paused, giving Tenno a chance lift his bound hands in... well, he was mostly just sticking his hands in the air, but she could tell it was supposed to be a wave. "Tenno, this is Amella. She's the boldest trader in Oddment. Actually the only trader in Oddment, but, um. She drew her sword against these bandits here and fought probably twenty of 'em, all so I could jump ship and escape."

There it was. A grin, albeit a feeble shadow of what Corrin knew Amella was capable of. And for a moment, Amella caught Corrin's eye.

Some of the aforementioned bandits gave them both dirty looks.

Corrin reasoned that they couldn't kill her horribly until they were done having her lead them around, so she wouldn't bother being terrified of slighting them for now. She was tired of terror. She'd been terrified so much that she might've just run out of terror to feel, anyway. So she kept talking, pointy weapons and imminent doom be damned.

"And this is Turner. He's a ship's captain, knows the sea like the lines in his palm, and he's good with a sword, too. And Bruin over there, he took a bolt to the shoulder and didn't even faint. And Chevira, she taught me how to tie the tightest sailor knots I've ever seen." Bruin grunted. The corners of Chevira's lips quirked, a ghost of her usual easy smile. Corrin opened her mouth to keep going, then stopped. That was all of them. There should have been one more, but there wasn't.

Turner cleared his throat. "We used to have a man named Vinny with us. A good cook, and a good sailor." He bowed his head, solemn. "A moment of silence for him. He was taken from us violently, needlessly, before his time."

They fell quiet. The *drip drip drip* of water from a stalactite echoed in the distance.

"Stop with the melodramatics," grumbled one of the bandits. He had his back propped up against a stalactite and a whetstone in his hand. It rasped along the edge of his cutlass. He had hair pale as ash and eyes grey as the weapon he sharpened, and he had the lax posture of one who felt that he had the upper hand. "So the paunchy man died, what of it? That's life. You live, you suffer, you die on the flick of a blade." He paused, giving the words time to settle and itch beneath Corrin's skin. Even for a criminal, making light of someone's death was a terribly insensitive thing to do.

Especially when it was, at least partially, his fault.

Something inside of her blazed and sparked. *How dare he.*

"Stuff your knife in your own gut, then," said Corrin. "If that's all life is to you."

Tenno inhaled sharply. Amella smile-grimaced at Corrin like she was torn between intense pride and intense pain.

The bandit looked unimpressed. "I could run you through with my blade right now, fishbone."

Corrin's hands balled into fists. The rope dug in painfully. She ignored it. "But then the Bandit King would run you through with hers, because she wants to keep me around. I'm useful, you see."

"But you won't be useful forever. I, on the other hand? King can always use a capable fighter." He put his whetstone in his belt pouch and swung his cutlass through the air. It made an audible *swoosh*. "Soon as you get us through the Gloamwood, you expire. And if you're rude to us, your expiration might be a bit more unpleasant, if you get my drift." He pointed his weapon at Amella. "That one needed to see a blade against someone's neck to calm down. Do I need to do that with you, fishbone?"

This threat hit Corrin like a shock of icy water. Her words could get her friends hurt, even with the bargain she'd struck. The only value they had to the Bandit King, to Corrin's knowledge, were as a way to ensure her good behavior. And her friends could be hurt and still have that value, as long as they were kept alive; they could be bruised, and cut, and ill-treated... Corrin turned away from the pale-haired bandit and said nothing.

"Hey, Corrin," said Amella softly. "I'm sorry."

"What for? It's my fault you got caught up in this."

"Alright, one, it's not your fault some outlaw jerk decided to be an outlaw jerk. And two, I—I told her which route you were taking. She was going to kill Turner, and I'm a terrible liar. And then she killed Vinny anyway."

A flicker of surprise, and something akin to disappointment, stirred in Corrin's chest. She'd never seen Amella cornered and cowed before today. She wouldn't have been able to imagine it; she'd always seen Amella as someone who was unbeatably strong, fearless, able to do anything.

But that wasn't fair, was it? It wasn't a fair thing to expect anyone to be all those things. For all her bravado, Amella was flesh and bone just like Corrin was, prone to illness and bleeding and needing to be soothed and stitched up. "It's alright," Corrin said, and her words rang true. "You said it yourself: it's not your fault some outlaw jerk decided to be an outlaw jerk."

"Given me a new title, eh?"

Corrin started and turned. The Bandit King loomed over her, a bowl of dates and dried meat in her hand and a grin twisting her lips. Her face looked shadowy and strange in the weak lamplight of the tunnels, and Corrin subconsciously shifted back, closer to Tenno.

"For future reference, I prefer King of the Outlaw Jerks." The grin shrank. "As refreshing as your spirit is, if I catch you calling me something without 'king' in it again, I will make you regret it." She set the bowl of dates and meats near Corrin's crossed legs, then reached for her, ignoring the way Corrin flinched back. But all the Bandit King did was take Corrin's sword and dagger, scabbards and all, and shove both weapons into the hands of her nearest underling. "Give me your hands, and I will unbind them. You'll eat with me."

"Do I get a say?"

The Bandit King arched her eyebrows. "You could refuse to eat. But I'll allow that only so many times. You're not useful to me starved and dead, little healer."

Corrin held out her hands.

The Bandit King untied them, as promised, and all of a sudden Corrin had more blood flowing through her fingertips. The Bandit King waited while Corrin flexed her wrists to get rid of the unpleasant tingles and numbness that plagued them, then nudged the bowl toward her. "You first. Let it never be said that I'm not courteous."

"Excuse me, but you killed a man."

"So I did."

"Why?"

The Bandit King shrugged. "To set an example, and to have one less mouth to feed. It's easier to get captives to cooperate when they realize their lives depend on it, you see." She paused. "You're not eating."

Corrin plucked a date from the bowl and forced herself to chew it. Stress, fear, and disgust at the Bandit King's callousness had impaired her ability to feel hungry. But judging from her friends' gauntness, she couldn't afford to forego food when it was offered, no matter how little she wanted to eat or how greatly she distrusted the person offering it. She swallowed. "Would you give my friends something too?"

"I will, later. But since you're the most valuable one, I'm inclined to make sure you're fed first." The Bandit King crossed her arms. "Now, outline for me the path we're taking. First, we cut through this mountain. And the edge of the Gloamwood is close to the far side, where we resurface?"

"Yes." Corrin remembered that much, at least. "I think there are some prairie lands and hills we need to cross first, and some copses before we reach the Gloamwood itself."

"Good. So we enter the Gloamwood, then, what, cut straight through? Veer north? Is there a hidden path?"

Corrin bought herself time by shoving a handful of dates and dried meat-morsels in her mouth. It was like trying to eat clay and wood chips. *I need to make something up,* she told herself firmly. *I need to tell a lie, one so good it sounds like a truth. One that makes her think I know the way for a little longer.* She wracked her memories. Troll settlements, sink-mud bogs, an ancient bridge. She couldn't remember where any of them were. But she could pretend the trolls were ahead of them and to the south. Sink-mud patches to the northeast. One of the rivers in the way, and a bridge over it if they went south enough. The path sounded plausible, even though it was improbable.

But if she told the Bandit King that path exactly, she'd have what she wanted—or *think* she had what she wanted—and decide Corrin wasn't useful anymore.

When Corrin's brothers told a fib, sometimes they just took the truth and twisted it. They did make their beds—except they hadn't made their beds that day. They did go harvest berries—except not the full bushel Mum had asked for. They didn't go clambering on the Lookout Rock—they went clambering on the walls of Oddment instead. So she'd tell the King she only remembered parts, and other parts she wouldn't know 'til she saw them, which was partly true. The Bandit King would just have to think Corrin remembered more than she did. Like where bits and pieces were.

Play pretend, she told herself. *Just play pretend, and weave in some truth to make it sound good.*

Corrin swallowed, and with a soft, hesitant voice, laid out a path for them. One where she knew where some of the trolls were and the general direction of the bog lands (or so she claimed), and where she'd remember the shape and narrowing of the river when she saw the water and walked along the shore. "There's no safe path through the Gloamwood," she said, "not really." A truth. "But I remember one of the better ones through." A lie.

"Hm." For a terrifying heartbeat, the Bandit King furrowed her brow, and Corrin thought the Bandit King hadn't believed her; but then she grinned and nodded. "Not bad for someone who's lost her map." She snatched a meat chunk from the bowl and plopped it in her mouth.

Corrin chewed on her lip. She seemed to have gotten on the Bandit King's good side, so perhaps… "I need to change my friend's bandages.

He's at risk of catching a sickness, and if he catches a sickness, it could more easily spread to all of us."

"Interesting argument. You realize that if I cut your friend down—the ill-tempered, blonde-bearded one, correct?—and left him behind, the risk would be removed."

Corrin clenched her fists in her lap until her knuckles turned white. "Begging your pardon, but I thought you wanted me mentally whole and helpful as possible."

"I'd prefer it, but if you need to be controlled with force, that's what I'll do." The Bandit King's eyes glimmered ominously in the firelight, dark and calculating. She could've been one of Death's creations from the stories, Corrin thought. A being more frightening than Death herself. Even Death had never murdered for the fun of it or to make other people submit, and everything about the Bandit King, from her predator's grin to her casual threats to the way she toyed with her dagger, screamed that she would. That she had. "But you seem too clever for that," added the Bandit King. She spoke like they were sitting down for a cup of tea and she didn't hold Corrin's and her friends' lives in her fists. "Tell you what: since you've been such polite and pleasant company, I'll grant your request." Her gaze shifted to something over Corrin's shoulder. "Limerick! Fetch this girl some bandages and water."

Incredulity cut through the dread that had taken permanent residence in Corrin's mind. *Limerick? The heck kind of a name is Limerick?*

The ash-blonde bandit who'd been bothering them before got to his feet, grumbling, and loped off toward a tent. He returned moments later with an armful of bandages and a canteen of water. "Not a word," he hissed, and shoved the supplies into Corrin's arms. She obliged him—not a sound passed her lips—but she did look questioningly at the Bandit King, her eyebrows raised. Did all the bandits have nicknames?

"Before he joined me, he was a bard." The Bandit King sounded amused. "His old name didn't suit him at all, so I changed it. Go on, now, treat your friend."

Corrin, still silent, shrugged off her pack. The Bandit King hadn't seen fit to confiscate their packs; she'd said something about them carrying their own weight. She dug around in it until she found the jar of salve, then shuffled over to Bruin, who watched her with an expression she couldn't read. He didn't protest as she peeled off the dirt-stained bandage across the shoulder, nor speak up when she murmured in distress at the sight of his wound. It was reddened around the edges, with a yellowed membrane coating it. Infected. Not good. It would heal slowly and messily, and she'd have to hope his body could ward off sickness in the meantime.

He grimaced while she soaked a clean strip of cloth and wiped it down, and he let out a soft sigh when she applied the salve. She re-wrapped the wound, mindful to make the bandage snug, but not too snug. "You're probably the most cooperative patient I've ever had," she mused, more to herself than to Bruin. "You just sat there while I yanked a bolt out of you. Remarkably difficult to do, that is."

Bruin's lips quirked.

"Um. Anyway. I would've rather doused it in antiseptic wash, but I'm hoping between the salve and the new bandage, it'll heal a bit better. It's going to scar something awful, though."

Bruin shrugged with his good shoulder. "I don't mind scars, so long as it still works."

Corrin gave his bandaged shoulder one last, gentle pat and put away the salve.

"Hold out your hands," commanded the Bandit King. Corrin started; she had forgotten, for a moment, that King was there, but there she was. With the ropes.

Oh, great, she's going to tie me up again.

Corrin hated the feeling of the rough ropes against her skin, the way it cut her blood flow and made her fingertips fall asleep. The binds seemed a smidge looser this time, but not loose enough to feel comfortable, let alone wriggle out. The Bandit King must have thought she would've tried something otherwise, even with Corrin's friends under her thumb and her bandits surrounding them, hard-hearted and bristling with weapons.

The Bandit King brought Corrin's friends food next, but she made them eat with their hands tied together. She didn't stay to make small talk with them either. It might've been the way Amella glared at the Bandit King like she wanted to skewer her guts, or the way Turner refused to engage, staring off at some distant thing nobody else could see. But Corrin had the suspicion that somehow, she'd curried the Bandit King's favor—in the sense that an interesting toy did, or a pet. Only until the Bandit King grew bored of her or decided she wasn't useful, and got rid of her.

It made her uneasy.

But maybe, just maybe, she could take advantage of it.

CHAPTER ELEVEN

The Slumbering Trouble

Corrin didn't sleep well. The tunnel floor leeched the warmth from her body, and bits of uneven ground dug into her sides and back, no matter which way she rolled. When she did drift off, it never lasted; she'd start awake with her heart hammering, a nightmare slipping away like sand through a sieve. She kept hearing things—the footsteps of a bandit pacing, Tenno's snores stuttering to a halt, the rustle of some unidentifiable thing moving. The noises echoed off the walls, so she couldn't tell where they were coming from. Once or twice, she thought she heard wingbeats. *Must be the bats,* she reasoned. *The sound's so quiet, though. Must be a ways off. I don't think they'd want to live too deep in the cave...*

She also had no sense of night or day underground. That didn't help either, especially when she'd spent several days camping under open skies.

The bandits took turns watching over them. First, it was Limerick, slouching by a stalagmite. He didn't say anything when she caught his eye, just looked away and took a swig from his canteen. The next time she started awake, she thought for a heartbeat that he was still there, closer, now; but no, he was gone. Someone awfully similar in appearance had replaced him. She had the same shade of pale hair, the same build, and the same slouching posture, but she was a smidge shorter and narrower in the shoulder.

The Limerick look-alike grinned. "Someone murdering you in your dreams?" Her voice was a murmur, quiet as the brush of a feather but not nearly so kind.

Corrin blinked. "Are you Limerick's kin?"

"That obvious, eh? Yeah, his sister. I go by Verse."

"Were you a bard too?"

"Can't imagine how you guessed. I'm the one who could play the lute worth a damn."

"Oh. Um. Why didn't you just keep doing that?"

"Long story. Go to sleep, before someone hears us and tries to stab you through." A beat of silence passed, during which Corrin tried to pick out more of Verse's features in the dark. Verse flashed her teeth in a smile that sent unease crawling down Corrin's spine. "You need to close your eyes to sleep, shrimp. Try not to think too hard about whether you'll open them again."

Which, of course, guaranteed that that was all Corrin could think about.

Eventually, the Bandit King decided it was time for them to move. Beddings folded. Packs were shouldered. Bandits grumbled and jeered at each other, and Corrin and her friends were herded to the front. Corrin plodded onward, leading them through the dark. Every once in a while, the tunnel branched, and Corrin pretended she knew which path to take. Sometimes one of them felt warmer or tasted a little fresher, and she'd pick that one. Other times, she'd take the one that looked bigger. But despite her choices, despite trying to steer them toward daylight and open air, it felt like they were spiraling down, down into the earth.

She and Tenno still had their packs on their backs (although they felt peculiarly light) and their weapons on their hips. The Bandit King seemed to think that there was no danger in making them carry their belongings, no risk that they'd draw their daggers or swords or try to make a break for it. Corrin reckoned she was right on that count. Their hands were tied, after all, and they were vastly outnumbered.

The tunnel broadened. The walls and floor grew craggier. The path ahead was riddled with furrows, as if a massive beast had gouged out the tunnel with its claws.

Something warm and heavy collided with Corrin, sending her sprawling.

"Sorry, so sorry."

Corrin blinked, dazed. She was on her back. Next to her was... Tenno?

"I tripped," he said. "Must have been a stray clump of dirt."

"You can't guide us if you can't walk," said the Bandit King irritably. She hoisted Corrin upright by the back of her vest.

Behind her, Tenno shuffled and muttered to himself as he struggled to get his feet under him. Corrin frowned. It was tricky to get up when they couldn't use their hands to help balance, especially in terrain like this. And it made it harder to feel confident about where they were putting their feet, since they couldn't catch themselves; it forced them to be more careful. At this rate, they wouldn't be able to move faster than an ambling tortoise. It increased the risk of hitting their heads in a fall, too, and head injuries could have dire consequences…

Maybe she could make the Bandit King see that, see all these good and logical reasons to unbind them that, strictly speaking, had nothing to do with how much Corrin would like to be free of the ropes or how that might grant her a sliver more of a chance of getting out of this mess… 'Course, it still boggled her that Tenno—coordinated, athletic Tenno, Tenno who knew solid footwork like Bathilda knew remedies—had tripped like that—

Wait a minute.

She couldn't catch his eye, and his expression gave away nothing. But she had a sneaking suspicion he'd done this on purpose.

In any case, she wouldn't let this opportunity slip away. Corrin turned to the Bandit King and said, "We're less likely to fall if you untie us."

The Bandit King turned and faced her fully, her eyes glinting dark as the tunnels they walked. "You want me to trust you not to try anything."

Corrin shrugged and tried to look nonchalant, even as her heart beat fast. "You've got us outnumbered about seven to one, and all of you've seen more fights than I have. Trying anything would end real badly. Didn't you say you thought I was clever?" Her expression tightened dangerously, and Corrin tacked on a hasty, "King?"

Silence.

Corrin waited.

"Only until we're out of the caverns."

The bandits untied their hands.

Corrin tried not to look too happy. It was kind of hard with Amella beaming at her from her left, though, and with Tenno whispering a "thank you" in her ear. It was a small thing, but maybe, just maybe, it would give them a chance.

They kept moving. The tunnel kept widening. She was seventy percent sure they weren't going down anymore, though it was hard to tell when the floor formed great ridges and crags like miniature hills. The air seemed warmer, and the darkness ahead of them less thick—

and then not thick at all. Perhaps the tunnel had sloped back up without her realizing it. *Is this it?* she wondered. *Did we pass through?*

The tunnel opened into a chamber so vast and well-lit that for a second, Corrin thought they were outside. But they weren't. The ceiling hadn't gone away, just stretched up to dizzying heights, and walls still surrounded them. Gaps riddled the walls and ceiling, cracks and holes that looked like the work of giant fists. Buttery bright shafts of sunlight slipped in through those gaps and illuminated a red mound that took up most of the floor. It glittered, vibrant, like a secret heart of the mountain. It was peculiarly shaped, with shadows and lumps in odd places…

…a shape like the fold of a giant wing…

*Death's scythe, it **is** a wing.*

Corrin realized what she was seeing now. A triangular head, with grey horns like a ram's. A crest of feathers, running partway down the curve of a serpentine neck until they tapered off into a scaly ridge. A set of bunched hindquarters, powerful, made to launch an enormous weight. A tail, curled around it and tucked near its chin. Massive paws stretched out in front of it, catlike except for the charcoal color of the claws and the scales in place of fur. And the size. By the Churikin, *the size.* Big as a hill. Corrin could've tried to climb it.

But attempting such a thing would have been madness. Even her brothers would know better than to climb on a dragon's back.

"Merciful Churikin," breathed Turner.

"Shut up," hissed the Bandit King.

SNRRRRRRRGH.

The dragon shifted. A ribbon of smoke drifted up from its nostrils. But it didn't wake.

Corrin gulped.

The dragon must have a way out of these caverns. It needed room to fly, places to hunt bears or griffins or sea monsters or whatever a creature of its size subsisted on. And since the way they came in here had started as smaller tunnels, there had to be at least one other tunnel, a massive one, that led to the surface. One they couldn't see from here. One that lay on the other side of this beast that could probably swallow them whole. It might be the only way to cut through the rest of the mountain.

The Bandit King stared at Corrin intently. She pointed to the dragon, then over it, to indicate what lay beyond. Then to the dragon again. She mouthed, *This is your shortcut? THIS is where your map led you?*

Corrin stifled a sudden urge to laugh. *Yes,* she mouthed back.

The Bandit King looked incredulous; Tenno tugged insistently on her sleeve; and Amella caught her eye and mouthed, *are you serious?*

Corrin nodded. And with her heartbeat in her ears and her breath bated, she tiptoed forward.

She kept close to the wall and willed her footsteps to fall softly, to not jostle a loose rock or knock against a ridge of stone. She paused and listened, because she thought she heard a whisper of movement, but no, she must've been mistaken... she was near its tail, now... if she reached out to it, she could probably brush those scales with her fingertips, those hard, jagged things as large as her face and plated like blood-red armor...

RRRRUMBLSNRRK.

She froze.

The dragon let out a snotty snore and slumbered on.

Clogged respiratory system, catalogued the medical corner of Corrin's brain. *It needs hot liquid, like boiled water or tea, and maybe a decongestant.* The smoke billowing from its nostrils caught her eye. *Unless, could it be its fire breath that's the problem? How does it breathe fire, anyway? How would it direct it anywhere? It would have to be attached to some launchable, combustible substance. If the substance is like a mucous, it might have been sleeping for a long, long while and let it build up. Maybe that's what's clogging it.*

So perhaps it's time to wake it up.

It was a lunatic thought, a thought she scarcely believed she was thinking.

But the thought stayed and spun, like a wheel gaining momentum, and it grew less absurd by the second. After all, not even the Bandit King's forces could repel a creature of this size. It could bat them aside like a cat batting away field mice, especially if it awoke in a temper, tail thrashing, scorching heat pouring out of its mouth... and it probably would, wouldn't it, if it was bumped or jostled out of a nice deep sleep? Of course, if it attacked, it might (*would*) try to hurt Corrin and her friends as well. But they would have a nonzero chance of surviving, if the dragon decided the Bandit King was more attack-worthy than they were. They had their hands free, their packs on their backs, and daggers at their belts. It was a risk, but also a chance.

And she didn't see another chance coming. If she didn't act now, there might not be an opening later—and if there wasn't, if they didn't escape, the Bandit King would strike them down and leave them dead in the Gloamwood.

Corrin thought of Sam's lucky rock, tucked in her belt pouch with her scant coins and fire-lighting flint. She pretended, for a heartbeat, that she believed in it.

Amella poked her from behind. *Move,* she mouthed, frowning.

And Corrin did. Probably not how Amella had in mind, though.

She bellyflopped onto the dragon's tail with a shrill, "AAAGH!" The dragon's scales scraped her palms and banged painfully against her stomach. Amella choked back a yell of alarm, and the Bandit King spewed oaths, but Corrin barely noticed—the tail shifted beneath her, stirring. She stumbled back. Her pack collided with the stone wall.

"*SNRRRGRAAAAAH.*"

The tail-tip flicked. A ripple ran up through the dragon's hindquarters and up its spine, and its head lifted, its neck twisting around and arching over its shoulder so it could look at the peon who had dared disturb its slumber. Its crest feathers rose and fell with its breathing. Its eyes were round-pupiled with sclera as yellow as egg yolk, like a hawk's. The way its wings fidgeted was birdlike too—but the shape of its snout was more like a snake's, as were the movements of its neck and tail.

The dragon's jaws parted. Corrin gulped. Those fangs were needle-sharp, and the two big ones looked long as her forearm. She quivered, or maybe the ground beneath her did—maybe both—as the dragon stood on its paws and circled around to face them. The back of its throat glowed an ominous orange.

"Sorry," Corrin squeaked to the dragon, and leaped to one side.

Fire crackled behind her. She felt the warmth against her back and the gust of rapidly heated air, and there was a smell like campfires and forge ovens and an acrid *something,* like one of Bathilda's most refined and revolting (though useful) elixirs. Corrin glanced over her shoulder. The spot where she'd stood a heartbeat ago was smoking and stained black. The Bandit King stood on the other side of the smoky spot. She had a tight grip on the hilt of her sword, and ash dusted her cloak and face. Her expression was frozen in a half-fearsome, half-fearful sneer as she stared up, up at the dragon. Amella, Tenno, and the others were on the other side of the smoking spot, too, with the Bandit King and her lackeys.

Lucky rock my foot, thought Corrin.

The dragon paused. Its focus shifted between Corrin and the forty-odd other humans in its den, its head twitching back and forth like a bird's. Its eyes narrowed, as if in thought—and Corrin got the sense that it *was* thinking, that this giant was intelligent and all the more deadly for it, because it was probably thinking of avenging its rude awakening, contemplating how best to rid itself of the mob of critters that had invaded its den. The dragon's tail whipped behind it, and its feathery crest bristled. Corrin quaked in her boots.

We did this on purpose, she reminded herself. *This was the plan.* But a part of her hissed back, *It was a foolish plan. Very foolish. We regret it. We're all barbecue now.*

The dragon's eyes settled on the Bandit King, maybe because she had the most belligerent expression. Its throat convulsed. Its jaws parted, exposing its fangs. It almost looked like it was going to barf.

"Scatter!" roared the Bandit King.

A glob of flame erupted from the dragon's throat, bursting across the floor. Corrin bolted. The cavern filled with the sound of pattering footsteps, people calling out to each other, the stench of the dragon's fire, and glinting, rippling scales and flaring wings. Everything seemed too bright, too red. At the same time, Corrin felt acutely aware of her heart quivering like it was trying to jump out of her rib cage. Air heaved in and out of her lungs. Her legs launched her to the far side of the cavern as if she were spring loaded—

—The dragon's tail-tip whipped into her side and sent her flying into the wall. Her bones rattled. Her breath was forced out of her, and she couldn't seem to draw it back in. Corrin panicked internally for a second, until her head cleared enough to diagnose, *winded, probably just winded and banged up a bit.* She staggered to her feet. The dragon turned toward her, fangs bared and an ominous light pouring out of its mouth —

"*OY!*" screeched Amella. "Look over here, you overgrown lizard!"

The dragon's head whipped around, and Corrin's heart stuttered with a mix of *thank you* and *what are you doing* and *no.*

"No, fight me!" yelled Tenno.

"Aaaugh!" yelled some of the more panicky bandits. There were fewer of them, it seemed. Maybe some of them had escaped back into the tunnel. Maybe some of them were the charred smudges on the walls. Had they not raided Turner's ship, murdered Vinny, and held her friends captive, Corrin might have felt bad for them. As it was, she figured, *Better them than me.* She hoped none of those smudges were Turner, Chevira, or Bruin. She couldn't hear their voices, and she couldn't see them.

The cavern lit up with orange flames. Somewhere beyond the dragon, Amella shouted an oath, which meant she was alive and not a smoldering crisp. *Good,* Corrin thought, *now please stay uncrisped, somehow,* ***please.***

Corrin kept running, fear and adrenaline coursing through her veins. She could see multiple exits up ahead, now, some small, some large, most dark as pitch. One stood out from the rest, enormous, yawning wide enough to admit a dragon. Corrin raced toward it. It wouldn't keep her safe. The dragon would surely follow, eventually. But if she could get out without it noticing her leave…

…if Amella and the others stopped being so darned noble long enough to follow her out…

Out of the corner of Corrin's eye, she saw the dragon's paws dart forward, trapping a section of wall just to the left of the tunnel. She knew that move. She'd seen Tiptoes and the other village cats do it many a time to catch a beetle or a toy. The dragon had cornered someone. She hoped it was the Bandit King. Corrin was almost at the tunnel—

"*FINE, SCALY FACE, I CAN TAKE YOU!*" yelled Amella.

Oh for the love of WHY.

The dragon drew its head back like a snake poising to strike—

"*PICK ON SOMEONE YOUR OWN SIZE!*" Corrin yelled. Which was a remarkably absurd thing to say. There probably wasn't a creature within a month's hiking radius that matched the dragon in size, and if there were, it sure wouldn't be Corrin. But it worked. The dragon whirled toward her and away from Amella. Its wings extended, webbed like bat wings but thicker, blotting out the beams of light coming in from behind it. It swiped at Corrin with one leg, paw curved in a hook. She flung herself to the side, stomach smacking the cold ground, and the swipe just grazed her, sending her rolling…

"*SCREE.*"

A tiny, red blur sped past the dragon's nose. The dragon chased it instinctively, snapping its jaws, but the blur escaped by a feather's breadth. It dodged the fire the dragon spat at it, too, and then dove *through* it, came out glimmering orange-gold-yellow like an ember itself. Like… like…

Corrin put together the call and a memory of bright feathers, of soaring wings and a long firebird's tail, and it all tallied up to *Junior.* Her heart leapt. Bless that firebird. Forget every uncharitable thought she'd ever had of it being spoiled or disloyal or abandoning them.

How did a bird, a little feathery being with no weapons and scarcely a twentieth of her size, pluck up the courage to fly at a dragon, in the confines of a cavern? Where had Junior even come from?

An arrow whistled through the air and sank into the dragon's wing. The dragon roared and flapped furiously, sending a gust throughout the cavern. Stones rattled. The air bit Corrin's face.

Corrin ran into the massive tunnel, the one that had a dim light spilling out of it. It sloped sharply upward, at such an angle that she'd basically have to climb it. "Troll bites," she muttered. She sought a handhold on the stone. It wasn't an impossible climb—not as steep as a wall or tree, with plenty of grooves and knobs she could hook her fingers on—but as she went up, and up, and up, her lungs strained and her arms ached. She could swear the air was getting thinner… and she could still hear the dragon, its roars echoing up the tunnel, its fire crackling somewhere behind and below… and people were still shouting, the voices too distant for her to pick out, but she hoped desperately that some of them were her friends…

Feathers brushed her cheek, and Corrin leaned back just in time to see Junior zip overhead. The firebird chirped and soared up and to the right, where there was a smallish hole, a branching path off the main exit. It wasn't pitch dark, which meant it must go somewhere. Junior perched on a spur of rock next to it and waited, preening, while Corrin scurried toward it.

She ducked into the narrow tunnel and leaned against the wall. She breathed out. *Safe. Ish.* "Good bird," she whispered, and scratched Junior behind her crest feathers. Tenno had often scratched that spot in thanks or praise, and Junior seemed to favor it.

Junior closed her eyes and cooed.

"This is an awful lot to ask, but do you think you could go back for your owner? And for my friends?"

Junior's eyes opened and gleamed like drops of oil in the dim light, and she tilted her head inquisitively.

"Amella, she's a woman with short-shorn hair who'll probably be trying to save everyone's skin. Braver than anyone you'll meet and a bit mad. Can you make sure she doesn't die being heroic? And Turner, he's tall and thin with greying hair. He always looks melancholy, but he's a kind person and better with a sword than you'd think. Probably composing his own eulogy in his head. There's Chevira, she's got dark skin and she's not that big, but she's a skilled sailor and the deftest knot-maker I've ever met. 'Cept I think she's scared out of her wits right now. And Bruin, he's the big blonde guy, wide shoulders, barrel chest, acts grumpy most of the time but can sit there stoically while someone yanks a piece of metal and wood out of him. He has a shoulder injury, so that'll be bandaged, hopefully easy to spot…

"Help them, okay?"

Junior crooned. It was a comforting sound, like a hen reassuring her chicks. For a heartbeat, Corrin rested her palm against Junior's warm back, a silent *thank you, a sorry for asking this of you.* Junior blinked and rustled her feathers. And then she departed in flurry of wingbeats, leaving Corrin to crawl through the tunnel alone.

The sound of fighting faded behind her. The tunnel was dimmer than the big one it had branched from, but it grew lighter as she made her way along. It had patches inside of it that looked like the innards of a geode (Amella had shown her what one of those looked like, once)—glittering clusters of blues and purples that reflected scraps of light. Finally, she saw a patch of daylight up ahead, blindingly bright after so many days in the caverns, and she hurried toward it with renewed vigor. At last, Corrin squirmed out through a craggy exit and sat on the edge of a precipice.

Puffs of cloud drifted across the blue skies above her, and a cascade of rocks and scrubby brushes sloped down below her, descending into tree-peppered hills. The woodsy patches thickened, and thickened, and if she cast her gaze out, they became a blanket of lush green that stretched far to the north and south. Its vastness reminded her of the sea—except this was a sea of leaves, dark and still, and it didn't gleam in the sun.

That's the Gloamwood, Corrin thought, with an instinctive certainty and a dread deep in her bones. *It must be.*

She turned around and traced the rise of Mount Cauldra behind her, tilting her head up, up as she searched for its peak. She could see where the shrubbery gave way to bare gray stone and where the stone became coated with snow and ice, but the top of the mountain was lost in the clouds. Corrin took a deep breath and let the cool, thin air settle in her lungs. She tucked herself closer to the tunnel entrance, away from the precipice below. She felt the aches in her arms and legs acutely, now, and a pounding in her head, and her muscles felt all quivery and jelly-like as her adrenaline drained away.

I have to keep moving, she reminded herself. *The Bandit King might still be back there.*

But I can stay here and catch my breath, just for a minute. One measly, miserly minute…

A roar shook her, and she jolted. The sound had come from higher up the mountain, a ways north. Fire spewed from the mountainside. Corrin scrambled back into her tunnel with a rabbiting heart and peered around the lip. She watched as a red shape with wings followed the fire. The dragon cast a shadow on the mountain, stretched wide by the angle of the sun and the slope of the land, then flapped its wings and wheeled north. Toward the griffin highlands. The dragon probably dined on griffins. Anything smaller than a griffin couldn't be more than a snack, after all, and what other than a dragon could dine on a griffin?

Corrin almost missed the speck that followed the dragon—a red speck, silent and swift, that hovered for a moment and then angled toward her. The speck grew in size and detail as it approached, until Corrin could make out the wings and the coal-black talons, the curve of a hawklike beak and beady dark eyes. Junior chirped once, then glided down and landed on her shoulder. Junior's momentum would've made her stagger, if she'd been standing. As it was, she leaned against the wall and let Junior dig her claws into her vest for purchase. She mustered a faint smile when Junior cooed in her ear.

"Good bird," Corrin murmured.

Junior chirped.

Corrin extended her arm as she'd seen Tenno do many times, turning it into a perch, and Junior shuffled onto it readily. Her forearm dipped under Junior's weight. "How'd it go?" Junior simply looked at her, and she remembered that, for all Junior's evident intelligence, the firebird had never spoken a word of human language. Her vocabulary was limited to *bob-yes* and *shake-no,* plus some hard-to-interpret vocal tones and gestures. Yes-no questions it was, then. "Were you able to help Tenno and the others escape?"

Junior hesitated, then bobbed her head.

"You did?" Corrin's chest lightened, and her eyes grew misty with relief. "So they're okay."

Junior ruffled her feathers and shifted her wings in a shrug, as if to say, *I'm not actually sure about that.*

"Oh." Corrin bit her lip. "Did you see what happened to the bandits? Um, all the other people who had weapons, the ones who tied us up."

Junior tilted her head, as if working through what Corrin was asking. Eventually, she shrugged.

"I'll take that as a you don't know." Corrin rested the arm with Junior on it against her knee, supporting the added weight. Her thoughts whirled. Junior had been able to help her friends get out, but neither of them knew whether her friends were okay now. The bandits might still be lurking about, and if they were, and they found her, they'd try to capture her again. Junior didn't seem sure if her friends were alright, which could mean they were hurt, or it could be that the Bandit King caught up to them again. She dearly hoped they weren't back in the clutches of the bandits. It'd make the fire and terror she'd gone through scarcely feel worth it.

But she was beyond the Bandit King's reach, so there was that, at least. For the moment. Maybe, if she could just find out where her friends were…

"Junior, can you lead me to where they came out?"

This time, Junior shook her head emphatically.

"Why not?" Corrin frowned. "I thought you helped them. Wouldn't you know where they came—"

More emphatic head shaking.

Corrin groaned in frustration. "Okay. I could—I could circle around and look for them." Even as she said it, she didn't like the idea. If she went back and wandered around looking, she might stumble back into the bandits' clutches. But she didn't want to leave her friends behind again. She had jumped ship and fled, back when that was all she could do. But if they had escaped and were injured, she could treat them. Also, the thought of going into the Gloamwood alone made her cold with fear. "Or maybe you can? Could you circle back around real quick and look?"

Junior shuffled uneasily, ducking her head and ruffling her feathers.

Corrin frowned. Had the dragon's roaring and fire shaken Junior up? Did Junior feel too scared to leave her again? She could understand that; her heart was still beating fast, and the dragon fire still burned bright in her mind's eye. But why hadn't Junior stayed with Tenno? Surely Tenno would be a more comforting presence than Corrin was. Unless Junior had lost track of Tenno while they were evading the dragon, and so she'd latched on to the first friendly face she saw…

Tentatively, Corrin reached for Junior's head and smoothed the feathery crest. Junior stilled and cooed softly at her. "Alright," she murmured. "It's okay. Um, let me think… let's see… How about I find a safe place to camp, and we'll hide there and think until you're ready to fly again? Or until I come up with something better. Whichever comes first."

Junior didn't shake her head or shuffle. Corrin took that as assent.

"Okay then." She crept back out of the tunnel mouth. It was quiet. She could see a way down the mountainside—several, actually—that would give her some rock and scrub brush cover. Not much, but if she hid her hair and Junior inside her cloak and moved carefully, she should be hard to spot. And if she went far enough, she could reach that patch of trees over there, or that one, or—

*Is that a house? Is that a **village?***

She stared hard, picking out inorganic shapes and the brownish grey of stone and wood. A cluster of unnatural structures rested near the base of the mountain, tiny from this far up but unmistakably buildings. But as she looked more closely, she realized that it looked abandoned. For one, there were no signs of people—no movement, no noise, and there surely would be when the sun was this high and bright. For two, one of the houses didn't have a roof, and another had a wall that had fallen to pieces. Green spread across some of the buildings, softening their edges. It reminded her of Oddment, with its thick blankets of ivy and its repurposed ruins.

And that, perhaps, is why she mistook it for a safe space and headed toward it.

CHAPTER TWELVE

Interlude: The Aftermath

In the chaos of writhing scales and fire, Amella had lost sight of Corrin. It felt like she'd lost a kid she'd been responsible for. Seventeen wasn't too far off from childhood, heck, was still considered childhood up in the desert lands. And Corrin was just so… so small. A wisp of a lass, with big green eyes, hair bright as fire, and a slightness that worried Amella sometimes. *She's clever,* Amella reminded herself firmly, as the dragon belched flames over her head. The bandits scrambled around like rodents caught in a wildfire, panicking. That was probably what Corrin was going for when she woke the blasted thing. *She's mad, but she's clever. She'll be alright.*

A red blur sped past her. Amella almost mistook it for a stray bit of fire, but then it shrieked. She knew that sound: a firebird.

What the—

"*SCREE.*"

It soared up, past the dragon's snout, and the dragon chased it with snapping jaws. In that moment of distraction, Amella scanned the cavern. The Bandit King—*murdering scum*—stood several paces away, barking orders to the few minions who'd listen. Turner crouched off to her left, his sword drawn. That big guy Corrin had introduced to them (*Tindo? Tenmo?*) watched the bird, and she swore she could see his face light up—

Something enormous and heavy slammed into Amella's side, and she went flying into the wall. *Crack*—her elbow. *Crack*—the back of her skull. Her vision flickered in and out of focus. A giant red whippy thing lashed ahead of her… ah, the dragon's tail. Dragon didn't seem to be looking at Amella, fortunately for her. She couldn't see what it was snarling at, though. She hoped to the starlands it wasn't after

Corrin.

"*SCREE.*"

A bundle of crimson feathers flew past her face, shrieking, and on impulse, Amella went after it. The bird doubled back at the last moment, brushing past her shoulder, but it had gotten her to an opening in the rock wall. A tunnel stretched ahead of her, faintly lit. A way out.

She took it, hoping her friends would follow.

Amella crouched on the north side of the mountain, watching the dragon fly overhead. Going for the griffin highlands, looked like. Perhaps it would bring the population down. She wondered what would happen to the dragon if it ran out of griffins to eat. She supposed it would head west or venture north and terrorize human settlements. Or maybe it would have its meal of griffins and bears and whatever else, and then go straight back to sleep. When was the dragon last said to be awake, anyway? A few hundred years ago? That was what the bards would say. Seemed like half their stories happened three hundred years ago.

Amella shook her head. *Move,* she told herself. *Look for your allies.* And she did, ignoring the throbbing in her head and her arm as she traipsed around the mountain, angling east, searching for familiar faces. Her good hand rested ready on the hilt of her sword.

She found a cluster of three bandits arguing on a spur of rock. They looked burned and battered. *I could take them,* Amella thought, her heart rate picking up and her blood singing with anger. But no. She had more important things to do. So she kept to the shadow of a ridge and snuck past. She paused just long enough to catch a snippet of their conversation, listening keenly as their voices drifted down the mountainside.

"—should do we do?"

"Go back and find the King—"

"You can't get me back in there, I'm done, I'm not doing this anymore—"

"You freakin' coward."

"If wanting to freakin' live makes me a coward, then fine. I don't get it, why'd we go after some lass with a story about magical fruit? We could be plundering caravans, making easy money. The King's insane."

"What if she hears you said that, you idiot?"

"What if the rest are dead?"

Dissidence. Music to Amella's ears. She slipped past and away, grinning fiercely.

Her grin faded with the sinking sun and the growing weariness in her feet. She looked around, crept along, and drew her sword at bunny rabbits that sprang out of the scrub bushes, but she traveled for hours and saw neither foe nor friend. Dark thoughts ate at the corners of her mind. What if Corrin hadn't been quick enough? What if the dragon had scorched her or snatched her in its jaws? Turner mightn't have escaped alive either, or Bruin, or Chevira. And what about Oddment, where the sickness must have gotten worse? The bandit's words echoed in Amella's mind, placed in a new and more troublesome context: *What if the rest are dead?* What if Amella was alone?

A shape moved farther down the slope—a human shape, with light brown hair like deer's fur and a step that seemed too quiet for their size. The person turned to her, and with a jolt, Amella recognized his face. *Tenjin—Tenso—whatsit?*

"Oy!" she called.

The man started. Saw her. Waved.

Amella picked her way down to where he stood. "Glad to see you breathe," she said, and extended her hand. He accepted it, smiling warmly, and she grinned back. The man was built like a bear and carried a formidable broadsword, but he was obviously a kind fellow. And young—younger than Amella by at least a couple decades, though older than Corrin. His beard was patchy, like he was just growing into it, and his face round at the edges. Amella might not know him well yet, but she'd spoken true: she was glad he'd made it out. "Corrin introduced us, but in case your memory's spotty as mine, m'name's Amella."

The guardsman chuckled. "My name's Tenno. Corrin told me a lot about you... Er, before we got captured."

"Aw, I'm touched." Amella let go of his hand. "What do you say we move before something finds us?"

Tenno nodded and gestured for her to walk with him. She had to take an extra half step for every one of his.

The two of them headed northeast, around the mountainside and away from the setting sun. An eternity of plateaus and high-grassed fields stretched northward from the base of the mountain. A massive red shape chased smaller, browner shapes over the plateaus. As Amella watched, the red shape shot a blazing stream of fire and scattered the smaller figures, making them shriek. Looked like the dragon was hunting the griffins. It must've been a nasty shock for them, being preyed on instead of doing the preying.

Serves them right, she thought with a flicker of satisfaction.

"You haven't seen Corrin, have you?" asked Tenno, and Amella's attention snapped back to him. "Or any of the others?"

Amella shook her head. "You?"

"I haven't seen them out here." He kept his voice low, and he checked their surroundings constantly, eyes flicking back and forth and a hand resting at the hilt of his sword. He sounded worried. "I saw —what's your friend's name, Turner? I think he dodged a blast of fire and ducked into a shadow or corner somewhere along with a couple of others, but I don't know what happened to them after that. I lost sight of Corrin early on, but—but I asked Junior to look after her, and since Junior's not back yet, she must still be alive somewhere."

"Junior?"

"My firebird. I trained her to help with military operations."

"Ah. Explains why she flew in that dragon's face."

"I hadn't told her specifically to do that. I'd just signaled her to keep back and wait for an opening to help—"

"Hey, I'm not complaining. Brilliant bird. She found me an exit. Distracted that dragon at some key moments, too."

Amella scanned the terrain. A black bear lumbered out of a clump of trees ahead and stretched out on the rocks. A serpent slithered across their path, sinuous; it uttered a soft *hssssss* as it passed them by. No signs of people, friend or otherwise. She could see some of the eastern lands, now—the copses that dotted the hills and grew until they merged into woodland, the woodland that sprawled and thickened until it became a sea of dark green… The vast forest carried the echoes of a hundred bard's stories, the tales of Death making the trees grow so thick and the monsters so fierce that no one could get through.

Amella had long ago stopped believing in those tales, at least in the literal sense. Even so, she felt like they must contain a kernel of truth. This growth seemed unnaturally dense.

Tenno sucked in a breath.

"Scary, isn't it?" said Amella.

"I—yes. Yes, it is."

"She told you she meant to go in there, I take it?"

"Yes. Even my captain couldn't dissuade her."

"I'm thinking she hasn't been dissuaded now, either. We should try to pick up her tracks there." Amella pointed east, between the far side of the mountain and the Gloamwood. "Either she's already made it that far, or she is going to." Amella ignored the whisper of doubt in her mind, the *what if she couldn't*, the *what if she didn't survive and the firebird didn't either*. Corrin hadn't given up, after all, despite all the what ifs—not when she'd leapt into the sea, not when she'd seen Amella and her friends tied and defeated, not even when she'd been taken prisoner herself. Nor when she'd first come knocking on Amella's door for help, when Amella's answer had been, *Only if you come with me.* "And I'll be starred if I give up on her now."

Turner was getting too old for this.

His bones ached. His joints were stiff. His breath wheezed. And his sword, skilled though it was with decades of experience behind it, wasn't as quick or as sharp as it used to be. He'd had more than his fair share of close scrapes and near-death experiences, and by all rights he should be planning his retirement on the outskirts of Miritown. His ship might have rested easy on land; her timber was growing old, like he was, but it would've held up sheltering him on stable ground. But his old friend had roped him into another adventure, and he'd scarcely escaped with his life and limbs yet again. And now, here he was.

Specifically, here he was on the south side of Mount Cauldra, sitting with an inscrutable Bruin and a trembling Chevira. The firebird had guided them. It had wanted to get them across the cave, Turner suspected, but swerved when the dragon blocked their path and left them at the inner entrance to this tunnel instead. They'd kept going until they'd found the exit, a craggy gap in the mountainside. The bird must have been the guardsman's; Turner remembered seeing it fly off his shoulder. Brilliantly trained bird, if he was right.

Firebirds must be more trainable than cats. But then, perhaps Dragon would have helped Turner just as well, of his own volition.

The sun blazed orange and low to the west. To the south, the badlands stretched before him, fields that he knew would be riddled with wyrms and wolves and other fearsome creatures. He didn't know what had happened to the bandits. They could be dead, or they could be prowling around the mountain. He didn't know what had become of Corrin and Amella, either. Most likely nothing good. Amella was the sort to take risks, to be brash and throw herself in the path of danger. He'd seen her do it; he remembered helping her hobble back into town while she clutched a boar's tusk in her fist. And Corrin, oh, the lass had been so young, and just learning how to swing a sword… And who knew what had become of Dragon?

The thoughts hurt.

But he refused to push them away. He had to acknowledge them, and he had to accept the probable outcome and move on. Even if Amella and Corrin had survived, by the grace of the Churikin or by sheer, preposterous luck, Turner wouldn't know where to begin looking for them.

He did know that Chevira and Bruin were alive, though, and that he could guide them back to the peninsula. He needed to get them to safety; or, at least, he needed to try. They were his shiphands, after all, and he their captain, even though they'd lost their ship.

"We'll report this to the guards," Turner said.

Chevira's trembling lessened. Bruin simply looked at him and nodded.

Turner moved his weary bones once more and led them west.

Verse crouched with her brother and her King in an offshoot tunnel, her heart hammering. It was dark and cramped. Safe. The dragon's roars faded, but the stench of ash and burned flesh remained. This would make one heck of a song if she were still a bard. (Or so Verse told herself, wrenching her thoughts from her racing heart and the ache in her ribcage.) Yeah. A song. A story for her to recite, with the shield of distance between her and the dangers within it. She couldn't think of a good lead-in, though. Whatever. Wasn't like she had to sing for her dinner anymore—sing and steal and slip away—not when the Bandit King had taught her how to plunder.

The Bandit King stood in front of her and Limerick, shoulders squared and back turned to them. Verse could just make out her outline, dark against a patch of dim light.

Next to Verse, Limerick trembled and murmured oaths like a prayer.

Verse's nose crinkled, and she elbowed him. "Get a grip," she said. "That's life, right? Charred and crushed on the flick of a blade."

"I was talking about *stabbings*."

"What, you'd rather bleed than go out in a blaze of—"

"Enough," said the Bandit King. Her voice snapped like a whip. "We've lost the captives."

"Our captives, stars, we've lost everyone," said Limerick.

Verse rapped the back of his head. "Apologies for my idiot brother."

The Bandit King acknowledged her with a grunt and stepped out into the chamber. Verse hesitated, then followed, Limerick trailing after her. She peered around the Bandit King. She glimpsed scattered bodies, blackened and damaged beyond recognition. Her stomach churned. She'd seen dead people before, struck down many a target herself, but this... the scale, the extent... She tore her gaze away and focused hard on the Bandit King's back instead: the dark brown hair like a beast's mane, her whole and sturdy neck, her singed cape, the ripple of cloth as she moved...

The Bandit King glanced back and caught her eye. Her lips curved with amusement. "Too much for you, Verse? You look ill."

Verse swallowed. "I'm fine."

"Hm." The Bandit King didn't look convinced, but she didn't push the matter. She scanned the chamber, eyes narrowing. "I see twelve bodies. By my last count, we numbered well over thirty. What does that tell you, Verse? Limerick?"

"We're not all dead?" suggested Limerick dryly.

"Not even half of us are dead," corrected the Bandit King. "But only three of us are here."

"So everyone's scattered," said Verse. "Should we try to round 'em up?"

"We'll see who we can find. But first, we'll see who we shouldn't look for." The Bandit King made her way around the chamber, pausing to inspect the remains of the fallen. Sometimes, she'd identify the body with a glance; other times, she'd kneel down and nudge their face into better view, or run her hand thoughtfully over a distinct piece of clothing or weapon. Sometimes she'd mutter to herself or pose a question to the empty air. King evaluated the remains just as she would the tracks of wild deer, or the weather patterns at sea, or the movements of whatever poor souls she planned to ambush.

King did not grimace, nor grieve, nor show any sign that the fate of her followers troubled her. She never did. The Bandit King valued her people while they were of use to her and discarded them when they weren't. The dead bodies were just people who had lost their value, no more, and so she examined them with detachment. It left Verse feeling chilled and unnerved, though she'd told herself many a time, *The world's a cold, brutal place. Get used to it.*

At least King provided value in return: protection, tactics, leadership, power. Equivalent exchange. Verse and Limerick had reaped rewards aplenty for their service.

At last, King straightened and addressed Verse and her brother. "All twelve of these are ours. We'll check the adjacent tunnels for survivors, but I don't want to linger here too long."

"Yeah, let's get out of this death trap," agreed Limerick. "Regroup and... then what?"

The answer was obvious. They should cut their losses and head southwest of Mount Cauldra, away from the dragon and the peninsula's guards. They could camp by the trading route that wended through the Bristleback mountain range. That road was full of pinch points and shadowy twists, which provided opportunities to jump on unwary travelers. Verse knew this because it was one of the Bandit King's favorite prowling grounds. Traders knew that path was dangerous, whispered of its risks in the taverns and around the festival fires, but they still used it. They had to; it was the only way to the mining settlements. Verse waited for the King to dust the soot off her cloak and say as much, to chart their course for easier winnings.

The Bandit King scowled. "We're going after the healer."

Right, we're going—wait what?

"Twice she's slipped through my fingers, now. We won't let her slip again."

A beat passed.

Verse cleared her throat awkwardly. "Not to rain on your bonfire, King, but how do you know she's even alive? The dragon might've had her for a snack."

The Bandit King frowned and shook her head. "No, she escaped. I caught a glimpse of her ducking into a tunnel."

Troll bites, Verse swore silently.

"She knows our faces. She'll cause trouble if we let her walk free."

And then the Bandit King scowled, thunderous, and all hope of giving up on this high-risk chase left Verse, blown away like dandelion seeds in the wind. This wasn't about tactical implications, was it? This was about the King's pride and anger. She always had enough power, combat skill, and sheer ruthless vitriol to seize what she wanted, but now, something had escaped her. The Bandit King probably didn't know how to accept that. So she wouldn't. Which meant the odds of convincing her to cut their losses were nil.

Double troll bites.

"We head east," said the Bandit King. Her voice was laced with venom. "This target, Corrin, didn't turn back before. She won't turn back now."

Verse traded glances with Limerick. He looked as uneasy as she felt.

"Boss," he tried, "if she's really continuing on into the Gloamwood, she's probably good as dead anyway."

"She should've been good as dead with the dragon or when she leapt into the sea, and yet, she is not. Besides, if she's continuing on to the Gloamwood, she might still lead us to that legendary fruit." Something else flitted across her face, something other than stung pride and simmering anger. Hunger, sharp and vicious, made the Bandit King's mouth twist and her eyes gleam. She turned to Verse, who suppressed the instinct to step back. "Those stories you once sang carry a kernel of truth. They must. And Corrin has a map in her head. What if the fruit truly does heal all ailments? What if it stops aging? Wouldn't you like to see which parts are true for yourself, Verse?"

This is nuts, Verse thought. *Look at what's happened to us so far. It's not worth it.*

And yet, her curiosity burned.

She looked to her brother. Limerick flattened a hand and tilted it from side to side. He wasn't sure about this. He didn't like it. But he was leaving the call up to Verse.

Verse took a breath. "Alright. We're with you."

CHAPTER THIRTEEN

In Ruins

Corrin stepped cautiously among the ruins, the back of her neck prickling. Most of the buildings had once been stone cottages and halls. Built with rocks from the mountain, if she had to guess. But now the stones were crumbly and overgrown with moss. The walls had holes in places, and the wooden roofs rotted and sagged. Twilight had arrived, and with it came a creeping chill and deepening shadows. Thistles and wildflowers obscured what might have once been paths. *Blue fingerlings for congestion,* she thought, as she avoided the bristly patches and gravitated to the more useful plants. It was second nature for her to identify herbal remedies, and it calmed her, a little, to lean into that habit. *Dandelions for bitter tea. Night's lace to help sleep…*

Tiny, iridescent creatures flitted among the wildflowers. Corrin mistook them for dragonflies at first, but then she knelt down for a closer look.

Fairies?

They were humanoid. Kind of. Less so than the elders' tales claimed. Stories always painted them as having human-shaped torsos, legs, and heads and wings that sprouted from their shoulder blades. But these fairies had blue skin instead of peach or brown, no hair, and four arms instead of two. Their fingers were proportionally large and spindly, and their eyes were black, even in the sclera. They were bigger than garden spiders but smaller than tarantulas, about the size of Corrin's thumb.

Two sat cross-legged on bowing leaves and chattered in a high-pitched babble. It sounded like a different language. Lots of vowels, interspersed with angry-sounding shrills and clicks. The chatter had gaps where Corrin felt *something* in her ears, a tension that almost hurt, but heard nothing. Seemed like their voices were reaching pitches that her ears couldn't make sense of. That was something else the stories had gotten wrong. The elders had said that fairies spoke in human tongues, so as to strike tricky deals and warn heroes not to cross them.

Junior chirruped inquisitively, and Corrin absentmindedly scratched the firebird's head. She extended her other hand, palm up, and watched as one of the fairies buzzed near it. Corrin held her breath. The fairy alighted on her palm, delicate as a butterfly. Its wings stilled and folded. It peered at her and said something in its incomprehensible fairytongue. Corrin didn't say anything in response, didn't dare breathe for fear of startling it away. The fairy cocked its head, then made a strange gesture with its hands and left.

I can't believe they're real, she thought.

The twins would love this. She wished they were with her so she could show them.

Except not really, what with the bandits and the dragon and all the deadly things that still lurked ahead of her, deep in the Gloamwood. Corrin exhaled. She couldn't take a fairy back with her—they weren't like flowers she could pick or glittering stones to be collected—so she'd just have to tell the twins as much detail as she could when she returned. If she returned. She hoped she could make it back. Her heart ached for Oddment and for the life that hadn't been in mortal danger all the time. It felt an age away, but it had only been, what, a month ago? A little more?

Time is strange.

Corrin picked herself up and carried on, scanning the buildings as she passed. She needed a rest spot—somewhere she could hide, but still be able to breathe—somewhere she wouldn't feel trapped. At last, she stopped at the entryway of what might have once been a… a hall? A village hall? It was a simple structure, a rectangle of ivy-draped stone walls with the tattered remains of a roof. The entrance was a hole in the wall, with no trace of a door—no scraps of rotting wood or rusted hinges, even, which made Corrin suspect it was intentional. Like the architect had designed this building to always be open.

It almost felt like this place was inviting her inside. And it was more spacious than the dilapidated huts around it, and its walls looked sturdy despite their age…

"What do you think?" she asked Junior. Her voice sounded unnaturally loud in the stillness.

Junior shuffled closer to her face, until Corrin could feel the softness of feathers and the press of a hard, small head against her cheek. Junior didn't have any commentary—at least, not any she could share. But her company was comforting, all the same.

Corrin crept inside. The ground was earthy and riddled with ferns and flowers. The air smelled like moss and petals. Long tables were laid out in rows—but they were made of wood, and wood-worms and fungi had taken them over. (The white puffballs were edible, and the blue buttons medicinal; Corrin plucked a couple of those as she passed. The redcaps and ink shelves were toxic.) The walls had grand arching windows, though little light came through them now, what with the sun hiding at the edge of the horizon beyond the mountain. Fairies flitted among the flowers in here, too, clustering in the corners. At the back of the hall stood a cabinet, and before it was an opening in the ground, ringed with stones.

Curiosity gnawed at her.

Corrin bypassed the opening, which led to a stone staircase with torch brackets affixed to the walls, and pried the cabinet open. Bits of rotted wood crumbled away from her fingers, and she peered inside, wondering, what did the people consider important enough to put in here? Surely something interesting. Maybe even something she could use.

Corrin reached in and pulled out the contents, one by one.

A silver bowl and a goblet, intricately engraved. Probably for ceremonies.

A bottle, filled with dark liquid that sloshed when Corrin picked it up. The cork smelled like wine so strongly that it made her nose wrinkle. One serving might've knocked even the likes of Amella flat, and that was assuming it wasn't poisoned. Could be poisoned or contaminated, with how long it'd been sitting here, though the seal looked snug. Corrin set it aside.

A silver dagger, with a ruby inlaid in its pommel. Pretty, but no better than her own dagger, function-wise.

A book.

Corrin opened it. The script was in an old style that she'd seen in a couple of Bathilda's texts, riddled with curlicues and symbols that modern scribes didn't use anymore. How old had Bathilda said those texts were? Five hundred, six hundred years? In any case, this seemed to be a book of stories. Some of them she recognized: the one about the Death goddess bargaining with the world-tortoise to let people keep living on its back; the one where the Churikin pilfered the fruit from

Death's portal-tree, the Tree of Life, and became immune to her sickle blade; the one where Death made the forest grow wild and thick, and crafted bog sprites and trolls and other terrifying creatures to protect it…

Mentions of the Tree were marked with inky dashes in the margins, like someone had been leafing through it and looking for each occurrence. That same someone must have scrawled the notes in the margins too—observations, questions, comments on the likelihood that each creature existed and where they might live and hide. The notes didn't use the same archaic letters as the text; they couldn't be more than a couple hundred years old, if that. And in the back, on spare pages, those notes were consolidated, sorted into paragraphs and accompanied with sketches of the creatures… sketches that seemed reminiscent of something Corrin had seen before, something… something she'd been carrying in her vest pocket, been counting on before she'd jumped into the sea and ruined it…

The hairs on the back of her neck stood on end. She turned to the last page, and she read the curly script there, neater than the marginal notes and with the same runes as the rest of the text, though in a different style.

Property of the People of Gailstone.

Corrin's gut twisted. This was the place Bathilda had mentioned. This was where Bathilda had witnessed the illness, where she'd needed the Gloamwood's fruit to save her patients. This was where she'd been too late, and two thirds of the population had fallen to the plague while the other third had left. Had it truly been a thriving village mere decades ago? Why did it seem so ancient, so long-decaying? And the book, those annotations—logically, they should only be decades old, but they seemed centuries old, too. Why didn't these puzzle pieces seem right? Why didn't the timing fit? Well, maybe Corrin had misjudged. Maybe degradation and decay worked faster than she wanted to think.

For a heartbeat, Corrin envisioned Oddment like this: mouldering away, abandoned. The parchment crinkled under her fingertips. The twist in her gut grew worse. Tears prickled at her eyes. If, after all of this, she had already run out of time…

Junior chirruped in Corrin's ear and dug her claws into her shoulder.

"Good bird," Corrin murmured, and took a steadying breath. She peered down the staircase. Was it possible Gailstone had kept more records down there? A copy of the map, maybe? She took out her flintstone and striker and crept down, showering torch brackets with sparks as she went. Some of them lit up. Some didn't. The ones that did were enough, and a soft orange light filled the staircase as she progressed. Junior chattered nervously on Corrin's shoulder.

"It's okay," she said to Junior. "I'm just going to take a peek. We'll head up soon."

She quickly reached the bottom of the staircase. The base opened into a small room with hulking shelves lining the walls. A funny lump sat in the back of the room, rendered indistinct by shadow. Corrin couldn't quite tell what it was—a mound of blankets? A pile of grain sacks? She took a step forward and struck a spark onto a torch just inside the room, and then an oil lamp sitting precariously on a crate. The air filled with the stench of ancient oils burning, and golden light spread over the floor and walls. Corrin could pick out jars and bottles on the shelves, now. The shape in the back still looked fuzzy. How strange. The light should have sharpened the edges of its bulk, made it clear where it ended and the wall began. It was mottled with black, brown, and gold. If she didn't know better, she'd guess it was a giant tortoiseshell cat—

It moved.

A pair of eyes blinked open and settled on her. They were lurid orange, and their oval pupils flashed red in the light. Cold dread tingled down Corrin's spine. An ear flicked up, pointy-ended and ten times the size of hers. The… the thing… growled deeply and heaved itself to its feet. It stood on its hind legs, almost like a human. But its legs were shorter and stockier and its arms so much longer and thicker. Its paws harbored a set of wickedly curving claws. It slouched forward, like it was meant to walk on all fours as easily as two legs. Its snout was squashed-looking, and its face was covered with fur. It bared its teeth. They flashed sharp and vicious in the firelight.

Troll, she thought. And then: *This is unfair. I just got away from the dragon.*

The troll's snout crinkled. Its eyes squinted. Its jaws stretched into a yawn, then snapped shut with a *click.* It stared at her like it was her fault for waking it up. Which, technically, it was.

Unfair, Corrin thought again, weakly. She reached for her sword.

The troll lunged across the room like it was immune to inertia, like it didn't realize something so bulky shouldn't spring so fast. It reached Corrin just as her sword rose, steel flashing, its point skimming the troll's chest. Junior screeched in her ear and surged toward the troll's face in a rush of crimson feathers—

The troll snarled and slammed Corrin's head with one paw. Her vision flashed with dark and light splotches, and she toppled over. Her back hit the ground, and breath *whooshed* out of her lungs. Her sight cleared and sharpened just in time to see Junior batted away like a fly. The firebird spun and flapped frantically to right herself, coming within a hair's breadth of the wall. The troll came at Corrin again. Her sword lay just beyond her fingertips—she turned and reached for it—

A heavy weight landed on her chest, and something hard and narrow pressed against her neck. The troll bent close to her face and narrowed its eyes. Corrin could've lived her whole life happily without knowing what a troll's morning breath stank like, but here she was. Her fingers curled around the hilt of her sword, but she knew, even as her heart rabbited and her arm twitched with the instinct to fight back, that the troll could kill her faster than she could kill it. She was doomed. *I've failed.*

Junior attacked the troll's face.

The troll roared and swatted Junior aside, harder this time, but its claw lifted from her neck, and Corrin twisted and stabbed at its chest—

—but the point scarcely made it an inch into the knotty muscle before the troll moved. It reared and seized the hilt between its meaty paws, wrenching it out of her grip and tossing it aside. It pinned her again, this time by the arms. Corrin trembled. Out of the corner of her eye, she could see Junior on the ground, staggering to her feet and shaking her head dazedly. ***Now** I'm doomed,* Corrin thought.

"Junior," Corrin said, "find Tenno."

It was a small thing, maybe a futile one, but she could at least try to make sure Junior didn't die with her. Maybe the bird could help her friend.

Junior ducked her head low and fluffed out her feathers, staring at her helplessly, then let out the most heart-broken call she'd ever heard from a bird. Corrin stared back, pleading silently. Junior stretched her wings, but she didn't move just yet.

The troll's ears twitched. It leaned in closer.

Corrin squeezed her eyes shut.

"Wyrman."

What?

The voice had not been human. Too low and growling. Also, she was the only person here, and the sound had come from right in front of her, right near her ears, which meant… but that was ridiculous…

Corrin chanced a peek. The troll's face was too close for comfort, but miraculously, it didn't look about to bite her head off. Not right that second, anyway. She still didn't like her odds for the next minute or so. The troll's snarl had shrunk, leaving just the tips of its teeth exposed.

"Krr catch wyrman." The troll's mouth moved with the words.

The stories hadn't said anything about trolls talking. Not a single one. What was this?

Corrin cleared her throat. "Yes. Um. You caught me. You caught a… a… human."

The troll's nose crinkled. "Hoo. Man? Wyyyrrr man."

"I—I think we mean the same thing. Wyrman, except it's human where I come from. How'd you learn to talk, anyway? I didn't know trolls could talk." From the way the troll's expression contorted, Corrin gathered she was talking too fast. She tried to slow down. It was hard. Her heart raced, her thoughts whirled, and the words wanted to spill out of her, hasty and jumbled, while they still had the chance. "Our stories never said anything about you talking. They just talk about you a—attacking anyone who goes into the Gloamwood. But, um, this isn't the Gloamwood and you're making word noises, so maybe is there a chance that you-could-not-claw-me-dead-and-I-could-talk-you-intolettingmego?"

The troll drew its head back, but its paws stayed planted on Corrin's arms. "Gloam-wood." It said the word as if it was chewing on it, tasting it. "Nurwood? Troll, krr?" It paused, then grinned. Its mouth bristled with sharp teeth, more terrifying than the Bandit King's could ever be. "No let go. Bring you harth. Wyddscatch."

"Wydd-what?"

The troll huffed. "Wyddscatch. Krr bairn be krr big. Krr walk far, hunt Wyddscatch, bring harth, purf strength." The troll shifted back, and in one fluid motion, it hooked its claws in the front of Corrin's vest and lifted her.

For an instant, she was standing—and then she was in the air, her feet dangling, the leather of her vest straining as it supported her weight. The troll held her out at arm's length, with the ease that Corrin might hoist a kitten. She felt as helpless as a kitten—a tiny, fragile creature with a speeding heart, with limbs too short to reach the eyes and claws too small to do more than sting. Blood congealed on the troll's chest and matted its fur, but the troll didn't seem to notice. Which meant if she tried to stab its arm with her dagger, it'd probably just blink at her and dash her head against the wall. It was probably going to do that anyway.

I'm dead. I'm dying. I'm troll food.

And of all the things she could feel, it was frustration that bubbled to the surface.

IT'S NOT FAIR.

Corrin kicked ineffectually at thin air.

The troll seemed amused by this; it grinned, and a rumble that might have been a laugh purled out of its chest. "Fierce small wyrman," said the troll. It jostled her, and she stilled. "Bring lif, show Krr big strong-skill-clever. Wyrman body-weak, det mind-strong. Tales say wyrman trick-monsters. Trick hands make clars and mouths shape trick groks."

What was it saying? Bring lif—bring alive? Take her alive? As a prize to show… what, to show it was big and scary? What would it do with her afterward?

Tie me up and slow-roast me for a feast, probably, she thought glumly.

Behind the troll's head, something red glided past and soared up the staircase. *Junior.*

"Grok," said the troll, and watched her as if it expected something.

"…Talk?"

"Ttttalk? Grrrrrok. Yus."

"Oh. Uh. I… live?"

"Lif. Stay wid Krr. Run, I catch more time and kill."

"I," Corrin pointed to herself, "stay—" she pointed to the troll "—with y—with Krr? Go home, harth, with Krr? Otherwise, you'll claw me dead?"

The troll—the krr—Krr?—grinned and nodded. Carefully, Krr set her down. The second Corrin's boots bore her weight, she staggered back and into the wall. Corrin's legs had turned to jelly, thanks to all that dangling and thinking she was troll food. Which she still might be, in the near but not (she hoped) immediate future.

Krr rumbled, "We go, move fast. I rest did, much strength now."

"Great," said Corrin weakly. "So after moving fast and reaching harth and all, what are you going to do with me?"

Krr's face scrunched in concentration. "What… going… me?" A single claw jabbed the front of Corrin's vest. "What do hooman-wyrman?"

Corrin nodded. "Are you going to eat m—the wyrman?"

"Eat? Hrr." Krr scratched its stomach with one paw, then grinned.

"May be, may be no."

Unfair, she thought again, with renewed vehemence. And then: *I've got to get out of this.*

CHAPTER FOURTEEN

An Unlikely Alliance

Corrin walked away from the Gailstone ruins with Krr at her back and nothing but a dagger to protect herself with. She still wasn't sure if Krr was its—their?—name or their way of saying "troll." She wasn't sure of everything Krr said, in general, because sometimes she wasn't sure which words the sounds were supposed to be. Most of the time, though, the words were the same, or similar, or close enough where she could kind of see how one matched another in her own language. If she tweaked a vowel here and twisted a consonant there, and did some mental topsy-turvy contortions...

Whenever her mind tired of puzzling over Krr's words, or trying (and failing) to find a way out of this mess, she wondered how two such different species shared so many bits and pieces of language. And how had humankind forgotten that they did? Had they known the trolls, once, before even the bards could remember? And when she tired of circling around *that,* she went back to talking to Krr.

"Why was Krr sleeping in the basement?" Corrin asked, as she stepped around a crooked oak.

"Base-ment? Hrm. Sleep... Krr sleep... Den?"

"Um. Yes. I think so. Den."

"Good den. Safe. Krr find, Krr need sleep, Krr take." Krr grabbed Corrin's pack and steered her left. "Go this way. No tree wyrms."

The trees thickened. Roots ran across the ground like veins that had risen to the surface of the world's skin. Corrin picked her way over them cautiously. The forest hummed with insects and smelled of damp soil, and the air grew cold as night settled in. It was harder to see now; everything was vague shapes and shadows and flickers of motion, and eventually, she slowed down enough that Krr lost patience.

"Carry wyrman," Krr huffed, and tossed her over their shoulder.

"Agh! Put me down."

"Wyrman turtle."

"I'm not a turtle, I just can't see!"

"Rrrr?"

"Wyrman no see. Dark."

"Eyens weak."

"Eyens very weak," Corrin agreed. "Wyrman sleep at night. Eyens better in the daytime."

"Daytime bright time?"

"Yes. Bright time. Unless it's raining or cloudy."

"Hrrmmm."

But they kept walking, or rather, Krr kept walking and Corrin rested on their shoulder, until the moon reached its zenith and Krr set her down. Krr nudged her toward a tree with low branches and a thick knobby trunk, and Corrin instinctively grabbed ahold of it. This was a good climbing tree, the kind her brothers would have scaled in a heartbeat back home. "You want me to climb this?"

"Yes. Climb. Sleep wid tree. Up-up-up."

Corrin obligingly clambered her way up, navigating by touch. She found a sturdy branch, thick around at the base as her leg, and crawled onto it. Krr followed with a grunt and mutterings too low to make out, until at last, the troll settled near her, in the junction where all the tree's branches met. Like the rest of the forest, Krr was difficult to see, little more than a stirring shape. Only their flashing pupils stood out. They blinked.

"Wyrman climb fast." Krr sounded impressed.

"Thanks." So she could climb as fast as a troll. Good to know. She was smaller and physically weaker, and her novice swordsmanship had done beans all in a fight, but perhaps she could climb to a place that couldn't support the troll's weight… no, then she'd be trapped up there… Could she outrun a troll? She hadn't seen Krr run across open land, but Krr had pounced so fast, back in the cellar. So she couldn't count on being faster, either…

"Why wyrman here?"

Krr's question startled Corrin out of her thoughts. She blinked; she processed; and then she asked, a touch indignantly, "What do you mean, why am I here? You took me here."

Krr growled. "Why wid dead harth, where no more wyrman? Wyrman do Wyddscatch?"

"Oh." Corrin chewed her lip, trying to figure out how to explain in language the troll would understand. "I don't live in the ruins, uh, the dead harth. I came from far away to find the Tree of Life. The Lif Tree? I need its fruit to help my people. They're sick." She paused. When Krr didn't say anything, she added, "They're going to die if I don't get back to them with the fruit. My teacher and I tried all the remedies we could think of, and none of them worked. Nobody was healing. We had to do something."

Krr rumbled and hrrrmed softly. "Wyrman leave harth, wyrman hunt lif give wyrman-kin. Wyrman no lif alone? Wyrman no do Wyddscatch?"

"That's right. You don't happen to know where the fruit is, do you?" She tried to remember how Bathilda had described it. "It would be purple, and it would grow on a big tree. The map called the tree the Tree of Life. Lif Tree. But I don't have the map anymore, so I was just… I was going to try to find it, anyway. We—the wyrmen—have lots of stories about the fruit, say it can heal any wound and grant immortality and even, in one story, bring someone back from the brink of death. I don't believe most of that, but my teacher told me it really can heal a plague. Says it's the cure for the sickness afflicting my village now."

Krr huffed. "Grok fast. Det Krr grekka grok. Krr grekka Lif Tree stories. Krr have many stories, too. Danger place."

"Really? Our stories said you—Krr—are the dangerous ones."

"Hah! Krr strong. Krr danger. But Lif Tree wid heart Nurwood—Gloamwood. Wyrman no grekka Gloamwood. Danger even for Krr. Grokkachur, bog trippers, Churikin. Churikin quick, have kill bite, make ikik." Krr reached out and snatched Corrin with their powerful paw, yanking her into the junction of branches with them. There was scarcely room; Corrin was smushed against Krr's side, and Krr's arm was wrapped around her, trapping her. "No run," they said confidently. "Stay wid Krr. Be Wyddscatch. Meet Krr-kin, Krr-kin pride wid Krr. May be, lif." Krr rumbled thoughtfully. "Grok wid Dono. Will see."

Oh, fantastic, Corrin thought. *So either I die, or I live but stay a captive, and everyone else dies.*

But before Corrin could respond, Krr yawned and said, "Sleep now." And with that, the troll closed their eyes.

Corrin stayed awake long after Krr's breathing had slowed. She waited and watched, and gradually, the arm trapping her loosened a smidge. She could shift. She could wiggle. She could, maybe, slip away while Krr slept, if she moved the arm and squirmed out and scrambled quick and quiet down the tree…

Except Krr would probably start tracking her the moment they woke up.

What if they never woke up, though?

She was hyperconscious of the swell and contraction of the troll's chest, their breath whispering out through their pointed teeth, and their fur, thick and bristly but softer 'round the stomach. The eyes would be vulnerable, too. So would the neck. Her heart pounded in her ears as she reached up with cautious fingers. She felt the thick ruff of fur, and underneath it the firmness of stabilizing muscle, and then—*there*. The troll had a carotid artery, just like she did. One slice there, and Krr would bleed out. And then she wouldn't have a troll chasing her, and she could continue on her quest to save Oddment…

The hand gripping her dagger trembled. Her stomach churned.

The troll snuffled and slumbered on, defenseless.

Corrin sheathed her dagger. She couldn't bring herself to do it.

She tried to justify it to herself, her inability to kill someone who seemed awfully blasé about possibly killing her. It wasn't foolishness, it wasn't a weak stomach. She had sensible reasons for doing what she did, didn't she? What if they woke up? What if they startled and lashed out, striking her down as she struck them?

What if she was safer with them than without? For now, at least?

Ahead was the Gloamwood, with all its beasts and sink-bogs and unknown pitfalls. Behind her was a mountain where a dragon had almost turned her to ashes, and also the Bandit King, who might still be alive and probably wanted her head on a pike. It seemed like everything around her was determined to kill her. But not Krr. Not yet for sure, maybe not ever. Krr wanted her alive, at least until they reached Krr's home village. And then… well, it kind of sounded like they were thinking of keeping her around. Like a kitten plucked from the streets, or something.

But they might get there and decide that she was worth more as a snack than a prize, or pet, or whatever she would be alive. Besides, she couldn't abandon Oddment to stay in a troll settlement for the rest of her life, however short or long that life may be. No, she'd have to find a way to convince Krr that Krr should let her go. Or she'd have to slip away and make it hard for Krr to find her again, somehow. Corrin needed a plan. An opening. Something. She needed to figure out what to do.

Corrin fell asleep enveloped in fur, with the stench of raw meat and mushrooms in her nose.

They left at daybreak. The canopy thickened until only the narrowest beams of sunlight filtered through. The plants grew strange. Some were plants that Corrin knew, but larger, coming up past her knees or growing thrice as thick. Others looked like variants or cousins that had evolved for the Gloamwood; they might have the right leaf shape and texture, but the color was slightly off, or vice versa. But some were unfamiliar, and they did things Corrin didn't realize plants could do. One plant had green petals with fringes that lay open, emitting a rotting smell until an insect landed inside of it—and then it snapped shut! Like a mouth! Another with thin shoots tried to curl around her finger when she touched it. Even the trees were different. Some had papery bark, and others had leaves like ferns, star-shaped leaves, or long leaves like streamers.

Krr had names for all of them.

"What's this?" asked Corrin, and prodded one of the fly-eating plants.

"Techung."

"This one?" She let the dark shoot curl around her pinky.

"Jrrin. No eat. Make bodin no move."

"It's a paralytic?"

"Para—ruh?"

"Nevermind."

"..."

"Is Krr your name, or is Krr your kin?"

Krr blinked. "Krr be Krr, Krr be kin."

Corrin searched for the right words."I..." She pointed to herself. "I'm a wyrman and my kin are wyrmen, but I am Corrin and my kin are not Corrin."

"Cor-rin?" Krr's eyes narrowed in concentration, then widened. "Corrin be namae."

"Um. Yes. Namae. Name."

Krr thumped their chest. "Makur. Makur be Makur, Makur be Krr. Makur be namae."

"Makur's your name. Okay, Makur."

Makur grinned. "Corrin good namae."

"Thanks."

* * *

They stopped at a stream that wended through the trees and babbled over rocks and exposed roots. Dark pebbles and reeds lined the shore, and peculiarly colored fish flitted about in the middle, weaving their way between underwater weeds and tree roots. "Kilifin," said Makur, and pointed to a vibrant red one with orange freckles. "No eat. Make belly ache, under-fur burn." Makur pointed to a glinting thing just beneath the surface. "Yigurfin. Can eat. Crunchy." Makur's paw flashed out, and the rippling surface beneath it burst into droplets. When the paw retracted, it had a silvery minnow skewered on two claws. Makur shoved the fish in Corrin's face. "Good snargak. Corrin try."

Gingerly, Corrin tugged the fish off Makur's claws. It was cool and limp and slimy, as all fish were when they first came out of the water. Makur watched her with wide, earnest eyes, and for a heartbeat, Corrin was reminded of Tiptoes. Sometimes, the pudgy little cat would sneak into the apartment and drop a grey, furry lump at Corrin's feet. She'd mew and gaze at Corrin expectantly, much as Makur was doing, as if to say, *Well? Aren't you going to eat this delightful dead thing that I've brought you?*

(In fairness, Corrin supposed she did eat dead things. They just so happened to be cooked, or skinned and stripped and dried beyond recognition. And whenever she went to do that, Tiptoes would wander after her, meowing urgently, as if accusing her of food blasphemy. It had taken Corrin weeks to figure out that Tiptoes was doing no such thing, but instead wondering why Corrin hadn't given the cat fresh milk or gamey tidbits in gratitude.)

Makur clicked their teeth and chomped the air pointedly.

Corrin screwed her eyes shut and took a bite out of the fish, chewing determinedly. It tasted of algae, oils, mud, and… And snot? Its flesh was tough and stringy, and it slipped around between her teeth. Her stomach, which had felt hollow moments ago, shriveled in on itself as if to say *no thanks, I'll eat myself, it's fine.*

But Makur watched her intently, and she didn't want to offend the creature who was twice her size, thrice her strength, and armed with sharp teeth and claws. Besides, she needed to eat, and in the broadest sense of the word, this was food.

She swallowed, shuddering as the cold, slimy gunk slid down her throat. Corrin opened her mouth to force out a thank you.

"Hngaguh."

Makur tilted their head and scrunched up their face in concentration. "Hng… gaguh?"

"I. Agh. Thaguh."

"Thaguh?"

"Th—" Corrin coughed and thumped her chest. "Thanks."

"Good snargak," said Makur uncertainly. "Yus?"

"Yus. Uh. I appreciate it, I really do. But I have other... snargak." Corrin pulled off her pack. It was lighter and less full than she would have expected, and when she opened it, she found some of its supplies missing. The dried meats and fruits. The bar of soap. The slingshot. Most of the travel biscuits. The jar of salve was still in there, along with spare bandages, the canteen, a comb, and a sleeping blanket, but too much was missing. She can't have used up all those supplies. One of the bandits must have picked through them, back in the tunnels.

It's enough, Corrin told herself firmly, and withdrew a travel biscuit. She bit into it. It was better than the fish, dense and salty and subtly sweetened with honey, but dry on her tongue and difficult to chew. She felt hyperaware of Makur's eyes on her, but she ignored the troll until she'd finished the biscuit, then withdrew another.

"Good snargak?"

Corrin hesitated; then, begrudgingly, she offered the biscuit to Makur. Makur pinched it between two claws, eyed it critically, and popped it whole into their mouth. Corrin's stomach ached with longing.

Makur swallowed and thumped their chest, much as Corrin had done. Unlike Corrin, they made no pretenses at thank-yous. Makur's fur bristled, and they picked crumbs out from their teeth with a disgruntled growl. "Rrr. Blurgh. Stick-tarth snargak. Dry, old. Bad snargak."

"More for me, then," said Corrin, and took out a third biscuit. She'd have three left after this one. She bit into it hungrily and tried not to think of her pillaged food supply, nor whether she'd soon be living on Makur's offerings of slimy fish. She also dunked her canteen in the stream, filling it to the brim, and drank.

Makur turned back to the water and waited, paw ready. *Splash.* Another minnow caught. *Splash.* A long, snake-like thing with blue-green skin. *Splash.* A fat fish with scales that looked black but glinted rainbow. Makur kept at it until six or seven fish lay in a heap, then plopped down and dangled them, one by one, into their gaping mouth. Bones crunched, and the pile vanished faster than it had grown. When Makur finished, there was one left—the snake-like fish—and they tossed it into Corrin's lap, startling her. "Eat," said Makur severely. "Corrin no eat old bad snargak. Corrin be starve. Makur want Corrin no starve. Lif, see harth."

Corrin considered the snake-fish in her lap. Its skin was like a frog's, soft and slimy, and its eyes bulged. Thin ridges ran along the top and bottom of its tail, which was flat, as if it had been pressed beneath a stone. It was interesting to look at, but she didn't want to bite into its skin, not after trying to brave the minnow's. She looked up at Makur, who looked back at her, then at the snake-fish, then up at her again. Then, cautiously, she drew her dagger. It was a move that could be mistaken for aggression. She knew how dangerous her dagger could be to the unguarded—remembered her hand trembling on its hilt while Makur slumbered beside her, unaware.

Makur narrowed their eyes, but they didn't leap on her or growl.

Corrin let out a slow breath and cut into the fish. She bisected and divided it as she would one of the frogs or salamanders she used to catch for Bathilda, removing the bones and organs and cutting the meat into small pieces. There wasn't time to make a fire, not with Makur waiting impatiently on the bank, so she took a skinless fleshy piece and ate it raw. To her relief, it wasn't half as foul as the minnow. It was pungent and a smidge oily, but it was also tender and savory, almost sweet. She ate a second piece.

"Good snargak," said Makur. They bared their teeth in a—a smile?

"Good snargak," Corrin agreed, and kept eating. She hoped she wasn't ingesting infections or toxins. *I'm probably not,* she mentally reassured herself. *It tastes like fish, and Makur seems to think it's safe to eat. And they're smart enough to name poisonous things. They were doing it earlier.* She tried not to think about how Makur had a troll's physiology and a troll's stomach, and what was safe for one species wasn't necessarily safe for another, and human bodies were terribly delicate and vulnerable things...

Makur growled. Not at her. Something else.

Corrin looked where Makur was looking—and promptly dropped her fish.

A rope of patterned scales and sinew hung from a tree not five paces from them and swayed, all seven arm-lengths of it (Makur-sized arm lengths). It ended in a reptilian head as big as her own, with beady eyes and a forked tongue that flicked out to taste the air. The creature was thick around as Corrin's leg.

Snake, thought Corrin numbly. She took a moment to reach this conclusion because snakes weren't supposed to grow that enormous.

They were supposed to be small and easily missed in the underbrush, or coiled up and rattling to say, *I am here, please leave me alone, I will bite you if you don't.*

The snake slithered down and touched the forest floor. It paused, as if it were sizing them up and deliberating over its approach.

Makur growled. "Serdra."

Corrin swallowed. "We should go."

Makur's ear twitched. "No. Serdra stalk, serdra wait, serdra hunt. Rahrg now."

"That—that seems like a terrible idea." Though, in fairness, it was the kind of idea Amella would have. She probably would've strode up to the massive nightmare of a snake and lopped off its head with her sword. But Corrin didn't have a sword with her. And even if she did... "Snakes are slow, aren't they? Unless they're striking? Can't we just—"

But Makur surged forward. So did the snake, which was decidedly not slow, and the two became a writhing mass of scales and fur. The snake bit into Makur's shoulder and wound around Makur's body. Makur's claws blurred through the air, swiping at the coils and the head. But the snake had too snug a hold, and the wounds they scored were shallow. Corrin stumbled back instinctively, drawing her dagger, but the snake paid her no mind. It was too busy pinning one of Makur's arms and ducking away from Makur's swipes. It curled around to attack the other arm.

Corrin couldn't tear her eyes away. Her legs didn't want to move.

Which was unfortunate, as it was the opportune moment to run away.

Makur made a sound halfway between a snarl and a wheeze.

Corrin took a step forward. *I'm a fool,* she thought desperately, her heart slamming against her ribs, *a tender-heart, a duft, a madperson.* But she took another step, and another, and she ran toward the fight instead—and as the snake bit into Makur again, she whipped out her dagger and severed the head.

The snake's jaws lost their grip, and its coils slackened. Makur shoved the snake off and shuffled out of reach, growling. Corrin took a shaky breath. The snake's blood had stained her dagger. "It's dead," she mumbled, more to herself than Makur. Because it was, just like that. She knelt and wiped her dagger on a fern. "Th-that was too close."

Makur stared at her with wide eyes, one paw on their injured shoulder. Their breathing was unsteady and their pupils large, and their fur bristled.

"I. Um. I-if you let me, I can help. I heal things. I'm a healer's apprentice, th-that's what I've been doing most of my life." Makur stared at her like they couldn't understand, so Corrin took a deep breath and tried again, forcing her voice to steady and her words to be simple and slow. "I heal." She pointed to their injuries. "Corrin help Makur. Yus?"

Makur's ears twisted back, then forward. They grunted.

"I'll take that as a yus." Corrin sheathed her dagger and approached Makur. She nudged their paw out of the way, which they permitted with a huff and a turn of their head. Blood matted their fur, and she had to pry away the sticky clumps to get to the snake bite. Or bites, as it turned out.

Dozens of puncture wounds oozed blood. None of the wounds were large, but they looked deep and torn around the edges. Judging from the alignments, the snake had bitten several times in the same spot.

Ouch, Corrin thought, and a murmur of sympathy escaped her.

"We're cleaning these," she said, and guided Makur into a sitting position for better access. She dunked a cloth in the stream and cleaned away as much gunk as she could, then dabbed on her salve, a green paste that had a sharp smell but felt cool and pleasant to the touch. The salve would soothe the damaged skin and help it regenerate. She just hoped the snake wasn't venomous. It shouldn't be, she didn't think, Bathilda had told her that snakes with venom in their fangs usually struck and drew back, but if she was wrong... *Don't think about it. Just treat what you can.* She applied gentle pressure with her hand, feeling for swelling. There was none. A good sign. The muscle twitched beneath her touch, though, like it wanted to recoil but had stopped itself. "Hurts?" she asked.

Makur bared their teeth. "No."

Liar, she thought. But she didn't argue. Bathilda had once told her that that was rule number one for dealing with difficult patients: don't argue when you don't have to. Don't give them reasons to be more difficult. *Doubly important with troll-beasts,* Corrin decided.

She grabbed her spare bandages and swathed Makur's shoulder. The muscles kept twitching and stiffened every now and then, and Corrin would pause, worried that Makur would lash out. But Makur never did; they kept their head turned away and their eyes fixed on something Corrin couldn't see. She wrapped the bandage snug, but not snug enough to cut off the circulation, and tucked in the end. "It's done," she said, and stepped back.

The result looked strangely flat and thin compared to the rest of Makur. Fur puffed out around the edges of the bandage, thick and tortoiseshell-dark in contrast to the white fabric. Makur ran their paw over the bandage and grumbled something that Corrin didn't know how to interpret. Their pupils had shrunk, though, and their bristling had subsided, so she hoped they weren't terribly bothered by her treatment.

She eyed Makur's chest—the fur was clumped with old blood there from when she'd flailed her sword. She gestured to it, and Makur let her clean that out as well. This one was a longer cut. Scabbed closed, but swelled around the edges. Infected. Corrin cleaned out the clumps with stream-dampened fingers, then dipped her hand in the salve jar and coated the scab in green. She smoothed the fur back over it. She couldn't spare a bandage. She only had the one left, and it wouldn't have fit around Makur's torso, anyway.

Makur huffed. "Corrin finish?"

"Yes—I mean, yus."

"Good." Makur rolled their shoulder, the injured one. Pink spots bloomed on the bandage.

"You should try to keep your shoulder still. No move, no hurt."

Makur grumbled, but they stopped rolling it.

Corrin went to the dead snake and picked up its head. Its eyes were like black beads, still and lifeless. Its tongue peeked out of its snout, limp and turning purple at its forked ends. The snake's scales were cool and smooth. Not too different, really, from the shy garter snakes that lurked in the woods near Oddment, except these scales were ten times bigger and thicker, and this snake had gone after a troll instead of field mice. And it could've had Corrin for a snack if it hadn't—and if she hadn't—

She tried not to look too closely at the truncation point, and she pried open its jaws. The snake's teeth were all of similar size, thick at the base, and milky white; they didn't look made to inject venom, just to pierce and grip.

Okay then.

"Corrin rahrg good."

She started; her fingers slipped, and the snake head thudded against her boot. Makur had ambled up behind her to peer over her shoulder, and they looked down at her now with bright orange eyes and one of the scariest grins Corrin had ever seen. The troll rumbled something she didn't catch—it almost sounded like a purr—and repeated, "Corrin rahrg good. Corrin small. Corrin hunt serdra. Weak, strong. Weak-strong wyrman be krr bidum." Makur reached for her, and Corrin flinched—but all the troll did was pat her head, like she would pat a herding dog or Oatmuncher. "Ikres Makur."

"Thank you, I—I think."

Makur ruffled her hair. Corrin didn't complain. She didn't have it in herself to care. It had probably been a tangled mess for a month, anyway. "We move. Makur, Corrin, go harth to krr-kin. Be good Wyddscatch. Lif."

Corrin blinked. She looked at the snake, and then at her hands, and then at Makur, and then at the snake again. "Do you think this could be your Wyddscatch?" she asked weakly, and pointed to the mess of coils that in all probability they couldn't carry. "It'd be more impressive. It almost ate us. I couldn't almost eat us."

Makur cackled in the back of their throat. "HarrraHAR. Serdra no Makur Wyddscatch. Serdra be Corrin Wyddscatch. Corrin be Makur Wyddscatch." Makur scooped up the snake's head and held it out to her as if they were offering a lucky rock, or a festival pie, or some other reasonable likable prize that wasn't a severed head. "Take, carry, show Corrin hunt serdra, show Corrin be krr bidum. Then krr be Corrin bidum."

Gingerly, Corrin accepted the offering. She wrapped it in fern leaves, added some flowers that might have been distantly related to lavender and carried a fresh, light scent, then wrapped it all in more fern leaves, and finally tucked it in her pack. Despite her efforts, she resigned herself to the reek of death that would inevitably permeate everything she owned.

(Everything that hadn't been pilfered, anyway.)

She stood up. They kept walking.

CHAPTER FIFTEEN

Interlude: Detective Work

As Amella led them on, Tenno couldn't help but recall everything Corrin had told him about her venturesome friend, weighing the descriptions, looking between the person in front of him and the person painted in his mind's eye. Amella had been larger than life in Corrin's stories. An adventurer who strong-armed men twice her size and took pieces of beasts and monsters as trophies. A seasoned traveler who knew the ways of the world as well as Corrin had known the ways of Oddment. A swordmaster. Someone with a big voice and a hearty laugh and a long shadow. Someone who was brave and bold and perhaps slightly mad.

When he'd first seen Amella, she'd seemed small and defeated. She seemed less small now as she led the way along the mountainside, with sharp eyes and a hand resting on the hilt of her sword, and Tenno could see the strength and worldliness Corrin was talking about. Her demeanor reminded him of some of his seniors in the royal guard; she would've done well there, he suspected, if she'd chosen to apply. But he still didn't see the mad boldness Corrin had described.

Honestly, if he were going to describe anyone as mad, it was Corrin. Her madness was just quiet, buried beneath her politeness and her fears. It was her determination to brave the Gloamwood despite the risks, and her willingness to gamble on a dragon.

"Huh," said Amella. "What's that?" She pointed to a red speck in the sky.

"I don't—"

The red speck grew until Tenno could make out wings, brilliant crimson feathers, and a beak black as coal—a firebird. It dove toward them and cannonballed into Tenno, its claws hooking into his leather shoulder pad. Its—no, her—voice chirped anxiously into his ear. Junior. Junior was back. Junior was no longer with Corrin. Corrin was either nearby or...

Tenno held out his arm, and Junior shuffled onto it. "Is Corrin okay?"

Junior neither confirmed nor denied. She ducked her head and shifted her wings up, a gesture halfway between a shrug and a cringe.

"The heck does that mean?" demanded Amella.

"It means either it's complicated, or she doesn't know." Tenno gentled his tone and ran a finger along Junior's spine. "It's alright. You did great. Can you do a little more for me? Can you guide us to where you saw her last?"

Junior bobbed her head and took off.

She led them to the ruins of a village. Tenno didn't remember ever hearing of a village that lived beyond Mount Cauldra, but then, perhaps he hadn't heard of it because it was ancient. The place was decrepit—the wood was rotting away, the roofs collapsing, and the ivy overtaking the walls. Furthermore, it was infested with fairies, which had a legendary avoidance of human settlements, so legendary that Tenno had never seen them or even been sure that they existed. Twilight made ghosts out of the fairies and nightmare shapes out of the decaying structures, and Tenno had to will himself forward. Junior guided them deep into this mess, toward the remains of a building that might have once been a town hall.

Amella followed him, close as a shadow. If she felt unnerved, he couldn't tell.

Junior soared over the fungi-infested remains of tables and hovered in front of a ransacked cabinet, over an opening in the ground. Tenno peered into it and saw stairs, spiraling down, down into darkness.

Junior landed on his shoulder.

"In here?"

"Scree."

He glanced back at Amella, who frowned but nodded. They descended the stone steps. Amella found a decaying torch on the wall, lit it (albeit with difficulty), and passed it to Tenno, so they could see where they were putting their feet. The stairs let out into a cellar, or what Tenno assumed was a cellar, from all the bottles and the smell of old beer. He cast his torch light across the floor, which had been crafted out of old flagstones and had a layer of dust and—and a dark reddish streak?

He knelt and examined it. It was a blood stain. Concerningly large.

Corrin?

His heart constricted.

Amella knelt beside him and swore. "What happened here?"

"I don't know."

He held up his torch, casting the light farther, and spotted a glint of metal. A discarded sword, with blood encrusted on the tip. It was simply made, with no ornamentation or sigils to distinguish it from another sword, but Corrin had been carrying one just like it. Which meant in all probability it was hers, and she'd gotten cornered down here by someone, or something, and lashed out at it, and then—and then she'd lost her grip on her sword and hadn't retrieved it. Tenno's drill instructor once said that a lost sword means a dead soldier. His stomach twisted. He thought, *She's not even a soldier.* And then: *She can't be dead. She made it past the* ***dragon***…

"Stars," said Amella quietly, and picked up the sword. "What happened here?"

"I—I don't know." Tenno scanned the rest of the room. But there was nothing more of interest, just the blood splotches and the old beer. "Looks like a struggle took place, and then the winner must have…" He trailed off. Something dark and fuzzy on the floor had caught his eye, and he knelt to inspect it. A hair clump? He pinched it with his fingertips. Not hair, no. Too soft for hair. Fur. It was thick, with black and brown strands, and sticky with blood. That answered one question, then. Some*thing,* not some*one.*

"Let me see."

Tenno started; Amella had crept up behind him without his noticing. Her dark eyes glinted in the half-light, and he wordlessly held out the clump of fur. Amella plucked it from his hand and inspected it, her brow furrowing.

"This isn't bear fur—not a solid color, it's got blacks and browns mixed. Not griffin fur, either, too dark. Sure as stars isn't human. There was some beast here. Mayhaps something that wandered out from the Gloamwood…" She grabbed Tenno's torch and cast its light back toward the stairs, then crouched down to inspect the base. "There's a bit more here. Speckles. More fur. So they fought, and then they left, unless—" Amella cut herself off and shook her head violently. "C'mon. Let's go back up, look for tracks. Clues. Something." She didn't give Tenno a chance to reply or wait to see if he was following her. She simply left, her shoulders rigid and her grip tight on the hilt of her sword. She kept the torch.

They searched. For hours.

And then they found the footprints.

There were two sets. One set looked like—it wasn't a bear print, exactly, too long and narrow—but it was of a similar size, with the kinds of footpad indents and claw marks he'd expect from a bear. The other set was a pair of boots, dwarfed by Tenno's own feet but too large for a child's. Possibly Corrin's. He hoped they were Corrin's, because if they were, that meant she had walked away from the mead hall. Which meant she was alive. Which meant she'd gone to the Gloamwood, walking the same path as the beast, probably with the beast, which meant... what? Was she a captive? But why? What would this beast—this thing, whatever it was, that was twice Corrin's size—want with her alive?

"I'll be damned," said Amella quietly. "Listen. Tenno. You know those old stories about the Gloamwood? The stuff that lives in it?"

"I—yes?"

"We might be dealing with a troll. I've never seen one, but it would fit... this. If the stories got them right."

Tenno swore.

"Yeah. Corrin might be walking and breathing, but she's in trouble." She paused. Considered him. For a heartbeat, Tenno saw Ragnor echoed in her expression: the way she seemed to measure him, the hard steely *something* etched in the lines on her face. It was striking, since she seemed so unlike Ragnor at first glance—expressive body language, casual mannerisms, a self-interested choice of profession. And yet, Amella carried the same fierce, selfless resolve as she said, "I'm going in after her. You coming?"

He thought of Corrin, hypothermic and weak, asking him to help her companions; Corrin, unyielding, saying that her life was hers to risk, refusing to stay where she would have surely been safe; Corrin, pale as milk and likely terrified to her core, but talking the Bandit King into keeping them all alive; Corrin, and how she'd forgiven Amella for telling the bandits where they were headed. Corrin and her mad idea with the dragon, and then her yelling at it from across the chamber, drawing it away. Corrin and her efforts to learn the sword. Corrin and her fondness for her brothers, which showed in her eyes and her voice even as she complained of their mischief. Corrin and her encyclopedic knowledge of medicinal plants. Corrin who seemed terribly young, and kind, and a bit timid, but who faced obstacle after obstacle and just… kept going.

Who had, over the course of their travels, become a friend.

Tenno's voice shook slightly as he replied, "Of course."

The corner of Amella's mouth quirked. She didn't speak, but she clapped him bracingly on the shoulder, and they set off for the Gloamwood together. Tenno ignored the fatigue that pulled at his eyelids and made his limbs heavy. He would keep going, and he would catch up. And he would rescue Corrin and accompany her through the Gloamwood, as promised.

Amella's torch burned, lonely but bright in her grasp.

The Bandit King crouched on the side of Mount Cauldra, swathed in her dark cloak and sheltered by a rocky overhang, and watched a lone light drift into the edge of the Gloamwood. She listened keenly, pulling her hood back. Nothing. Some crickets, sure. A breeze rustling the scrub brush. The breaths of what few followers she'd recovered; they crouched behind her, awaiting her command. But there were no wing flaps or distant roars, no crackling fire, no footfalls, no beasts snarling. Just the Gloamwood, inky black at this time of night, and the light disappearing into it. She watched it flicker out of view at the tree line and mentally marked that point.

The Bandit King turned back to her much reduced forces. The shadows half-hid them, but she knew them all the same. Verse and Limerick were the closest, side by side at her heels. They were resilient, those two, and interesting to keep around. Witty. Clever. Useful. She had four other followers left, with nothing remarkable about them other than the fact that they had stayed—which was, all things considered, extraordinary. Had she been younger and less powerful; had it not been her goal, her escaped target; or had it not been so grand a prize as a chance at immortality; she would have turned back herself. The golden rule of the streets, after all, was to look out for yourself first. Stab others before they stab you. Save your own neck. She wasn't even bothered that most of her followers had fled, really. She understood the rationality of it.

She could gather them back into her fold or crush them later, anyway.

As for the ones who were here…

"Sleep. I take first watch. We'll chase their tracks at sunrise."

Murmurs of assent rippled from her small troupe. Cloth rustled, and bodies scraped against rocky soil as they lay down. The Bandit King listened with amusement as Limerick sputtered a curse, then something about demonic thorn bushes, and Verse grumbled about idiot brothers.

Silence fell. They weren't asleep yet, though—the breathing wasn't right. Didn't surprise her. Her people were *her people,* after all, conditioned by the roughness of life to stay alert and wary of all the beasts that crept about at night. She drew her sword and let it rest across her knees, sharp and ready, and turned to the Gloamwood. She picked out the spot where the flame had vanished, making sure she'd remember the shape of the tree line…

CHAPTER SIXTEEN

The Dono

They traveled for two more days. Corrin kept hearing rustles in the canopy and thinking she saw things moving in the underbrush. Once, she'd spotted the glint of amber eyes and a moon-white face; but that had just been a ghost owl, and it had hooted peevishly at them and retreated. Other times, though, she couldn't identify the source. She'd catch a glimpse of movement or a glint of strangely colored scales or fur, and she'd tug on Makur's arm frantically and point. Makur would narrow their eyes and look, ears twitching, only to relax a moment later. "Takagur," Makur would rumble, or "Misetruh," or "Vikti," or some other foreign phrase, and ruffle Corrin's hair.

Only once did Makur stiffen, when Corrin spotted an acid green tail and the gleam of... of a stinger? "Petik," snarled Makur. "Make ikik." A massive paw on her shoulder and another at her back chivvied her away.

Since the words varied each time, Corrin gathered they must be names for different creatures, probably whatever things she was pointing out.

"Corrin fear," Makur observed on the second night. They'd tucked themselves into a cluster of roots at the base of a tree. Makur had their arm wrapped over Corrin's shoulders, drawing her in snug against their side. They still smelled like the poultice Corrin had used on them, fresh and minty with a trace of lavender. They also smelled faintly of blood, but Corrin tried not to think about that. The wounds hadn't reopened; she'd checked them herself each evening, with Makur sitting docilely while she parted their chest fur and peered at the faded pink-brown spots on their shoulder bandage. "Hear noise, jump, herth quick. Grek noise be lif end? Be beast hunt Corrin? Make ikik? Many noise no be danger."

"For a troll—I mean krr—maybe. But I'm wyrman."

"Wyrman quick eyes, quick ears, quick fake-claw. Many noise be small thing." Makur booped Corrin's nose—well, more like her entire face—with the pad of their paw. Ever since the near-death-by-snake incident, they'd become downright cuddly. Corrin didn't know how to feel about this. One the one hand, she'd rather be cuddled than eaten. On the other hand, she'd rather not be cuddled by a creature who could probably shred her or crush her on accident. Makur added, "Also. Corrin be wid Makur, be Makur Wyddscatch. Makur big, strong. Protect Corrin. Corrin safe."

"What about the snake? The serdra?"

Makur flattened their ears and growled. Corrin's heart hammered, and she tensed. But they didn't lash out, just shook their head vigorously. "Serdra. No many. Corrin beat serdra. Makur beat next time."

They walked on the next morning, silent and steady, until Makur suddenly threw their arm in front of Corrin. Corrin ran right into it.

"What was that for?" she demanded, indignant.

Makur grinned down at her. "Here be harth," they said. They gestured to the forest around them with an expansive sweep of their paws.

At first glance, it looked the same as the rest of the forest. It had the same tree trunks thicker than she was; the roots that wormed through the ground like veins bulging under skin; the clusters of ferns that came up to Corrin's waist and grew wild, spreading everywhere, bursting with green fronds that tickled when she brushed against them. The only notable things were the stream trickling its way through the trees; the log that lay across it, all scratched up and groove-ridden; and the odd little hills and mounds that swelled out of the ground like acne. Corrin didn't find any houses or halls or anything else that would suggest, *This is home. This isn't just another patch of Gloamwood.*

So she looked again.

And she saw.

The earthy mounds had holes large enough to fit a bear—or a troll. Burrow entrances, she guessed. Ferns and fallen branches obscured them, made them easy to miss if you didn't know to look closely, but they were there. Always adjacent to a tree, which always had a pattern of claw marks scored in its bark. And the grooves in the fallen log's bark weren't purposeless scratches and damage, but intricate whorls and glyphs. It was crafted, made into a bridge on purpose, even though the water was shallow enough to wade across. Maybe it was for children and the elderly, or maybe trolls just didn't like getting their feet wet any more than humans did. (Well. Most humans. Mischievous brothers excepted.) All of these little details, these things that she'd missed at first glance, coalesced into a small village. It was subtle. Kind of beautiful. Kind of hard to stop and appreciate it when Corrin had literal life and death worries weighing on her, though.

Also, it was missing something.

She asked, "Where is everybody?"

Because if this was a troll village, shouldn't there be more trolls? Little ones wrestling on even patches of ground and clambering up the mounds and trees, or doing whatever else troll children did. Adults up and about—perhaps keeping a lookout, or bringing back fresh meat, or carving signs and messages into the trees… or something. No crafting, probably, or commerce, seeing as Makur got by with their fur and claws. But still. Shouldn't at least a few be outside, even if only to lounge around?

Makur huffed. "Late bright time start. Krr sleep, krr go hunt."

"O-okay, so was this a bad time to come?" Corrin asked, even as she thought quite the opposite. She was standing in the troll village and none of the trolls were out to… well, to stare at her and look menacing, in the best-case scenario. Otherwise, they might try to convince Makur that Corrin was food and not a—*a pet? a friend?*—after all, or else simply decide that she was food and force Makur to give her up. Who knew what they'd do, really. Going by the stories she'd heard, she should have been dead when Makur first found her, but it seemed her people's stories had missed several crucial details.

Like the talking.

Human words, specifically.

Also anything about their culture, because it was clear that they had one. At the very least, they had a coming-of-age ceremony… hunt… quest? The Wyddscatch.

What are they actually like? she wondered. *What are my odds?*

A warm paw pressed against her back, startling her out of her thoughts, nudging her forward. Makur's voice rumbled in her ear, resonant and… amused? The spurts of noise sounded kind of like laughter, kind of of—

"Good time. We wake Dono."

—mischievous?

"Maybe we shouldn't bother them?" suggested Corrin. "I mean, um. They might not like us waking them up."

"Won't like," agreed Makur. They sounded gleeful. "Yus. Anger Dono. Fun. Det, Dono will like. Won't, then will. Surprise, I bring good Wyddscatch."

This did not sound reassuring to Corrin in the slightest. This sounded like trouble. She dug in her heels, but unfortunately, her resistance was futile. Makur pushed her along effortlessly. They crossed the stream, ignoring the bridge entirely, so water flooded Corrin's boots (*blech*), and entered a burrow that was indistinguishable from the others, except for the swirling marks on the adjacent tree trunk. The marks' pattern seemed unusually complex.

It was dark in the burrow. The air tasted like soil and humidity, and she felt more than saw her way along the tunnel, her fingers skimming the damp earthy walls. She glanced back. Makur was a dark, fuzzy shape behind her, blotting out the entryway, indistinct except for their orange eyes and glowing pupils. They grumbled at her hesitation and prodded the small of her back, and *ow,* sharp claws, did they have any idea how much those things hurt?

The tunnel opened into a chamber faster than Corrin would have liked (because now she'd have to face the creature that lived inside, and she could've lived happily without ever doing that, thank you very much). The walls fell away from her touch. Her boots sank into a layer of leaves and fronds instead of trodding on firm ground. Everything was shadows and vague hints of shapes—but then Makur came in after her and shuffled to the side, unblocking the tunnel. Faint light seeped in, letting her see outlines and traces of color.

The chamber had a scant few personal belongings. A large stick leaned against the wall, along with a slab of rock. A heap of small objects occupied a far corner, jumbled and too shadowed for Corrin to see in detail. A massive basin was shoved in another corner. Or at least, she thought it was a basin. It was vaguely basin-shaped. Other than that, though, all the chamber had was roots dangling from the ceiling and a thick carpet of leaves—and a lump of fur in the back.

That must be... Dono? The Dono?

The furry bundle had a smattering of silvery hairs mixed in with the dark ones. Its—their—side rose and fell with their breathing. They shifted and snuffled, which might have been cute coming from something smaller and less dangerous but in this context just made Corrin cross her fingers and hope they wouldn't wake up cross. Or hungry.

"*DONO!*" Makur roared. Right by Corrin's ear.

Oh for the love of the starlands, WHY.

The Dono jerked awake and jumped to their feet, baring their teeth —teeth that had a yellowish cast and were duller at the point than Makur's, smoothed and blunted by time. This troll was smaller than Makur, too, though still awfully large compared to Corrin. Their fur was shaggier and their shoulders narrower, hunched, reminiscent of some of the Oddment elders who suffered from bone degeneration. (*Best mitigated with tonics of milk and corifi plant.*) One of their ears had a tear in the membrane. (*Would've needed stitches to hold it together and heal whole.*) All in all, this troll—Dono?—seemed aged and painfully ragged.

Except for their eyes. Their eyes were vivid gold and piercing, focused. On Corrin.

"Good wake start, I back," rumbled Makur. "Bring lif wyrman Wyddscatch. Wyrman is krr bidum. Good, yus?" They puffed out their chest proudly.

The elder troll narrowed their eyes. They reached for their stick, ominously slow and deliberate.

Corrin drew back, but the Dono's wasn't looking at her anymore. They glared at Makur, who kept grinning even as the Dono hefted their stick. Corrin edged further away. Makur's grin faltered, finally, as the Dono shifted their grip and—

—poked Makur lightly in the chest. "Bibbinhead," they grumbled. Their voice rasped and creaked. "Bibbinhead bairn be fool. Big krr—" and here Corrin stopped understanding. The words came too fast and thick, too many of them foreign. She got the sense that the Dono was fussing over Makur, though, from the way they sniffed Makur's bandage and chest and tapped them repeatedly, muttering. They might have said "bibbinhead" a few more times. They certainly did when Makur growled and tried to swat them away. Corrin had the sneaking suspicion "bibbinhead" was the troll version of calling someone a fool.

Corrin swallowed and edged further back, then began to sidle around them. Maybe she could get to the exit. It would be nice to slip outside where it wasn't so dark, at least.

"Wyrman," said the Dono sharply. They pointed to her without turning around. "Stay."

Corrin froze.

The Dono traced Makur's shoulder bandage with one paw, while the other grasped their stick loosely. And at last they turned to her. "You. Wyrman." They spoke slowly, deliberately, as if they wanted to make sure she understood them. "Do this?" They tapped the bandage. Maybe she was imagining it, but Corrin felt like she heard something accusatory in their tone, like they thought she'd done something wrong.

"I—I just bandaged it, to protect the—"

"Do. This?"

Corrin gulped. "N-no. Serdra hurt. I fix."

"Hrr." And suddenly the Dono was in her face, scrutinizing her. They'd moved startlingly fast for an elder.

Corrin took a shaky breath. Her hand twitched, itching to grab her dagger hilt, but she stilled it and told herself firmly, *That's not going to help me here.*

She forced herself to stay still as the Dono peered at her, sniffed her face, lifted her arm, and poked lightly at her ribcage. They used the knuckle of their paw, and it was much softer and lighter than Makur's prodding claw from earlier. But she could feel strength behind it. If the Dono wanted, they could hurt her as easily as Makur could. Corrin's heart thudded against her chest as she thought, *Please don't think I'm food. Please don't think I'm a threat.* The Dono's untorn ear twitched. They were probably close enough to hear her heart beat.

At last, the Dono drew back, their face crinkled in displeasure. "Bones," they grumbled. "All bones."

Great, thought Corrin, *maybe that means they think I'm not worth eating.*

"Healer wyrman, yus?"

Makur, to Corrin's surprise, answered for her. "Yus. Good healer." They added helpfully, "Namae Corrin."

The Dono huffed. "Bibbinhead. Corrin. Good healer no eat?"

Huh?

"No bibbinhead," grumbled Makur. "Good Wyddscatch. Wyddscatch hunt Wyddscatch."

The Dono's ears perked up. "Wyddscatch hunt Wyddscatch? No sense making." Despite their words, they sounded excited. Their eyes grew round as gold coins, and their gaze seemed sharper, more probing. "Show," demanded the Dono.

...What?

"Serdra," said Makur. "Corrin have?"

Corrin blinked. Right. She had a massive decapitated serpent's head wrapped twice over in fern fronds and buried in her pack. It was full of sharp teeth and stuck in rigor mortis, and probably decaying and putrid, and she would rather handle it as little as possible. "I have," she confirmed.

The Dono and Makur watched her expectantly.

With a grimace, Corrin slipped off her pack and withdrew the snake's head. As expected, it smelled, a cloying mix of flowers and spoiled meat. She gingerly unwrapped it, exposing dulled scales. She willed herself to not identify the discoloration of the mouth, the exposed muscle and bone where her knife had cut through sinew, the —*nope, too late, nevermind*. Corrin's stomach churned. She hastily looked away and up, at the Dono.

Wide golden eyes blinked back at her.

She held the snake's head out, practically shoved it into the Dono's face, thinking, *Please,* ***please*** *take this thing off my hands.* Makur was mad, insisting she hold onto this. Or maybe this was a troll thing, and they just regularly lugged trophy heads back, and they were all mad. Either way, it was sickness waiting to happen.

The Dono grabbed it and held it up to eye level, nose crinkling.

"Makur made me keep it. It's… It's old, so it'll probably be riddled with disease. Um. Unclean. Make ikik. You should probably just burn or bury it."

The Dono lobbed the snake's head at Makur, who caught it deftly. "Bury," agreed the Dono. "Bury, feed Dono tree. Is good wyrman Wyddscatch. Small wyrman, big serdra." They bared a hint of teeth and turned to Corrin. "How hunt?" they asked. They grabbed Corrin's hand, engulfing it in their paw. Their grip was firm but cushioned by fur, their claw tips mercifully kept off her skin. They shook her hand emphatically. "This. This be no fur, no claw, no strong. Wyrman usen trick?"

"I—I think Makur did most of the work."

"Hrr. Makur lie?"

"N-no, I cut its head while it was distracted." Some explanation seemed to be expected, so she added, "I have a dagger."

The Dono blinked.

"Knife," Corrin tried. "Um. Fake claw. Metal. Here." She pulled out her dagger, resting it flat on her palm so the Dono could see. The Dono took it. Corrin wished they hadn't; it was the one tool she had to defend herself, now. She told herself that it didn't matter, she hadn't planned to use her dagger anyway, but handing it over still felt like snuffing out the last candle in a dark room, or shedding her leather vest and her boots and walking barefoot on treacherous ground. And the longer the Dono held the dagger—laying it flat; prodding the edge and hissing softly; obscuring the hilt in their grip—the harder it was to resist asking—

"Can I please have it back?"

The Dono considered her. Then, wordlessly, they offered her the dagger.

Corrin took it and put it back in its sheath. "Thank you."

"Wyrman trick." The Dono watched her intently. "Stories say be Punula trick."

"What's Punula?"

The Dono *hrrrr'd*. "Good ask. Punula, wyrman no grekka *Punula*?" What followed was a slew of words that Corrin couldn't understand, which was a shame, because the Dono sounded awfully earnest and eager to share. Their voice rumbled low and surprisingly soft, and they gestured with their paws. Several of the motions looked like slicing; others mimed pulling something open. The unfamiliar words were interspersed with "lif" and "krrkin" and "sleep." Finally, the words stopped. The Dono made a face like they were thinking hard about something.

Corrin hesitated. Should she say something? Nod politely?

"Har grekka," said the Dono suddenly. "Corrin no grekka, yus?"

"Yus. I'm sorry."

The Dono reached for her head. Corrin flinched back, and they froze. "Corrin be no harm," they said. "Corrin be wyrman, det, be good. I grok, Corrin be krrkin. I grok, be truth." They reached for her again, slower this time, and Corrin held still, let them rest a paw atop her head. The touch was gentle, gentler even than Makur's head ruffles, and she relaxed, just a little. *Okay. This is alright. They like me, I think.* The Dono rumbled at her, a wordless noise that put her in mind of Tiptoes pressing against her ankles, or Dragon curled up near her knee. It was a comforting sound. "Yus," the Dono assured her, "Corrin be no harm."

Makur huffed. "So. Good Wyddscatch? I no be bairn, yus?"

"Yus," the Dono grumbled. They waved their stick vaguely. "No be bairn."

Makur perked up. "Krrkin see."

The Dono huffed. "Fikah. Yus. Krrkin see. Det, Makur sleep. Corrin sleep." They nudged Corrin toward Makur, and then the both of them toward the exit. They said something about Makur and a den, and more about krrkin, and some other trolltongue that Corrin didn't grasp; and then they were all out of the tunnel, surrounded by vibrant greens and the light that filtered through the canopy. Corrin blinked and looked around.

The troll village wasn't deserted anymore. A pair of troll children growled and splashed each other by the stream. An adult stretched out in a sunny patch and watched them. There was a flicker of motion up high—another troll, clambering up a tree—and she caught glimpses of fur and movement in the underbrush. As the Dono led her and Makur through the village, troll heads popped up to watch them. Their eyes were various shades of orange, some closer to golden like the Dono's and others darker, closer to red. Their fur was mostly tortoiseshell, but some were dappled with lighter browns while others were black as crow's feathers. The troll children scarcely came up to Corrin's waist, but the adults all towered over her. Most of them dwarfed the Dono. Some were even larger than Makur. They all stared. Some bared their teeth and drew their ears back. Others merely looked curious.

The Dono addressed each of them in turn: *Wyrman be Makur Wyddscatch. Namae Corrin, krrkin, no harm.* Some of them narrowed their eyes at Makur and grumbled. Others simply looked for a heartbeat longer, then nodded and returned to whatever they were doing. One of the troll children rushed toward her and leapt. Corrin jumped aside, startled, and the child went tumbling with an "uff."

The Dono rapped the child lightly with their staff and growled.

"*RANA,*" roared the troll Corrin had noticed earlier. She assumed they were the parent. "No hunt… Wyrman? Be Wyrman, yus?"

"Wyrman," Dono confirmed. "Makur Wyddscatch. Namae Corrin, no eat."

"Cor-rin." The adult troll eyed her curiously, while their child rubbed their head and bared their teeth behind them. "Hingheket, Corrin. Be bairn? Small wyrman."

"I'm not that small," she protested, though at the moment, she did, in fact, feel that small. "My village would say I'm an adult. I'm old enough to take care of myself, and I've been studying healing for a while."

The troll's expression didn't change, which probably meant they weren't convinced. Or hadn't understood.

Which was fine. Useful, even. If they thought she was young and innocent, they might be more inclined to be gentle with her. Though there was the risk they'd think she should stay like Makur had suggested instead of continuing on her quest, and that wouldn't do at all…

The Dono rumbled something to the troll, who bowed their head, and shepherded Corrin onward.

They stopped in front of a burrow near the edge of the village. The tree next to it had a freshly carved pattern: a single whorl with three lines struck through it and a notch beneath it. The ground looked newly dug and smelled fresh. Makur stopped and stared at it with an expression that Corrin couldn't read.

The Dono clapped Makur on the shoulder, and said, "Good Wyddscatch. Makur strong." They bared their teeth in a grin. Makur bared their teeth back, but Corrin could swear that the response was muted, hesitant. The Dono dropped the grin and continued, their voice low and rumbling with solemnity. "Det, more porrent, be wis. Most krr see wyrman, grek kill. Dono also, may be see wyrman, grek catch kill." The Dono paused. "Makur see wyrman, grek inreska, grek, wyrman grekka maybe, maybe keep lif, may be krrkin." Makur shifted uncomfortably, while Corrin mentally struggled to translate. The trolltongue resolved to something like, *Most trolls kill humans but Makur see human and think—something?—and think maybe it understands, maybe it can be a troll.* Corrin frowned. *Be a troll? No, that can't be right…*

Also, I'm pretty sure that's not what Makur was thinking when they pounced on me.

Makur's ears drooped. "Makur see wyrman, Makur grek inreska Wyddscatch, grek keep lif purf Makur strong. No grekka krrkin."

"Cheng grekka also wis. Dono be pride." The Dono clapped their shoulder again and nudged Makur toward the burrow entrance. "New harth, new lif. We feast nurtime."

"Danku."

The Dono turned to Corrin. "Corrin be wis also. Kind. Be Makur Wyddscatch, det, try grekka, rahrg serdra, heal Makur. Stay wid Makur. Sleep good, feast wid krrkin." The Dono touched Corrin's head affectionately, and she, too, was nudged toward the burrow. The Dono turned and shuffled away, their back rounded and their weight heavy on their staff. Corrin watched them leave; then, when Makur called her name from inside the burrow, she crept through the tunnel.

It was a simpler burrow than the Dono's, with no personal

belongings that she could see, but whoever had built it had carpeted it with fresh leaves. Makur curled into a massive, fuzzy ball on one side of the den, leaving Corrin ample space to stretch out on the other side. She shed her pack and nestled it in the leaves. She dearly hoped the floor wasn't infested with giant spiders or venomous beetles. The Gloamwood seemed like the sort of place for those sorts of creatures. Still, if the trolls had survived this long, sleeping in places like this... And it was so comfortable, even more cushiony than her bed back in Oddment.

She was so tired. She hadn't noticed the fatigue before, but she felt it now, a heaviness deep in her bones and in her head and eyes. She must have been running on fumes and worry. She felt a chill, too, mostly in her fingers and toes, and she burrowed her limbs into the leaves. Corrin breathed in the smell of earth and sank into a dreamless sleep.

CHAPTER SEVENTEEN

The Feast

Poke. "Corrin wake." *Poke.* "Feast."

Corrin stirred and rubbed the sleep out of her eyes. Her head still felt heavy. She could scarcely see anything; it was nearly pitch dark. Makur hovered over her, their orange eyes wide and luminous and their paw readied to prod her. Her shoulder and back felt tender and tingly, like they'd been jabbed several times but not like any skin had broken. Makur must have been poking her for a while. She yawned and stretched out. Her joints popped, and leaves rustled around her. It had been a good rest, and long, she suspected, but she felt like she needed more. "G'evening," she mumbled, and rolled over.

Makur put their paw on her side and shook her. "Feast. Food. UP."

"Alright, alright, I'm up."

Makur growled. "No be up. Be down."

"One second." Corrin forced herself up to a sitting position, and then onto her feet. She latched onto Makur's outstretched paw, steadying herself, and let loose a jaw-cracking yawn.

Makur asked, "Why tire?"

"I d-don't know. It's been a long journey, I think."

"Hrr. Eat."

"Mhm... okay..."

She followed Makur out of the den. Her first impression was more darkness and shadows. Then she turned and saw a searing brightness: a writhing mass of flames that burned by the stream bank. Her heart jumped—but the fire was narrow, contained in a ring, and shadowy shapes paced around it. There were dozens of them, most larger than her, and it took her a few seconds and glimpses of bright, gleaming eyes to realize they were all trolls. The air smelled like wood smoke and charred meat, and through the bleary fog in her mind, she thought, *Oh. I didn't realize they cooked. Would've been awful nice when Makur caught those fish…*

Something tall and thin waved through the air, and the shapes settled down. Corrin blinked. The tall, thin thing was the Dono's staff, and holding it was the Dono, their silvery fur backlit by the fire and their teeth bared in a grin.

"Makur," boomed the Dono. They waved their stick again.

Makur ambled over to the Dono. Corrin trailed after them, and somehow, she found herself seated between the two trolls, a roasted chunk of… some creature… in her hands and a bracing paw against the small of her back. She nibbled on the roasted thing. It wasn't too bad. It certainly didn't taste poisonous, although, if she wracked her memory, she could list three… no, five toxic things that had no alarming flavor or odor… *Never mind that,* she told herself firmly, *I can't afford to starve, and the trolls are eating this stuff, look.* And indeed they were. Some held portions twice the size of Corrin's head.

Rumbles and growls floated around the bonfire. If Corrin tried, she thought she could distinguish Makur's and the Dono's voices from the others, but she didn't feel motivated to focus for long. She watched the flames flicker within their confines of stone and mud, and she let the noise wash over her, like lake water closing over her ears. She felt, distantly, the paw against her back stiffen and press more firmly against her. *Whoops,* she thought. *Almost tipped over, didn't I? By Death's scythe, why am I so tired?*

"*HARAHKET*."

Corrin started. The Dono's roar had been head-achingly loud.

The other trolls fell quiet. The Dono spoke again, still loud, but less so than before. Corrin tried to focus, now, to shake her drowsiness off and piece together the contents of their speech, and she thought she got the gist of it. Makur be adult troll. Travel far outside Gloamwood, hunt Wyddscatch, find human, capture human. Something something strength and combat skill and whatever else trolls think are important. Human and Makur rahrg giant snake, be allies, be blah de blah something something, win. Human named Corrin. Corrin sitting here with us. No eat Corrin. Corrin be trollkind—no, wait, ally of trollkind? *I'm a friend and not food. Hooray.*

Maybe it was her imagination, but she thought some of the trolls looked dubious. That was fair, she supposed. She felt dubious about them as well.

The Dono finished with their speech, and the chatter erupted again. Corrin watched as troll after troll ambled over, each one clapping Makur on the shoulder or cuffing them lightly on the head. Makur swatted each of them back and puffed their chest out, rumbling phrases like, "Yus, good Wyddscatch" or "Be wykrr now, yus."

There was one congratulator, though, that made Makur's ears flatten. This one had nearly the exact same shade of fur and eyes, but they loomed over Makur, half a head taller. They also grinned wider and cuffed Makur's head harder than the others had. Makur growled back and swiped at their face. They caught Makur's paw and rumbled something in trolltongue that she didn't quite catch. She did notice the tone, though. And she didn't have to be a master of trolltongue to understand it.

It was hostile.

The sleepy fog in Corrin's head cleared away. The hairs on the back of her neck prickled. She watched the fur rise along Makur's shoulders and spine. Makur returned the hard grip and brought their snarling face close to the giant stranger's. She felt a wall of furry muscle behind her and realized she'd instinctively drawn back, into the Dono's side. She looked up and over her shoulder, but the Dono didn't notice. They were watching Makur and the other troll, a hint of their yellowed teeth showing and their nose wrinkled in irritation. "Gut water krrkin," they grumbled, and heaved themselves to their feet. "Alltime rahrg."

Gut water... what?

And then it clicked. Gut water. The closest phrase she could think of was "water of the womb," and in Corrin's years of medical study, she'd seen how warranted the phrase was. Amniotic fluids gushed out of the womb at birth. To someone who didn't know the difference between womb and gut, or didn't care, it did look an awful lot like water spilling out of someone's gut... Well, water and a litany of other things that she'd learned not to be squeamish about. (Bathilda had hammered the importance of that into her, had lectured at length about the risks involved in having a child, and the pain. How vital it was to have a healer be there for them and be a comfort, a sense of security and safety as much as a source of expertise.)

Gut water kin. Of the same womb. That means they're siblings.

Makur's sibling drew their head back and squared the shoulders. "Challenge Makur," they said. They prodded Makur's chest. "*PURF RAHRG.*"

"*FIKAH,*" Makur spat.

A few of the surrounding trolls erupted into roars and cheers. And boos? Despite all their fur and foreign words, they sounded an awful lot like the rowdy bunches back in Oddment when they got too drunk at a festival. Shouting and yammering over each other and whooping, usually over something ridiculous like Elder Yelt attempting to dance, or two folks who'd gotten into some nutty competition of strength, or agility, or daring, or gastronomical fortitude in the face of unending pie. The trolls parted for the two siblings, letting them access an open spot farther from the flames, and closed behind them again, forming an enclosure.

"Raar," grumbled the Dono. They dragged a paw over their face. "Be *BIBBINHEADS*."

Corrin opened her mouth to ask what was going on, but the Dono cut her off with a grouchy, "Move, Corrin, we watchet."

"Watchet what?"

"Purfararg. Be Wyddscatch purfararg, purf Makur new be wykrr."

"I'm sorry, I don't understand. I mean, I no... grekka?"

"No need grekka. Makur Rakar be bibbinheads." The Dono huffed through their nose and chivvied her along, bringing her to the forefront of the spectators. Makur and their sibling—*Rakar?*—stood in the middle of the makeshift enclosure, in a spot with relatively even ground and only a few snaking roots. The two siblings faced each other. Rakar wore a grin, sharp-toothed and broad, like a festival mask. They rolled their shoulders, slow and deliberate. Makur bared their teeth, but not in a smile, and their fur bristled. The Dono leaned down and rumbled close to Corrin's ear, "Rakar be more big, be elder, tintur Makur much. Rakar want grok, Makur be small. Det, Makur be wykrr now, show strength, want show Rakar tintur no more, I grek." The Dono shook their head once more and grumbled, "Rahrg, alltime rahrg. Bibbinheads."

"Wha—oh." Corrin thought she understood the gist of it now. This kind of fight was part of their Wyddscatch traditions. And Rakar had a habit of antagonizing Makur because... because they were bigger? Because they were a bully? Corrin bit her lip. She hoped they wouldn't take this too far. The Dono didn't seem concerned, but Corrin had seen a few antagonistic sibling relationships back in Oddment. Not hers so much. Her siblings were mischievous, but also sweethearts and helpers. (She desperately hoped that they were still well, that she'd make it back in time to see them grow up strong and healthy.) But others, well... One sibling feud had resulted in a broken arm. And if a human family feud could end in broken arms, how did troll feuds end?

Aloud, she said, "I understand. Um, I grekka. Shouldn't we stop them?" She pointed to Rakar and Makur. "Stop, no rahrg, no be hurt?"

The Dono shook their head. "Is okay. This be Wyddscatch krrlifdo. Is krr right to purfararg, test strength, grek, Makur be strong, good rahrg, or Makur need more strength. Rakar use krrlifdo tintur Makur. Det, no danger, no end lif."

"Okay. If you're sure."

"Yus."

And then the Dono said, "*PURFARARG*."

The two siblings threw themselves at each other, colliding in a snarling mass of fur and claws. They rolled and flipped over each other, ears laid back. Makur landed on top, paws planted on Rakar's shoulders and eyes gleaming—but Rakar threw them off, and Makur hurtled into the stream with a splash. Makur sprang upright, sopping wet and spitting what was probably sailor's language in trolltongue, but Rakar was on them in an instant, tossing them back into the water.

Corrin winced. That looked cold. And painful. And overall dreadful and unpleasant, and—and then Rakar shoved Makur's head underwater and held it there. Makur thrashed, but Rakur didn't budge. They kept not budging. They kept holding Makur's head underwater as second after second slid by…

They're going to drown, she thought.

Before Corrin realized what she was doing, her legs moved. Her boots thudded across the forest floor, and her hand wrapped around the hilt of her dagger. She felt more than heard the "*STOP*" that tore from her throat. Rakar's head jerked up, eyes narrowing. They opened their mouth, to snarl something back or perhaps to bite the second she came close—

"*NO MORE,*" roared the Dono.

Rakar released Makur's head, and Makur came up spluttering.

Corrin teetered to a stop. Water sloshed over the lips of her boots and soaked her socks, sending a shock of cold running through her. She'd reached the edge of the stream. The bottom was muddy and sucked at her foot when she stepped back. Heart hammering, she watched Makur cough up a mouthful of water and take heaving breaths.

Rakar thumped the small of Makur's back and bared their teeth in a grin. "I win. Makur no bairn, may be. Det, Rakur more strong." They turned to Corrin, still grinning, and she froze under their stare. The frantic impulse to act had deserted her, leaving only trepidation and the shaky aftermath of her surging heart. Rakar cocked their head and asked, "Makur Wyddscatch want purfararg Rakar? Wyddscatch also hunt Wyddscatch, yus?"

"No purfararg Corrin," growled the Dono. "Corrin is krrkin bidum, det, wyrman no krr. Hunt Wyddscatch, det, no big, no wykrr."

Rakar tilted their head, then shrugged. "I no grekka. Grekka Dono grok und I obey, det, no grekka Corrin. Is lif, no hoblek. Makur hunt Corrin truth? Wyrman be Wyddscatch?" Rakar shoved Makur's shoulder, and they stumbled, their ears flat. "Makur hunt wyrman or wyrman hunt Makur?" A sudden, deep chortle rose from Rakar's throat. "Makur need hunt more Wyddscatch, may be. May be still bairn."

Makur scowled. "I no bairn. Be wykrr."

"Wyddscatch truth," said the Dono firmly. "Rakar go hunt more feast snargak. Makur go dry."

Rakar snorted, but they obligingly turned and ambled off into the trees. They melted into the shadows in an instant. Makur stared after them for a moment, then shook their head, scattering water droplets, and trudged toward the bonfire. None of the other trolls intercepted Makur, though a few reached out to pat their head or shoulder as they passed, and one of them—the parent Corrin had met earlier, she realized—muttered something that might have been a reassurance.

The flames still burned strong, sparking and crackling. Makur sat inches away from the fire, their back to the stream, and wrapped their arms around their knees. Gradually, the other trolls dispersed, breaking off into clusters of twos and threes and picking spots near the flames or in the trees. A few of them grabbed portions of meat from a pile on Makur's right. They edged around Makur without speaking and departed quickly.

The meat pile was almost up to Makur's head. Suspiciously large, considering that the Dono had sent Rakar to gather more. Corrin had the feeling that had just been a tactful way to get Makur's sibling away from the festival.

The Dono *hrr'd* and shook their head. "Bibbinheads," they muttered, and leaned on their staff. "I lif much time, is much watchet bibbinheads."

Corrin cleared her throat. "Um. Dono?"

The Dono peered down at her. "Grok."

"It looked like Rakar was going to drown Makur." When the Dono tilted their head quizzically, Corrin tried again. "I grek, Rakar end Makur lif. Not okay."

"Hrr. Corrin worry. Corrin be big softiclaw, be kind. Det, krrkin strong, ken hold breath for long time. Und Rakar obey Dono grok. I stop purfararg, yus?"

Corrin bit her lip.

"Go. Eat snargak, grok Makur. Be kind." The Dono nudged Corrin gently toward the bonfire.

Corrin approached hesitantly, hyperconscious of the twigs cracking beneath her boots and the rustle of her shifting clothes, but Makur didn't stir when she drew close to them. They didn't protest when she sat next to them either, and when she reached out and lightly touched their injured shoulder, they scarcely glanced at her before turning back to the fire. Corrin surreptitiously inspected the bandage, relying on proximity and the blazing firelight to see and her fingertips to feel. The fabric had been drenched and stained pink all through. She would have offered to change it, if only she'd had bandages to spare. But at least it didn't seem to be getting pinker, which meant it probably hadn't reopened. *Okay,* she thought, *looks like the bites didn't get agitated. That's good.*

She drew her hand away and wrapped her arms around her knees, copying Makur. "That was a harsh, uh. Purfararg."

Makur's ear twitched.

"I would've been terrified. I... be scared of purfararg."

Makur shook their head. "Wyddscatch krrlifdo, purfararg no end lif."

"I don't like it."

"No need like. Corrin no be krrkin." Makur paused, then amended, "Corrin be bidum, be krrkin by Dono grok, det, no be *krr* krrkin."

"Alright then." Her words stalled, and the crackling of burning wood filled the silence between them. Eventually, she asked. "Are you okay?"

Makur snorted. "Purfararg no rahrg for lif. I okay."

"I'm glad." Makur stared at her uncomprehendingly, so Corrin amended, "I happy Makur okay. I want Makur be okay."

Makur let out a small huff. "Corrin soft."

"Yup. Soft and small and fussy like a mother hen, I am."

Makur's face wrinkled. "Mother? Hen?"

"Mother. Mama, mum, ma, mom, parent?" Makur continued to look confused, so she pieced together an explanation that might translate. "I be in my mother's gut water, and then when I be bairn, my mother gives me food. I be like mum, mother, a little, in bone and face."

Makur's expression cleared. "I grekka Corrin grok."

Corrin smiled faintly. "And a hen is, uh. Fat bird. Big bird that lay eggs, good food. Hen bairn be chicks. Mother hen fusses over chicks. That means they worry."

"Aaaah." Makur poked Corrin lightly in the chest. "Corrin worry much. Det, no bird, be wyrman."

"Yup. It's just an idiom. A figure of speech," she clarified, "so it sounds like one thing but doesn't mean it literally. The words, the... the grok? They mean something else together that's not what they mean by themselves." Makur tilted their head and wrinkled their nose. Corrin didn't know how to translate this one. How was she supposed to talk about the nuances of language when a language barrier was the problem in the first place? So instead she shrugged and said, "Yus. I'm wyrman and I worry much. About a lot of things."

Makur huffed. "Truth."

Corrin took a deep breath, in and out, and watched the embers glowing near her toes. She shifted her feet back.

"Corrin was plan rahrg Rakar for Makur. Yus?"

She blinked. "I... yus? I grek? I kind of panicked."

Makur showed a hint of teeth, and they burbled from deep in their chest. "No be Corrin purfararg. Det, danku. Corrin fistiruf, good krrkin." They reached out and patted Corrin atop her head. She huffed and ducked, and Makur nudged her shoulder, burbling again. "No be krr, be wyrman wid small fake-claw. Det, be good krrkin. Danku." They snagged a chunk of roasted meat off the pile and proffered it. "Hanger? Need food? Eat. Is good."

In truth, Corrin didn't feel much like eating more, but Makur was looking at her expectantly, so she accepted the morsel with a murmured thanks. She nibbled on it. Now that things were calmer, with Makur seeming okay and Rakar presumably off wrestling snakes or fishing or doing whatever else the troll village typically did for food, the hum of fear and worry that had sharpened her senses ebbed away, leaving her feeling tired again. Her limbs felt leaden, her head heavy. She yawned. "M'going to... need to sleep... Need to be well rested so I can find the Tree of Life. I've got to... g-got to get the medicine..." She listed to one side and felt a tickling against her cheek, and then the comfort of a solid, furry mass supporting her side. It was soft and very warm.

A discontented growl rumbled overhead. "Corrin still want softseed? Be danger, grekka? Krrkin harth be safe. Dono grok Corrin krrkin."

"I grekka." She couldn't seem to keep her eyes open. "But my… my people… wyrmankin… they're sick. My da's sick. My siblings, m-my gut water kin." Urgency sparked anew in her heart, and she struggled against the fatigue to put that feeling into words. "Your gut water kin is a jerk. Bad. A, um. Bibbinhead. But my gut water kin are good. My da's good. My people are good." She paused as a thought bubbled sluggishly to the surface of her mind. *No, that's not quite right, it's not so simple.* "Except some of them not always, like the guards who wouldn't come with me or that little bugger who picks on Petuni and my brothers. I want to—to feed him bitter medicine sometimes. But they're okay. Mostly good."

She took a slow, deep breath. The air smelled smoky and woody, and her face was warm, so warm. She'd been explaining something important… that her people were good… that her people… *oh right.* "They need help. Need me. I've got to, g-got to heal them. Got to bring them the medicine, from the tree b'cause nothing… nothing else was working."

It was quiet. Ish. There were sounds, rustles and voices and crackles, but they all kind of blurred together in her ears and sounded far away. She couldn't be bothered to pick them out. She said firmly, "Need the Tree. Need the Tree of Life."

Makur said nothing.

Corrin must have gotten up at some point, must have been escorted to bed (or to the den, rather), because somehow she ended up with leaves against her cheek and no more firelight glowing through her eyelids. It was dark and peaceful, and the air was soothingly cool and still, and so she sank into the leaves… into a sea of images and sounds and vague impressions that slipped away from her nearly as soon as they appeared, like minnows slipping through her fingers…

And then a horn blared, and she awoke with a start.

CHAPTER EIGHTEEN

Interlude: The Riddle Beast

Amella and Tenno took turns keeping watch beneath the shelter of a crooked old tree, and they got moving as soon as sunlight started filtering through the canopy again. Amella took the front, Tenno following closely with Junior riding on his shoulder. He was the guardsman, true, and she could tell his training had been good from the way he read the moss and handled his weapon. But he had deferred to her, confessing that tracking wasn't his strong suit and that Junior couldn't search effectively in a forest this thick and dark.

So even though the tracks here were easy to lose in the undergrowth and the beasts were all sorts of unknowns that sent shivers of apprehension up her spine, Amella squared her shoulders and acted like she knew what she was doing. She tried to believe that she did, in fact, know what she was doing. *You've tracked many a beast in your lifetime, Amella,* she told herself firmly. *No reason to be lily-livered now. Your junior's counting on you.*

Unfortunately, the tracks had gotten muddled on a patch of ground by a stream, trampled over by hundreds of tiny pawprints. The set she'd chosen to follow had seemed about the right size, but now, something was nagging at her...

"If you don't mind me asking, where'd you learn to track?" asked Tenno. "You're awfully good at this."

"We haven't found them, so don't start the hero worship yet, eh?" Amella grinned. "But if you must know, my ma taught me these things when I was but a sprout. My parents were professional questers before they turned to merchantry. They'd settled down a bit when I was born." The thought of her parents came with the phantom ache of grief, but it also brought happy memories, good times full of adventure (and some misadventures) and raucous laughter. She held the memories close. They kept her warm in dark places. "Only a bit, though. Not many people with kids will brave the northern deserts to reach the resource-rich southern lands, but they did."

"You followed in their footsteps?"

"Aye. I quested for a bit too, then switched over to merchantry. It's lucrative, gives me creature comforts, and I get to pick what treasures I hunt instead of taking on commissions or working by someone else's orders. Depending on how a merchant operates, it can be a fine line between my profession and questing." Amella knelt to inspect a footprint in a soft patch of peat, rendered in fine detail, and the good humor brought on by her reminiscing vanished. Now that she looked closer, something didn't seem right about their shape. She could swear it was wider and shorter than it should be. She frowned. "Hey, do me a favor and take a look at this. Does something about it seem off to you?"

Tenno obediently crouched beside her. "It looks like a big beast track to me. What am I looking for?"

"Something about the shape's… Hm. Listen. Forget about trolls for a minute. Imagine this is a track from your own homelands, from a beast you've seen and would recognize. What does it look like to you?"

Tenno frowned and tilted his head one way, then the other. "It looks like a mountain cat's," he decided at last.

"Aye. Shorter, and with four toes. I thought maybe the fifth was just smudged or wiped out before, they don't always leave the clearest imprints, but…"

"Shoot. You think we're following the wrong set?"

"Yeah." Amella's hand curled into a fist. "Dammit. Sorry about this, but I think we'll have to—"

A branch snapped up ahead, and Amella froze. The forest around them was full of mist and boggy ground, thick with drooping strands of leaves and strong-smelling flowers. Twice in the past five hours, Amella had menaced off a cluster of bog sprites, grey humanoid creatures with spindly sharp fingers and glowing spots on their chests that looked deceptively like splotches of sunlight. But that snapping branch couldn't have been a bog sprite. Little ne'er-do-wells scarcely came up past her boot. Something heavier had to have made that sound…

A hulking figure stepped out of the underbrush.

Junior twittered nervously.

"Oh dear," said Tenno softly.

Oh dear, in Amella's estimation, was a woefully inadequate reaction to the beast in front of them. It was a massive cat-like creature, roughly the length of a mountain lion and probably twice as heavy. Its fur was black and yellow striped, like a wasp, and a thick ruff protected its neck. Its head was proportionally huge, broad as the beast's own shoulders and drooping low. Its ears were large and keen, held stiff, like any cat who had spotted a target. And its eyes, oh, its eyes were unsettling, a deep blood-red with pupils that reflected a ghostly green. It glared balefully at them. Quills rose and bristled along its back and tail. The beast bared its teeth. Amella gripped her sword tightly, the back of her neck prickling with unease. The teeth should have been all fang, but the ones in front were flat and square, like a person's. It wasn't right, seeing human-like teeth in a beast's mouth. It didn't fit.

"Right," whispered Amella to Tenno, "you flank right and I'll flank left, no sudden moves—"

"I can hear you, you know," said the beast.

Amella nearly jumped out of her skin.

Junior fell silent.

By Death's scythe, what **is** *this thing?*

"Would you look at that." Its voice was deadpan. "You ridiculous creatures, you're always shocked when I start talking to you. *Flabbergasted.* As if you think only humans can speak in human tongues. But then, I don't suppose most of you survive to see a Riddle Beast more than once."

Well I'll be darned, thought Amella. She knew of the Riddle Beast, or at least knew stories of them. The olden tales painted them as a servant of Death, a bristling monster that devoured anyone they deemed unworthy, which in their eyes meant not clever enough with words. Her ma had delighted in telling her stories about the Riddle Beast, largely because they always had riddles, but unfortunately, Amella had never taken a liking to them. They'd frayed at her patience, and she'd always wondered why the hero didn't just draw their sword and poke the Riddle Beast full of holes. That worked well on most everything…

Well, except the dragon, and the bandits who'd outnumbered her twenty to one. But those were rare exceptions. She could take this beast. Probably.

She could damn well try, at least.

The Riddle Beast prowled closer. Amella drew her sword. Out of the corner of her eye, she looked to Tenno. She expected him to be standing ready, his weapon held strong in his meaty grip.

Only he wasn't. He had one hand on his sword hilt, but the other was raised, palm open. *Stop right there,* said the open hand. *Easy, now.*

"Excuse me," said Tenno with an air of forced calm. "But do you have business with us?"

The Riddle Beast stopped and swiveled its ears toward him. "Isn't that refreshing. Of the dozen humans I've dealt with, four of them tried to fight me, five froze, and three screamed and tried to run. Never mind that if I'd wanted them dead promptly, I would have stalked them and pounced from behind... Yes. Yes, I have the usual business with you. The business a Riddle Beast always has, of course." Its tail flicked. "I'm bored. Play a riddle game with me."

Amella tried to surreptitiously kick Tenno's shin—*come on, soldier, let's take this thing down*—but Tenno ignored her. "What are the rules, and can we win something?"

"Besides the right to walk away alive?" The Riddle Beast rumbled out a laugh. The sound was deep and rough, and sinister as a laugh could get. "You might be able to ask me a question. A favor. Something. Then again, you might not. It depends on how reasonable your request is, whether I decide I like you enough, or, sometimes, simply whether or not I'm in the mood to grant boons." It licked its paw pad, tongue rasping over toughened skin, and swiped it over their ears. "I will ask as many riddles as I feel like asking. I decide when you've answered enough to entertain me. I will tell you when I am done, or else, if you've failed too many times, I'll either devour you or chase you out on my territory. Again, it depends on what mood I'm in." It stepped closer, but it still wasn't within stabbing reach.

Cunning beast, Amella groused silently to herself.

"I will grant you three wrong guesses. Perhaps more, at my discretion, but that's not likely. Since there are two of you buffoons, please feel free to discuss between yourselves before submitting an official answer. But please, don't take too long. Don't make it boring."

Their eyes locked on Amella's weapon.

"And for the love of fresh fish, you daft fool, put the sword away."

Not a chance in the starlands, you overgrown ball of fur.

"Amella," said Tenno quietly, "maybe we should—"

"Nope."

"But if we can ask a boon—"

Amella ignored him and stared down the Riddle Beast. "I will lower it. That's as good as you're going to get from me." She let her sword drop to her side, but she didn't sheathe it. She ignored the Riddle

Beast's grumble of discontent and said, "I've lived a few decades too long and made too many bargains to be shoved around by the likes of you. Now here's *my* rules. First, if you pounce, I'll stab you full of holes." She lifted her sword and jabbed at the air in front of her for effect. The Riddle Beast flattened its ears and snarled. "Second, we won't be held up for more than three riddles. We've got someone we need to find, you see." Amella took a deep breath and lowered her sword again, and she forced a bit of the fire out of her voice—the fire, but not the steel. "Lastly. If you want to quit and run, we won't hunt you down. Heck, we didn't mean to track you down this time, either. You can go on your merry way and prey on hapless bog sprites or claw tree trunks to smithereens, or whatever else you do, and we'll carry on with our quest. Do we have a deal?"

The Riddle Beast's teeth disappeared, and it held its head high, eyeing Amella speculatively. "Ten riddles."

"Three."

"Twenty."

"Two."

"Forty-two."

"One."

The Riddle Beast's tail thrashed in irritation. "Seven."

"Zero. Keep pushing, and I'll fight you."

The Riddle Beast's quills flared in warning. They weren't just along its back and tail, Amella realized; the quills spread down its sides, though they were smaller and blended more and more with fur the farther down they went, disappearing near the belly and the tops of the leg joints. Corrin probably would've wanted to know if they were venomous, or if they might have medicinal properties. Well. If the lass could get past her boot-shaking fear, at least. Then again, she'd gotten past her fear enough to wake a dragon—to *think* of waking a dragon, that mad lass—so…

"Hmph," said the Beast, and its quills flattened. "You can't afford to fight me, even if you could win. Can't risk getting wounded for your quest, can you?"

Argh. Seastorms and dragon dung, the beast's right.

"That's what I thought." The Riddle Beast sat back on its haunches and curled its tail around its paws. "Five riddles. I will promise no fewer. Do we have a deal, O Bargain Driver?"

"…Yes."

"Excellent." The Riddle Beast's ears flicked forward, and Amella could swear the corners of that unnerving, half-human mouth were curled into a smile. "First riddle: what is an origin, an action, and a thing that dwells beneath the earth?"

I hate riddles, Amella thought sourly.

An origin… an action… a thing beneath earth…

Tenno's voice rang out, bright and confident: "A root."

Huh. Good on you, Tenno.

The Riddle Beast blinked. "That one was too easy, wasn't it?"

"No, no," Tenno said hastily, "it was a good one. I was just lucky enough to think of the right word, and, uh… well, we're surrounded by trees and roots, so that probably helped."

"Hrrm. Well, let's try a longer one." The Riddle Beast lifted its head and puffed its chest out self-importantly. "Second riddle. There is a thing that hungers but has no stomach, that devours but does not eat. This thing is lively, but it fears the liquid that grants life. What is it?" The Riddle Beast fidgeted with its forepaws and looked smug. "Now how's that for a riddle? It's a puzzling one, isn't it?"

"Yes," agreed Tenno. "Also, the answer is fire."

"*WHAT?* Too fast!"

Junior shrilled in alarm at the outburst.

Tenno rested a calming hand on his bird's back. She settled. He smiled politely. "Again, I had an unfair advantage. My companion Junior's a firebird, so of course, fire's one of the first things that comes to mind for me."

The Riddle Beast's tail lashed. "Fine. Fine! Enough with your platitudes. Third riddle." It cleared its throat and made a show of raising and lowering its spines.

Posturing like a growth-stunted rooster, Amella thought. *Oooh, scary. Well guess what, I've dealt with more fearsome beasts than you.*

"What has four legs at sunrise, two legs at midday, and three legs at sunset?"

"A human," said Tenno promptly. "The day is a lifetime. A person is a baby at sunrise, adult at midday, and an elder leaning on a staff at sunset."

"*ARGH.*"

"Sorry, I've heard that one before. It was a family favorite." He sounded genuinely apologetic, which, by Amella's reckoning, was a baffling and profoundly foolish sentiment to waste on a beast who was holding their lives hostage—for time-wasting games, of all things. "If you like, we could throw in an extra riddle—"

Amella cut in. "*NO*. We agreed on five and we're sticking to five, Tenno. You don't go throwing bones to the beast who threatened to gut us."

Tenno flushed. "Oh. Ah. Right."

"Fine," growled the Riddle Beast. "*FINE.* I'll fulfill our agreement. But this one, *this one* is sure to stump you." The Riddle Beast cleared its throat and forced its bristling quills to lie flat, with visible effort. "Fourth riddle. What is heavy forwards, but not backwards?" It waited several beats, and when no answer came, it preened. "See? You're stuck on this one, aren't you? Remember, if you don't solve it, you lose. I'm sure you'll make a delicious meal."

Amella was half-tempted to call off the game and leap straight to the sword-fighting. "I'm sure you'll love being poked full of holes, you puffed up unicorn's—"

"I'm thinking," interrupted Tenno quickly. "Just give me a moment, please."

"Argh, *fine.*"

The Riddle Beast rumbled happily. "Of course. I'm an excellent sport, if I do say so myself, which I do. I'll even repeat the riddle for you: what is heavy forwards, but not backwards?"

Tenno repeated the riddle aloud. Paused. Said it again, slowly. And then his expression cleared, and he tapped his fist against his palm, smiling. "I have it! This one's a play on words. The answer is *ton,* which is a Staltian standard measurement for massive amounts of weight, but then you spell it backwards, and... And... Excuse me, but how did you know about a human-standard measurement? And, uh, written spelling?"

The Riddle Beast blinked with all the innocence of a street cat, which was to say, none. "Oh, I've been around a while. Heard a few things. Was taught a few things by my mother, too, may she rest in peace in the shadows and hearts of trees."

"Uh. Alright. Anyway, we've now solved four of your riddles, which leaves one more."

"..."

Four out of five. Stars, Tenno solved those fast.

Curiosity prickling at her, Amella asked, "Were you one of those kids who liked wordplay jokes and riddle games?"

He rubbed the back of his neck and smiled ruefully. "Well, I was one of those kids who was subjected to them, all day, every day. My dad used to love passing the time with them, back when I worked with him in the forge and we'd be waiting for metal to soften or melt. I guess after a while, I had to get decent at them, eh?"

"*AHEM.*" The Riddle Beast flicked its tail restlessly. "Since you're so 'decent' at this, can we carry on with the game?" Without waiting for a response, it continued, "See if you can answer this last one, interloper." Its voice had a decidedly stressed edge to it now, and its ears flicked anxiously. "Fifth riddle." The Riddle Beast hesitated.

Amella suppressed a grin. *Lost its confidence, eh?* she thought. *Serves it right.*

Then the Beast said, "What can you keep after giving it to someone?"

Amella looked to Tenno. For a heartbeat, she swore that she saw a glimmer of realization, the ghost of a smile tugging at his lips. But then she blinked, and no, she must have imagined it. His brow was furrowed, and he mumbled to himself, ticking some indecipherable items off with his fingers. Was he stumped this time? *Come on,* she silently urged him, *you're the riddle enthusiast here, aren't you?*

The Riddle Beast looked triumphant.

Tenno turned to her, frowning. "That one has several answers that technically qualify, doesn't it? A story, advice, kindness... You can share any of those, but you don't lose them, right? You remember the story and advice. After you give someone kindness, you remain kind." All those answers sounded right and reasonable. And yet, none of them seemed to fit. She just couldn't put her finger on why... ah, and he was still talking. "I mean, hopefully. It's possible for someone to take advantage of your kindness, and you could become less kind as a result. But you don't have to, and it's terribly sad if you do, isn't it?"

"Can't believe a mushy heart like you is a guard," Amella muttered to herself.

"Sorry, what did you say?"

"Ah, nothing," said Amella quickly. "You're right, you still have all those things after you share them, don't you?" Her thoughts churned, and the fingers of her free hand drummed against her hip. "They don't quite fit, though. They're technically correct, but I think the real answer would be... How to put this?" She searched for the words. Blasted words. Words were difficult. "Seems like... It'd have a ring to it, you know what I mean? Like a bard's song or a poem, or a story. Like maybe the words should fit in more than one way..."

Curse those tricksy, Churikin-forsaken words.

...Wait.

"Words," Amella mused aloud. "You can give words. *I give you my word.* And if I give you my word, I'd better *keep my word.*" She smacked her temple. "Oh for the love of the stars. Took us long enough, didn't it?"

Tenno beamed at her.

The Riddle Beast huffed, but it didn't look altogether displeased. "I suppose I won't be eating you after all."

"Won't be getting stabbed full of holes, you mean."

Tenno's smile disappeared. "*Amella.*"

"It's true. Now act your age and chortle with me."

Tenno took the deep, slow breath of an overly sensible sort who was willing himself patience. Amella was ninety percent certain she'd seen Corrin do the same thing at least once. And Turner, Turner had definitely made that face and taken that breath. And, come to think of it, so had the vast majority of people she interacted with for more than a few minutes... *Ah, well, I suppose the world is full of overly sensible sorts. No levity to be had.*

The Riddle Beast's rumbling voice startled her out of her thoughts. "It was a good riddle, though, wasn't it? I almost had you."

"Yes, you did," agreed Tenno quickly. Suspiciously quickly. Amella narrowed her eyes, but alas, he wasn't looking at her. "It was an excellent game, really put us on our toes."

"Good, good. I was a bit out of practice, so..."

"I wouldn't have been able to guess. You've trumped my dad's riddles, that's for sure."

The Riddle Beast preened.

"Speaking of words," continued Tenno. "You said that you might grant us a boon. Do you feel up to it, by any chance?"

Internally, Amella updated her mental profile of Tenno. Under his name, she'd already catalogued descriptors like *giant, friend of Corrin, guardsman, too much of a bleeding heart for a guardsman, too polite for roguish humor,* and *daft enough to keep his weapon sheathed around a monster and then try to reason with it after it professed an interest in eating us.* Now, she had another couple to add. Firstly: *A ridiculously clever head for riddles.* Secondly: *Manipulative as a politician, when he sets his mind to it. Should consider changing his career.*

"Up to it?" The Riddle Beast lifted its head proudly. "Of course I feel *up to it.* As for whether I will, well..." They made a show of standing and stretching like a house cat in the sun, if a house cat were a hundred times larger and armed with bristling wasp-colored quills. Tenno waited. Amella bit back her impatience. At last, the quills flattened, and the Riddle Beast continued. "You did help alleviate my boredom. You made for a good game, a very good one indeed. Suspenseful. Close at the end, there." The Riddle Beast rumbled, not quite a growl but too deep and rough to be a purr. "I have decided that I like you. So yes, go ahead, request a boon. Make it a weighty one, while you're at it."

"Thank you so much," said Tenno. He finally looked at Amella, smiling faintly, and gave her a surreptitious thumbs up behind his back. "We're here because we're looking for a friend of ours, who we think was taken by trolls. Her name is Corrin. She's smaller than both of us, with red hair and freckles. If you've seen her, could you help us find her? If you haven't, could you take us… perhaps…" He hesitated. He looked to Amella again, this time with a flicker of uncertainty in his eyes and in the wavering of his smile. He was clever, daft, manipulative, and brave, and *oh fire ghosts no wonder he and Corrin got along*, but he was also inexperienced in matters such as questing and leading. Leading in particular.

You'll be amazing at that someday, by my reckoning, but for now…

"If you haven't," Amella finished for him, "could you guide us to the nearest troll village?"

The Riddle Beast flicked its tail. "You're certain about that? Trolls are nasty creatures. Big barrels of fangs and aggression, and they've no patience for riddles."

"We're sure," said Amella firmly.

The Riddle Beast considered them carefully, then said, "All right, I'll guide you. But on your own heads be it when we find the trolls."

They trekked with the Riddle Beast back to where Amella had first lost the trail, that patch by the stream that was all scuffed up and muddled with a hundred footprints. And snake prints, as it turned out. The Riddle Beast was quite emphatic about the smell of snake, specifically of slaughtered snake, and of the Gloamwood's various scavengers who had come to clean up the leftovers. "It also smells like human," the Beast reassured them, "yes, definitely some live human here." It wrinkled its nose. "And troll. Eurgh, trolls *reek*."

"Can you tell which way they went?" asked Amella.

The Riddle Beast circled the area, snuffling. "Hm… I think… yes, this way." It bounded off, and Amella and Tenno had to run to keep up. The Riddle Beast didn't seem used to setting a pace for beings with shorter strides. And since Amella would prefer to reach Corrin sooner rather than later, she'd let her legs seize before she asked the Beast to slow down. Tenno seemed to feel similarly. Or perhaps the military had simply drilled him until he could no longer feel fatigue. She'd heard legends about Stalt's armored finest. Then again, those slackers back in Oddment didn't live up to them, not even close.

Probably wasn't the military, then.

They stopped for the night.

The Riddle Beast assured them that it would wake up in a trice if danger drew near, but Amella and Tenno took turns keeping watch, all the same. During Amella's watch, Junior kept starting awake and cooing softly, even as Tenno slept peacefully on his blanket.

Amella wasn't sure how to quiet Junior. She seemed to be a sensitive creature, and Amella didn't do so great with sensitivity. Case in point: her failure to realize she was bothering Corrin, back on Turner's ship. She could still picture the frustration that had burst out of her, and how it all had seemed so sudden, even though it had, apparently, been building up for weeks… And then the two of them, sitting belowdecks while the storm raged overhead, with Corrin scuffing her boots and Amella feeling wrong-footed, clumsy, trying to understand, to figure out how to make things alright again…

She hoped Corrin was okay. She hoped the lass would hang on until they caught up with her.

The darkness seemed unusually thick, like it was not just an absence of light but a substance, obscuring everything beyond their tiny cluster of bodies. Noises seemed magnified. The Riddle Beast's ears twitched now and then, flicks of motion that Amella could just barely pick up. Amella was feeling twitchy herself.

Junior chirped nervously.

"We're fine," Amella promised, as much to herself as to Junior. She patted the hilt of her sword. "We've got each other. We'll be alright."

Junior quieted.

They left before the crack of dawn.

They reached troll territory when sunlight had scarcely begun to break through the canopy. "See here," said the Riddle Beast, nosing a claw mark scored deep into a tree. "This is a border marker. The trolls' hunting grounds begin here, and they don't take kindly to other large beasts wandering into their land." It sniffed haughtily. "Not even ones who are gifted in language, such as myself. They've no courtesy. None whatsoever." The Riddle Beast turned back to them and narrowed its eyes, scrutinizing, warning. "You're absolutely certain you want to barge in, now? The trolls remember the old days as well as you, I'm sure. They'll be bitter toward your kind."

"Beg pardon?" asked Tenno politely.

"You know. The wars. The failed negotiations. The captives, the damage, how your kind eventually emigrated because the forest was too hostile. I was scarcely more than a kit at the time, but I remember my mother's stories."

What?

Out loud, Amella said, "I've never heard of humans trying to negotiate with trolls, let alone living in the Gloamwood. All our stories say they're the servants of Death and that the Gloamwood is a cursed place." She paused. "I haven't seen anything supernatural here, yet, but I can't imagine us living here. Place is overrun with flesh-hungry beasts."

The Riddle Beast's quills rose along the back of its spine. "What do you *expect* me to eat? I'm hardly built to live on leaves and bark, you know."

"Actually, I once heard a theory that we came from here," said Tenno thoughtfully. "Not a popular one, mind, but an interesting one." Amella turned to him in surprise. He scratched the scruff on his chin and frowned pensively back at her. "I had this friend back in the military who was a history buff. She used to go poking around the capital archives at night, just to see what ancient records and stories she could find. Sometimes I'd talk her into a game of castles and dragons, and we'd get to chatting between turns. One night, she let slip that she'd found the work of some hare-brained archaeologist that suggested some of us had come out of the Gloamwood. 'Course, the theory undermines some of our favorite origin stories, and existing support for the theory is sparse.

"But there's definitely enough to make it possible. Some madman actually investigated near the Gloamwood's edge and found a crypt he thinks was pre-Staltian. It had human bones in it, along with some strange drawings that I guess he didn't know how to interpret, though my friend said she had some ideas. And she said something about early agricultural records, I think mentions of breeding certain plants to better handle the local climates, which means we must have gotten them from somewhere else… say, here."

"I—what? Really?"

"Really. That's about it, though." He paused. "And there wasn't anything about us trying to communicate with trolls. Not a word."

"You're sure your friend wasn't off her gourd?"

Tenno smiled faintly. "I believe in her. She was eccentric, sure, but she was also brilliant. She ended up receiving an invitation from the Imperial Academic Counsel, and she quit basic training to join them. I missed our castles and dragons games, but I think the Academic Counsel was a better fit for her. At least, I hope so." He grew pensive again and turned to the Riddle Beast. "But if this theory was right, and you were old enough to remember us living here... Um, I hope you don't mind me asking this, but how old are you, exactly?"

The Riddle Beast's quills flattened, and it lifted its chin proudly. "Over a millennium. I've seen and lived through eras you can scarcely dream of. My word's a better source than any of your dusty, half-forgotten books."

"Is that so?" said Amella. "You remember the specifics about these wars you were talking about? Or what happened with the compromises, and why they failed?"

"Pah. The details were beneath my notice."

"Uh-huh. Sure."

"As I was saying, I doubt the trolls like your kind. They probably view you as trickster demons of some sort, or as—how did you put it?—servants of Death herself." The Riddle Beast paused for dramatic effect. Amella thought, *Beast's a blasted showboat, it is. But if I want to make use of it, I'd better keep playing along.* And so she suppressed her eye roll as the Beast went on to ask, "Are you certain you want to go this way? Are you absolutely, one hundred percent committed to walking into this den of doom? Because I'm not. I intend to leave you to your fate the moment the trolls are upon you."

"Yes," said Amella and Tenno in unison. Their voices rang strong amid the hush of the Gloamwood.

"*Sssh,*" hissed the Riddle Beast. Rather hypocritical of it, considering how much it had been talking—but its next words, at least, were scarcely more than a whisper. "Fine. I won't question your resolve again. Stay close to me, now. I can guide you close to the village's edge, but you're on your own from there. Assuming they don't find us first." And without another word, the Riddle Beast stalked onward, its paw-steps more cautious than before. Amella followed suit, stepping lightly with a hand on her sword hilt, and she could hear the soft rustles of Tenno trailing behind her. They kept on like this for several minutes, stopping now and then as the Riddle Beast paused to taste the air or flick its ears toward some sound too far off for Amella to hear—until suddenly, the Beast's quills bristled.

"Troll," it murmured, and jerked its head toward a shadowy patch of forest.

Amella squinted, and indeed, she could see the dark shape of a creature moving in the undergrowth. The shape stepped out behind a trunk, and Amella's breath caught. *Death's scythe,* she thought, *that thing is **huge**.* It had to be nine feet tall, at least. Its stance was two-legged, almost human, but its frame was too broad, its arms too long and clawed at the ends, and its fur thick as a bear's. Something white and curved glinted on its chest, swaying as it moved, along with the deer it had slung over its shoulder. And then the thing—the *troll*—paused. Its ears twitched.

Its eyes landed on Amella.

"Have fun with that," said the Riddle Beast sardonically, and sprang off into the undergrowth.

"Thanks a lot, you scaredy cat," Amella grumbled. She ignored the tingle of trepidation that ran up her spine, as she had with the dragon, the horde of bandits, and every other beast or thug she'd resolved to fight in her not-so-insignificant lifespan, and drew her weapon. Beside her, Tenno did the same. It was a fearsome beast, but it was alone. *We can handle this,* she told herself firmly. *We've got this one, easy. It's two against one, all it has is its claws, and the both of us aren't half bad with the sword. It'll be like hunting a bear. A massive, clever bear with a grudge, that's all.*

The deer hit the forest floor with a *thump,* and the troll raised the white thing to its lips. The call of a war horn pealed through the forest.

Oh, COME ON.

CHAPTER NINETEEN

Reunion

Corrin scrambled to her feet. "What was that?"

Makur grumbled and rolled over, their ears pressed flat and their face tucked in their arms. Noises that were probably meant to be trolltongue rumbled out of them, but all Corrin heard was a muffled mash of vowels and consonants, something like, "Mgrhrruhruhgh." She prodded Makur's back, and then their side, and finally, a single orange eye cracked open. Makur unblocked their mouth enough to say, "Is no bright time. Go sleep." And then they curled into a giant furball and rolled away from her, snuffling.

Corrin was contemplating shaking them when the noise rang out again, distant and deep—and this time she was sure of what it was. The guards in Oddment and the elders both had horns that sounded like that. The elders used them to call the village together for a meeting or ceremony. The guards used them to signal warnings.

Makur's ear flicked upward, and they abruptly sat up. "Hrr. Be blorg. Near is danger."

"No grekka. What?"

Makur heaved themselves to their feet and bounded toward the burrow entrance, only to pause on the threshold, as if they'd almost forgotten something. They turned back to her with narrowed eyes and pointed at her fiercely with one claw. "Corrin stay," they said sternly. "Blorg danger. Corrin be wyrman, small wid no fur, no claws." They curled their paw into a fist and thumped their chest. "I deal wid it. Krrkin deal wid it. Grekka?"

Corrin understood the *stay* and the *danger* bits, and that Makur and the other trolls would supposedly handle… whatever this horn meant. But she couldn't help but remember the snake that had almost strangled Makur, or how Rakar had held Makur down in the water. She also recalled the last time she'd heard a horn, and the forty-odd bandits it had united. What if this horn was the Bandit King's? She tried to imagine the trolls fighting the bandits. The trolls were a fearsome bunch, and Makur could best Corrin any time of day, but against someone who really knew how to use a sword... who made their livelihood taking captives and lives they had no right to...

"Corrin stay in den. Yus?"

"Nope," she said, and stepped forward. Her heart beat fast. What was she doing? She didn't know, really. But she was going to do something, if she could. "I'll come with you."

Makur growled. "Danger."

"I'm coming," she said resolutely.

"*ARRR. FIKAH.* Hardhead wyrman." Makur whirled around and barreled outside.

Corrin followed as fast as her feet could carry her.

They joined a river of fur and bared teeth that sped away from camp. It seemed, at first, like an unfathomable number of trolls; but then Corrin realized she could only pick out seven counting Makur, and it only seemed like there were so many trolls because each troll was so much—so big and fast and fluid. Corrin ran past the Dono, who leaned heavily on their staff and watched her go with an unreadable expression. She passed the enormous troll parent that she'd met, who was out with their child again but had stopped to watch the group running by. And then the village was behind them, distant, nearly indistinguishable from the rest of the Gloamwood.

Corrin's boot caught on a tree root, and she pitched forward into Makur. Makur gave her a flat look and grumbled something she didn't quite catch, but was probably along the lines of, *Bibbinhead wyrman. Can't even run straight.*

The horn sounded again, closer this time.

The troll at the front growled a signal, and all of a sudden the trolls split, loping off in two different directions. Corrin stuck close to Makur and one other troll, who treaded astoundingly lightly for such large creatures, until they stopped and crouched behind a tree trunk. Cautiously, Corrin peered around it.

A single troll half crouched, half stood with an ivory horn at their lips. They had their ears pressed flat against their skull, and their fur rose along their spine. Across from the troll, two people stood side to side, their swords at the ready—and Corrin's heart leaped.

Tenno! Amella! They're alive! They're here!

Even at this distance, Tenno was recognizably a giant of a person, with meaty arms and broad shoulders and scruffy, light brown hair. His sword was held defensively, on a slant and ready to parry. Amella kept her hair distinctively short-shorn, and she was poised more aggressively, her sword level and ready to stab. She'd shifted slightly in front of Tenno. Corrin caught a glimpse of red flapping anxiously above them, and her heart leaped even further.

Junior!

Two of the trolls crept up behind them. Tenno turned so he and Amella were back to back. Corrin felt rather than saw Makur tense next to her, muscles bunching, sinking deeper into a crouch.

They're alive and they came for me and they're about to get pounced on by trolls oh viper bites.

Corrin tugged frantically on Makur's arm. "They're friends," she hissed in Makur's ear. Makur looked at her uncomprehendingly, teeth bared, eyes narrowed, and she recalled that she'd never heard Makur utter the word *friend.* She rephrased: "They're good. They're my kin." She jabbed her own chest with her thumb. "Corrin's kin."

Makur's eyes widened, but their aggression didn't drop.

"Oi," said Amella. Her voice echoed through the trees, proud and sharp and inviting a fight. "One wrong move and I'll spill your guts, you blasted trollbeasts." Which was an understandable reaction and in keeping with her usual, well, Amella-ness, but probably the least helpful thing she could've done. Corrin could practically feel the spike in tension, the crackling tempers and the clenched teeth. "You've taken one of ours. You've trapped Corrin somewhere, haven't you? Give her back!" Again, Corrin should've seen it coming from Amella, that burst of daring and protectiveness. It warmed Corrin's heart, made it swell with gratitude and affection and a desire to rush out and embrace her. But again, it wasn't helpful.

Corrin needed to calm everyone down, approach carefully and explain, gently, no sudden moves—

The trolls crept closer. Makur growled.

No time.

Corrin leaped out from behind the tree and sprinted to Amella and Tenno. Amella whirled, her sword jabbing on instinct, and Corrin skidded to a stop with a steel point inches from her chest. Her heart rabbited.

"H-hi," she croaked, as Tenno's and Amella's eyes grew wide and round as coins. Amella's weapon dipped, and the beginnings of an incredulous grin curved the corners of her mouth, exposing a hint of yellowed teeth—

A snarl shook Corrin's bones from behind. She whipped around.

"Danger," Makur growled. They stood at their full height, bristling from nose to tailbone. "Catch Corrin? Take Corrin away?"

"For the love of—*NO!*"

Amella's sword rose.

"Corrin, get behind me, let me at that beast—"

"*NO.*" She pressed her palm against the flat of Amella's blade and pushed it to one side. She used her other hand to poke Makur's chest. She felt hyperaware of everything: the rustling leaves, the trolls who had stilled but remained on edge, her own heartbeat pounding in her ears, the humidity collecting on her skin. "No fighting, I'm fine, everything's *fine.*"

"But it *took you.*"

Makur bared their teeth. "Wyrmen take Corrin? Makur rahrg. Makur protect."

"*NO, MAKUR. STAY.*" Makur's eyes widened in bafflement, or affront, or possibly both, but Corrin forged on before they could respond. "These are my kin. My friends. They want to know I'm alright. Want to know Corrin live, no hurt." She batted at Makur's paw, which had started to reach out to grab her waist, and said firmly, "No." Then, she turned to Amella.

Amella's mouth was open, but whatever words she might have readied had died on her tongue. Her gaze flitted between Corrin and the troll. Her eyes were so, so round. Corrin had never in her life seen her this gobsmacked.

Corrin mustered up a ghost of a smile. "They took me captive, but then I won them over. We, um, we battled a giant snake together. Terrible fearsome creature, probably would've swallowed us whole otherwise." She watched Amella's sword dip again and a bit of the tension leave her shoulders. Behind her, Tenno hadn't dropped his guard in the slightest. He wasn't ready to attack, but he looked, well, he looked like a guardperson. On alert and ready for the situation to get worse. Corrin softened her voice and said, "The stories we know left a few things out. Did you know they can talk?"

"No," said Tenno. His voice was quiet, cautious. Junior drifted down and alighted on his shoulder. The poor bird hunched nervously, her head drawn in and her feathers ruffled, and he murmured soothing nonsensical babble to her. To Corrin, he amended, "Actually, we did hear some interesting things from the Riddle Beast, which suggested that... well, it's a long story. Perhaps we should discuss this later?" He glanced behind him. Three of the trolls had crept a smidge too close for comfort. One looked like it was itching to pounce, but the other two leaned forward with their ears perked, as if trying to listen in. One had its face scrunched in concentration, and the other looked decidedly grumpy. Corrin would wager they understood just enough to feel thwarted by the rest of the unfamiliar human babble.

Oh, and there were also another three trolls behind the one with the horn...

...and one who had drawn level with Makur when Corrin wasn't looking. They were a good head taller and bigger in the shoulders, with dark fur and lurid orange eyes and—*oh fairy bites,* Corrin thought, *that's Rakar, isn't it?*

Rakar scowled. "Too many wyrmen. Wyddscatch bring danger. Catch them." They shoved Corrin aside with one paw.

Corrin tried to resist, but her boots skidded uselessly on the dirt. She smacked their forearm. Unfortunately, that didn't seem to affect them either. But then she glommed onto their arm, yanked, and shouted, "Bibbinhead!" and they sure took notice then.

Rakar glared at her and bared their teeth. "Wyddscatch stay out. We catch."

"No."

"*YUS.*"

"*NO.*"

Rakar's massive paw lashed out and smacked the side of Corrin's head. She staggered, her vision going splotchy and her head spinning. Distantly, she heard Amella's furious shout, a troll's snarl, and a yelp of pain. A warm hand grabbed her shoulder, steadying her. Tenno said something that she didn't quite catch. Whatever it was, he sounded worried, which was concerning, because if Tenno was fussing then there was probably something to worry about. She blinked away the splotches and forced herself to focus.

Rakar had a massive gash bleeding on their arm, but they'd put Amella in a headlock. Her sword arm was trapped against them. Her free arm socked them repeatedly. Unfortunately, Rakar wasn't budging.

That's not good.

"Are you okay?" asked Tenno urgently.

"M'fine." Corrin blinked again.

Makur roared invectives at Rakar, who roared back. The other trolls hadn't sprung yet, but some of them were thinking about it, judging from their bared teeth and bristling fur. Tenno had drawn Corrin close to his side protectively, and he brandished his sword at a troll who had ventured too close for comfort. The trolls who weren't thinking about pouncing watched Makur and Rakar fight, visibly entertained. One of them cheered when Makur cuffed Rakar on the head. Rakar seemed too torn between holding Amella and dealing with Makar's assault to fight back.

"Death's scythe," said Corrin quietly. Then, louder, "Would you bibbinheads *STOP!*"

Makur paused mid swing. Amella stopped striking and looked at Corrin, bewildered. *Bibbinheads?* she mouthed.

"Bibbinheads?" whispered Tenno, bemused.

"Bibbinheads," said Corrin sternly. "Grok Dono. Dono will know what to do. Let them walk."

Makur dropped their paw. Rakar didn't budge.

"Let her go, please. She won't hurt you." Corrin locked eyes with Amella and willed her to listen. "She'll be good. Right?"

Amella's expression contorted into one of confusion, then incredulity, and then, finally, a hard mask that could have been carved from stone. Corrin feared for a moment that Amella wouldn't listen; but then she spoke, and though her voice was all steel and anger, it wasn't the refusal that Corrin had feared. "Alright. I won't strike the troll-beast, as long as they don't strike you again. But if they do hurt you, I will spill their entrails and lop off their heads." Amella dug her fingers into Rakar's forearm, close to the bleeding gash. "You understand that, you giant muttonhead?"

Rakar growled.

Corrin's heart sank.

Makur looked at Corrin, then Rakar, then Amella. "Let go," they rumbled. "Is Corrin kin. Bring to Dono."

Rakar narrowed their eyes. "Makur be soft. Wyddscatch have Makur snargak from paw."

Makur bristled, but their voice remained level. "Rakar be bibbinhead. Grok wid Dono. Dono wis."

Tenno spoke softly in Corrin's ear. "What are they saying?"

Corrin shushed him.

"Raar. Makur be no wykrr. Makur be bibbinhead bairn."

Makur swelled with fury, and Corrin thought for sure they were going to lunge and then Rakar was going to hurt Amella and there'd be a brawl and someone would get stabbed and she and her friends wouldn't have a mouse's chance in a cat's gut of getting out of this unscathed. But then Makur went still. They looked back at Corrin, and at Tenno who stood protectively beside her, and then again at Rakar. And they deflated. Their snarl dropped. Their fur flattened. Makur's eyes were narrowed and their ears twisted back in ire, but all they said was, "Dono grok iffen Makur bibbinhead. Be danger, I be bibbinhead. No hurt Corrin kin. Yus?"

Rakar blinked; then, miraculously, they let Amella go. "Fikah."

Amella scowled at Rakar and stepped away with exaggerated strides, her right hand resting pointedly on the hilt of her sword. Rakar bared their teeth, but they didn't try to snatch her up again. Amella stalked up to Corrin with flinty eyes, and for a heartbeat she looked thunderous, like she was angry, like she was going to roar at Corrin for, well, everything. But next Corrin knew, Amella's arms were around her, embracing her so fiercely that her ribs creaked. Amella's breath warmed Corrin's ear as she said, "You have no idea how glad I am to see you alive."

Corrin hugged her back and buried her face in Amella's shoulder.

"You're not leaving my sight from here on out. You hear me?"

She nodded.

Tenno wrapped them both in a hug of his own, warm and snug, and Junior cooed. Both Tenno and Amella seemed awfully reluctant to let go. Corrin didn't mind this; she wanted to keep them close and never let them go again, herself. But eventually, Makur grumbled with impatience, and they all stepped back from each other.

Makur said, "Go harth, yus?"

"Yus," Corrin confirmed.

Rakar growled and shoved their way to the front, grabbing their deer carcass on the way. The other trolls fell in behind Rakar, rumbling excitedly to each other, except for Makur and a couple of others who gathered behind the humans, forming a rear guard. Makur shuffled up beside Corrin, giving Amella and Tenno wary sideways looks and twitching their ears this way and that, like they suspected her friends of mischief. Which, in fairness, Amella might have done if the circumstances weren't so fragile, what with her love of dreadful irritating jokes.

Corrin reached out and touched Makur's shoulder. It was the

uninjured one, so her fingertips sank into thick fur. "Thank you," she said, and meant it. Keeping their temper around a murderous bully of a sibling seemed like an awfully hard thing to do.

Makur huffed. "Corrin be much hassark."

"Yus," agreed Corrin. She didn't know what the word meant, exactly, but she got a sense of the feeling behind it. And that was enough.

"Bibbinheads," grumbled the Dono, and shook their staff as if trying to flick water off of it. "Wyrmen bibbinheads, krr bibbinheads. Raar."

Corrin smothered her desire to laugh. She, Amella, and Tenno were seated cross-legged near the Dono's burrow, crammed knee to knee despite the ample space. Junior had stayed on Tenno's shoulder, pressing close to his cheek as he offered her head-scritches. Makur and Rakar were there, too, but they stood off to one side with their heads ducked and ears pressed back. Each troll had tried to explain what had happened to the Dono, rumbling in rapid-fire trolltongue and constantly cutting each other off, voices rising. Eventually, the Dono had whapped both of their snouts with their staff and barked at them, calling them bibbinheads and grumbling an order that probably meant, "Go one at a time." So first Rakar, and then Makur, delivered their account in brusque growls and emphatic gesturing; and at the end of it, the Dono rapped them again, lighter this time, on the tops of their skulls.

The Dono leaned heavily on their staff. For a heartbeat, Corrin envisioned Bathilda standing in their place, short and ancient and exasperated by her patients' propensity for never-ending foolishness. Then the Dono turned to Makur and rumbled in a deep, markedly non-human voice, and the mental image vanished. "Catch one Wyddscatch, more follow. Catch tri wyrmen now, and wyrmen bring fake-claws. One wyrman, small, no much hassark. Tri, big hassark. Hmph." They pointed their stick accusingly at Corrin. "Corrin is krrkin, det, more wyrmen no. More wyrmen come? More follow Corrin? Be hassark, be danger?"

Corrin blinked up at Amella and Tenno. Even when they were all sitting down, their torsos were a smidge taller than hers. "I don't think… Was Turner coming too? Or Bruin? Chevira?"

Amella let out a long, slow breath. "I don't know what became of them. But if I know Turner, he would've turned back. He would've tried to persuade the others to go with him, too, if he was able to find them." Wry but fond, she added, "You've met the man. He's the fatalistic sort. Probably thought the lot of us dead."

Tenno spoke up. "Or he thought we'd regroup in the port city, or he's seeking out my superiors… or he weighed the risks and went with the choice he thought the most likely to save the most lives. Or, well." His voice gentled, but somehow, his kindness made his next words cut deeper. "He might not have made it. It's a miracle that *we* made it. That was a risk, you know, when you woke that dragon. And I gather it was a risk you knew you were taking."

Corrin's throat tightened. She nodded.

"Hey," said Amella. "We were stuck between a dragon and a bunch of bandits. Tough decision. I would've picked the natural disaster over the horde of cold-blooded killers, too, if I were mad enough to think of doing it." Corrin ducked her head, swiping at her prickly eyes, and Amella wrapped an arm around her shoulders, bracing her. "Look, Corrin. Between the lot of us, we got exposed to a plague, raided, captured, threatened with death to keep us in line, attacked by a pissed off dragon, kidnapped by a troll, attacked by a giant snake, threatened with death *again* by a Riddle Beast and subjected to their blasted word puzzles…" Amella cracked a grin. "Seems like more than our fair share of misfortunes, eh?"

Corrin didn't know whether to laugh or cry.

Amella kept talking. "And now we're deep in the Gloamwood and surrounded by trolls, and instead of trying to eat us like all the legends say they should be trying to do, the trolls are talking to us, because somehow, you convinced them to. No idea how, but you did. So here we are, all alive and together. By the stars, Corrin, that's an incredible thing. *You've done* incredible things."

Amella paused for effect, or perhaps to gather her next thought. Then, the arm around Corrin's shoulders tightened into a sideways embrace. Amella promised, "We'll get that miracle fruit of yours, too, and we'll bring it back to Oddment. We'll stop that plague, and Death herself will throw up her hands and say, 'You win.' And then some bard'll write a song about the girl who stopped the celestial scythe, and meanwhile you'll get to chase your brothers all over Oddment, study your medicine, and pet the village cats to your heart's content. And perhaps you'll decide one day you want to go on adventures again, except this time Death will leave you well alone, because she's already thrown enough peril at you to last a lifetime."

Tenno nodded. Junior cooed, a soft query with an up-tilt at the end.

Corrin took a heaving, shuddery breath and hiccuped.

The Dono, who had waited and watched them this entire time, huffed, as if greatly put-upon by the water that leaked out of Corrin's eyes and the sniffles she couldn't quite stifle, or perhaps (and more likely) by how long Amella had spoken in a language that they could only half grasp. "What this?" they rumbled, and gestured to the tear streaks on her face. "Corrin be sick? Eyen ikik?"

"M'fine." Corrin tilted her head back to meet the Dono's eyes, which were bright and round like polished coins. Rakar had lost patience and wandered off somewhere, but Makur had stayed nearby; they watched her with a round-eyed expression similar to the Dono's. So Corrin explained, for both their benefit, "The eye water doesn't mean I'm sick. It just means..." She paused, searching for the words to say this in a way the trolls would understand. "It happens to wyrmen sometimes because of feelings. Angry, sad, happy, scared, and tired, if the feelings too much, they be water and come out of our eyens. Like this." She pointed to her cheeks, which were thankfully drying by now. "I'm okay. Not hurt. But I'm tired. Also scared. I need to know the krrkin won't hurt my wyrman kin."

"Krrkin no hurt Corrin kin," promised the Dono. "Det, Corrin kin no hurt krr. No make danger."

"We'll be good guests. We go soon, anyway. I rest with wyrkin, eat, maybe, then leave."

Makur scuffed the ground with their foot and screwed up their face with displeasure.

The Dono merely looked curious. "Hrr. Where you go?"

"I need to find the Tree of Life. It has fruit..." And slowly, with carefully chosen words and gestures, Corrin explained where she had come from and why she needed the fruit from the Tree of Life. The Dono listened intently as she described her homeland and her people, as her hands shaped the ruins and ticked off her family members. She described the sickness as best she could, miming the symptoms and all the remedies she tried, and then explained that her people had a wise healer, and that the healer had sent her out here. She told the Dono that a "bad wyrman" had come after them, that she'd been separated from her friends... and then, well, she'd run into Makur, and the Dono knew what happened after that. "And now I'm here," she finished, "and I need to keep going. I know it's dangerous. Makur told me, Tree of Life is deep danger. But if I don't find that fruit, I can't heal them."

"Und Corrin is healer," said the Dono. They leaned heavily on their staff and nodded to themselves. "Yus. Is har, no have power, no ken help. Lif Tree softseed have power. We krrkin have stories. Det, Makur grok truth, be danger. Will show you. Come wid me." They abruptly turned and lumbered off, pausing just long enough to make sure Corrin was still there. She was; she'd gotten to her feet, but she hadn't moved, uncertain of what the Dono wanted from her. The Dono huffed. "Come wid me," they repeated. "I show you stories. You grekka truth Makur know, truth krrkin know. Is impurrent." They swiped the air with their staff, then stomped off into the undergrowth.

Makur jerked their head as if to say, *Come on,* and followed the Dono.

Corrin took a deep breath and willed her weary feet forward. Amella and Tenno followed at her heels.

CHAPTER TWENTY

The Trolls' Tale

The walk seemed arduous to Corrin; they clambered over roots and up hills, and Makur snarled at strange creatures in the undergrowth thrice. Her skin was sticky with sweat by the end of it. But Amella and Tenno scarcely seemed to feel the distance, and timewise, it didn't seem that long. Perhaps, if Corrin had had a moment longer to wonder about her fatigue, she would have also noticed that her fingertips were cold and her face flushed, and she would have begun to worry. But instead, she was distracted when the Dono stopped short.

They pointed at a dais and a series of stone columns in the middle of a clearing and said, "Stories be scribble there."

Amella said quietly, "I'll be starred." A pause. "Seems out of place, though, doesn't it?"

Corrin tried to look at it the way Amella did. She saw rocks too evenly shaped to be hewn by nature, and exposed ground that someone had to have cleared on purpose, because it went from soil to tangles of undergrowth in a single footstep. The columns and the dais were weatherbeaten, but someone had kept the moss and vines at bay —the trolls, Corrin guessed. Pictographs looped around the columns, painted on with deep earthy hues of red, blue, and purple. They were vivid, even though the rock underneath was worn.

"Come," said the Dono. They took Corrin's hand and guided her to one of the stone columns. "Usen eyen. Story is impurrent. Grekka scribble?"

"I don't know. Let me look..."

Now that she could see them up close, it was clear that some of them had been redone. Some looked more faded than others, as if they'd been sitting there for decades; others looked like they could have been painted yesterday. She could see, too, where old, faded lines peeked out from underneath the new, as if the artist's brush (or finger? claw?) had wavered.

Subconsciously, Corrin reached up and touched her fingertips to the writing, the way she did sometimes when Bathilda gave her an old medical tome to read. She'd always liked to imagine the person who, at some point, had picked up a quill and a bottle of ink, who'd noted whatever knowledge they'd gained so it would outlive them. She would imagine hands scrawling letters across a blank page—sometimes large, sometimes small, but always deft, capable of blending herbs and stitching people back together. It was harder to imagine trolls doing the same; their paws were large and thick, and their claws seemed like they would get in the way. Even so, maybe they'd painted with the pad of one digit, or maybe they'd whittled a stick and held it sideways in their fist. Corrin remembered she used to write like that when she was first learning how…

But she'd never written in pictograms.

Even the most ancient books in Bathilda's library mostly had phonetic runes, with the rare pictograph sprinkled in—but nothing like this. It was interesting, she thought, that spoken trolltongue was so close to Staltish while their written languages were completely different. Corrin studied the pictograms curiously, walking around the column, noting which ones reoccurred. She could sort of tell what some of them were. Or guess, at least. Tree, troll, probable human (stick figure wielding pointy triangle), round shapes that might have been fruit, and a vague, blobby shape wielding a sickle, or something like it, which made her think of Death… But others stumped her. They were too simplified and abstracted—or else, perhaps, represented something that was highly abstract to begin with.

Corrin frowned. "Um. I think… I need help to grekka."

The Dono rumbled gently. "Be fikah. I help."

"Thank you very much." She pointed to several of the recurring pictograms in turn. "Lif Tree, krr, wyrman, fruit—I mean, softseed… Death? End lif?"

"Yus, yus, yus, yus, no." The Dono tapped the sickle wielder with one claw. "Punula. No end lif. Ikik end lif." They pointed to a pictogram of a being hunched over, surrounded by wavy lines. "Rahrg end lif." Another, more complex pictogram: a claw tearing jagged streaks in the air. "Det, Punula help. When lif end, und when krr sleep und see things…" The Dono paused, peering around the column, then pointed to a different symbol. A jagged shape like a rift or a tear, with two lines running through it. "Punala open—" they said a few words that Corrin didn't understand, then saw her expression, stopped, and amended, "Place. Open place. See other place."

Corrin blinked. "Punula... bridges realms? And sleeping and seeing things... Dreams? You believe—oh, that's interesting." It sounded like the trolls' Punula was roughly analogous to the humans' Death, guiding spirits to another realm. Except Punula didn't end lives, just took care of them after they ended, and had a connection to dreams that Death lacked—or, at least, lacked in the tales Corrin had been told back home. "Wyrman, um, I haven't met anyone who grek—who grek sleep place is real place."

"No grek? Inresting." The Dono bared their teeth in a smile. "Punula is good story. Det, less purrent now." The Dono nudged her hand to the top of the column. "Try grekka *this* story. Iffen no grekka scribble, asuk."

"Okay. Danku." And so, Corrin set about learning to read a new language. She focused on learning the most commonly recurring pictograms first. Basic vocabulary, at least for this story. If she had the most common building blocks, she could use that context to intuit the other ones and start guessing at the approximate meaning of sentences. She named the pictograms aloud, sometimes struggling to translate the human word to the troll word, and the Dono either confirmed or kindly corrected her.

Then Corrin started looking at the sequences together. Grasping greater meanings, or approximations or summaries of them, at least.

"Nurwood, sky, and underground were—" She held her hands away from each other. "Separate."

"Yus."

"Wyrmen in sky. Krr underground. Punula and Life Tree in forest."

"Yus."

"Punula make holes for tree, so roots go deep and branches high, and Life Tree grows big. Krr, wyrman enter Nurwood through holes."

"Yus. Good."

Corrin felt like she was missing a lot of the finer details, but the Dono was encouraging her to move along, so she did. Maybe it wasn't important that she got all the finer details, though. She just needed to understand enough. Understand the danger the Dono spoke of. "Tree grows softseed. Wyrmen and krr eat it. Eat it all, rahrg each other. Wyrman, um... Mean? Make traps?"

"Yus." The Dono patted Corrin's shoulder. "Det, Corrin be kind, I grekka. Corrin be krr bidum."

"That's good," said Corrin awkwardly. "I'm glad we're friends. Bidum. Even though the story wyrmen aren't nice. Um. Anyway. Then, one day..." Corrin paused on a depiction of a round-bodied creature with a curlicue tail and exaggerated fangs. She read ahead, grimaced, then continued. "One day, the Churikin come through the hole in the sky and—and start biting everyone."

"Yus," said the Dono solemnly.

"Everyone gets really sick. They die. End lif. So many wyrmen die, they leave the Nurwood. Krr die slower, and stay."

"Yus."

"Lif Tree... eat bodies of krr? Be sad? And Punula be sad?"

"Yus."

"Starts growing more softseed again. Then, Punula... does something. To the Churikin. Grok?"

"Yus."

"Churikin start eating softseed. Stop biting krr. Krr... no eat softseed anymore. Don't live at Life Tree. But when lif end, krr body go to Life Tree." Corrin was crouching, now, running her hands over the pictographs at the base. The end of the story. The lesson in the tale. "What you're saying is... what this story is saying... is that the Life Tree lets Churikin eat its softseeds, so they're not hungry and don't bite krr, or anyone else. But if the Churikin don't have enough softseeds, they will start biting again, make everyone ikik."

"Yus." The Dono placed a paw on her shoulder and turned her to face them. Their expression was solemn. "You grekka now. Is danger, Lif Tree. Must eat softseed. Det, no much. Tree need much softseed, peacekeep Churikin. Take only softseed Corrin need, help Corrin-kin. No more."

"I grekka," she confirmed. Then she asked, "The krrkin make this, yus?"

"Yus." The Dono released her. "More stories too. Inresting, learn sometime. Det, you need softseed, yus? Go soon." The Dono pointed between two trees. At first, it seemed as if that direction held more wild undergrowth, like the rest of the forest; but if Corrin looked closer, she could see the beginnings of a narrow path. It was the kind of path paved by footsteps, and nothing else.

"Yes," Corrin said. She reached up and touched the Dono's shoulder, echoing their gesture from moments before. "Thank you."

The Dono's lips curled into a yellow-toothed smile, and they rumbled gently.

Corrin went over to Amella and Tenno, who had gone up to a different column and were inspecting it curiously. They listened intently as she relayed what she had learned. She explained that the Churikin had something dangerous in their mouths, maybe venom or maybe a different kind of sickness, and that the fruit warded it off somehow; and that the trolls stayed away and didn't eat the fruit themselves most of the time, because the bounty kept the Churikin from wandering to other parts of the forest and biting them. Corrin pointed out the path, and she concluded with, "If you get bitten, you need to eat the fruit too."

Amella frowned. "Sounds like this fruit fights the Churikins' disease, but what if it doesn't fight ours?"

Amella's question raised a prickle of doubt in Corrin. On the one hand, Bathilda had seemed so certain that the fruit would cure Oddment. It had worked for her in Gailstone, after all. Something about that account still niggled at Corrin—Gailstone's ruins had seemed older than any living human should be, even Bathilda—but she brushed it aside. Bathilda's understanding of medicine and the world ran deep, and she always explained it, always encouraged Corrin to seek it. Corrin trusted Bathilda. On the other hand, Amella raised a valid point: sometimes a potion that banished one illness did nothing for another. What if Bathilda was wrong? What if the fruit's curative properties didn't apply as widely as she'd thought? What if the illness Gailstone had caught was enough like the Churikins' disease, but Oddment's was too different? What if, after all this effort and peril and loss, the fruit didn't save them?

But this was Corrin's last hope. And hope was better than nothing.

"If it doesn't work, then it'll be terrible," said Corrin honestly. "But Bathilda thinks this fruit will help us, and I'll believe in her 'til I can't anymore. We have to try." Corrin turned to the Dono. "I go to krrkin village, get my things, my pack, and after that I leave, find Tree of Life."

The Dono rumbled their affirmation.

Makur growled unhappily, but they didn't protest with words.

Corrin turned to head back. But as she did so, the world tilted and spun. Her vision spotted and blotched around the edges. Corrin had just enough wherewithal to drop to her knee and think, *Well this isn't good,* before her vision went entirely.

She was dimly aware of loud voices and a hand on her shoulder, and of the ground beneath her feet. She focused on her breathing, told herself to *inhale, exhale, head down, inhale, exhale.* Gradually the light came back, then colors and shapes. Features came into focus: dark eyes, dark skin, short-shorn hair, a sharp jawline, puzzle pieces that joined together bit by bit until they became Amella. A worried-looking Amella, at that.

"You with me?" she asked.

"Yes," said Corrin. Her own voice sounded distant. She took another deep breath. She didn't try to stand up yet because she still felt weak and lightheaded, but she tried to think, to diagnose herself: why had she fainted? Not hunger; she'd eaten seared meats from the festival aplenty last night, despite her lack of appetite. Perhaps it was dehydration. That would be an easy fix, since the trolls' stream water was clear and good to drink. Corrin breathed again, mentally checking for other signs—and realized that her face felt hot, her hands cold. This... No, this wasn't just dehydration. This was sickness. And the symptoms seemed like...

The realization hit her like a physical blow.

This is what happened to my da. And Petuni. And the others back in Oddment. This is how the plague starts manifesting.

"I think we should go," she said, and tried to will her weakness away so she could move. Unfortunately, it didn't work.

Trolltongue rumbled nearby, low and too quick for her to understand.

"Aye," Amella agreed, "we should go, get you lying down somewhere. Tenno, carry her for me, will you?"

Tenno slid one arm behind Corrin's back and the other under her knees and picked her up as easily as Corrin might've lifted a child. She felt a peculiar sense of déjà vu. This was how they first met, wasn't it? Her half-conscious and him carrying her up a hill, and up stairs, and into a bed. The ground was far away, but Tenno's arms were thick and sturdy, his hold secure. He felt like comfort. "We're taking you back to the village," he said to her. He sounded too kind, like how Corrin would when she tried to reassure the dangerously ill.

Or maybe that was her projecting. She knew better than many would in her position, after all, just how sick she was.

CHAPTER TWENTY-ONE

Last Legs

Back at the village, they set Corrin down by the stream. Makur hovered nearby and growled at the other trolls if they came too close (with the exception of the Dono), and Amella refilled her canteen and made sure she drank. The Dono lumbered off and came back with a pawful of sharp-smelling herbs, which bore a vague resemblance to a kind Corrin would use if she needed to stay up for a long time. Bathilda probably would've scolded her for accepting a strange plant so readily, but she did, and it helped. Her mind worked a little faster. Some of her strength came back, and soon she was sitting up and asking for her pack, and if anyone had any food because at this point she was feeling hungry, though perhaps not as hungry as she should have felt. When Corrin's (much battered and lightened) pack landed in her lap, she dug through it for her cloak and swaddled herself in the thick fabric.

"We need to go," Corrin said again, more clearly this time. "To the Tree. M'sick."

"We've gathered that much," said Amella dryly. "Look, I don't think you should be trying to move anywhere. How about we stay for a while, or you ask one of us to go to the Tree and come back?"

Corrin shook her head. "Need the fruit."

"Okay, but I can *get* the fruit."

"S'faster if I go." Corrin mentally braced herself and gathered her feet under her, and slowly, she stood up. It was like someone had tied sandbags to her bones. It was terrible. This was the most exhausted she'd ever felt in her life. Was this what her da and the others had felt? Had the onset been so quick and sudden for them? But chances were good that she'd caught the illness before she left on this quest, from her patients, so it must have been inside of her for a while. Maybe the sickness festered and bided its time until it saw the opportune moment to strike, or maybe it just took a while for the body to realize that something was wrong. If that was the case, then she wanted to eat the fruit sooner rather than later. She had to get strong again quickly, so she could bring it back to Oddment.

But standing was so difficult.

She wished she could borrow the Dono's staff.

Corrin shook her head (which also took more effort than it should have) and took a wobbly step.

Tenno said, "I don't think that's a good—"

"I help," interrupted Makur, and swooped in before anyone could protest. They grabbed Corrin by the waist and plucked her off the ground, lifting her dizzyingly fast. Next she knew, she was on Makur's shoulders, her legs draped over their chest.

Corrin clung instinctively, nestling her fingers deep in the ruff of fur around their neck and hooking one foot over the other. She felt like a small child on a parent's shoulders, except she wasn't riding on her da's shoulders, she was riding on Makur. On a troll. She hadn't ever imagined that she'd ride a troll. (Or talk to one. Or be one's guest.) If Corrin weren't so tired, perhaps she would have felt excited, or nervous, or at least a smidgeon apprehensive. As it was, all she felt was faint surprise, and all she thought was, *Oh. This is surprisingly comfy. So soft.*

"Corrin no ken walk," Makur said, addressing the Dono, Amella, and Tenno. "I walk for Corrin. Small, easy help."

Amella looked wary and had a hand on the hilt of her sword, and Tenno, while less overtly preparing for trouble, seemed uncertain about this arrangement. As for the Dono... Expressions flickered across their face that were too subtle and quick for Corrin to grasp. Didn't help that their face was covered in fur.

"Are you alright up there?" asked Tenno. He had to tilt his head back to meet Corrin's eyes, now, which was fascinating thing to witness. It made her feel tall. *Being tall is fun,* she decided, and then realized she said that aloud when Tenno's eyes crinkled with mirth. "Yes," he said, his voice shaking slightly, "it is fun sometimes. And now I think I know how you feel whenever you talk to me."

Corrin "mhm"'d and rested her chin on the crown of Makur's head. Fur tickled her nose.

Amella grabbed Corrin's pack and slung it over one shoulder.

"Okay. This is a strange solution, but if it gets you to the cure you need, I'll take it. Let's go."

"Yus," agreed Makur. "We go now."

The Dono growled and thumped their staff against the ground. "Okay," they said. "I grekka. Det, travel wary, is danger. No be bit by Churikin. If be bit, eat softseed. Come home no ikik, Makur. I want you have much liftime."

"Yus," said Makur solemnly. "I grekka."

And then they shifted, and the whole world swayed and turned. Corrin was no longer looking at the Dono or her human friends, though she could hear their footsteps, crunching twigs and fallen leaves behind her. Makur led the way back (and it seemed much faster this time) to the stone clearing with the pillars and the dais, and then onward to the ancient path that was nearly hidden in the undergrowth. From there, they walked for a long time. Or, at least, Corrin thought it was a long time. Maybe. Her sense of time felt slippery and vague.

The steady back-and-forth rhythm of Makur's stride lulled Corrin into the hazy boundary between waking and sleeping. She caught snatches of Amella and Tenno murmuring to each other, and of Makur rumbling something rough and curt. Visions of trees and deep shadows were all around her when she was awake and followed her into dreamland when she dozed off, and sometimes, she wasn't sure of the difference. Sometimes, it seemed like the tree branches were reaching for her, or like the vines that dangled down wanted to curl around her arm or her fingers and steal her from Makur's back. Sometimes, she saw glowing eyes and strange faces watching her from the canopy or the underbrush.

There was a dark greyish scaly thing with a long snout, which turned and scurried away with a hiss when Makur growled at it; and there was a pair of bright orange eyes that burned like flames from the shadows, but when Corrin blinked and looked again, trying to focus, they were gone. Small furry creatures with dappled golden coats flitted across their path. But when she went to mumble in Makur's ear about them, they were gone, and Makur murmured to her, "Sleep." Butterflies with iridescent wings grouped around a bush of blood-red berries. A moth with feathery antennae and an eye pattern on its wings hovered near a flower with thorny, purple petals. The flower lunged and snapped shut, missing the moth by a hair's breadth.

She knew she was awake for the carnivorous plant, because when she pointed to it and asked, "What's that?" Makur had named both the plant and the moth in trolltongue. The plant was a "rabluchur." The moth was a sound that made Corrin think of moonlight.

She buried her face in Makur's fur and rested for a while. When she woke up, she was more awake and energized than she'd felt since the fainting spell, but it was dark.

She was lying on the ground by a flower patch that smelled like honey, which probably meant it was a variant of honeysuckle. Makur sat next to her, watching her with bright orange eyes that were round with worry, and Tenno and Amella were rolling out their cloaks by her feet. It was very humid. Water had beaded on her skin, cool and less sticky than sweat, and when she sat up and reached out to touch Makur's arm, she felt it in their fur, too. The closest she'd ever felt to this was an early summer morning, gathering toadstools near a boggy patch while the air was thick with mist.

It was misty now, she realized. It wasn't just nighttime making everything harder to see; the mist blurred the edges of things.

"Are we close?" Corrin asked.

"Yus," said Makur, and brushed the top of her head with their paw. Their claws worked lightly through her ponytail, tugging out snarls. Corrin grimaced. The tugging hurt a little. It reminded her of her mother's hurried combing, when she rushed to get a far younger Corrin cleaned up and tidy before the solstice festival.

She asked, "Why did we stop?"

It was Amella who answered. "I'm sorry, but we need to rest. Badly. We've been going all day." She paused. Insects chirped and hummed in the background. Corrin could just make out her silhouette, the blurred boundary where her steady shoulders and her bent knee ended. "Are you feeling any better?"

Corrin gathered her feet under her and stood, interrupting Makur's fussing. She could carry herself alright, now, and she could take a step or two without wobbling, but she still felt tired. And even though the night air was warm, and her face flushed with fever, she felt shivery and cold on the inside. She also felt an aching hollowness in her gut. She mentally weighed all of this against how she had felt before she'd had a chance to rest, and she decided it was an improvement. "A bit," she said, and sat back down. Makur instantly resumed the head petting and hair combing. "I can walk, and I feel like I could eat something."

"That's good." Amella rummaged in her pack for a moment, then passed Corrin something small and hard. "Have a travel biscuit. Sorry it's not more."

"S'okay. Thank you." Corrin nibbled on the biscuit. It was hard and tasteless, but it curbed her hunger. She listened to Tenno and Amella argue about who would take first watch. (Tenno insisted, gallant as ever, that it was his duty as a guard to see to their wellbeing. Amella was having none of this, though. "You won't wake me up for my shift," she accused him mutinously. "You'll let me sleep until morning and then not get any yourself.") Makur stopped fiddling with Corrin's hair, opting instead to wrap their thick, furry arm around her shoulders and draw her in close to their side. Corrin didn't protest. Trolls, provided they weren't trying to bite your head off, made for comfy pillows.

But before she could drift off to sleep again, she saw something enormous shift in the shadows. Something with reflective pupils that caught the light, and with long fur or spines or quills bristling across its back, though which, she couldn't tell. Corrin knew it was real, had to be, because when she tugged on Makur's chest fur and pointed, she could feel Makur stiffen, muscles bunching and coiling.

"Is grokkachur," growled Makur, their grip growing uncomfortably snug. "Is danger."

Tenno and Amella both startled, and Corrin heard the whisper of swords drawn.

The creature stepped closer. Corrin could tell that it had a tail, now, and four legs with paws like a cat, if a cat were a thousand times the size a cat should be. Its head was massive, even compared to the rest of it, but also cat-shaped. It was striped—like a wasp or honeybee, maybe, though she couldn't tell the color of the lighter stripes in the gloom. It stopped several paces away. Its tail flicked. Its pupils flashed green. And then it spoke, not in the vague noises of an everyday animal or even in a complex foreign language, but in polished Staltish.

"You have terrible kin," groused the strange beast. "Absolutely terrible, no appreciation for riddles at all."

It's talking, thought Corrin numbly. *But I have no idea what it's talking about.*

Makur rumbled a wordless warning.

Amella still had her sword out, but inexplicably, she was relaxing; and even more inexplicably, Tenno was sheathing his. "Beg your pardon," he said politely, "but what kin?"

The beast huffed and sat on its haunches. "Your kin who are searching for you. They knew you by name. There were several of them, reeking of fire and sweat and blood. Incredibly rude, they were." It tipped its head to one side and fixed its gaze on Tenno, who stood still as stone, while Amella swore beside him. Corrin felt lost and a bit irritated. Clearly whatever it had said meant something to Tenno and Amella, and clearly, it knew them, but the puzzle pieces clacked uselessly in her head; she felt like she was missing some, or perhaps she just couldn't put them together properly because she was tired and sick, and the sickness was fogging her mind… But the beast was still speaking. Its nose wrinkled in distaste as it continued: "I thought they might be like you, you know. Sensible humans with a healthy respect for a Riddle Beast, obliging, with clever little minds to provide some entertainment. But they were nothing like you. They tried to threaten information out of me, those hooligans."

So it's—they're?—a Riddle Beast, Corrin thought, and a puzzle piece clicked into place. Amella and Tenno had told her they'd met one, hadn't they? This must be the one. And the Riddle Beast had said other people were looking for them, aggressive people who smelled like blood… Could it be Turner? Could he be madder and braver than Amella had predicted? Or could it be the bandits? They had tracked her to Mount Cauldra, after all, and aggressive and bloodstained sounded about right for them.

Knowing her luck, it was probably the bandits.

The Riddle Beast's gaze alighted upon Corrin, half hidden though she was by Makur's protective hold, and their pupils dilated with interest. "Is that little one the friend you were looking for? And what's the troll doing with you? I could grant you another boon, perhaps, and take care of it for you. In return for another riddle game."

Makur snarled.

"That's not necessary," said Tenno quickly. "The troll's with us. Yes, the third human is the friend we were looking for, so thank you again for pointing us in the right direction. But please, could you tell us more about the people who were coming after us? How many were there? What exactly did they look like?"

"Like most humans, they were ugly creatures with borrowed hides. There were… hrm. Six, perhaps? Seven? Enough to be a bother, however many there were. The leader was a tall she-human in a cloak, and two of her deputies were pointy-featured, with pale hair. The leader was not one for bargains. She took me for a mindless monster at first, then thought she could coerce answers out of me. What a fool." The Riddle Beast paused. They licked their paw, slowly, deliberately, their tongue rasping over fur. "You're lucky that I like you, you know. I wouldn't have bothered to find you and warn you otherwise. It would have been more entertaining to sit back and watch, see if the interlopers could catch you unawares. They're no friends of yours, is that correct? They don't seem the sort."

No, Corrin silently agreed, her heart sinking into her stomach, the Bandit King was not someone she would call a friend. She doubted any sane person would call the Bandit King a friend.

And it had to be her. The description fit too well.

"Yeah, not the sort," said Amella. "You said they're after us?"

"Yes."

"Dragon spit. They're headed this way?"

"A day behind, at a human's pace. That's assuming the Gloamwood doesn't devour or disorient them." The Riddle Beast growled with discontent. "Their stupid leader is fierce, unfortunately, and quick with her blade, so they might find their way to you after all."

"Please tell me you didn't tell them anything." Tenno's voice was strained.

"Of course I didn't. I ran aw—ah, that is to say, I decided they weren't worth the trouble of dismembering, and I left them to flounder on their own."

"I guess you wouldn't be willing to come with us, would you?"

"No. This is your problem, not mine." The Riddle Beast's eyes flashed, and they shifted their attention to Corrin again. Their lips curled back, baring teeth longer than her fingers. Corrin's breath caught, and her heart stuttered with an instinctive fear. She imagined this was how mice felt if they saw Tiptoes coming after them. "You reek of deadly sickness, small one. Anyone who comes near you risks becoming contaminated."

She gulped. "My name's Corrin. And I'm looking for the Tree of Life."

The Riddle Beast shuddered so violently that their spines rattled. "Yet another reason for me to stay away from you. That place is a curse."

"But it has a cure."

"Only the desperate go after that cure."

Corrin forced herself to sit straighter and look the Riddle Beast in the eye. "Well, by my reckoning I'm pretty desperate."

"Yes, I suppose you are." The Riddle Beast studied them all for a moment, their tail swishing, their pupils luminous and eerie. Corrin couldn't help but think the stories hadn't done them justice. They hadn't conveyed how massive they were, or how deep their voice was, or how polished and selfish-silvery their words were. "This is where I say good-bye, then. Try not to get pounced on, will you?" And in a blur of moving shadow and the *hsssssss*-crackle of disturbed undergrowth, the Riddle Beast vanished.

"Dammit," said Amella, with feeling. "I bet it could've swiped the Bandit King's head off if it weren't such a scaredy cat."

They all slept in shifts. Even Corrin was up part of the night, though technically she wasn't supposed to help keep watch, sick as she was and convinced as the others were that she should sleep. The trouble was she couldn't sleep, not for long, so she ended up staying awake with Makur. She saw the nighttime darkness thin out and the first greenish gold dapples of sunlight slip through the canopy. She listened to Makur's steady breathing, and to her own, which was lighter and shallower and had a slight rasp to it. The rasp was troubling. It meant the illness had begun to interfere with her respiratory tract. And soon after Petuni had started wheezing, she'd been bedridden. Corrin had to get to the fruit, quickly, and then back to Oddment, and to Bathilda, and her mortar and pestle and tools for medicine-making—before Petuni's breath stuttered out, before her da's hands went cold, before the plague took her mum and her brothers and smothered the sparks of Bathilda's seemingly never-ending vitality.

Makur's eyes grew narrower and narrower, and at the break of dawn they slid shut. But they snapped open a moment later.

"We go?" Corrin asked Makur quietly.

"Hrr... yus."

And so they woke the others and carried on. Corrin walked for what seemed like an awfully short time before she tired, and Makur hefted her onto their shoulders again. She rested her chin on Makur's head and watched as the Gloamwood's trees grew fatter and taller, and the light fainter. The birdsong faded away. The underbrush scarcely rustled. Even the cicadas and crickets didn't buzz here. But she could swear she saw flickers of movement in the trees and a glimpse of a thin brown tail. The farther they went, the more Corrin couldn't shake the feeling that she was being watched.

The trees grew thicker still, and the space between their mighty trunks broader. At last, they gave way to a vast space carpeted with rolling green moss, peppered with patches of peat-bog and wavering tendrils of steam. It was the sort of steam Corrin would expect to see from a brewing cauldron of medicine. Except there were no cauldrons here, only holes in the earth filled with roiling water. There were funny brown ridges too, thick around as a troll and nearly as tall, with a rough texture like bark—in fact, it *was* bark…

And if she traced one of the bark-covered ridges back through the clouds of steam, it led to a tree trunk. It was thicker than the watchtower back on the peninsula; broader than the inn back in Miritown; massive enough, it seemed, to house a village. And if Corrin looked up, and up, and *up*, that trunk grew into branches that bowed under the weight of hundreds of thousands of leaves, vibrant green and star-shaped. Since she could see their shape so well from all the way down here, they had to be large, the size of both her spread hands at least. Purple fruit nestled among the leaves, half hidden, as if someone had tucked them away in the hopes that no one could find them.

She imagined the goddess Death, a shadow in the folds of her cloak with a gleaming sickle blade in hand, drifting among the leaves and adjusting them so that they better hid her fruit. Her fingertips would be smoky black tendrils that took and lost shape at will, if one were to go by the stories.

Actual hands, dark but small and decidedly solid, darted out from a cluster of leaves and plucked one of the fruits. A tiny head popped up. It was flat-faced and had round, gleaming eyes that were yellow as egg yolk, and its mouth stretched to encompass the entire fruit as the creature shoved it into its mouth. As Corrin watched, bewildered, more heads appeared to stare curiously at them. Dozens of heads. Dozens of pairs of eyes. The air filled with chatter.

Corrin thought, *Those must be the Churikin.* Then: *For critters with plague-causing bites, they're awfully cute.*

Not that their bites could hurt her anyway, not more than bites from any other creature of their size, at least. Not when she was already sick. They could hurt her friends, though. Her friends would need to stay back. Then again, they might already be infected, might need to eat the fruit themselves. What if they caught the plague from her by traveling with her, resting with her, staying on a ship with her in close quarters? What if the illness had gotten into Amella even earlier, back in Oddment? What if it was incubating, waiting for a moment of weakness to sink its teeth in?

"Churikin," growled Makur. "Churikin be danger."

"Yus," Corrin agreed. "Det, I'm already sick. Bites no hurt me no more. I go."

Makur's shoulders turned rigid beneath her, but they did not stop her from unhooking her legs from around their neck, or from swinging and sliding gently off. Their ears folded back as Corrin stepped around to stand in front of them. Makur watched her worriedly, their eyes wide and uncertain.

Corrin willed her tired self to be steady and mustered a faint smile. "You stay here for a bit, okay?"

"Why?" whined Makur.

"What do you mean, stay here?" demanded Amella.

Corrin turned to her. "You aren't sick yet. Hopefully. Besides, maybe I'm small enough that the Churikin won't mind me too much. You, though—" and she grinned, amusement bubbling up inside of her —"you're terrifying."

"Corrin. Look around. Have you noticed that *no other animals live here?* Don't you think there's a reason for that?"

"Pretty sure there's a bug or two, if you look closely enough."

"Not funny."

Silently, she thought, *Huh, well, I thought it was. S'pose you can't humor everybody.*

Tenno interrupted. "Corrin, why don't I try sending Junior up? She's quick, and she can fly—augh!"

Junior had nipped his ear. She chattered anxiously, pulling her head in like a turtle. Maybe the Churikins had dredged up a primal fear that ran deep, deeper than even wolves or bears or dragons could incite. Maybe Junior had used up all her courage on the dragon, and now it was taking her last reserves just to stay with them in this dark forest, with its thick canopy and warm, damp air that clung to her feathers. Or maybe she would have a harder time outmaneuvering hundreds of small, agile tree-climbers among branches than she had a giant beast who breathed her favorite element in a vast chamber, and she knew it.

In any case, she clearly wasn't willing to fly up there.

Tenno deflated and flattened her crest feathers with his finger. He petted her wings and murmured soothingly. Gradually, she calmed down, but she still hunched low, like she meant to glue herself to his shoulder and never let go. "I can't force her to go," he said apologetically. "And since I can't force you to not go, please, take this." He stepped forward and unfastened something long, thin, and wrapped in leather from his belt.

Befuddled, Corrin nonetheless took the bundle and unwrapped it. A leather grip peeked out, and then a hint of glinting steel, a sharpened edge. It was that old sword she'd found on Turner's ship. She still had its empty sheath belted at her waist; she'd simply forgotten it was there, what with her loss of the weapon upon encountering Makur, and then the monstrous snake, and the troll village and her introduction to the Dono, and the Wyddscatch brawl between Makur and Rakar, and her burgeoning fatigue, and her reuniting with Amella and Tenno, and then her illness. The sheath was light, scarcely noticeable without steel to weigh it down.

"I've been meaning to give this back to you. I think you dropped it in your struggle with the troll."

"Their name's Makur," Corrin corrected as she slid the sword into its sheath. "Thank you."

"Be careful."

"I will." Corrin turned and started toward the tree. The mossy peat depressed under her weight, though she trod lightly, and she had to sidestep bubbling mud patches and roiling pits full of water. She could feel the heat radiating up from the ground and through the soles of her boots. The steam condensed and beaded on her skin. She stayed between two roots that hemmed her in on either side like low bumpy walls. She peered over them to see if the ground on the other side looked any different, if it held anything interesting. It didn't, and Corrin didn't feel much inclined to clamber over if it wouldn't do her any good.

She scanned the ground around her for fallen fruit. If she could find some that weren't spoiled, she wouldn't have to scale that massive tree, nor risk bothering the Churikin up in the canopy, where they'd be far more mobile than Corrin was. But there were no fallen fruit, not even rotten ones. Either the Churikin had picked the ground clean, or they ate the fruit before it had the chance to fall. Perhaps that was why there was only the one Tree of Life and not an entire grove of them. Or perhaps not. Perhaps this tree had simply grown too big first and there wasn't room in this boggy patch for another one; and perhaps this type of plant was adapted specifically for this kind of soil, squishy and warm with a certain nutrient profile, and couldn't grow anywhere else.

Corrin stopped at the base of the trunk. This close, it loomed over her like an insurmountable wall. *Nothing for it,* she told herself firmly, and heaved herself up onto the nearest root.

And then she was stuck.

Back in Oddment, she would scale the walls by using the vines that blanketed them. Failing that, she'd always find some hole, a protruding stone brick, or crevices and gaps where she could grab a hold or plant her toes. She'd climbed plenty of fat trees back home, too, but there was always some trick she could use to make up for her lack of claws or climbing feet. Even if there wasn't a low branch for her to grab or a helpful slant in the trunk, she'd be able to get her arms and legs halfway around it and shimmy up, her stomach close to the bark. But the Tree of Life had no vines and no slants, and certainly no low-hanging branches, and it wouldn't have crevices to dig her fingers into like a ruined stone wall. Corrin placed her hand on the bark and felt for anything she could use. It was rough, but not uneven enough for her to grab ahold of anything.

She reached into her pack and fished out a coil of rope, gauging its length, trying to figure out if she could use it. Perhaps if she looped it around the trunk in lieu of her legs, or if she fastened one end to a rock or a stick or something of the sort and flung it up to catch on the closest branch… but no, that wouldn't work either. Even the rope was too short to reach around, or to catch on a branch and still dangle all the way to the ground.

Corrin stepped back and frowned.

Another option would be to lob rocks at the tree branches until the fruit fell down. She had a funny feeling the Churikin wouldn't like that, though. They might even come after her, like a horde of giant, angry bees with teeth instead of stingers.

"Hrr," rumbled Makur from behind her—close behind her, so close that she could feel the warmth of their breath on the back of her neck. Apparently they'd decided her request for them to stay back was more of an advisory suggestion, and they had elected to ignore it. She turned to face them. Makur blinked slowly back at her and spoke. "Lif Tree is big. Corrin is small, no claws. No climb, yus?"

"Yus. I can't see a way to get up there."

"I help," said Makur decisively, and plucked Corrin by her waist, settling her securely onto their shoulders. Corrin locked her feet together and fisted her hands in the fur around their neck, clinging close to the back of their head. Makur dug their claws into the bark, piercing it as easily as needles did cloth, and pulled themself and Corrin upward. They were quick and sure for such a large creature, climbing paw and foot and paw and foot in a steady rhythm, and all of a sudden they were ten feet off the ground and stretches of bark were slipping toward them, past them, beneath them. The branches overhead grew more distinct, more detailed, and in another several heartbeats Corrin would be able to reach up and touch the leaves—

—but the Churikin swarmed down from the branches, numbering in the dozens and baring their tiny sharp teeth, chattering ominously. Before Corrin could react, before she even thought to draw her sword, Makur backpedaled. "Churikin," they growled, and scurried down the Tree of Life twice as quickly as they climbed. "Churikin," they said again, like a curse, as Corrin slid off their shoulders. Makur hugged her close, protectively, much like her mum and da used to do when she was small and upset over something or other, or when she'd been out wandering past twilight and worried them. "Bibbinhead Churikin be danger. Too many. Makur no climb tree, Corrin no climb tree. No climb, no climb. Danger."

"I need to get to that fruit somehow, though."

"No climb," said Makur adamantly.

Frustration roiled inside of her. She'd made it. She'd found the Tree of Life. The fruit was literally right over her head. And yet, it was out of reach. How, she wondered, had the trolls ever gotten their paws on it? They must've braved the hordes of Churikin, once. They must've braved the angry swarming and the bites, even though Makur wouldn't, even though Makur had scrambled back down with ears laid back and anxious growling at the first sign of trouble. Corrin wished she had Makur's claws and strength. She wasn't afraid of being bitten. She already knew she was a dead woman walking, and that her patients were too, if she didn't get to the fruit.

And then a voice spoke, a voice Corrin hadn't heard since the caverns of Mount Cauldra, and her heart stuttered with dread.

"I've finally found you, little runaway."

CHAPTER TWENTY-TWO

Downfall

Corrin forced herself to face the speaker.

The Bandit King stood atop a root, her mane of hair bedraggled and her face smudged with grime. Her cloak, once splendid, had tears in the fabric and mud splattered at ankle level. Her boots were so dirt-streaked that they looked like they were made of earth. A still-healing wound beneath a ripped sleeve mottled her arm a sickly pink-purple. But her eyes were sharp and clear and her shoulders thrown wide, and the steel of her sword glinted bright and ominous as she held it ready with one hand. The corners of her mouth were quirked up in amusement.

Corrin didn't understand what the Bandit King was laughing at.

"You couldn't hope to combat me, so you woke a dragon that could've killed us all," said the Bandit King, casual as someone talking about livestock or a ripe berry patch they found. "I'll have to admit, that takes a certain kind of ruthlessness. I wouldn't have expected it from a healer."

Corrin didn't say anything. She couldn't think of anything to say.

Four heads popped up behind the Bandit King, peering over the root. Two had ash blonde hair and pointy, sharp-edged faces. They seemed familiar; and when Corrin cast her mind back, she recalled a pair of siblings with odd names, making light of death and loss. Limerick and Verse. They'd said they were bards once. Corrin couldn't put names to the two others, but she had vague memories of their faces on the mountainside and in the caverns. They all looked as worn down as their leader, dirt-smudged and hollow-cheeked.

Five of them and four of us, Corrin mentally calculated, *and one of us is a troll and another of us is a guard, and the third of us is Amella. But the fourth of us is me, and I'm sick, and I'm about as useful in a fight as a fishbone on the best of days. And they were able to hunt us down.* She did not like what this was adding up to. Even so, she rested her hand on the hilt of her sword, curling her fingers around the worn leather.

"Corrin kin?" Makur asked, and pointed at the Bandit King.

"No," said Corrin quickly, "they're danger."

Makur bared their teeth and growled.

The Bandit King laughed. "That's right, Corrin. I'm dangerous." She leapt off the root, boots thudding heavily on the soil. "So you've allied yourself with those beasts, have you? Interesting. What did you do? Hold them at knifepoint? Use sleights of hand and make them think you were a goddess? Bribe them?"

"I asked nicely," Corrin said wryly. Which was, technically, not accurate. Makur had taken her captive of their own volition, but she hadn't left Makur to die when she'd had the chance, and she'd done the one thing she knew she could do: she'd healed them. And then they had unilaterally decided that Corrin was a friend and under their protection. Corrin had never asked, really, never requested that they come along, that they help her reach the Tree of Life. They'd just picked her up and said they would. But the spirit of her answer was true, in a way.

All she'd done was be kind.

Corrin said, "You could've done the same to me. Back when you found me in the tavern, I mean. Could've said you'd like to work together, that you'd like to have some of the fruit too. Could've meant it, maybe, and maybe I would've listened. Maybe you wouldn't have killed Vinny and no one would have died in the dragon's den." Corrin paused, then continued: "But you asked to take my map instead, and if I'd given it to you, you would've just absconded with it and never kept your promise. And if you'd thought to ask to come along, and if I'd let you, you would've stabbed us all in the back the moment we reached the Tree of Life. Isn't that so?"

The Bandit King inclined her head. "Even in your sheltered, backwoods naîveté, you were too cautious to make it that convenient for me."

Corrin was beyond the point of dread. Instead she felt a deep weariness, down to her bones. Part of it was the sickness, but another part—the heart of it—was from being hunted and chased and hunted again, from getting attacked and almost dying so many times, and from constantly having to watch her back, feeling like danger could be lurking in her shadow.

The worries that had followed her out of Oddment were enough on their own. The threat that the Bandit King had added, though, that was the worst. Because the threat wasn't necessary. Because if the Bandit King hadn't decided to be a murdering knave, so much pain and death could have been avoided.

"Why are you like this?" she asked the Bandit King tiredly. "Really, why? Why hurt all these people who wouldn't mean you any harm otherwise?"

For a heartbeat, Corrin thought she might have caught the Bandit King off her guard, might have seen a flicker of surprise cross her face. But a moment later, the Bandit King scoffed and asked, "Why not? Why share when I can conquer?"

Heavy footsteps approached Corrin from behind. She glanced back and saw Amella stomping toward her with a scowl. Tenno moved with her, harboring an expression that could have been carved from stone. Junior circled anxiously above them both.

The Bandit King held her free hand up in a fist.

Her lackeys leaped and scrambled over the root, drawing daggers and sickle blades. Makur roared and surged forward, lips curled back, fur bristling. Amella and Tenno moved to flank Corrin. Corrin drew her own weapon, but it felt so much heavier than she remembered, so slow—and everyone was moving so fast, steel clashing with steel, claws flailing. A blade lashed out at her. Corrin moved to block, heart jumping, thinking, *too slow too slow come on arm WORK*—but then Tenno was there, parrying the strike with a flick of his wrist. He stabbed, his reach long and his sword quick as a snake. The bandit crumpled.

"Yellow-bellied donkey manure for hearts," cursed Amella from beside her. She took a wild swing at Verse, who sprang back. Verse's brother, Limerick, darted forward to attack, but Amella switched focus in a heartbeat—she blocked him—her sword flashed, and he screeched in pain, stumbling back—Verse swore, and Amella was forcing her back again—

Makur roared with fury and pain. A figure sped past them, a blur of dark fabric and steel and blood, and a sword lashing out toward Amella's side, and Corrin's heart surged with terror—she forgot her fatigue, forgot every thought except *no* and *stop it, I have to stop it*—she lunged for the weapon-hand arm—

Her sword swung true and bit through flesh and bone, and the

Bandit King shouted in pain. The Bandit King's weapon glanced off Amella's side instead of piercing it, angled awry by Corrin's strike. Corrin breathed out and watched the Bandit King stagger. She readied herself to keep fighting, whatever it took to make them to leave her friends alone—

And then Tenno stabbed the Bandit King through the gut.

Adrenaline and fury sang through the Bandit King's veins as she swiped and ducked and lunged. Monstrous paws sailed over her head and past her, or clashed against the edge of her sword and came away dripping. And then her sword bit, and the trollbeast stumbled back—she saw an opening, a chance to slip past—and before her was that blasted trader, wielding her weapon like a fiend, pushing Verse back. The trader's side was exposed; she wasn't watching her back, wasn't guarding her periphery. A stab through that blind spot would take her down, put an end to all her irritating defiance and hamstringing scruples. That would leave the others open. The Bandit King would target the guardsman next, and then she'd take care of the healer, Corrin—that will-o-wisp of a lass with the soft, cowardly heart, who threw her luck to dragons and trollbeasts because she was too weak to make her own.

All these calculations raced through the back of her mind, second nature, even as she moved in to strike—

Pain lanced through the Bandit King's wrist. Her hand seized. Her vision burst and spotted. She couldn't feel the hilt of her sword anymore—couldn't feel the tips of her fingers—and then she saw the glint of metal and the blade embedded in her wrist. The hand holding the hilt of that blade was small and thin. Something recoiled inside her at the sight—the wielder's grip looked so pitiful, so insignificant and fragile, everything the Bandit King spilled blood trying not to be—no, *was not*—she shouldn't have been vulnerable to someone so weak—

Something rammed into the small of her back, narrow and sharp and searing. She'd been stabbed. She knew this instinctively, immediately. She recognized it. She'd been stabbed in the back before, and the feeling had been similar to this, an impact near her spine and a tingling and, finally, a blaze of pain that forced her to notice. But no one had dared stab her in years. She'd gotten too strong, too watchful, too good at seizing control and making them too terrified to dare. And it had never been so deep, never been felt beyond skin and a few inches of muscle…

The tip of a sword poked out of her stomach. It had run her through. And then she felt the blade sliding back, and the sword-tip disappeared. An iron smell filled the air.

Shit.

The Bandit King crumpled.

The air was thick and heavy. Darkness crept in on the corners of her vision. Faces swam in front of her: the troll's, beastly and sharp-toothed, sparking her fear—no, *fight* instinct; the guardsman's, blank as a stone; the trader's, fierce and dark; and lastly the healer's, ghost-white and wide-eyed. But where were her people? Why weren't they avenging her, attacking her killers (no, no, *enemies)* from behind when they had the chance? And then she realized: they wouldn't. Of course they wouldn't. She'd lost, hadn't she? If she didn't win, they wouldn't gain anything from fighting for her. So they had no reason to anymore... none... at all...

Someone pushed insistently on the Bandit King's shoulders. The world tilted. Something was supporting her back, now, and the edges of the world kept wobbling. Clouds of leaves were far above her, loaded with purple spots and the flickering movements of squirrels... no, not squirrels, squirrels didn't have flat faces, squirrels didn't have pointy teeth or make sounds that low in pitch...

"—too much blood," a voice was saying quietly, "can't fix it—"

It was the healer girl. Corrin. Her hair swam in the Bandit King's vision like a patch of fire, and her face kept blurring. Dark spots swarmed over everything: the leaves, the tree demons, the healer. The other faces close behind her. The trader's voice grumbled, hard and angry—"not worth fixing, trust me"—and a deeper voice murmured something the Bandit King didn't quite catch. A massive hand rested on Corrin's shoulder. She was shaking. Or perhaps the Bandit King's vision was wavering. *Focus,* she told herself, *stay awake, you weakling, or what do you call yourself King for?* But even her thoughts felt unsteady, like she couldn't quite follow them through, like they were slipping away from her. The pain dulled, and coldness overtook her. Everything was damp. Her back felt wet and sticky.

"—be easier on you if you fall asleep," said Corrin. "Please."

The Bandit King could not go to sleep. It felt important to impress this upon the girl crouched over her, though it was hard to say why. Something about needing to fight. A strange feeling, like she would float away and never be able to come back. The darkness crept in, obscuring Corrin's hair, and her cheeks. All that was left now were her eyes, green and strangely bright. The Bandit King tried to speak, but it felt like too much effort to push air past her lips. Her protest, half-thought and half-formed, wheezed and died in the back of her throat. The cold felt distant now. Like she was feeling it through a barrier. Like someone else was feeling it, and she was merely witnessing it. Like this was a dream.

It was dark.

It was silent.

And the Bandit King knew no more.

Amella was a fiend. She blocked every strike, parried every stab. Her weapon swung wild and quick, and for a heartbeat Verse envisioned her in a story. She'd be suited to it. She looked and acted the part.

Death's scythe, she's terrifying, Verse thought.

But then Limerick joined her. Verse felt the assurance of two-on-one, of fighting with the one person she could trust to watch her back. It was a different safety than that granted by the Bandit King, less fragile, less conditional. He was her idiot brother, sure, but he was her idiot brother no matter what she did. He stuck by her. Kept trusting her, for some reason, to make the hard calls and keep the both of them alive.

Between the two of them, they'd break through this trader's defenses eventually. The trader was no Bandit King, after all, nor was she a legend, nor an immortal like some hero in a song. She was a hot-headed fool who had fought a battle she knew she couldn't win, and she'd gotten herself captured. She'd been beaten. She'd screwed up. She'd screw up again.

Amella's sword bit into her brother's ribs.

Verse saw red. "You *viper.*"

She stabbed. Amella blocked. Tremors ran up her arm. Stab, block, slash, block—she was being forced back, *damn it—*

A blur of motion crossed her periphery, and Verse saw a mess of dark fabric and metal and blood.

The Bandit King fell.

The Bandit King never fell, not in all the seasons Verse had known her.

Verse stumbled back, away from Amella's barrage. The air reeked of iron and felt thick and heavy with humidity. Her brother slumped against the trunk of the Tree of Life, his hand pressed to his side and blood seeping out beneath his fingers. The ring of metal against metal stopped. One of their group was sprawled on the ground, unmoving and unseeing with a hole in his gut. Another fled, sprinting across the clearing and away from the snarling troll. His gait was uneven, his shirt bloodied. Alive for now. But probably done for.

Verse might be able to name them, if she were close enough to see their faces. But she couldn't identify them from a distance. They were practically strangers to her, insignificant compared to herself and her brother. Insignificant compared to the King. Banditry was a cutthroat business in the most literal sense; it didn't pay to be forthcoming or work closely, unless the Bandit King demanded it of you.

Amella stayed back, close to the healer. She still had her sword pointed at Verse, but her attention had dropped, turned to the Bandit King. The troll straightened. The guardsman's face was blank. Stone-like. Blast, that was unnerving.

Limerick coughed. "The—the heck happened?"

"Boss got stabbed," said Verse quietly. "Rest are dead or gone."

We should leave, she thought. *The boss is done for.*

But Verse stayed, transfixed, and watched as the troll straightened up and bounded over to her boss's prone form. She listened to the snatches of—of words?—between the troll and the healer girl. She kept her sword at the ready and a hand firmly on her brother's shoulder, and she listened to his wheezing breaths and muttered curses. As the healer sheathed her sword, Verse realized, *It's red. The shrimp struck someone.* When the healer placed her hands on the Bandit King's shoulders and made her lie down, Verse subconsciously tightened her grip on the hilt of her weapon. *What in Death's name is she doing?* she thought, as the healer hunched over the Bandit King.

The healer was a mess of bright red hair, bony limbs, and lightly moving fingers, of fidgets and murmuring that was too quiet to make out. At last, she drew back, shaking her head. "She's dead," she said. She sounded upset.

What do you have to be unhappy about? Verse wondered. *You won the fight.*

Limerick's breathing was shallow. His eyes were screwed shut, his face twitching. Verse wrapped her arm around his shoulders bracingly. She couldn't carry him, she realized, not if she also needed to hold her weapon, which she did. And she wasn't certain of the way back, either. She'd been following the Bandit King. She'd assumed that the Bandit King would bring her back out of here again. That was their exchange. The King led, and Verse followed. Somehow she'd never pictured the King falling short.

The Tree of Life loomed over her. Mist from the pits of boiling water created a haze, and the other trees around this mess of humidity and massive roots all looked the same, dark and distant and strange.

Verse had no damn idea what to do.

The healer and her companions were turning away from the Bandit King now. The guardsman spotted Verse and quickly leaned down to say something to the healer, who caught Verse's eye. Verse tensed. The wisps of steam blurred the healer's expression, fuzzed the corners of her mouth and made her look paler than Verse remembered. The healer started toward her, the trader, the guard, and the troll following close behind.

Corrin, Verse recalled, *her name is Corrin, and she's a threat.* Verse moved to crouch in front of her brother. She ignored the voice whispering in the back of her mind that this was a futile act and her brother was dying anyway.

Corrin stopped several paces away.

"What do you want?" demanded Verse.

She opened her mouth to answer.

"Don't move," said the guard sharply. He pointed his sword at Verse. Behind him, the troll growled.

Verse scoffed. "I'm not stupid enough to attack you right now."

It was Amella who replied this time. "That's great," she said dryly. "Would've been even greater if you hadn't been stupid enough to chase us into the Gloamwood, either."

"Hey, you're the ones who went in first."

"Aye, well." Amella shrugged. "At least we had a good reason to go in here. You, though, don't have a plague to stop or a friend who needs a miracle cure." Her focus shifted past Verse for a heartbeat. "At least, you didn't before you followed your idiot of a boss in here. Chasing some fairytale, right? Some nutbar idea about immortality?" Amella paused, letting the words hang in the air; and then, when Verse didn't reply, she asked, "So what now? Your boss is gone, you're outnumbered, and the only companion you've got is on his last legs, from the looks of it. Why aren't you scurrying off?"

Verse said nothing.

"Would you like me to look at him?" Corrin asked. The words came out thin and raspy, flat. She sounded half dead, like her spirit was already drifting from her body, resigned, waiting for Death to swoop in and cut its last threads away. It didn't sound right, coming from her. Sounded eerie. This was the same shrimp who'd leaped off a ship and pissed off a dragon just to have a chance at escaping them, after all.

Something twisted in Verse's gut. She mentally shoved the feeling out of the way and buried it. "What, so you can make sure he's finished off?" she asked. "Got a poison vial tucked away somewhere, or are you just going to use your pointy piece of steel there and do it the old-fashioned way?"

The guardsman and the trader both looked ready to run Verse through. But Corrin threw an arm up in front of the both of them and said quietly, "It's alright."

The guard looked like he wanted to argue, but the trader, after taking a long, hard look at Corrin, grabbed his arm and said, "Let's trust her on this one." He lowered his sword, though he didn't look happy about it.

Behind him, the troll shuffled and grumbled gibberish at Corrin. To the troll, Corrin said firmly, "No Corrin-kin. No good. Det, no danger." It was a load of half-language gibberish to Verse, but the troll seemed to understand it; it backed off, its ears twitching backward.

And then Corrin came right over and sat down within three paces of Verse, leaning back against the nearest root. She wasn't facing Verse, exactly, but she wasn't looking away either. Now that she was closer, Verse could see how thin and worn her face was, and that her eyes had a glossy sheen. "I don't like hurting people," Corrin said simply. "Even people I don't like. Which is important, because I really don't like you." A pause. "Or your brother. He's a jerk."

"What do you want, then?" Verse demanded.

Corrin smiled wanly and pointed up, at the fruit that grew far out of reach. Or, well, it could've been the demon squirrel things—the Churikin?—that were all over the canopy. But all things considered, Verse seriously doubted she meant the Churikin. Not that it made a difference.

"Can't help you with that. So what do you want with *me*?"

"Let me try to help… what's his name… Limerick?"

It used to be Ephraim, Verse thought. "Yeah," she said. "Limerick. And you just told me you hate his guts, so, no."

Beside her, Limerick hissed through his teeth and curled in on himself.

Corrin frowned. "Not hate. M'too tired for that." She took a deep breath, and it was then that Verse noticed the strain in it, the way it rattled. But she didn't have any injuries that Verse could see. And then she put that together with the thin face and the pallor, and it clicked.

She's sick, Verse realized. *Probably the same sickness her village had. She's dying.*

Despite this, Corrin sat upright. She kept talking, her voice weary and flat but sincere nonetheless. "I trained to be a healer because I like to help people. Stitch 'em and bind 'em back up, or give them tinctures to chase out their illness. Makes me feel like I can do something. Your brother's in bad condition, and I'm right here. So please, let me help."

Verse looked between Corrin and Limerick. She ran some calculations. Weighed the odds. It wasn't that she trusted Corrin. Trusting someone who'd been your captive was a special kind of idiocy. But her options were either risk losing her brother to this shrimp's anger or incompetency, or definitely lose him to his wounds. The risk was better than the certainty, simple as that. "Fine."

Corrin crawled over to inspect Limerick's wound. She brought out a jar of green gunk and dabbed it on, muttering reassurances while he flinched and cussed her out, half coherent. Verse gripped his shoulders and held him still. And then Corrin cut off one of his shirtsleeves and bound it tight over the wound. The bandage turned red fast, too fast, and after Corrin applied pressure to it and counted under her breath, her fingertips came away bloodstained. Verse's stomach lurched; that seemed bad. But the little healer merely frowned and budged Limerick over until he was level on his side, with his head resting against Verse's knee. A mumbled string of incomprehensible gibberish left his lips. Verse would've bet her finest dagger he was still cussing Corrin out, though perhaps not as ardently as before.

Verse thought fervently, *You idiot. Stay with me.*

Corrin drew back. Her shoulders drooped. "I'm sorry. Wish I could do more. He needs stitches or cauterization, but I don't have the tools. Best I can do is slow the blood loss."

Limerick seemed to breathe a bit easier, at least, in this position. His eyes remained shut, but some of the tension around them disappeared. He grumbled something that might have been a dismissal, or perhaps a thank-you, but came out more like "mrrgrhrrurr."

"Yeah, well," said Verse gruffly. "You didn't make it worse."

Corrin's companions had stayed in place and watched. They looked uncertain—the humans did, at least. The troll was difficult to read, what with the animal eyes and the bristling fur everywhere. But at last, the trader turned and muttered something to the guard, who nodded shortly, and the two of them came over, the troll trailing after them with its teeth bared. "Oy, Corrin," said the trader, her eyes dark like coals and her hand resting on the hilt of her sword. "You done healing the lowlife who tried to stab us?"

Corrin let out an exasperated sigh and nodded.

"Alright, then." For a moment, the trader stared at Verse like she was sizing up her weak spots—like she was going to attack. The guard seemed similarly intent, though more reserved. A firebird, of all things, fidgeted on his shoulder. And then the moment passed, and the trader addressed Corrin again, her voice gentling. "You're hanging in there, kiddo? You weren't hurt, were you?"

"I'm alright."

The troll said more troll-gibberish. Corrin repeated herself to the troll, and they lumbered over. Verse's heart nearly stopped, her instincts screaming that this thing would eat them all; but all the troll did was crouch down beside Corrin and wrap its massive, furry arms snugly around her. Its chin rested on the crown of her head, and a deep rumble purled out from its chest. Corrin peeked over the beast's arms like a baby peering out of its swaddling. She didn't seem in the least perturbed by the massive predator clinging to her, not even with blood gunking up the troll's paws. It was nuts. If Verse were in her shoes, she would've been shaking in her boots and trying to stab the beast.

"Good," said Amella, apparently no more bothered by this than Corrin was. "So. We still need to get the fruit down from the tree, somehow. And you tried to scale the tree with Makur, but from back here it looked like the Churikin chased you two off the second you sank your claws in the trunk. Is that right?"

The troll (*Makur?*) growled. Corrin mumbled an affirmative.

Amella frowned. "Thought the Dono said we needed to get the fruit. That suggests they expected we'd be able to get it. We missing something?"

Verse considered asking what in the starland's worst tempests the Dono was, then realized this would draw attention back to her and Limerick and decided against it. The guard watching her was already enough to make her tense.

Makur spoke. "No grekka. Det, krrkin no go here for long time. Lose grekkit, maybe. Dono grekka, maybe, det, Makur no."

Amella said, "I didn't get all that, but sounds like you have no idea."

Makur's only response was to grumble and embrace Corrin more tightly.

Quiet fell. The trader's brow furrowed, and she crossed her arms. The guard continued to watch, though he softened for a moment as he murmured a reassurance to his firebird. (Verse knew a few legends about firebirds and their cunning. She'd never put much stock in the details, but she wondered now if they held more truth than she imagined.)

And then, out of nowhere, Corrin asked, "Um. Excuse me, bandit—Verse?"

Verse started.

"You were a bard, right? Do you know any tales about the tree?"

A flicker of pride stirred within her, an old pride that had been buried and half-forgotten in her pursuit of security, in all the knifing people from behind. "Sure I do, shrimp." Verse scowled. "Wouldn't be a bard worth my salt if I didn't know our origin stories."

"Anything that might help us?"

Verse's first instinct was to scoff. A bard's tale was just that: a bard's tale. A flight of fancy. A bit of magic cast with some plucked strings and pretty words, with the truths woven in so seamlessly with the fiction that it was nigh impossible to tease out those precious strands. But then she paused, and thought again, and, well, what else did they have to go on here, other than old stories? And how many had she learned, had she needed to learn, to vary her performance and earn her pittance of coins and food? There was the story about Death bargaining with the celestial turtle. The one about the conscription of the Churikin. A dozen tales about reckless heroes surviving the Gloamwood through some uncommon skill or wit, like the riddle master and the Riddle Beast, and the piper who escaped Death and her Churikin by playing them a melody…

She'd liked that one. She'd liked any story about musicians, since music was half her trade.

The Churikin were still watching them from above, interspersed among the leaves and the ripe purple fruit.

"There's a story about a piper charming the Churikin," said Verse at length. "Don't know if you've heard of it."

"I haven't." Corrin's face scrunched up in thought, then brightened. "Could you sing it?"

Verse blinked. Considered. Shrugged. "Sure. Why not?"

Taking care not to disturb her brother, Verse removed the case strapped to her back and flicked the clasps open. Inside, her lute nestled in a lining made from her spare cloak. The instrument was worn and wooden and dull from lack of use, but when she plucked the strings with her fingertips, it still sang to her. She lifted the faithful instrument and cradled it tenderly, bracing its neck against her shoulder and its rounded body against her stomach. She strummed a few chords. Her hands felt clumsier and stiffer than she would have liked, but she still remembered the fingerings. She remembered the melody, too, and the words, and as she started the song, the rasps and gruffness smoothed out. And on the loom of rhythm and sweet melancholy notes, she wove a story.

There once was a man who wove his songs
On a flute he'd carved with wood and heart.
He traveled, played, and lived and loved
And found this world too dear to depart.

And though he aged, and the Churikin came,
This clever piper played them for fools!
He soothed them to sleep, and gave them the slip,
And for a time, alive he remained.

But Death herself came searching for him,
And she was far more tricky to shake.
"Your time has come," so she proclaimed.
With shadowed hands, she raised her scythe.

But the man thought fast, and made his plea:
"I beg, a bargain may I strike?
Let me play you a melody, sweet and bright,
In trade for more of this precious life!"

At this, the reaper sighed and said,
"See if it stirs me; see if I'm moved.
I promise only the chance to try."
For Death was weary, with naught to lose.

He held his flute and drew a breath,
And wove a tale on notes alone.
Sincere and soft and melancholy,
His song spoke straight to heart and soul.

Death to her great surprise was swayed.
Somehow, somewhere, he'd struck a chord,

And though she seldom bends her rules,
Fell Death will always keep her word.

"I give you two decades, to live and love,
But in the end, you'll come with me.
For I've an oath to the celestial turtle:
All souls to guide, my pledge to keep."

And so the piper kept weaving his songs
On the flute he'd carved with wood and heart.
He traveled and played and lived and loved
Until at last it was time to depart.

When Death came calling once again,
Proclaimed herself with hand outstretched,
The man was weary; his soul craved rest.
He went to the starlands without protest.

They say he plays to this very day,
On that flute he'd carved with wood and heart,
His sweet melodies among the stars
To comfort souls after they depart.

Verse closed her eyes as she played, focusing on the twang of her strings and the tale she had to dredge up from old memories, like a treasure she had to dig out of the bottom of a trunk. No one else spoke. A rustling started up, but she dismissed it as forest noise, perhaps the wind through the trees or the scuffling of small creatures in the branches. When she finished, she took a deep, slow breath and opened her eyes again—and nearly dropped her lute in shock.

The forest floor had turned into a sea of Churikin. There had to be dozens, no, hundreds of pup-sized creatures with brown-dappled fur, flat faces, and glinting, beady eyes. They sat on roots and seemingly every patch of ground they could find, right up to the edge of the boiling water pits. Some of them were within a stride of Verse herself, though they gave Corrin and Makur a wider berth. They had round bodies and practically no neck, but their limbs were disproportionately long and slender. Their tails curled over them in curlicues, and their hands were fine-fingered, human-shaped. It was like someone had made a fat fuzzball of a creature and then decided they needed to move around, and so they'd plastered on body parts that had once belonged to something else. They reminded Verse of another myth she'd heard, another version of the land's origins, in which Death crafted the things from coconuts.

However they'd come about, they were freakishly weird.

The Churikin bore their tiny, needle-sharp teeth in grins reminiscent of festival masks, and they clutched bright purple fruit to their chests, like kids clinging to sweets they'd bought for a hard-earned pittance.

Why're they looking at me like that? she wondered, with a beat of trepidation. *What're they going to do, swarm me and try to have me for dinner?* Instinctively, Verse took her fingers off the lute and reached for the hilt of her sword.

But they didn't attack.

Several of them crept forward and dropped the fruit near her toes, and then darted back, chittering. Before long, Verse had a small mound of the things at her feet. The fruits were round, the size of her clenched fist, and covered from stem-base to end in a vivid purple fuzz.

The Churikin tilted their heads this way and that and chattered more. One of them mimed holding something large and striking it with their hands. *A lute,* Verse realized, *they're mimicking playing a lute. They're bribing me for more music.*

A low, coarse laugh escaped her. "I'll be starred," said Verse. "This is the best tipping crowd I've ever had."

CHAPTER TWENTY-THREE

Recovery

Corrin waited and listened as Verse played another song, and then another, and the mound of fruit grew at her feet. Verse recited Death's bargaining with the celestial turtle. She sang a story about a hero who fended off an invasion of trolls. (Makur did not like this one. Corrin had to prod them and tell them to stop growling.) Another song about a war between two rival tribes, before the realm of Stalt was formed. A tale about one of the first Staltian kings, who was once a vindictive fool but then learned patience from her servant, who had a silver tongue and a knack for clever pranks. Another song, this one a lullaby, from an unnamed parent to their likewise unnamed child. The crowd of Churikin dwindled, until eventually, most of them were back in their tree and only a few were curled up on the ground, their eyes half open and their chittering softened to contented mumbles.

Verse ended her song and set the lute aside. "You think this stuff would help my brother?" she asked, and pointed to the mountain of fruit in front of her.

"I don't know," said Corrin honestly. Makur was holding her awfully tight, and she had to strain to get enough breath in her lungs. Or maybe that was just her illness getting in the way. "I only know they can help with sickness. M'not sure if they would help with blood or flesh regeneration. But I think they should be safe to ingest, if you want to try."

That, apparently, was good enough for Verse. She shoved one of the fruit against Limerick's lips, and Limerick, after some prodding and a few grumbled threats, bit into it.

His face screwed up in disgust. "Tastes like worm slime and skunk juice," he complained.

Corrin wondered when, and why, he would have tasted a concoction of worm slime and skunk juice. She'd never found that combination in the medical texts, not even in *Remedyes Moste Foule And Potente,* with its chapters of intestinal extractions and disgusting gunks (which in truth were to be considered with skepticism; Bathilda had explained, in depth, why this one and that one and that other one would do more harm than good). But it didn't surprise her that the fruit tasted foul. Many good medicines did.

What did surprise her was how quickly color crept back into Limerick's cheeks, and how, mere minutes later, he sat up. He grimaced and kept his arms wrapped around his bloodstained middle, but he looked well as a patient after a stitching and three days' rest—if Corrin ignored the dirt and the stained bandage, and that when he took a hand off the wound, it still came away with traces of red.

"I'll be starred," said Limerick. "It actually works."

For a beat, no one said anything.

A grin spread wide and crooked across Limerick's face. "Hey—hey Verse, you got all this with your music? You sat there and played, and they brought you all this fruit?" A pit of foreboding formed in Corrin's stomach as he added, "So it's ours by right, isn't it?"

Verse clapped a hand over his mouth and hissed, "Shut up."

"Mmph." Limerick narrowed his eyes at her, but he couldn't be bothered to remove her hand.

Verse grabbed another one of the fruits and, with a lazy flick of her wrist, tossed it toward Corrin. It arced through the air, blurring as it passed through a cloud of water vapor, and plummeted toward her—right at her face, and she couldn't help but wonder if Verse had done that on purpose. Corrin couldn't move to catch it, so enveloped she was in fur and muscle, all swaddled in Makur's concern; but then the arms entrapping her loosened, and a dark blur shot out and caught the fruit. Next she knew, Makur's massive paw was inches from her face, with the fruit skewered on two of its claws. Makur's growl of satisfaction rumbled against her back. "Corrin eat," said Makur. "Eat, heal, feel better. Corrin be strong wyrman."

Corrin gingerly pried the fruit off Makur's claws. It was fuzzy and slightly squishy to the touch, with a pungent sweet smell she usually associated with an overripe harvest. It looked strange and of questionable edibility, in truth, and if she wasn't desperate and hadn't heard the legends or seen it heal Limerick unnaturally fast, she would rather have dissected it, perhaps brought it to Bathilda to mash into tubes and test with heat and other implements.

But as it was, she bit into it. And somehow, Limerick's description fit perfectly. Corrin had never tasted worm slime, much less a skunk. But she had held plenty a worm and smelled the residue of a skunk's spray, and she imagined that if someone took a worm and doused it in skunk juice and maybe left it out to sit in the damp for a few days, it would taste like this. She had to force herself to swallow. A shudder ran down her spine, and her stomach churned with distress as the mouthful slid down her throat. It felt sticky and thick, and she was half convinced it was spoiled—but it wouldn't have been attached to the Tree of Life if it was, surely, wouldn't have been plucked and offered up as tribute by the Churikin.

She kept nibbling on the fruit, waiting for it to take effect. One minute passed, then two.

And little by little, she noticed its effects.

Warmth crept into her fingers and her toes where before she'd had a chill. Her head felt lighter, not in the spinning unstable way that meant fainting was imminent, but in the clear and steady way, in the sense that it suddenly felt like less work to hold it upright. Her limbs felt lighter too, and her heart quicker. Her breathing became a smidge easier, even as it kept a raspy edge. And the forest looked more vivid. Details were sharper, more in-focus. Leaves were a deeper green. The sunbeams slipping through the canopy were a brighter gold. The steam that drifted up from the boiling springs shimmered.

It wasn't a world-tilting change, this shift in perception; it wasn't like she'd been transported to another forest, or like she was suddenly seeing things that weren't there before. It wasn't like she felt quite up to full strength, either. No, she could remember feeling even lighter and stronger than this, back in Oddment. Like when she was chasing her brothers or climbing trees in pursuit of nuts or herbs. Or when she was traipsing about the forest with her da, learning how to use a slingshot. Or when she babbled to her mum about what she'd learned from Bathilda while they kneaded dough for bread, her small hands pressing enthusiastically next to her mum's sure and deft ones. But she'd forgotten how well she could feel in her haze of fatigue, and now she could remember.

She stared at her half-eaten fruit, stunned. She could count on one hand the tonics she knew of that took effect this fast. Most of those weren't true cures but instead relief from symptoms. True recovery was supposed to take longer, because it was always harder to dig down to the roots of a problem and fix it for good. But this...

Amella stepped in front of her and peered at her face. "You were making some interesting expressions there," she said. "How're you feeling?"

"Better," said Corrin, bewildered. "Much better."

"Glad to hear it." Her voice was warm and her grin broad with relief. "So I take it we should pack up the pile of fruit and get out of here, right?"

"Yes, I think—" Corrin began. But then she remembered the dead.

The Bandit King and the follower whom Tenno defeated, whose name she did not know, lay prone and lifeless nearby. A few of the Churikin sniffed the bodies curiously, and one of them bared its teeth, like it was thinking of taking a bite. Corrin did not regret that they were dead, not when they would have killed her and her friends—and had, in fact, killed Vinny and probably many others—but the thought of leaving them to be carrion sparked an unease she didn't know how to explain. The dead didn't need their bodies, even in the stories where their consciousness somehow persisted, but the people of Oddment never left the dead to be scavenged, no matter how despised they were among the villagers. They were always burned to ashes and cast out free in the wind, with a recitation of wishes for safe passage to the starlands.

"I think we should take care of them first," Corrin said quietly, and pointed.

Verse scoffed at this. "You took care of them alright. They're done for. Bit late to be a bleeding heart, don't you think?"

"Maybe we could start a pyre here, gather some undergrowth or branches and spark 'em with flint—"

"Not gonna work in this humidity," said Amella, her grin flickering and turning wry. She didn't accuse Corrin of being foolish or ridiculous, or too soft-hearted, or complain that Corrin was giving kindness to gone-for lowlifes who didn't deserve it. Perhaps Amella understood the unease Corrin couldn't rationalize; perhaps she even felt it herself. "But what was that tradition the, uh, Dono was talking about? Something about feeding some of the dead to the Tree? Burying 'em near the roots, probably? Though they don't make for brave and honorable fertilizer, not by a long shot."

"Give to Tree," growled Makur abruptly. "Danger wyrmen, weak bad not krrkin, det, bodin is bodin and feed tree is good. If gruk truth, stories grok be dead den. I bring dead bodinses, I find, I bury them there." A warm weight settled on top of Corrin's head—Makur's paw, with its squishy pad and just enough pressure to remind her of the immense strength behind it. Makur's strength was reassuring instead of intimidating, now, after all of their protection and fussing and help. "Corrin come wid."

Amella frowned, and behind her, Tenno's brow furrowed. Corrin had struggled to parse all that herself, but she provided a rough translation: Makur thought that it would be good to bury them, to nourish the Tree, and claimed that there was a special place to do it somewhere around here. They said that they would take the bodies, find the special place, and handle the burial, and that Corrin should accompany them. The implication, she guessed, was that Amella and Tenno would keep watch over Limerick, Verse, and the pile of healing fruit. Corrin thought this was a reasonable plan, and she said as much. "You can definitely handle them," she concluded, and pointed at Verse and Limerick. Limerick, who had moved as if to creep away, froze; Verse yanked him back by the collar of his vest. She wouldn't look Corrin in the eye.

Tenno glanced back at the scuffling siblings, his expression hardening, and he kept them in his periphery even as he addressed her. "Corrin," he said worriedly, "just a few minutes ago you could barely stand."

"I'm feeling better, I really am. 'Sides, Makur will look after me."

"I protect Corrin," said Makur solemnly, and ruffled her hair.

"They'll be fine," said Amella confidently. "Let's you and I watch the troublemakers, and wait for Corrin's swift return."

Tenno didn't look reassured, but he assented.

And so he and Amella positioned themselves on either side of the bandit siblings, while Corrin trailed after Makur—right after insisting they eat a fruit, that is, to help heal the wounds they'd gotten in battle. (Several deep gashes in their arms and side. Makur tried to shrug them off, but Corrin would have none of it.) After eating a fruit and scrunching their face in disgust, Makur strode over to the bodies and slung them over their shoulders like a farmer hefting feed sacks. (Corrin tried not to look too much at their faces, or the bloodstained clothes, or the gaping wounds that were beyond fixing.) Makur led her around the base of the trunk. They stopped now and then to squint intently, as if trying to recall something, and grumble under their breath. They wended their way around boiling springs and clambered over roots, pausing to give Corrin a boosting paw as she scrambled over the low walls of knobby rough bark. Eventually, Makur stopped and pointed. Corrin nearly ran into them from behind.

"There," rumbled Makur.

A dark tunnel yawned open at the base of the trunk. Unlike the burrows in the troll village, there were no ferns or other plants to conceal it, and no etchings in the trunk above marked it. Instead, whoever had dug it out had marked it with two stone statues, roughly chiseled. As Corrin drew near them, she was better able to gauge their size and make out their features. Both came up to her waist and had yellowish-green lichen growing on their heads and shoulders and backs, though not on their faces. One of the statues had giant paws and feet and a head vaguely reminiscent of Makur's, though the ears were missing. The other was hunched, with a single hand extended and clutching a walking stick. Their head was strangely shaped; it took Corrin a moment to figure out that the shape was the folds of a cloak's hood, and that the giant protrusion coming out of their face was a pointed nose.

She reached out and traced the hunched figure's face with her fingertips. The features must have been craggy once, but they'd been worn smooth with time. The eyes were deep, narrow holes gouged on either side of the nose; Corrin tried to stick her fingers in them, but they were a smidge too narrow. The statue had no eyebrows or beard, and no hair spilled out from underneath the cloak hood, which also covered the spots where the ears would be. But overall, the figurine seemed more human-like than the other one. Corrin couldn't help but think of Bathilda, plodding along with her staff and cloak. Of course it couldn't be Bathilda, but then, who had made this Bathilda-like figure and why? And why would the trolls have kept it, when their history with humankind was war-torn and mostly forgotten?

"We go," growled Makur impatiently, jarring Corrin out of her thoughts. They led the way into the tunnel.

The tunnel continued down for several paces, then opened into a vast chamber. It was a luminous goldish-green, brighter than expected for an underground room. Corrin squinted, befuddled, and then she saw the light source—strange fuzzy stuff, maybe moss or lichen, or perhaps some kind of mold or fungus. Whatever it was, it grew in a thick carpet on the ceiling and crawled down along the walls. Rows and rows of small mounds filled the chamber, and the luminous stuff grew on those too, in varying quantities. Corrin would bet her dagger and half her medical supplies that they were burial mounds, and that the hero-trolls of centuries past lay beneath them, decaying bit by bit into the soil. Judging by the growth on top of them, they'd been left undisturbed.

There were also dozens of roots, some thin as ropes and others thick as Corrin's waist. They dangled from the ceiling in dark, twisted clumps and wended their way along the walls, like giant veins. A few of them spread along the floor and snaked around the mounds protectively. The glowing fungus didn't grow on the roots, only around them.

The air was earthy and damp, so thick that it felt like a burden to breathe, and there was a strange smell in the air, something sharp and acidic. Corrin wrinkled her nose.

"Stink," grumbled Makur, scrunching up their face.

"Yes," Corrin agreed wholeheartedly. "Stink much."

Makur stomped over to a flat patch of ground and tore through the soil, scooping out great pawfuls until they'd made two shallow holes. They laid the bodies to rest inside, and then they heaped the dirt back over them: first their feet, and then their legs and chest, and at last their necks. Together, Makur and Corrin patted the dirt down, smoothing it like a blanket. Corrin reached over and brushed the eyelids shut. That was also something her people did, just before the bodies were burnt to ashes and cast upon the wind. If Corrin only looked at their faces, she could almost pretend that they were sleeping.

But she knew too well how to look for the movement of breath and feel for a thrumming pulse, and she'd long ago learned the meaning of a chill beneath her fingertips and a person's absolute stillness. And she'd seen the injuries too clearly to forget them, no matter how much earth she blanketed the bandits with.

"This is the part where I'm supposed to say something to you," said Corrin quietly to the Bandit King's face. "I'm supposed to wish you safe passage to the starlands, I think, maybe say a piece about the life you lived. But I didn't really know anything about you, other than that you were trying to hunt me down and you wouldn't hesitate to kill my friends. And I'm not sure I'd want you to get to the starlands even if they exist. You'd probably terrorize everyone you met there."

Corrin paused and reconsidered. "I guess you wouldn't be able to harm spirits, not any more than they could harm you. I'm not sure I can find it in me to wish you well, though. You're already getting a better sendoff than Vinny probably got anyway, so... goodbye." And with that, she covered their heads and finished the burial. For good measure, Corrin peeled some of the glowing fungus stuff off the walls and laid it protectively over the mounds.

She wiped her hands, shedding clods of dirt and bits of luminous residue, and turned to address her friend. "Alright, Makur, I think we're—"

But Makur was gone.

No, not gone. Over there, near the back of the chamber, prying something open.

"What are you doing?" asked Corrin, bewildered. "What's that?"

"No grekka," said Makur, without turning around. "Will find."

"Are you sure you should do that?"

But Makur had already tossed aside a flat, grey slab with a grunt of satisfaction and reached into the thing it had been covering, which appeared to be a stone basin. Corrin felt a prickle of unease—she felt like they shouldn't be doing this, that they were disrespecting this grave site by prying into this thing—but at the same time, her curiosity burned, and her curiosity was stronger than her worries of offending long-lost ghosts. She crept up to Makur's side and watched as they withdrew something light brown from the basin.

They let their find rest flat on their paw, and together, Corrin and Makur stared at the object in bewilderment. It was a book. It was a smidge large for a human's hands but too small for a troll's, and it looked older than Bathilda's most ancient medical volumes, its leather cover faded and worn from repeated handling. Either the title had been worn away, or it had never had one. The edges of its pages were greenish yellow, tinted a shade similar to the lichen. Corrin could scarcely believe it was intact. She felt like if she tried to touch it, it would come apart.

"What this?" Makur asked. They prodded the book's spine with one claw. Corrin winced internally—books were precious, and a book this old especially so—but it held together.

"Don't know. Can I read it?"

"Hrr. Usen eyen." Makur passed the book into Corrin's waiting hands.

It was thick and heavy, and the leather was soft from sitting so long in a damp cave. It smelled like must and earth. Corrin opened it carefully to the first page, which was nearly as deeply yellowed in the center as it was around the edges. Glyphs that must have once been inky black and sharp had long since fuzzed at the edges and faded to grey. Some looked like more intricate versions of their modern Staltish counterparts, others like the ones in some of Bathilda's older books, and even a few like the trolls' pictograms, but the rest... well, she'd have to guess from their context, or skip them altogether.

The first page was some kind of meeting record. It listed names, half of which Corrin couldn't pronounce, and then:

The cross...gathering lasted for ... All we did was bicker. Maddening.

Could not reach agreement on land ... Will try again next full moon. Slip calming draught into everyone's drink and food, maybe.

Dono Frurtha says I scary, be good troll, be fierce guardian. Such a joker. I said I'm trying to be a wisewoman, and the tribe leaders are fools. Frurtha owes me fish. I knew nothing would get resolved today.

The next page contained several diagrams of the human body, as well as a bisection of... a fruit? The fruit from the Tree of Life? The shape was right, and the fuzz on the outside, although maybe that was just the ink. The journal keeper had labelled several parts of the human body with great care. The heart was called *soul-center, must never stop beating a person's life-rhythm.*

Corrin frowned at this. The heart was necessary, yes, but she'd hardly call it a soul-center. All it did was pump the blood and support the head. If someone lost their heart, they died. If someone hurt their head badly, or if the innards up there started to decay, they might continue to live but lose the things that made them who they were—their memories, their personalities, their ability to think, their relationships, their identity...

She grimaced internally and kept reading.

The stomach was noted as a *vat of burning liquid, soothe with milk-tonics.* (An apt description, Corrin would give the author that one.) The veins, and the blood that ran through them, were described as *life network, fed by the bones and the soul-center.* The fruit, though, was labelled with uses. Different parts had different descriptions.

The outer layer: *Peel and eat, it becomes the flesh to fill in the wounds.*

The inner flesh of the fruit: *Purifier. Purger of the death-curse. Can be salted and stored in ... for ...*

The seeds: *Unknown.*

The following pages had records on how well the fruit remedies worked on her patients when prepared this way or that, with personal notes interspersed. Raw and sliced, the fruit failed to cure a boy who had a stomach sickness (*or food poisoning?*); he needed bedrest and infusions of hot water and *furuk* leaf juice, and a tonic to *purge the vat full empty*. But it helped him recover astonishingly fast afterward. Dono Frurtha had visited and offered fish as promised, and they were good fish. Cooked well ... and savory. Someone with a gash from a ... had responded well to ingesting the fruit skins alone, but not to having them bound upon the surface of the wound. The ... and the Donos of ... and ... regions had come, and the author wanted to smack them broadside with her staff. *The ingrates. If they take too much from the Tree, then Death's curse will start biting us, can't they understand? Can't I stab it through their thick breastbones?*

The juice fermented when kept in a corked gourd for a few days, and its effects were *inconclusive. Can't tell if this ... helped the lass recover faster or made the sickness worse, for a short while.* Frurtha was hurt badly (and maybe Corrin was imagining it, but she thought the fuzzing was worse on this page, and the lines a bit wobbly). Three days in deep sleep. Used all tonics. Frurtha woke up. Would be okay. The ... who had struck her could go ...

Corrin flipped through faster, now, skimming over the penned paragraphs and building a narrative out of the pieces as she went. Makur waited patiently as she mumbled her way through, prodding her only when she forgot to speak altogether.

The Churikin seem restless lately. Chatter at me more when I play my whistle. Giving me less fruit. They are unsettling. I will play to them less and expect less, for a while.

Compromise failed again. Bibbinheads.

Not bringing me tributes as they once were. I have been eating more of the seeds. Feel stronger even though eating less. Strange.

If I plant seeds from the Tree of Life, they do not grow. Not sure why.

Finally a peace agreement. Maybe will last more than a single rainy-season dry-season cycle.

Frurtha's daughter Krurr is the new Dono. I gave Frurtha back to the earth and to the Tree. She is buried near my bed. She said she wanted to stay here. I must honor my old friend's wishes.

The Giving Ceremony was held today.

... son has begotten a child. ... hair is grey through all its roots, yet mine is still full black. She ages, yet the face I see when I look in the river is smooth. Why? Will I not grow old? Will I outlive my younger sister? Never see Frurtha or my other loved ones again, never follow them to the underworld?

I think this is the work of the fruit seeds. Perhaps I should stop eating them. But they sustain me... and my people, they need a wisewoman. They are not wise. They are bibbinheads.

Have shared my suspicions with Krurr. She agrees, better I stay around. Would like to increase fruit harvest so Donos can stay longer with me. Perhaps human tribe leaders too.

The Churikin bit me. Suspect they're underfed. I must stop taking from the Tree.

Meeting with leaders devolved into shouting match.

BIBBINHEADS. BIBBINHEADS. BIBBINHEADS.

I will not be a part of this war.

Too much loss. My people are leaving. May the spirits be with my great grand nieces. But I cannot imagine living anywhere but here.

Finally, I am old. My bones are brittle, and I wither.

Krurr has come to live with me. She tells her tribe to not hurt me, to honor her mother. She is not such a joker as Frurtha was, but is strong and good company. Brings me fresh herbs and fish. Likes my whistle. I teach her to play. Other trolls stay away, most of the time. Krurr often has to go check on them. Says they're afraid of the Churikin, but they don't want to be near me. Wonder if they're telling war stories around the bonfires and making us out to be demons.

Sick. But this is alright. I have lasted far past my harvest-time.

The remaining pages were blank.

Gently, Corrin closed the book. She could envision its author sitting here, hair turned grey and fingers crooked with arthritis, penning those last words with a weak and weary hand and laying the book to rest in this basin. She couldn't help but think of Bathilda, creaky and old and wise with a sharp witty humor, and all of a sudden the voice Corrin imagined in the journal's words sounded like her.

She imagined this Bathilda-like person studying the fruit and the tree; outliving her sister and her best friend; railing against the other elders, then losing friends to the war; then watching her people go, while she stayed to fade into obscurity. Corrin pictured Krurr burying her and coming up here once every blue moon to pay respects. Maybe that troll had carved the statues at the entrance. Maybe she had passed all these stories and history on to her child, who told their child what they could remember, and perhaps, eventually, someone had told the Dono who'd welcomed Corrin into their village.

She imagined the humans fleeing the Gloamwood. Perhaps they colonized the lands that would become Stalt some centuries later, or perhaps humans had already settled there, and the ones from the Gloamwood merely assimilated. She could almost see how the bits and pieces of their stories would be recast from song to song, becoming more thrilling and fantastical with each retelling. The storytellers would make themselves the heroes, and of course an epic tale needed terrifying enemies. They would keep the trolls' strength in battle but forget to mention that they could talk. They would remember rumors that the fruit had stopped a person's aging and speak longingly of its immortality-granting properties, but they would forget the price of taking too much.

Makur swiped gently at Corrin's cheeks with the back of their paw. "Be eyen ikik," they said. They sounded worried.

Corrin sniffled. "M'okay. It's just, it's a sad journal."

"Hrr." Makur patted her back sympathetically. "It sad. Det, it old. We can get softseed now. Heal. Corrin be strong, have much lif."

Corrin allowed herself one last, hearty sniffle, then leaned over to lay the book back in the basin. It wasn't the only object in there, though. Within the bowels of the stone container rested a rusted sickle blade, slightly longer than Corrin's forearm; a woven blanket of faded green, riddled with holes; other journals, each older than the last; two ceremonial bowls made from a cracked geode, painted on the outside and covered with pinkish-white crystals on the inside; and a plump, flute-like instrument that could sit in the palm of her hand. She was half tempted to look at the other journals or examine the bowls in more detail. But then she remembered Amella and Tenno waiting just outside, and her siblings and mentor waiting back in Oddment, and Corrin hefted the heavy stone lid back into place. She and Makur hurried outside and back to the clearing where they'd left their friends.

Corrin heard the strumming of Verse's lute before she spotted the thief and her brother. They sat cross-legged, with Limerick leaning back on his hands and Verse playing a jaunty tune. Amella leaned against the trunk of the Tree of Life several paces away. She looked comfortable, but her hand rested on the hilt of her sword. The second she spotted Corrin and Makur, she brightened and waved heartily.

Tenno, meanwhile, had seated himself upon one of the roots. He frowned intently at a scrap of parchment laid out on his knee while his quill hovered just above it, dripping ink. Junior wheeled over Tenno's head and chattered at Tenno impatiently. He scribbled something at the very end of the parchment, rolled it up, and tied it to Junior's leg; a moment later, the firebird was off, a flurry of bright feathers darting up through the canopy. Tenno offered Corrin a wan smile and said, simply, "Status report. For Ragnor."

Corrin winced internally. Right, Tenno had deserted his post to accompany her. Didn't seem like the sort of thing the military would forgive easily. She hoped their success would better his chances…

"All buried and done with?" asked Amella brightly.

Verse's music stopped.

"Buried," Corrin confirmed. She considered telling them all about the cavern with the peculiar lichen, the journal she found, and everything she'd learned about the ancients—about the wisewoman who'd once lived here, the compromises between trolls and humans, and the fruit's bizarre ability to halt age. And then she remembered how the Churikin started biting when they didn't have enough fruit to eat. The war that ensued once everyone heard about how the fruit could help them live indefinitely and wanted the supply for themselves. If they knew… What if they wanted to take more, again and again?

Makur and the other trolls knew better because they'd stayed here and remembered the consequences of taking too much. Tenno, she hoped, would understand the need to leave immortality to tall tales and legends, and Amella might be content to have had a grand adventure. But what if she was wrong? What if they were too tempted?

As for Verse and Limerick, well, they were bandits. They'd take as much as they could in a heartbeat, Corrin was certain of it.

So all she said was, "I think the fruit'll keep better if we salt it. Can you all help me?"

CHAPTER TWENTY-FOUR

Returns and Goodbyes

Limerick and Verse, to Corrin's bewilderment, asked if they could stay with them until they were out of the Gloamwood; but their motives became clear when they explained that they might have, maybe, utterly forgotten how to get out of this place. They'd rather risk their softhearted once-captives and a "tamed troll" over the Riddle Beast, giant snakes, man-eating plants, and whatever else might try to devour them in the Gloamwood. Amella protested, saying (rightfully) that they were "a couple of untrustworthy, yellow-bellied, murdering scum-lickers." But then Tenno noted that Limerick and Verse would probably try to follow them anyway, and he would prefer to keep them close at hand, under observation, instead of leaving them to lurk in the shadows. His tone was mild. The steel in his eyes was not.

So Verse—and Limerick, after Verse gave him a warning pinch to the arm—helped Corrin, Tenno, and Amella stuff their packs full of fruit. Corrin pretended not to notice when Limerick pocketed one. His injuries hadn't healed fully, after all.

They all stayed the night at the edge of the Tree of Life's clearing, near one of the hot springs. The humans ate a dinner of scrounged up hardtack, and Makur caught and devoured some many-legged critter they'd found in the bushes. (Corrin politely refused the tidbits of raw meat they offered her.) An awkward quiet hung around the bandit siblings, but that was all right with Corrin. No one drew knives. No one brawled. No one so much as said a barbed word, nor made cruel light of the dead. Verse even offered to take some of the watches, but Makur growled, and Amella and Tenno both vetoed this idea immediately.

Corrin slept better than she had in ages. The next morning, they hastened back along the winding path, through the undergrowth, and into the troll village, resolutely ignoring Verse's mutterings about their insanity and Limerick's whining queries of whether they really, *actually* had to pass through troll territory. As they drew close, trolls started popping out from behind trees, and Limerick and Verse tried futilely to hide behind Makur and Tenno. Corrin asked Makur to tell the other trolls that the new wyrmen wouldn't harm them, and to please stop baring their teeth and flexing their claws like that. Corrin also hoped she wasn't lying, that Verse had a death-grip on her dagger hilt by pure reflex and not because she was planning to stab anyone, and that Limerick's twitchiness didn't mean he was about to flee the way they'd come.

But Makur merely huffed out a chortle and said, "No be krrkin, try to hurt Corrin, yus? Good be scare. Grekka we strong, can beat them iffen they be danger."

And so the intimidation continued, and Corrin was left trying to reassure Verse and Limerick in vain until Makur led them to the Dono's abode. The Dono was sleeping, much as they had been the first time Corrin had met them; they were a bundle of silver-speckled fur at the back of the cave, their side rising and falling gently. And, just as Makur had done last time, Makur crept over and gave the Dono a rough shake.

The Dono's eyes cracked open, and with a deft paw, they grabbed their staff and jabbed Makur lightly in the chest with it. "Bibbinhead," they groused, and jabbed Makur again. "Bad wake-up. You be scarce wykrr. Und you take long time. You find softseed? What slow you?" Then they looked past Makur and spotted the quantity of humans crowded in their den, and their eyes grew round as gold coins. They sat up abruptly and pointed at the group with their staff. "What this? You catch more wyrmen? This be hassark."

"Yus, we bring softseed," said Makur. "Be har. Churikin bare tarth, no let us climb."

The Dono rumbled discontentedly. "Hrr. Yus, Churikin be hassark headhurt. How bring softseed?"

"Punik," explained Makur seriously, and the Dono murmured a curious "a-hruh?" Makur nodded solemnly and continued. "Det, yus, be hassark headhurt. Und new wyrmen, be no Corrin-kin. Be danger. Det, we beat them. That one—" Makur pointed at Verse "—she make punik, Churikin give softseed. Wyrmen say they no harm us, no danger." Makur bared their teeth. "We no let them be danger. They hurt

Corrin, they hurt krr, we beat. They no stay longtime. They leave Gloamwood. I make sure. Okay?"

The Dono grumbled and heaved themselves to their feet. "Yus. Okay." They shuffled past Makur and up to Corrin, and they peered at her intently, their face uncomfortably close. At last, they drew back with a satisfied rumble and said, "Corrin is better. Heal. I be glad." They patted her on the head. "Stay nurtime, little one. Eat good snargak und sleep." The Dono then turned to Verse and Limerick, who tensed, but the Dono didn't say anything, merely narrowed their eyes and curled their lip. Next Corrin knew, the Dono was prodding Makur's shoulder with their staff, saying, "Go, I sleep now," and shooing them out.

A grumbling Makur went first, followed by Tenno, who kept glancing behind him warily; then Limerick and Verse, who looked decidedly squirrelly; and then Amella, clambering confidently up after them. Corrin followed quietly behind. But at the tunnel entrance, she hesitated. She looked back.

The Dono had already set aside their staff and curled into a ball, but their eyes were open, gleaming in the dimness.

"Dono," said Corrin tentatively, "we buried the Bandit King in the crypt… the… the burrow under the Tree of Life."

"Hrr? That so?"

"I didn't know what else to do with her."

"I grekka. That is fikah." The Dono blinked. "Det, you need grok more?"

"I also—there was this… this stone container. It had a book, thing wid scribbles, and some other things. Grekka the book? Usen eyen on the scribble?"

"No. Never take what dead keep." The response was low and growling, but sedate. Corrin couldn't tell if it was a reprimand or a simple statement of fact. "I grok, iffen dead bodin keep it, let lif bodin no gruk no more. We lif now, not in old time and old grekkit. Det, curiosity is strong, I grekka. You usen eyen book. Det, then you leave book wid dead, yus?"

"Yus," Corrin confirmed. "Det, it was scribbled by a wyrman, I grek. She used to live there, and the wyrmen and krr used to live together, and the leaders would come together for meetings and things. They had trouble agreeing, rahrg much, but they compromised, sometimes. And the human, the wyrman, when the others left, she chose to stay." Corrin bit her lip. "It was a long time ago."

"Long old time, must be," agreed the Dono. "Det, why you grok? What you want asuk me?"

"Do you grek wyrman and krr can be better? Do you grek we'll start grok to each other again? Do you grek we can come to the krr harth und not rahrg over the fruit, someday?"

The Dono rolled languidly up to a sitting position and considered her, silent and thoughtful. At last, they bared their teeth in an approximation of a smile and said, "No all wyrmen. No many, maybe. Det, you grok wid krrkin now, yus? Corrin no be krr, det, be krrkin, I grek." Their voice was warm. A mere week ago, Corrin might not have been able to hear the kindness in all the rumbled syllables, but she could now, and it drew a smile out of her. The Dono pointed at her chest, approximately where her heart should be. "More wyrmen und more krr be kind like you, then, yus. We grok more, maybe."

The warmth didn't recede completely, but it did lessen as a note of warning slipped into the Dono's tone. "Det, Gloamwood belong to krr, grekka? I grek, many wyrmen no like you. No be kind. Be danger. Danger for wyrmen und krr both iffen we rahrg." The Dono held three claws to their lips and swiped them downward. "You come harth, det, don't bring many wyrmen here. Don't bring to Lif Tree, don't show how to take softseed. Impurrent. Asuk for hassark und danger. Grekka? You give lif-grok?"

Corrin swallowed and nodded. "I grekka. I promise."

"Good. Make Corrin-kin promise too." The Dono yawned and buried their face in their forearms. They made noises that were too muffled for Corrin to interpret as words, but she recognized it as a dismissal, all the same. She left the Dono to sleep and went outside.

It was twilight. Fireflies glowed all along the stream and around the underbrush. Makur and the others had taken a seat by the stream bank and gone to wash their faces. Corrin joined them, sitting cross-legged between Tenno and Amella. They drank from the stream and refilled their canteens. Verse and Limerick muttered to each other in low voices while Tenno watched them, ever vigilant. There was no bonfire or pile of hunted meat to feast on tonight, but Makur brought them a troll-sized armful of roots and berries, brighter and more varied than what Corrin would find near Oddment. "Corrin likes plants, yus?" they said. When Corrin hesitated—she didn't know some of this flora, after all, and what toxins it might contain—they screwed up their face and nibbled on one of each type of plant they brought. Makur gulped and said unconvincingly, "Is good. No make ikik, no danger. Mother alltimes make me eat these... Blurgh, plants."

Tentatively, Corrin tried a root that looked like a cousin of one of her favorite stew ingredients. It was dense and slightly sweet, with a bit more tang to it than she was used to, and it settled comfortably in her stomach. Delicious. She grinned and took a bigger bite, while Makur wrinkled their nose and grumbled, "You be strange." Makur must've liked vegetables about as much as Corrin's little brothers did, which meant they'd brought them purely for Corrin's and her companions' benefit.

Judging from Limerick's and Verse's expressions, the bandits had a similar aversion to perfectly good plant matter. Nonetheless, when Amella and Tenno copied Corrin and none of them dropped dead, they ate.

Troll passersby lingered to observe them. Gradually, a few of them approached—first a child, who prodded Corrin's boot curiously; then the child's parent, who grumbled something that sounded vaguely apologetic and whisked their child away; and then one with red eyes and a tortoiseshell pattern in their fur, who pointed at the lute case strapped to Verse's back and asked, "What that?"

Verse edged away and side-eyed Corrin. *The stars does it want?* she mouthed.

"They want to know what's in your case," said Corrin brightly. "You should play for them."

Verse hesitated; then, cautiously, she brought out her lute and began to play.

The troll promptly sat down and listened, entertained, as did the next troll who came by, and the next. One of the trolls, a smaller one with fur the color of bread crust, bounded off and came back with a drum. They sat with the drum held close to their chest and supported Verse's melody with a downbeat. Verse preened and strummed her chords harder; Limerick mouthed *showoff* at her and rested back on his elbows, smirking. A group of troll children came and clapped their paws along with the rhythm, and some older ones—Makur included—sang like drunks at festival time (if said drunks were an octave lower and growly).

Tenno looked like he was trying hard not to smile, and Amella sang along with the trolls, grinning broadly, every bit as raucous and off-key as the rest of them. Corrin, for her part, curled her fingers around the lucky rock in her belt pouch and thought of her brothers, her mum and da, and her mentor Bathilda. She hoped they would still be there when she returned. She hoped they'd have more festival nights like this: sitting side by side, enjoying music and good health together.

They slept overnight in Makur's burrow and departed early the next day. Makur led them through a bog rife with bog sprites; across one of the Twin Rivers, over a decrepit bridge that threatened to break under their combined weight; and finally to the edge of the Gloamwood, where the trees thinned and grassy hills rolled out before them. From here, Corrin could see the way to the ruins of Gailstone; she could even spot the crumbling walls in the distance, maybe even pick out which one had once been the mead hall. It was the longest one, she thought, the part of the ruin that was just a smidge taller than the rest.

Makur stopped under a crooked oak. "You go this way, far, yus?"

"Yes. Danku, Makur."

Makur nodded solemnly.

Corrin beckoned for them to lean down, and she undid the bandage around their shoulder and cast it aside. She inspected the sites where the wounds had been. Soiled though the bandage was from blood and wear, the wounds had healed clean, with no sign of infection or agitation. She couldn't even see a scar. "You've healed up nicely," she said, and clapped them lightly on the shoulder. "Not swollen or irritated or anything. Much better than I'd hoped for, honestly."

She'd meant to say her goodbye and hurry onward, but before she could, Makur enveloped her in a hug.

Corrin reciprocated as best she was able, wrapping her arms around them and nestling her fingers in the thick fur that covered the small of their back.

"You come harth, sometime," they said. She could feel their voice rumbling through their chest as clearly as she could hear it resonating in her ear. She could also hear their heartbeat, slow but steady, louder than her own. "Corrin, you be good bidum. You heal me. Makur harth be Corrin harth, any time. You come and grok, want rest in Makur den, I will alltime say yus. You no gruk way through trees, be confuse, I help. Und iffen Rakar or Riddle Beast be danger, try hurt you, I rahrg wid you. I protect." Their grip tightened for a heartbeat. Then they let go, gave her one last, fond head-ruffle, and prowled away, back into the depths of the Gloamwood.

Corrin felt sad to see them go, to an extent that surprised her; and as she led her companions onward, she caught herself thinking of returning someday. Maybe she could convince Amella or Tenno or some other brave soul to accompany her. Or perhaps she could make it here alone.

CHAPTER TWENTY-FIVE

Second Chances

Mount Cauldra jutted upward ahead of them, its peak wreathed in clouds. Corrin scanned the skies for a red shape, but there was none. Up north, griffin-ish shapes glided along sedately (though she could swear there weren't quite as many as before). She hoped the dragon had landed somewhere to rest, and not, say, flown west to terrorize Staltian lands and towns. She wasn't sure what the guards would do if they were faced with a dragon. When she asked Tenno, he wasn't sure either, though he had ideas.

"One strategy, I think, would be to bring our heavy artillery to the towers." His brow creased, and Corrin could imagine thoughts like little fires lighting up in his mind as he talked and worked through his answer. "But of course, that has mobility limitations, in which case... Hm. There's an old battle record we reviewed in tactics training: a couple hundred years ago, an army had to travel southeast to drive one off. Some lucky shots got its eyes and pierced its wings. Excellent example of targeting the weak points in a resilient threat. But it took something like three hundred piercing hits to persuade it to go away. There were also massive casualties, mostly burns and concussions, some fatal. It was terrible. It would probably be just as terrible if it happened again." Tenno smiled wanly. "Let's hope this dragon stays in the griffin highlands."

Verse and Limerick trailed after them. Verse had wanted to split away at the edge of the Gloamwood; she'd grinned crookedly and said she and her brother had places to be (though she didn't specify what places). But Tenno had set his mouth in a grim line and ordered her to accompany them to the peninsula. It wasn't safe out here, he'd argued, but Corrin read the hardness in his face and concluded silently that he wasn't thinking of their safety. No, he was thinking of innocents' safety, or maybe some kind of justice. Maybe retribution.

Verse and Limerick must have intuited the same, because Verse's crooked grin vanished, and both their expressions closed off, turned into cool masks.

It was dark before they reached the remains of Gailstone, but Corrin insisted on continuing until they did, and Tenno agreed; the ruins were too convenient a shelter to pass up, and besides, they needed to hasten back to Stalt as swiftly as their feet could carry them. Limerick, under Amella's supervision, gathered the firewood, while Verse watched Corrin roll out blankets and put together a fire pit in the shelter of the decrepit mead hall. They got a red blaze crackling and roasted local flora and fungi for supper, but they didn't talk much. Verse didn't seem inclined to play for them, and no one seemed willing to ask. Corrin reckoned it was still awkward to share a camp with people who'd threatened to kill you—or, she supposed, to share a camp with people you'd threatened to kill, and who were now keeping you captive. But more than anything, they were all tired.

Amella took first watch.

The fire burnt down to a pile of glowing embers. Amella sat cross-legged near the campfire's dregs, facing Verse and Limerick so she could keep her distrustful gaze on them—or attempt to. However, much to Verse's amusement, the weak light wasn't enough to keep her alert. Amella's eyes kept drifting shut, her chin dipping down, until she'd startle and straighten up. Each time this happened, her eyes closed for longer, and her head dipped farther. Verse's amusement turned to a flicker of hope, and then to impatience and suspense. Verse lay still as a corpse and took measured, silent breaths. She kept her eyes partially closed, surreptitiously watching Amella nod off, start, and nod off again.

Fall asleep, she mentally urged. *Come on, fall asleep. Give us an opening.*

Verse had spent the evening silently contemplating what to do. She knew what the steel in the guardsman's voice meant. He intended to escort her and Limerick into the realm's custody, probably to execute them—or worse, throw them in a dungeon where they wouldn't see the light of day ever again. Worst of all, they'd probably confiscate her instrument and destroy it.

Because bandits weren't musicians. Bandits, in the eyes of the weak and threatened, were scourges upon society, meant to be shut away or purged. Verse had learned that well from the Bandit King: from the plans she'd laid out and calculations she'd made before each attack, but also from the stories she'd told of a dark wooden cell in the northern mountains. From a scar, bone-white and puckered, bared proudly on the Bandit King's forearm. From the nights when she'd called Verse over to eat supper with her and saw fit to share her thoughts on survival, on prey and predator.

"We do what we need to thrive," the Bandit King had once said. It was a week after Verse and Limerick had joined her, the night before their first raid together. "We just draw our lines differently. We fight. Take more by force than most. I have no compunction against killing a person to get what I want. So the country's military hunts us as they would hunt beasts, even as they preach their pretty little lines about 'protecting the people' and 'seeing to it that justice is done'. The ugly truth is that they're scared of us, and so they're willing to kill us, same as we would them. They just won't admit it. I will." She'd flashed a grin, sharp and wolfish. "That's the difference between me and them. I don't lie about what I'm willing to do, not to myself and not to you, songbird."

Now Verse considered her captors and thought, her leader had missed something. As irritatingly self-righteous as they were, these people didn't start things. They reacted. They finished them. The Bandit King was like a panther, and these people were like mountain goats. Or slumbering bears, maybe. The overgrown guardsman—what's his face, Tenno—yeah, he'd definitely have to be a bear. Not Corrin, though, she couldn't be a bear. Too small, not strong enough. She was more like a rabbit, or something. Though, that didn't quite fit either; she'd need to be something with more grit, something that would run and hide first but would fight back, in the end. Hedgehog? They hid, but they bristled.

Or perhaps a fox. A cunning, tricksy little fox.

Amella's head dipped once more. Verse waited with bated breath for her to start, for her spine to snap straight and for her to turn and check that her captives hadn't moved. But that didn't happen. Amella's chin rested heavy on her chest, and she slumped over. Her sword hand slackened and dropped. Her breathing slowed, and as the embers flickered down to almost nothing, Amella snored.

Verse turned to her brother and prodded him sharply. He stiffened, then rolled over to face her. She could scarcely see his face in the dark, but she knew, instinctively, that he understood her intentions.

Limerick silently got to his feet. Verse did the same. She led the way around the traces of orange light, away from the slumbering Amella. She stepped cautiously over Tenno's feet, holding her breath, willing him not to notice her. She'd rather not deal with that guy. Death's scythe, he was terrifying. A King killer. Loaded to the brim with self-righteous anger, even if he put on a kind face for his companions.

Thankfully, neither he nor Amella stirred.

"The fruit," Limerick hissed in Verse's ear.

Verse stopped short. Right. The cursed miracle fruit from the cursed tales that the Bandit King had dragged them into the Gloamwood for (well, for that and for her cursed pride). The fruit that, to Verse's amazement, seemed to have the supernatural powers that she'd used to sing about. The fruit that had healed Limerick when he was bleeding on Death's threshold. In a sense, she could claim that it was hers by right, hers to eat and prolong her own and her brother's life. Even though Corrin had led them there and was intent on taking it back to her sick village, Verse had sung and played for it. The Churikin had given it to her. It was tantalizingly close, now, stowed in packs mere paces away from them.

Unfortunately, their captors were using said packs as pillows.

Verse didn't like her chances of a clean getaway if she went rummaging around their pillows. She'd skip those odds and take the safe escape, thanks.

...Well, she supposed she and Limerick could always stab them and run off with the prize...

That would probably work. So that was an option worth considering. She didn't feel guilty at the thought of killing Tenno, seeing as he would happily see them dead (or clapped in irons for the rest of their lives, which, no thanks; if her life was over, she'd rather it end quickly). And Amella had tried to kill her in that sword fight, she was certain of it. No tears shed there. That left Corrin. Corrin would, from a tactical standpoint, be the easiest to overpower. She had a sword and seemed to have some idea of how to use it, sure, but she wasn't a seasoned fighter like the other two. Not that it mattered if Verse was attacking them while they slept anyway, but...

Verse inhaled and told herself to draw her dagger.

Her hand clutched the hilt so hard that it hurt.

She couldn't bring herself to do it.

Dammit. She'd thought the bandit life had forced all the soft-heartedness out of her.

Limerick tapped her shoulder. His eyes glittered in the starlight, and his hand rested on the hilt of his sword. Verse set her jaw and turned back to the encampment, fully intending to let him to get on with it—

—but Corrin rolled over, and her open eyes caught the moonlight.

Verse grabbed Limerick's shoulder. *Wait.*

Corrin watched them both, like a startled fox cub that wasn't entirely sure what they were, or what they were going to do, and knew well enough to be cautious but didn't know quite well enough to be scared. Verse stared back to her, heart hammering. One yell from this shrimp would wake the other two. They could sprint for the mead hall's entryway, try to outrun them. Maybe succeed. Probably not.

Corrin tilted her head in a silent inquiry.

Verse let out a shuddering breath and tugged Limerick back. She pressed a finger to her lips. "We'll go," she whispered hoarsely. "We won't stab you, or bother you, or take anything of yours if you just let us go." Verse wasn't sure why she bothered pleading like this, when she wasn't even sure whether Corrin could hear her properly. Probably not. Probably couldn't understand a flaming word. But she didn't dare speak up, for fear of waking Tenno or Amella. She silently willed the little healer to give her and her brother the benefit of the doubt—to do the thing that Verse most assuredly would not, in Corrin's position.

Corrin nodded and mimed tying her mouth shut.

Verse's face nearly split in two from grinning. She grabbed her brother's wrist and led him out of the mead hall, quick, before Corrin could change her mind. In seconds, they were out of the mead hall. Past the ruins. Striding across moonlit grass and creeping through shadowy copses. Clambering up the incline of Mount Cauldra, feeling as much as seeing the way forward, ears straining for chasing footsteps or the subtle rustlings of wild animals, stifling the urge to jump at a ghost owl's shriek.

They made it to a rocky outcropping on the east side of the mountain and stopped. A darker patch several yards above them marked a tunnel entrance. The griffin highlands stretched out to the north.

"So what now?" asked Limerick. He didn't make jibes about her leaving the fruit behind and the healer girl alive. Verse had expected him to.

Now, she leaned against a boulder and crossed her arms, thinking it over. They were bandits without a leader. The armies of Stalt would know to watch for them, whether they conducted more raids or not. If they went back there, they'd be constantly on the run, thieving and fighting to get by whether they wanted to earn an honest living or not. They might be caught. Or they might manage. They wouldn't manage as well as the Bandit King had, either way. Neither of them could match their leader's tactical skills or ruthless prowess. They just couldn't.

And forget the Gloamwood. Corrin could navigate that maze of shadows and befriend its monsters, but Verse wasn't going back in there. Never again. Not for a king's ransom. Not for immortality. Not even for the best audience she'd had in years, because that audience was a mob of plague-carrying squirrelly things. She'd been having nightmares about their creepy crinkled faces and needle-sharp teeth. She probably would for weeks.

"Not sure," Verse admitted. "We need a fresh start."

"What, you've lost your stomach for stabbing?"

Ah, there it was. The verbal jab. Verse didn't have to see her brother's razor-edged grin to know he was wearing it. "Yeah, actually," she said. "I'm done. You?"

After a beat of surprised silence, he replied, "You know what? Yeah. If we can be."

Verse bit her lip. So no Gloamwood, no Stalt. South into the badlands would be suicide, and even if they made it through, they'd end up back in Stalt territory again. If they went north, though, maybe got around Mount Cauldra and walked the precarious path between Boar's Tusk Peninsula and the griffin highlands, stuck to the shoreline or stowed away on a merchant ship…

She'd heard stories about the north. Met a few storytellers and traders from there when she was a kid. It was a scorching land, covered in deserts where prickly cacti, venomous snakes, and scaled beasts proliferated. Human settlements clustered around oases. They formed camps. Trade towns. Fortresses. The people were fractured into a dozen nations, which had fragile truces and short-lived wars over resources. But they all shared the same hardiness and the same lilting language, and they collectively referred to the region as Lurin.

Some excellent stories originated there. Verse could remember the echoes of them: songs about tricksters and mirage palaces, and accounts of massive crypts built from sun-baked bricks. And dragons. Too many dragons for her liking, but hey, she didn't have a lot of options here.

Perhaps they'd like to hear some foreign stories. She'd have a new one to offer, too: a tale about a healer who'd charmed a second chance at life from the trolls.

"Ephraim."

Her brother started. "Yeah? Verse—uh. Emilia?"

"Let's start over in Lurin."

CHAPTER TWENTY-SIX

The Road Home

When Amella roused and saw that the bards were gone, Corrin pretended to be unaware, pulling her makeshift blanket over her head and hiding like a turtle. The fabric blocked out the faint light of dawn. Amella's shout woke Tenno, who shouted back, harsh and frustrated. Only then did Corrin poke her head out from under the blankets, pretending to have just woken up. When they both turned to her and demanded to know if she'd seen anything, she pressed her lips together and shook her head, wide-eyed.

Tenno let out a long, slow breath, and when he next spoke, his voice was quieter, albeit tense as a taut lute string. "Alright. Okay. They're gone, then, nothing to be done about it." He raked his fingers through his hair. "I'm sorry for shouting, Corrin. I didn't mean to startle you. It's not your fault. And Amella, I'm sorry for snapping at you. We're all exhausted. I just—they're a threat to innocent people, and I meant to take them in. That's my job, to bring people like them to justice. I failed at it."

"Dragon dung," said Amella. "I'm the one who fell asleep on my watch shift, not you."

Guilt prickled at Corrin. She felt like she'd let Tenno and Amella down. She felt like she would let them down further if they knew she was lying.

But she'd thought—she'd hoped—that Verse and Limerick wouldn't go back to thieving and killing, now that they'd been through the Gloamwood and Limerick had almost died and they'd worked together and made a fragile sort of truce. She'd thought that if she gave them this second chance to walk away, then perhaps they'd make good use of it. And she'd felt like, after Verse had helped her retrieve the fruit and then let her have all of it without protest, Corrin owed them that chance. She crossed her fingers and hoped that her instincts were correct, and she hadn't made a tremendous mistake.

Corrin could at least dissuade her friends from blaming themselves, though.

"It's okay," she said quietly. "You've both done an awfully good job of helping us stay alive. That's more important, isn't it?"

Tenno's shoulders slumped. "I—yes, of course."

"That's true," said Amella. She knelt down and ruffled Corrin's hair. "We're all glad you're still with us."

Corrin nudged Amella's hand off, smiling.

Amella straightened. "Alright. We've got a long road ahead of us and a village to save, so let's get moving."

The three of them traveled from dawn to dusk, driven by the weight of the miracle cure in their packs and Corrin's burgeoning sense of urgency; she'd get caught up thinking of her da and little Petuni, of Sam's pleading eyes, and of Bathilda's warnings of the plague's implacability, and her feet would move faster without her noticing, until Tenno drew attention to her huffing and gently reminded her to pace herself. They cleared swathes of land in a blur. A half day hiking up Mount Cauldra. Three in the tunnels; the dragon's cavern was mercifully empty, and between the three of them, they recalled their way through the maze. Two days crossing the first leg of wildlands to the west.

One incident with a griffin that had wandered far south, but Amella and Tenno took care of it. Corrin took care of the gash on Amella's arm.

And then they met the platoon.

They'd just crested a large hill. Corrin spotted them first: a contingent of people on horseback, patchwork armor glinting in the sun. A firebird soared above them. Corrin stopped short and stared.

"What—" began Amella, then stopped short as well.

Tenno took one look at the platoon and said hoarsely, "They came."

Junior dropped out of the sky like a stone and landed on Tenno's forearm, chirruping excitedly. He babbled just as excitedly back, declaring how glad he was to see Junior safe, what a brave bird she'd been, what an excellent job she'd done. The platoon broke into a canter and met them near the top of the hill. Armor clinked. Hooves pawed the ground excitedly. Faces grinned.

Ragnor dismounted his steed and strode up to Tenno. He was not smiling. "You disobeyed your captain," he said. His voice held no inflection. It was the sort of unreadable flat that, in Corrin's experience, meant that some sort of severe discipline awaited the recipient. A week of all-day supervision and hard labor. A month of no desserts. Expressions of abject disappointment, which made a person feel deeply and painfully guilty. Such expressions, by her reckoning, were the most foreboding discipline of all.

Corrin wilted, and Ragnor wasn't even directing this at her.

But Tenno stood tall and rigid and said, "I was protecting one of our citizens, sir. As you can see, we have returned safely. The Bandit King has also been dealt with, as per my report." Junior shuffled up to his shoulder and nestled there contentedly. "We have retrieved the fruit that Corrin was seeking, and we have good reason to believe this medicine will cure the village of Oddment, as she thought it would. Unfortunately, the two bandits who were with us have escaped. For this, sir, I sincerely apologize." Tenno ducked his head. Corrin could swear she saw a tremor run through him. "Please take into account the results of my judgment, but I understand if this means expulsion from the force."

Ragnor said nothing.

Corrin's heart twisted. "Sir," she said, "he saved my life."

Ragnor gave her a piercing look.

And then he stepped forward and clasped Tenno's free shoulder. When he next spoke, his voice wasn't level in the slightest. "You've no idea how glad I am to see you well. Come. We'll bring you back to Oddment with all due haste."

Ragnor had all three of them mounted on horses. Tenno got his own horse, which carried him and all three of their packs, while a sturdy dun carried both Amella and Corrin. Corrin was not used to riding horses; she'd pet them and accepted rides from an elderly neighbor who owned an old plow horse, but she'd never mounted one and certainly never steered one. Tenno had to pluck her off the ground and plop her down on the saddle.

"Hold tight, Corrin," said Amella with a grin. As if Corrin weren't clinging to Amella for dear life already.

The dun nickered and loped forward.

Under most circumstances, Corrin would have preferred to walk. She felt much more comfortable on her own two feet, or at least with a person (or troll) who could hold her legs in place. The dun's gait rocked her back and forth, and she felt like she could tip right off without the horse even noticing.

But the horses ate up ground more than twice as fast as humans could, and time was everything now.

One of the guards, a woman with a metal-plated cap and an easy grin, debriefed Corrin and Amella as they travelled. They'd done a sweep of the land and found an old sea captain named Turner with a couple of men following him. (Corrin's heart leapt. "He's alive?" Amella demanded, and then made a noise suspiciously like a sniffle when the guard confirmed that yes, he had survived, and he was waiting for them in the watchtower.) Oddment had been placed under quarantine weeks ago. No word of deaths yet, but last they'd heard from the healer ("Bathilda," Corrin supplied helpfully), some of her patients were within days of it. The elders. The children. The vulnerable. Each word of ill tidings fed the anxiety in Corrin's gut until she felt ill.

Corrin willed their horses to move faster and farther, even as her legs grew sore.

They reached the peninsula, and there Turner met them, grey and rake thin but more or less healthy, with Dragon winding around his ankles and purring profusely. He bore Amella's rib-cracking embrace without complaint, and though he didn't quite smile, Corrin could swear his greetings were fonder and less somber than normal. They found Oatmuncher chewing contentedly away in the military's stables, and Amella threw her arms around his fluffy neck with a shout of delight. They didn't take long for pleasantries, though; the guards bustled them all onto one of Stalt's navy ships, armed by a full platoon and bolstered along by both sail and oars.

They sailed south to Miritown. By Turner's reckoning, they moved fast, faster by spades than he could have taken her in his old ship (may her poor besieged timbers rest in peace).

But to Corrin, it felt like a lifetime.

It was cool and bright in Miritown. While the north had been warm, fall had settled in down here, making the winds brisk and the air chilly. The townspeople bundled up in cloaks and extra-thick doublets and scarves. Buskers still played on the streets, now with gloves shielding their fingers. Folks sheltered under the awnings with steaming tidbits of food and mugs of hot tea, chattering merrily. It was as if nothing were wrong, nothing at all.

And yet.

The guard at the docks reported that three people had succumbed to the plague in Oddment. Amella cursed. Corrin's heart lurched, and her throat constricted. The guard looked greatly discomfited as he added, "You realize that if your medicine doesn't work, you can't come back out, don't you? We can't risk the sickness taking root in the rest of the realm."

Corrin's vision blurred. She nodded and hurried onward.

Amella suggested that they stop by the Cuddly Bear—"just a quick visit," said Amella, "let Ida see your living, breathing face. Y'know she seemed darned worried about you last we talked." But Corrin balked; there was no time to stop, not when they were so close and some of her neighbors had already died; and the others caved to her urgency. Turner listened to this exchange gravely, then walked with them to the edge of town in silence. He stopped where the main path passed the last dwelling, an old riverboat turned into a cottage, and at last, he spoke. "I will visit Ida," he promised. "She'll be glad to hear you're well."

"Thanks," said Corrin hoarsely.

Turner gazed upon her, solemn. "Take care. Visit again when your town is healed, lass."

She sniffled. "I will."

From Miritown, Corrin, Amella, Tenno, the unflappable Oatmuncher, and an escort of four guards marched on to Oddment. It took them but a day and a night, and they arrived 'round midmorning, when the sun had chased the dew away but not the chill. The ruins of Oddment rose ahead of them, with its crooked towers and ivy-blanketed walls. It seemed peaceful, except for the contingent of guards patrolling atop the parapets.

Their escort stopped twenty paces away from the wall, with the exception of Tenno, who stayed with them up through the entrance. He signaled the guards above the gate. They lowered their bows and let them through.

The air smelled of wood smoke. Cats wandered the streets, but not people. Doors were shut tight. Corrin couldn't hear the rattle-bang of the smithy's tools, or the reedy complaints of the elders, or the cackling of small children. There were no gossiping neighbors clogging up the porches, nobody squeezing past or calling out a friendly hello. All she could hear was birdsong and the rustling of small creatures, and the thumps of guards' footsteps high above.

The atmosphere was all wrong.

"By the starlands," said Amella quietly.

"Alright, Corrin," said Tenno softly. "Where should we start?"

Corrin bit her lip. Where to start, indeed.

Bathilda.

Bathilda would know what to do.

"Let's go see my teacher."

CHAPTER TWENTY-SEVEN

Healing and Forgiveness

Bathilda's door was open, unlike the neighbors' doors, and an overpowering aroma of lilac and girdroot and a dozen other herbs and spices wafted out of it, along with a purplish smoke. Light flickered and glowed from inside, and finally, Corrin heard human noises: shuffling footsteps, a knife chopping on a cutting board, a curse. She motioned for Tenno and Amella to keep behind her and entered without knocking.

Bathilda hunched over her work table, her back turned to the entrance, her cloak swishing around her feet and her cane propped up against a seat next to her. Her bun seemed even wispier than Corrin remembered, and her gnarled hands worked furiously. "Keep the fevers down," she muttered to herself, as she tipped a handful of slivered root into a beaker. They hissed as they hit the liquid. "Keep their insides from burning up... Temper the acid with, where did I put —"

Corrin cleared her throat.

"One Churikin-darned minute."

Bathilda turned around.

Her eyes, a washed out grey and almost otherworldly in her shadowy home, grew round as coins. "Corrin!"

Corrin fumbled for a hello. She meant to say "I'm back," or "It's good to see you," or perhaps, "How is everyone?" What came out was, "You didn't think I'd come back, did you?" It sounded more accusatory than she meant it to.

But Bathilda seemed to take it in stride. Or perhaps she was so glad to see Corrin that she cared nothing for feet in mouths or accidental rudeness. "You took your time, lass. By the spirits, it's good to see you."

Bathilda grabbed her staff and hobbled over to embrace Corrin. It was the boniest hug Corrin had had in a long time, and Corrin returned it carefully, fearing for the brittleness of her mentor's bones and thinness of her limbs. She could swear that Bathilda's wrinkles had doubled in the time she'd been gone. That shouldn't have been possible. Bathilda had been as wrinkly as Corrin could imagine a person becoming.

But she was warm, and her cloak smelled of medicine and smoke.

Bathilda released her and leaned heavily on her staff, a new life in her eyes. "You found the fruit? The Tree of Life?"

Corrin shrugged off her pack and opened it, showing Bathilda the bounty she'd brought with her. "Amella and Tenno are carrying more."

"Tenno?" She peered past Corrin and made a "huh!" sound. "That's a strong-looking friend you've found yourself. Where'd you meet this one?"

Tenno, who had to duck a bit to fit inside Bathilda's home at all, rubbed the back of his neck nervously and cleared his throat. "I'm a guardsman from Boar's Tusk Peninsula. Corrin ran into some trouble with bandits near the peninsula, so, er, I helped. I went with her into the Gloamwood." Tenno paused. "Her cleverness did more for me than my sword-hand could do for her, in truth."

"Hah! Good. Means I've taught her well. But never mind, never mind—all of you, come with me. We need to distribute this cure, and quickly." Her expression sharpened. "Amella, Tenno, each of you take a section of Oddment, and visit all the apartments along the edges. Amella near your abode along the western wall, Tenno to the east. Don't wait or knock; many aren't fit to answer the door. Give one half a fruit to each adult, one quarter to each child. That should be enough to jumpstart recovery and keep the worst cases back from the brink. With luck, we'll have reserves for follow-up doses to the most severe cases. Track the names of all you help, write them down, and report back to me."

Amella and Tenno rushed out the door.

"Corrin, you come with me." Grimly, Bathilda added, "Little Petuni first. She's the worst off. The girl's clinging to life by a thread."

Petuni lay on death's doorstep.

She was gaunter than any child should be, her complexion pallid. Her dark hair stuck to her forehead, and she lay limp beneath her bedcovers. Her parents, who were similarly ill, lay in sleeping pallets on either side of her. Her father, Drey, sat up as Corrin entered, his breath catching, something akin to hope crossing his features. Her mother, Farin, lay still as a corpse. But she yet lived; her eyes tracked Corrin, and she rolled onto her side as Corrin rushed to Petuni's bed. Corrin feared, for a moment, that Petuni had stopped breathing, that she was well and truly gone, and Corrin's heart stuttered with dismay. But as Corrin's fingers ghosted over Petuni's lips, she felt the barest hint of breath. Small and weak, but present.

She's alive. Thank the stars. Please, hang on.

"Petuni?" Corrin called, and gently touched her cheek. "Wake up, please?"

Petuni didn't stir.

Please!

Corrin tried again. "Petuni, I made it back. With medicine." She shook Petuni's shoulder, insistent. "I promise you all the elderberry jam and sweet bread in the world, but I really, really need you to take this medicine. Please."

Petuni's eyes cracked open. She said nothing. She stared blankly, as if she couldn't see Corrin's face, or perhaps was simply too weakened to care.

Corrin's heart sank. She slipped her hands beneath Petuni's head and back and physically lifted the girl farther up the bed, positioning her so she was slumped against the pillows and headboard. Petuni did not protest, did not say anything, and did nothing to help herself stay upright, though Corrin thought, maybe, she finally saw a hint of recognition flicker in Petuni's eyes.

"One quarter of the fruit," instructed Bathilda from behind Corrin. She passed Corrin one of the life fruits, wrinkly and sickly sweet. "No more. Squeeze the juice into her mouth first."

Corrin withdrew one of the fruit, cut off the prescribed portion, cradled Petuni's jaw, and squeezed the juice into her mouth. She massaged Petuni's throat, silently willing her to swallow. *Please!!*

Petuni swallowed.

Corrin waited, holding her.

Petuni blinked. Her chapped lips parted. Her voice, whispery and feeble, reached Corrin's ear. "Cor…rin…?"

"Yes. Yes, it's me." Corrin's mind whirred. With Petuni as light and frail as a leaf in Corrin's arms, still so weak, Corrin questioned whether this single quarter of a fruit would be enough. *Bathilda said it would be. She was so certain. And we need to make sure we've got enough to go around. But maybe—she might need an extra—*

"The flesh," said Bathilda firmly. "And skin. Have her eat that too, all of it."

"O-oh. Yes." Corrin pressed tiny pieces of the squeezed-out piece of fruit to Petuni's lips and coaxed the girl into nibbling it.

Petuni did so with agonizing slowness. But each nibble seemed to make her marginally more alert, and she managed to finish it. "Corrin," repeated Petuni, her voice strengthening. A murmur instead of a whisper. "Sam said… but… Where did you *go*?"

Corrin breathed out. "A wild land up north, which I'll tell you about when you're feeling better."

Petuni frowned, and her voice gained a stubborn edge. "I'm better."

Corrin mustered a smile. "That's a brave lass. But you need to get even better. All the way healed."

Petuni blinked slowly.

"More bedrest," said Corrin firmly.

Had Petuni been feeling half her usual self, she would have protested immediately. As it was, she sank into the pillows and mumbled, "Okay." Which told Corrin that she still *really* felt lousy. But at least she was lucid. Talking. Peering up at Corrin's face.

She'll be okay. I think.

"I need to get medicine to everyone else," Corrin said.

"Sam? And—and Frendel?" Petuni's tone turned pleading. "They stopped visiting."

Another stab of fear ran through Corrin's heart. She turned to Bathilda, a frantic question on her lips.

Before she could ask it, Bathilda answered. "Your family's alive, even your da, though he's in poor shape. But yes, Sam and Frendel have caught the illness, as has your mother. I put them all on bedrest. Or tried to! Your mum refuses to lie down for long. She fetches me herbs, now. Most stubborn and insistent helper I've ever had."

Corrin's panic eased, and she managed a wan smile. *That sounds like Mum, alright. Okay… Okay, I can still save them.* She addressed Petuni gently. "Yes, sounds like they're sick. I'll make sure to get this cure to them, quick as I can." An idea struck her, and she reached into her pouch and withdrew the small stone Sam had given her. *It's just a silly rock,* she thought. *It didn't do anything, except make me think of him. But maybe that's not nothing. And maybe Petuni'll appreciate it. Small enough to still believe in superstitions, she is.* She pressed the rock into Petuni's hand and folded the girl's fingers around it. "Sam gave me his lucky rock for my travels. I'm back now, and he'd probably be real happy to let you hold it for a while. So keep it safe for him, and you can show it to him when you both feel better. Okay?"

The barest hint of a smile graced Petuni's face. "Okay."

"Good." Corrin nearly leaned in to kiss Petuni's forehead, but she caught herself at the last moment and refrained. Corrin hastened over to Drey, while Bathilda bustled over to Farin.

As Corrin passed Drey his dose, his hand clasped hers, firm, almost desperate. "Thank you," he said fervently. "Thank you for saving my child."

A lump formed in Corrin's throat. "You're welcome," she said thickly. After a few rapid blinks and a steadying breath, she added sternly, "Make sure you eat all of that. Every single bit."

And with that, Corrin swept out of the apartment, followed by a surprisingly swift Bathilda.

That was three. Just the rest of Oddment to go.

Bathilda led the way into Oddment's other apartments, one by one: shadowy cramped places, some with fires crackling in their hearths and others with nothing but a feeble lantern. Corrin's neighbors lay sweating in beds and reclined limply in chairs. Some greeted her with hoarse voices. Some wheezed and grimaced and told her to stay back, lest she catch the plague too. Others said nothing, for they were asleep. Under Bathilda's guidance, Corrin drew her dagger and cut off pieces of fruit. She pressed the fruit to chapped lips, returning greetings gently and becoming selectively deaf whenever anyone tried to warn her off.

Between apartments, Corrin recounted everything to Bathilda. Miritown. The sea voyage. The Bandit King. The trolls. The Churikin. The bards. Bathilda listened with little comment, except for her eyebrows that rose and rose and the smiles that grew and vanished: proud, fond, incredulous. In turn, she recounted for Corrin the decline of the people of Oddment, and how a quarantine was put in place a mere two weeks after she'd left. She described the guards who brought them supplies, but were too afraid to come close; the measures they'd taken to try to stop it from spreading; how it had spread to most, anyway; how she, Bathilda, had been making rounds day after day; and how they'd built a funeral pyre a mere three nights ago.

She told Corrin the names of the dead.

Jallen: the smith who could talk forever about his craft. He had never minded when Corrin, in turn, tentatively talked about medicine.

No more would he tell her about melting points, or listen patiently as she explained why she was applying a burn salve or how splinting his finger would help the bone repair itself.

Inrit: a boisterous elder with silver curls and stories to share whenever Corrin brought her salve for her joints. Evelyn's mother. Her lively voice was simply gone.

Melia: a seasoned hunter with hair the color of a grouse and a quiet, steady way about her. No more would she cross paths with Corrin in the woods and smile, nor greet her when they met in town.

Corrin's heart twisted and cracked.

"All their friends and family are devastated," said Bathilda, as they came closer to the center of town. "But at least most of them are still alive."

At last, they reached Corrin's home.

Her mum sat with Tiptoes on her lap, dozing. A half-finished bowl of soup rested on the table, long since gone cold. Mum was thin and awfully pale, and when Corrin brushed her forehead, her skin was flushed, feverish. But she woke when Corrin nudged her shoulder, and her gaze was still bright and sharp, her hands kind as she exclaimed over Corrin's return and brushed wisps of hair out of her face.

"I have medicine," said Corrin quickly, and pressed fruit into her hands. "You should eat—"

"We must get this to your da and brothers." Her mother turned on her heel and staggered off to her da's chambers.

The sight of her da, frighteningly ashen and still in his bed, hit her like a stab to the gut. But when she checked him, she could feel his pulse in his neck and breath leaving his lips. His skin burned with the furnace-like heat of fever, and sweat beaded on his brow, which was creased, as if he were caught in the thrall of a bad dream.

She shook his shoulder.

His eyes cracked open. "My good lass," said her da hoarsely. He grasped her hand. "I'm so glad to see you safe. So glad."

"Sssh. Eat this."

He did, and some color returned to his face, a spark of brightness to his eyes. He embraced her. He wasn't strong and sturdy as Corrin remembered; he trembled, and she had to support the small of his back with her own skinny arms. But his strength would return with time, she hoped. Her hope grew and her heart lightened as her mum kissed his forehead and murmured fond chidings in his ear, her eyes sparkling.

Corrin moved onto her brothers' room, conscious of Bathilda trailing after her. She was eerily silent.

Her brothers, at least, were awake, but it hurt her heart to see them so clearly unwell. They huddled together in their twin bed, covers drawn to their chins, cups of tea forgotten on the bedside table. They looked pale, and their foreheads were clammy to the touch. Sam remained listless as she cajoled him into eating his portion of the fruit; but Frendel, at least, showed a spark of interest in the purple chunks she handed him.

"What is it?" he asked.

"You know how I left to find a medicine to help everyone? This is the medicine. It'll make you feel better. Da already had some."

Frendel eyed the fruit suspiciously. "Does it taste like the gunky stuff you gave me when I had the sniffles?"

"Nope," said Corrin brightly.

Frendel frowned at her, as if looking for signs of deceit; but evidently he saw none, for he stuffed the fruit into his mouth and chewed. Moments later, his face contorted in disgust, and he shuddered as he swallowed. "You lied," he accused. "This is gross! It's worse than the gunky winter potion!"

"But you didn't ask if it tasted better. You asked if it tasted the same." Corrin smiled and ruffled Frendel's hair. "What matters is that this'll make you feel better, even if it tastes like skunk juice and rotten eggs and whatever other gross things you want to compare it with." She leaned in conspiratorially. "You wouldn't believe how far I had to travel to find this medicine for you. I went so far that I saw fairies, and had to jump ship because of bandits, and—"

"What?" asked her mum. "Corrin, honey, exactly how far afield did you go?"

Corrin flushed. Right. Her mum probably wouldn't be pleased to hear the details. Corrin might never leave Oddment again if she told her mum the tale in full, what with all the bandits and the dragon and near deaths and the *actual* deaths and the Gloamwood, and the trolls who could've had her for supper if they'd wanted to. Once upon a time, she might not have minded the restrictions of her mum's worry; she might have been content staying in Oddment for the rest of her days, within friendly old walls and shouting distance of the neighbors she'd grown up with. But now, the thought of never venturing out again; of never stopping by the Cuddly Bear; of never sailing again, or wandering afield with Amella; of not keeping her promise to Makur…

"A ways north," she said quickly, "just to the edge of Stalt."

Behind her mum, Bathilda's eyes twinkled knowingly, and she signaled Corrin with the briefest of winks.

Frendel's eyes were wide as an owlet's. Sam not so much, but at least he was watching her.

"Look me in the eye and repeat that, young lady."

"I went a ways north," Corrin said stubbornly, "and we can talk about this after you've taken your medicine and healed, okay, Mum?"

"...All right."

Her mum took the medicine.

She healed.

Her da healed.

Her brothers healed.

The rest of Oddment healed.

It took two weeks.

Corrin spent that time mixing supplemental remedies with Bathilda and running from door to door, distributing fruit rations to those who still needed it and coaxing fed up patients to swallow yet another bitter concoction.

Of course, remedies for sickness could do naught for grief, and though Corrin's efforts had helped Oddment tremendously—had saved most of their lives, had made it so most of them would be okay —some hearts would stay cracked and weighed down by loss long after the village as a whole recovered. Indeed, Corrin felt the atmosphere of grief whenever she stopped into those cracked hearts' apartment. She gave them their curative doses and offerings of food. Fresh elderberry jam, pickings from the woods, anything she and her mum and da could spare. Each gift felt like a paltry solace, like it was far too little. But their gazes became a mite less glassy, perhaps, when she brought them these things, and some even thanked her for trying. For making it back to them. For saving all she could.

Amella helped Oddment as best she could, too, mostly with anything involving heavy lifting. But she also stopped by the worst-stricken's homes and brought in her good spirits, her raucous laughter and wild tales.

Tenno stayed in Oddment as well. He helped with fixing doors and distributing blankets, food, and water, and he took shifts with the other guards to watch over everyone. He didn't have time to talk with Corrin at length—none of them had time for leisure; their hands were too full—until one evening, when the village was mostly healed and most everyone could breathe a bit easier.

Corrin sat on one of Oddment's walls with her legs dangling over the side and Tiptoes curled in her lap, purring. A pastel blend of pink and orange seeped across the sky, setting the undersides of clouds aglow. The sun was a burning orange disk, half concealed by the horizon. The air was cool and crisp. Corrin kept her fingertips buried in Tiptoes's fur and her cloak wrapped around the both of them. A thick-knit scarf coiled around her neck.

"Corrin, may I join you?"

Corrin started, but it was only Tenno. She patted the space beside her, and he took it.

They sat side by side without speaking, watching the sun go down. The orange grew dusky, and the light pinks turned to purple.

"It's nice out here," said Tenno. "Do you come up often?"

"Mhm. Sometimes I bring snacks, and sometimes my brothers come with me. They aren't the best at sitting still, but if they've tuckered themselves out enough, they can manage it." She tickled Tiptoes under the chin, and the little cat tilted her head up, her eyes narrowed in bliss. "It's especially beautiful when it's snowed, and I think the first snow will be here soon. You can tell it's coming when the cold makes your nose go numb. And once that first snow comes, the ground's buried in sparkling white stuff until mid-spring. We get green shoots fighting their way out before it gets properly warm and melty."

"Interesting. We don't get strong winters around the peninsula. No snow, just more rain and a bit of a chill." Tenno's forearms were conspicuously bare and riddled with goosebumps, and he rubbed them subconsciously. His expression turned sheepish. "I forget what it's like to feel this cold. I probably should've bundled up."

"Probably," Corrin agreed. "If you struggle to stay warm, you won't have enough energy to fight off sickness. And if you don't bundle your fingers and toes properly, they can freeze off." She grinned. "Like when you swim in a cold ocean and your toes turn blue."

"Please don't remind me. That was terrifying."

"You weren't even the one who went swimming."

"That's why it was so terrifying."

There was a lull; then, Tenno turned to face her fully. "I came up to tell you something in particular."

Corrin blinked. "Oh?"

"I'm leaving in two days to return to my post on the peninsula."

"Oh." Corrin was surprised by how much that saddened her. But then, she had gotten used to having him around, to his kind and stalwart friendship. He'd come all this way with her, after all, and stayed when no one else from the escort would set foot inside Oddment's walls. And the other guards had said he wouldn't be able to leave while the quarantine was in place. Though, come to think of it, most everyone was recovering now... "So the quarantine...?"

"The captain here thinks it's safe to lift it. I think Ragnor would like me back up there, to help us round up the last of the rogues. From what I understand, some of the Bandit King's followers are still wandering the countryside." Tenno scratched the back of his neck. "I think he'd like me back, in general. Something about being a giant person with a sword really seems to help with stopping mischief."

"Or he misses you."

"Or he misses me," Tenno agreed. He cracked a smile. "He's not the most social of captains, but he's a good man. There's something about dealing with danger and trouble together that forges connections, you know?"

Corrin hummed in agreement. Of course she knew.

It would have been nice, Corrin thought, if Tenno could have stayed longer. She could have waved to him and chatted over inanities and stopped over with tea, and maybe he would have started practicing the sword with her again. But perhaps—perhaps, if he were to stay—he'd miss his comrades and Ragnor more than she would miss him. Perhaps he would miss the peninsula and its gentle weather and its thriving fisher's port, as she had missed Oddment and its seasons and cats and walls cloaked in vines.

"S'why you want to go back so soon, isn't it?" asked Corrin gently. "For your friends and comrades up north. You miss them too."

"That's part of it," agreed Tenno. "The other part of it is just... I want to do my duty as a guard. Be prepared to protect, to get rid of threats and spare innocent people from pain and loss. That's important to me, perhaps the same way that being able to heal Oddment is important to you." He tilted his head and considered her. "You're a healer because you want to help people too, right? Help them feel better, the way Bathilda helped you? After a fashion, anyway." Tenno cracked a smile. "I know you said you didn't feel much, but I don't imagine getting stitches was the most comforting feeling."

Corrin said wryly, "No, but it sure was interesting. And I was a curious child."

Tenno grinned. "Ah yes. Interesting. So you told me."

Corrin nudged him playfully, and he laughed. Corrin let his laughter wash over her, deep and warm.

Eventually, his mirth faded, and his gaze shifted away, out toward the horizon. His voice softened again, turning somber. "Well, in my case, I… It was a little different, for me. Curiosity doesn't usually factor into joining the military." His hands fisted in the fabric of his knees. "I really did want to protect people in a way that I wish—well. Wish I could've done for my dad."

His words hung heavy in the air, and Corrin sensed a shift in the atmosphere. She had a strong suspicion about where this was headed—toward the fragile, squishy innards of his heart that she hadn't pried into on the road, for fear of hurting him. She didn't pry now, either, merely waited and listened.

Tenno's shoulders slumped, and he braced his hands on the cold stone of the walkway. "My mom and dad were both smiths. Mom still is, actually; she crafts masterpieces in her forge to this day. My sister, too. But anyway, I was… I was fourteen. Traveling with my dad in a small caravan to Valencia, to help sell some gear he and Mom had crafted. It, uh. It included some very finely made swords. And we had to walk along the trading route in the Bristleback Mountains, and, well… there was this shadowy mountain pass."

The beginnings of sadness and sympathy stirred within Corrin. This story, she knew, would not end happily.

Tenno continued. "We got jumped by bandits. Possibly members of the Bandit King's forces, in retrospect—it would make sense, given the pattern of banditry in the area and when we suspect she rose to prominence—but if so, I… I couldn't make out their faces in the dark, and there were too many voices, mixing together." He paused, gathering himself. "My dad grabbed one of the swords and told me to run. But—well—they got him." Tenno took a shaky breath. "They came after me next, and I… I ran, like my dad had told me. I was lucky. We were getting close to an outpost, and a patrol of guards was doing rounds at the edge of it. They protected me, mobilized to salvage who and what they could from that caravan, and got the survivors to safety. Not that there were many." His voice was edged with bitterness.

Corrin was at a loss for words. But perhaps that was for the best, because Tenno still had more to say.

"I never wanted to feel that helpless again. I wanted to protect people, like those guards protected me. I wanted to be able to *do* something the next time someone I cared about was threatened. And I wanted to bring down anyone who would kill the innocent." His hazel eyes were flinty, his jaw set. "So, as soon as I was old enough—around your age, actually—I enlisted for basic training. And, well, you know the rest. I completed training, was eventually stationed out on Boar's Tusk Peninsula." His expression softened again, and his voice caught slightly as he continued. "You came staggering out of the water with blue lips and trembling legs, and... You were so determined to save your dad and your home. To press onward into danger, with killers at your back and without a single friend at your side. And I'd be damned if I left you to face that alone. Not when I was strong enough to help, this time."

Corrin wanted to swipe the dampness from the corners of his eyes and slather salves on the still-tender scars of grief that he'd shown her. But this was not a thing to be treated by medicine, nor was it a thing to be stoppered and swept away. So she wrapped her arms around him—as best she could when he was so much bigger and broader, at least—and hugged him tight. She didn't say a word, but the gesture, she hoped, spoke volumes.

Tenno sniffled and hugged her back. "Thanks," he said quietly. Then: "I don't think I can ever forgive them. The bandits, I mean. They're monsters, more so than any other creature."

Corrin thought of Verse and Limerick and how she'd let them slip away in the night, and she felt a dreadful mixture of guilt, sorrow, and disquiet. They had done terrible things, yes, but she wanted to hope they could do better. Those two, at least. Verse could make beautiful melodies, and she'd given Corrin the fruit and left peacefully with Limerick in tow. Maybe they could make more music. Maybe they'd do less stabbing, with the Bandit King gone and her forces scattered. Corrin wanted to hope. She wanted to believe she'd done the right thing in giving them that chance.

But she tried to imagine admitting this to Tenno, tried to imagine how she could get him to understand, and... she couldn't. She couldn't imagine anything other than him getting terribly upset. And she understood why he would be. She could forgive him for not forgiving.

Corrin tucked her face against his shoulder and mumbled, "S'okay."

He held her for a moment longer, then released her. "Thanks," he said again, and managed a small, lopsided smile. "I'm going to miss you, you know, much as I miss my comrades up north already."

"I guess," she said quietly, "I'll just have to venture north one of these days to visit you."

"Best keep your swordsmanship sharp, then. You never know what trouble you'll find on the road."

She hummed her agreement.

They lapsed into silence and watched as twilight fell.

CHAPTER TWENTY-EIGHT

Bathilda's Tale

Three days after Tenno's departure, most everyone had healed and the first snow had dusted Oddment in a thin layer of glittering powder.

Corrin knocked on Bathilda's door. It was shut against the cold, but she'd left her healer's symbol hanging on the peg outside. The intricately woven vines and crow feathers held strong, and the bell at the end gleamed.

The door creaked inward, and Bathilda peered up at Corrin curiously. She was bundled up so thoroughly that she was scarcely more than a wrinkled face and a shifting pile of fabrics, except for the arthritic hand that poked out to clutch her staff. She leaned heavily upon it, and she seemed even smaller and more hunched than usual, somehow. Even so, Bathilda greeted Corrin with a broad smile and croaked, "Come in, before your nose freezes off."

Corrin hastily shut the door behind her and fed Bathilda's fire more wood. It crackled and grew, and the room became distinctly brighter and warmer. Better for Bathilda's joints. They got stiff and sore in the winter, and her tinctures could only do so much to alleviate the discomfort.

"Aaah," said Bathilda contentedly as she stumped over to the hearth, "that's a fine heat. Thank you, m'dear." She sank into one of the armchairs. Both chairs were worn and patchy, but the cushions were plush and comfortable, made to cradle tired and frail bodies.

"Of course." Corrin glanced around the room. The herb bundles hanging from the ceiling were much reduced, and the shelves emptier than they ought to be, but her table was laden from end to end with equipment: jars of poultice, mortars and pestles, vials of potion, pots, probably half her store's worth of herbs and pickled animal parts...

The last couple of dried fruit rested amid the mess, and Corrin drifted over to peer down at them curiously. One was split open. The seeds were missing. There were three small jars next to it, full of dirt but with no sign of sprouts.

Corrin pointed to the jars and said regretfully, "Those aren't going to grow."

Bathilda huffed. "Don't say they won't until you've tested the theory, lass. It can't hurt to try."

"But someone did."

"Oh?"

Corrin joined Bathilda by the hearth. Her fingers interlaced, separated, and interlaced again. "I found something else by the Tree of Life. See, Makur and I had to bury the Bandit King and her follower..." And so she described the tunnel entrance that led under the tree, and the two strange statues that guarded it. She described the crypt, the mounds guarded by the glowing lichen-like substance, and the stone container that she'd found there. The journal. The records. The wise woman and her experiments. Her longevity.

The seeds' failure to grow anywhere else in the Gloamwood. The records of war due to the fruit scarcity and people's hunger for immortality. How the healer had stayed behind while her people left.

Bathilda listened through all of it without interrupting, her brow creasing deeper and deeper.

"I think the seed needs some specific balance of nutrients in the soil by those springs. And the climate probably has to be just right, too. Or maybe there's something else, some other reason the seeds just won't grow." Corrin paused, then added quietly, "I'm sorry. I didn't tell you before now because I didn't tell Tenno and Amella, or anyone else. They're trustworthy folks, I know they are, but if they passed it on someone who wasn't, I thought, what if it started another war? Or what if they just... What if they were too tempted? Immortality's awfully tempting. Enough so that the Bandit King decided to chase it, even though she only heard about it from stories."

"Aye, young one. I know all too well the lure of immortality." Bathilda said no more than that; she seemed to be waiting for some kind of reaction.

Corrin blinked. She thought of Gailstone and the details that hadn't fit right, and gradually, a suspicion surfaced. "Bathilda, how old are you?"

"Old as dirt." Her eyes twinkled.

"How old is the dirt?"

"So you're going to press the point, eh?" Bathilda folded her hands in her lap. They didn't lace together as easily as Corrin's, thanks to their knobby joints and arthritis. "Alright then, lass. Given all you've done on my word and map alone, I'll tell you: I am five hundred and twenty-seven years old." Bathilda lifted a hand, signaling *I'm not done;* and with great effort, Corrin held back the tide of questions that wanted to burst out of her. "And as you must have reasoned by now, I could only live this long by eating the fruit. I had to have a dose, oh, every twenty years, or else I'd begin to age."

"I—I don't understand. That means you had to get the fruit from the Gloamwood, again and again and again."

"Not quite. I could store the seeds for decades. I could also drink its extract, brewed down to its essence, to better my health. I have only needed a fresh harvest once per hundred years. And as you can see—" she gestured to herself, to her wispy white bun and her papery wrinkled skin "—I stretched that boundary. I would go for an extra twenty, oh, thirty years, and let myself grow a bit older, a bit creakier."

"But you've still had to get the fruit, sometimes. Or… Or you had to have someone else get it."

"That's quite the frown you have!" Bathilda poked Corrin lightly with her staff. Corrin's frown only deepened. "Listen to me for a spell, will you? Trust your old teacher, one more time."

So Corrin sat. And she listened.

Bathilda began: "I was born deep in the Bristleback Mountains, though when Stalt was still young and fractured, some of us referred to that mountain range as the Dragon Spine. Smart whip of a lass I was, like you, and in my small village, I studied the arts of healing. I learned how to suture skin, to set bones, to brew medicines and quell my squeamish patients. It was difficult, very much so, because our people hadn't aggregated half as much medicinal knowledge. I was guessing and inventing, and sometimes failing, and sometimes someone would die for my failures.

"One day, my teacher fell ill. 'Twas not a plague like ours, 'twas something else—I believe a kind of infection that these days, I could cure without the Tree of Life's aid—but we hadn't learned how to treat it yet. Not effectively. I couldn't for the life of me clear the mucus in her airways or make her breathing rattle less."

Bathilda gazed into the flames, her pale grey eyes reflecting the flickering light. Her expression was difficult to read, but Corrin thought, maybe, she saw a trace of sadness, a hint of regret. "I had a dear friend. Reina was her name, and she had a grip as iron as the metal she worked and a heart as mighty as her forge. Reina saw me try, and fail, and try again, and one eve she pulled me aside and suggested we set out for the Gloamwood.

"The tales we tell of the Gloamwood have changed since then, but the core truths at them didn't. The Gloamwood was rife with monsters, and most who ventured in got caught in its shadows, never to return. At its heart thrived a tree whose fruit could cure any illness, could stall Death herself. And only the most foolhardy, the most desperate, would try to take it.

"By the turtle's back, I was desperate."

Corrin heard the intensity in Bathilda's voice, heard the ghost of that desperation, and understood it all too well.

So it was no surprise when Bathilda told her, "I said yes."

A wry smile upturned the corners of Bathilda's mouth. "We found our way. We survived—though not as spectacularly as you did! We tiptoed around the dragon, and we did not befriend the trolls. Reina killed one who tried to kill us, in fact. We did not charm the Churikin with music, either, but took climbing picks and axes and fought our way to the fruit. We cured our own ailments with the fruit, then cured my old teacher, then ate what we had left over. All was well. Time stood still for us, for a while; we saw seasons pass and our friends grow old while our joints stayed strong and springy as they'd been a decade ago."

Corrin's mind whirred. So Bathilda and her friend had eaten the fruit to cure themselves, and that had been enough to delay their aging? Then, what would happen to Corrin, and to everyone she'd treated in Oddment? She wasn't aging yet, not really. She had just barely reached adulthood. And none of them had eaten as much as it sounded like Bathilda had. And yet—what if—

"I can see the questions beetling your brow, my lass," said Bathilda fondly. "Best address them now, before I continue."

Corrin stuttered, trying to detangle her thoughts and put them in speakable order. Bathilda gave her a moment to gather herself, and Corrin finally managed to ask, "Do you think the doses we—um, am I and our neighbors going to live unusually long?"

"Hm! A good question." After a moment's thought, Bathilda said, "I believe the dose was small enough that the effects won't be all that noticeable. A few years extra for the folks who are older than you, perhaps. But you yourself... well, you're so young, and as far as I could tell, the fruit never delayed growth, only withering."

"Oh. I see." Corrin felt both relieved and slightly disappointed. "Well, that's alright."

Bathilda's eyes twinkled. "I'm glad... although that's certainly not how my first home reacted! Ahem, back to the story... The village saw how we didn't age. They wanted what we had—Reina and myself, and my teacher.

"Buoyed by our previous success, Reina and I agreed to guide them. We wanted more of the fruit for ourselves, as well. We had mapped our path, you see. And so we went back again, this time with half the village behind us."

Bathilda's eyes grew haunted, and her shoulders sagged with the weight of her next words. "Most of us didn't survive. Reina did, and I did, and we even got to the fruit. But the cost... Ah, we'd been so reckless. So foolish. I ate the fruit because I did not want all our efforts to be for nothing; we had survived, so we might as well live as long as we can. In my hands I held the power to avoid death; of course I would use it! But Reina refused. She told me she would rather age and move on to the starlands. She told me this fruit was a curse."

The power to avoid death, and the toll had already been paid. The terrible, nightmarish toll... Corrin could see Bathilda's logic. In fact, she thought Bathilda's response more logical than Reina's. At the same time, she internally quailed at the consequences of their poorly chosen adventure. Reina must have quailed, too. It was still difficult for her to imagine Bathilda being foolish, but their decision to bring the village into the Gloamwood to battle through it... well, Corrin needn't say it. Bathilda knew.

"I shouted at her, accusing her of waste and abandonment, and she shouted back at me. Our friendship fractured. We made amends with time, but I scarcely aged while her hair turned gray, and one day, I had to see to her funeral rites." Bathilda's voice shook with grief; but before Corrin could say so much as a feeble "m'sorry," Bathilda shook her head, lifted her chin, and continued:

"From there, I traveled from town to town, land to land; I'd settle down for a decade or two, teach my healing methods and learn some in turn, and then I'd move on. I even crossed the border into the lands of Lurin a few times. I stayed in Stalt's capital thrice, each time assuming a different name. Once, I was the head physician for the king! But most of the time, I dwelled in small and distant settlements, places like my old home—or like yours.

"Reina was wrong, or so I thought. This longer-than-natural life was not a curse, not to me. I invented a plethora of medicines and treatments and met so many people, and I did not regret it, even as I outlived and missed my friends. I had time to watch stories, technologies, and language morph through the ages." A wistful smile graced Bathilda's face. "I enjoyed my life, and I was quite inclined to do whatever I could to keep it, thank you very much."

Bathilda's smile faded. "But my oldest friend was also right, in a way. I had nightmares of Death's sickle blade. And it seemed that just as I'd started to resign myself to growing old and creaky, some sickness would strike, some disease that my remedies wouldn't cure. Once, it was an affliction that struck the king on my watch. Another time, it was a plague that swept through the peninsula. And once—I was not lying about this, lass—once, it was Gailstone. But scarcely anyone remembers Gailstone because it fell to ruin nearly two hundred years ago."

Corrin's thoughts whirred. Two hundred years ago. *That* was why those ruins she'd found had seemed so ancient, as had the writing in their book. It made sense now. And didn't, because Bathilda's story was astounding. Dreadful. Incredible. Upending Corrin's sense of reality, a bit.

And Bathilda wasn't done.

"I would find reason to send someone into the Gloamwood in pursuit of the legendary fruit. I would pick someone I believed would be brave, clever, and likely to come back out again. I would tell myself that it was necessary—that the King couldn't die now, lest their unsuitable sibling seize the throne and bring Stalt to its knees; that I could not watch a plague devastate an entire populace when I knew a way to stop it; that I was a healer, a medic, and these risks and sacrifices were always for a good cause.

"I would always eat a portion of the fruit and save its extract and seeds for the following decades. I convinced myself that my life was worth prolonging, that it served the greater good to prolong it. No one knew medicine as well as I did. My wisdom had averted tragedies. I could teach others some of it, could take on apprentices, could meet with my fellow healers; but 'tis difficult to convey in one lifetime what I've learned over many.

"And then I moved to Oddment. And I met you."

Corrin straightened in surprise at the shift.

Bathilda beamed, her expression alight with such warmth and pride that it took Corrin aback, shot straight to her heart and pulled unexpectedly on its strings. "Corrin," Bathilda said, "you are remarkable."

Before Corrin could recover and respond, Bathilda continued.

"At first, you were a toddler like any other, with a chubby face and tiny hands, and a child's shaky grasp of language. And then you were seven, teary-eyed with blood gushing out of your forearm, and by the time I was done patching you up, you'd learned what the veins and arteries are, and why a healer might sew up skin like the everyday person sews fabric.

"By nine, you knew most of my cold remedies by heart. By ten, you could name the major organs and muscles, and you could deduce when to apply heat and when to apply cold, when to splint and when no splint was needed. By eleven, you had memorized every bone in the human body and knew the various ways they could break, and which breaks were easiest to recover from. By twelve, I could trust you to help me remove an arrow or sew up a wound yourself. At fourteen, you were reading some of my centuries-old textbooks. And at sixteen, you were helping with my medicinal research and treating patients without supervision. They trusted you. As did I.

"You are the most brilliant student I've ever had. You are also one of the most kind, and quick in a crisis."

Quick in a crisis? When had Corrin *ever* been—

She remembered saving her brothers from drowning. Swiftly treating the guard who got shot with the arrow. Rushing to stitch up knife wounds from a neighbor's kitchen accident. Helping diagnose and providing an antidote for a case of poisoning, when someone had misidentified berries they'd gathered. And, more recently, patching up Bruin, escaping the Bandit King, rescuing Makur from the giant snake…

Oh.

Bathilda gazed upon her knowingly, proudly. Her ancient hand reached over and rested lightly upon Corrin's young one. Bent fingers over straight ones, wrinkled skin over smooth and freckled. Warmly, Bathilda said, "And so when all of Oddment fell ill, I entrusted you with this dangerous quest, because I truly believed you the most likely to succeed. I'm very glad you did, more so than I know how to express." She squeezed Corrin's fingers. "Thank you for going, and for coming back whole and well. Thank you for becoming the brave, gentle soul that you are. And thank you for letting me rest easy, my dear. Because I can, now, knowing that this world and these people have you."

Bathilda withdrew and reclined in her armchair, finally finished. Her eyes had gone soft and misty, her smile fond.

Corrin felt so many things at once that she could scarcely begin to untangle them. She felt sad and betrayed, warm and gratified, and still peculiarly confused, and she was at a loss for what to say in response. Her eyes prickled, and she swiped dampness off her cheeks. When she finally did speak, her voice was all clogged and nasally. "S-so did you have some of the fruit this time? A-are you going to stay awhile longer?"

"Aye, child."

"A-and... Did you..."

"I did not hoard the seeds, no. Though I did plant a few, as you deduced, just to see if it would work this time." Bathilda gestured to the pots of dirt. "Wishful thinking on my part, I know. But by my reasoning, it couldn't hurt to try while I had them. I'd never tried this particular soil in this particular town, so I thought, perhaps." She sighed. "If we could find a way to grow them, it would mean a tremendous leap in medicine. They're a general strengthening agent, a stimulant for the body's defense and repair mechanisms unlike anything else I've seen. They're of surprisingly limited use against the winter sniffles, though."

Corrin cracked a smile. It was common healer wisdom: one could not banish the winter sniffles, but only treat the symptoms.

"I think you've had enough of running about for a bit, hm? How about I brew us a pot of tea, and we let ourselves stop and relax for a while?"

Corrin acquiesced. Bathilda pulled out her dented tea kettle and set the water to boil, and soon enough the two of them had cups in their hands, tendrils of steam rising from the contents: a concoction of chamomile and lavender, with the dried leaves and petals unfurling at the bottom. The tea smelled sweet and the hearth crackled merrily, and the ceramic cup warmed Corrin's hands through to their joints. She blew the steam away and sipped, as did Bathilda.

Peace settled over her like a blanket. She had done it. She was home. Oddment had healed. And in this moment, all was well.

CHAPTER TWENTY-NINE

Epilogue

Winter followed on the heels of Oddment's recovery.

The first snow was barely a dusting. But over the course of the next month, more dustings came, and then the first blizzard. When it abated, it left a clear sky and powdery snowdrifts heaped up to the waist.

Frendel burst out the door, whooping in excitement. Sam trailed cautiously after him, and Corrin followed, breathing in the crisp air and listening to the crunch of snow under her boots. She watched Frendel tug enthusiastically on Sam's arm and drag him up, up atop the walls; watched him stick his tongue out and urge Sam to do the same; watched the ghost of a smile curve the corners of Sam's mouth, though he still seemed distracted and worried. Petuni had shaken off the illness, just like everyone else who had been fed the fruit from the Gloamwood. But being so near death for so long had left her weak, underweight, and dispirited, more cautious than Corrin remembered. Every time she opted to stay inside, to hide from the world and sleep more than most children her age slept, Sam worried incessantly.

Corrin tried not to fuss. *She just needs time to recover. She'll be okay… and I've got to take Sam's mind off his worries.*

So she crept up behind her brothers and lobbed a snowball at Frendel's back.

"*AAAAA! SISTER MONSTER!*"

Corrin grinned. She was already shaping another snowball. It packed together nicely—the weather was just warm enough for the snow to stick—and thanks to her leather gloves, it hadn't turned her fingers numb yet. "I am the dread snowbeast," she intoned, and dodged Frendel's loosely assembled counterattack. Sam kept back, but she could see it: a laugh burbling up inside him, making his eyes crinkle and his smile broaden into something more genuine. "Are ye puny adventurers trespassing on my wall? Shall I strike you down with my wintry powers?" She held up her hands and curled her fingers like claws. "Raaaaar!"

Frendel teetered precariously close to the edge, his arms full of snow. Corrin tensed and readied herself to lunge forward and catch him, but Sam caught his sleeve and kept him steady. Frendel straightened and declared, "We are the deadly duo! We shall defeat you, foul winter beast!"

Sam giggled.

"Back me up," Frendel stage whispered.

"We'll defeat you," said Sam obligingly, and snatched some snow from Frendel's arms.

"Hey! That's mine!"

"It's too much. We need to throw smaller amounts. Like this!" He packed his helping into a neat little ball and hurled it at Corrin's stomach. It hit the sturdy outer layer of her winter doublet and burst apart.

"Aaaah!" Corrin cried. "How dare you use my wintry domain against me! I am wounded! I must retreat!"

"See?" said Sam triumphantly.

The twins followed the attack with more missiles—Frendel's loose and clumpy, Sam's compact and carefully shaped. Corrin waved her clawed hands wildly and backpedaled, taking care not to step too close to the side. She pretended to roar and made threats of various kinds. "I'll string you up by your boot laces," she warned, as Frendel and Sam advanced on her. "Or drop you in the lake and turn your toes into ice blocks. I'll munch on you for breakfast, mix you in with—agh—winterberry soup—I must devour you—no, no, I cannot die here—argh!" She swooned dramatically and fell backward. The snow and her doublet muffled the impact. "You have slain me," she said, as she lay belly up and held aloft a single, twitching hand. "Done me in by my own snow. I am defeated. Gone. Death by—oof."

Frendel and Sam piled on top of her, cackling.

"Aye," said Corrin solemnly, "you've done me in. Not a breath of life left in my body. Not a trickle of power left in my fingertips—oh wait—" Quick as a squirrel, she grabbed two handfuls of snow and stuffed them down the backs of Frendel's and Sam's necks. They shrieked. "'Tis the curse of the snow beast's spirit! My vengeance before Death guides me to the—ppbbthagh coldcoldcold!"

The twins had shoved snow in her face.

Corrin brushed it away, then went limp. "Okay," she said, with the air of one resigned to her defeat. She heaved a sigh for effect. "You win."

Frendel whooped. Sam grinned.

"If you could get off me now, that would be much appreciated."

Sam obligingly scrambled off. Frendel didn't move.

Corrin grabbed him by the shoulders and shoved him back, just enough for her to squirm out from underneath. "You're a poor winner, you are," she accused him. "Once a person's down, you're always supposed to do the courteous thing and let them get back on their feet. Especially when that person's your dear beloved sibling, your blood relation, the pure heart who lets you hide with her during thunderstorms and helps you find elderberries. Also," she added, her tone turning ominous, "the person who knows foul potions and poisons as well as metalworkers know their ores."

"Uh-huh," said Frendel, clearly not believing her.

Before Corrin could respond, a small voice called out from below: "Hi."

As one, Corrin, Sam, and Frendel peered over the ramparts.

Petuni was bundled up to her ears in a thick cloak, scarf, and hat. She peeked out from between the folds and rested a mittened hand on the vines that crawled the walls, a glint of determination in her eyes.

"Hello!" called Frendel, grinning.

"Petuni!" cried Sam joyfully. He scrambled down to greet her, nimble as a squirrel. Corrin watched with a spark of fondness as he steadfastly accompanied Petuni up the vine wall, giving her little boosts and steadying her whenever she faltered.

Eventually, the two children clambered over the ramparts and plopped down next to Corrin. Petuni wheezed from the exertion and slumped against Sam, who politely stayed put for her. He looked a smidge concerned.

Frendel frowned at Petuni and Sam, then addressed Corrin. "Hey, can you tell us about your quest again?"

Sam turned to her hopefully.

Corrin considered it. She'd told Frendel, Sam, and Petuni the story at least five times. But in each retelling, she'd change a few details, make the story a little bit new. Sometimes she wrestled the trolls and sometimes the dragon talked, and sometimes the firebird whispered in her ear. Sometimes she mentioned the Riddle Beast, and sometimes she didn't. Sometimes she added a sea monster to the voyage. Sometimes the Bandit King had claws and fangs, and other times she was human, but larger than life. Sometimes Corrin claimed that Death herself had awaited her at the Tree of Life, ethereal and shadowy, with a glimmering scythe just like in the olden tales. Other times, she spoke of the Churikin and of how she'd ridden on Makur's back, and how the trolls were all right, really, if you could sway them into being friends. "They're very soft," she'd said. "Like cat fur, but thicker."

She decided that this time, she'd add a hidden fairy village to the ruins, and the Bandit King would ride a griffin and have scales on her arms, and Amella would defeat the griffin while Tenno defeated the King. She drew Sam, Frendel, and Petuni close, and they all sat on the wall with their feet dangling, sides pressed together, as Corrin picked up the familiar threads of adventure and rewove them.

Halfway through her retelling, a red blur sped at her out of seemingly nowhere and cannonballed into her knee. She blinked down at a heap of crimson and orange feathers, fire-bright against their snowy surroundings.

A crested head with beady black eyes and a curved hawk's beak popped up. The body underneath straightened. Wings flared out, once, then snapped back in. The firebird dug its talons into her pant leg for stability. It—*she?*—stared up at Corrin expectantly and cooed.

"Junior?"

Junior chirruped and stuck out one leg, to which was fastened a small scroll. Her feathers fluffed up against the cold, and she shifted impatiently as Corrin undid the twine bow that held the message in place. The moment it was off, Junior shook out her talons and nestled up against Corrin's stomach, making vague complaining sounds. She was very warm, Corrin noticed, warmer even than Tiptoes.

"What's that?" demanded Frendel.

"Her name's Junior. She's a firebird."

"Like the one who defeated the dragon?"

"Yes, the very one. Braver than the biggest warrior, she is." Corrin tried to open the scroll with her kludgy leather-clad hands, then decided it was far too troublesome and shed one of her gloves. The cold made her skin tingle, but she could feel when her fingertips caught the edge of the parchment. She unrolled it and peered at the contents. It was written in a hand that started out neat but grew less and less tidy until it was nearly illegible at the end. It looked as if the author were running late and trying to cram in the last bits quickly. Or maybe once he started writing, he was just bursting to tell her…

This was from Tenno, she assumed. Had to be, given the method of delivery.

Both the twins leaned in to read the letter along with her, and Petuni peeked over Sam's shoulder.

Dear Corrin,

I hope this finds you well! Are you keeping your hearth well fed with wood? Eating enough warm food? Bundling up? Please don't let your toes turn blue. I realize you know this better than I do, so I will trust that you're doing all of the aforementioned.

This may surprise you, but I never did make it back to the peninsula. A firebird from Ragnor carried orders to make for the capital instead and take a post there. I arrived a fortnight ago. I think it's grown even colder here than it has in Oddment, though less snowy (or so I've heard). The winds howl along the main roads, and we get blasted with ice. Junior hates it. I think she'll be glad to visit you.

Ah, I'm getting off track. My deployment to the capital was no coincidence or standard military rotation (we're switched around every few years… usually along with our captains). The king wanted to meet with me and hear my account of the Gloamwood.

I had never met the king before. They're an eccentric character. But they're a good enough character to be all right with me questioning their ideas, and based on our historical records, that is more than can be said for some of our ancestral rulers.

Please remember that as I get to the main point of this letter.

After I described your quest, the perils of the forest, the alliance you forged with the trolls, and the efficacy of the fruit as a medicine, the king decided that they wanted to meet you—and potentially appoint you as an envoy. To the trolls, specifically.

You would have only me, one or two other trained guards, and Amella (if she is willing) come along to accompany and protect you. Their reasoning is sound; they think a smaller number and familiar faces will help with kindling friendship instead of distrust. Even so, I do not like this idea. I especially do not like the idea of sending you with such limited backup. Who knows what dangers we might encounter before reaching the trolls? Or what if diplomatic efforts go awry, and we lose their goodwill?

Let me emphasize that you do not have to agree to the king's request. If you want to go back to Oddment after talking with the king, they won't stop you.

They seem insistent on at least meeting with you, though.

I will visit at the first sign of spring and offer you an escort to the capital.

Wishing you all the best,

Tenno

Corrin read it again, and then once more, to confirm that she hadn't misunderstood. The king wanted to meet her? Wanted to have her be a diplomat?

And apparently, the king wanted to send Corrin, Tenno, and Amella back to the Gloamwood, with maybe one or two more people, after hearing Tenno's account. Corrin wasn't sure what to think of the king's willingness to take that risk. If Tenno's report spoke of all Corrin had faced during her quest—the dragon, the giant snake, the tenuous trust Corrin had gained from the trolls and what they would have done to her if she hadn't—Corrin's first thought wouldn't have been, *I should send them all straight back into the jaws of danger, to broker treaties with the trolls when we could leave well enough alone! Yes, brilliant idea!*

What did the king hope to gain? Surely they wouldn't bother building an alliance with the trolls unless it could benefit either themself or Stalt. Perhaps they thought they could acquire more of the fruit? Perhaps they were tempted, despite all the trouble and warnings?

She hadn't told Tenno of the fruit's life-lengthening properties. But he'd witnessed its effects as a healing agent, not just with curing the plague but with hastening Limerick's recovery from a stab wound, and he had clearly highlighted it in his report. That alone might have been enough to interest the king. But Tenno must have informed them that the supply was limited, that it all came from the one tree guarded by the Churikin; that if the critters lost that food source, they'd run amok and spread disease with their bites…

Maybe the king thought they could make use of even a small quantity of the fruit. Or maybe they thought they could trade other goods with the trolls—foreign plants and meats and the like. Or maybe they were interested in trading knowledge, or in friendliness and the long-term, fuzzily defined potential to help each other in times of trouble. Somehow. Despite being separated by weeks of journey and a mountain at their closest border.

"You have to take us with you," said Frendel, startling Corrin out of her thoughts.

"No," she said on reflex. Then, after having a heartbeat to actually consider what he said: "Not a snowflake's chance in the forge. It's too dangerous for ten-year-olds—"

"We're eleven now."

"Eleven-year-olds. Same difference. You aren't old enough for these kinds of adventures."

"What's so special about being an adult?" demanded Sam.

Corrin turned to stare at him, startled by his defiance. Sam was almost never defiant. Mischievous, yes. Tricky, yes. Inclined to try to charm and squirm his way out of trouble, perhaps. But he'd never been the sort to push back and argue. That had always been a more Frendel-y thing to do.

"You almost died," Sam said. "You're seventeen and you had my lucky rock and you still might've never come back."

And oh, his words sank in like a dagger to the heart. He was right. They could have lost her forever. And he was acutely aware of that, it seemed. She hadn't really been thinking of that when she'd told and retold all those stories of her adventures to the twins. She could've made the dragon's fire a smidge less close to crisping her, or not mentioned how she'd almost been shredded by troll claws.

Sam continued. "If we came along, then we could help you. You may be an adult, but you're not that much bigger than us. We'd be stronger together." And then came his owlet eyes, wide and brimming over with sincerity, twisting the knife.

Churikin curse it.

Corrin mustered up her resolve against his pleading face and said, "It'll be safer this time. The Bandit King's gone, and I've already befriended the trolls. And I'll write you. I bet Junior would gladly carry letters between us." She caught herself, caught what she'd just implied, and hastily added, "That's only if I go back to the Gloamwood. I might just go to the capital and tell the king I'd like to go straight home. I could tell them I'd rather chase you 'round Oddment and through the woods, make elderberry bread with Mum, and give no more thought to adventures."

Sam gave her a long, hard look. Eleven-year-olds, in Corrin's opinion, shouldn't be giving looks like that. "You're not going to do that, though. You want to go back, don't you?"

Corrin opened her mouth to protest.

She paused.

And she closed it.

Because by Death's sickle blade, Sam was right. While she'd rather never run into the dragon, fight giant snakes, or worry about being pounced on by creatures or bandits again, she'd like to travel with Amella and Tenno. She'd very much like to see Makur. And while she didn't know what kind of treaty the king had in mind and what could come of it, perhaps it could lead to something good. Maybe mended bridges, maybe new ones.

"You're right," Corrin admitted. "I do want to."

"So if it's going to be dangerous, we should come with you to help," said Sam confidently. "And if it really is not going to be so dangerous, then there's no reason for us not to come with you."

Well, that's a scarily convincing argument, she thought.

But no, his argument had a hole in it. They were forgetting something vital, and Corrin swiftly pointed it out. "Best of luck convincing Mum and Da of that. They'd much rather have you around, you know."

The twins shared a look. Corrin didn't like that look. It was the sort of look they shared right before they got themselves into mischief. And Petuni, wan and quiet though she was, looked like she was contemplating aiding and abetting them.

"Tenno won't be here 'til spring, anyway," Corrin said quickly, "so there's no need to think about it now." She stood up. Her knees crackled and popped, and her joints felt stiff. "I should go see if Bathilda wants my help. Why don't you go hunt and forage with Da and Mum? We've had pickled roots and dried meats three nights in a row." She chuckled as they grimaced, and she watched them scramble down, down the walls and scamper off toward home, with Petuni in tow. Da and Mum were likely snuggling in front of the hearth, as they were wont to do during winter.

Corrin tucked Tenno's letter in her vest pocket and put her glove back on. She took a moment to flex her fingers, get blood flowing through them again, then clambered down as well.

However, she did not make for Bathilda's home.

Instead, she made her way to a familiar door near the gate, with a massive boar's tusk mounted upon it and the ever-unflappable Oatmuncher drowsing outside. Oatmuncher was cloaked in a beast of burden's blanket, thick as Corrin's bedcovers twice over. She paused to pet his nose, and he blinked contentedly. She crunched her way past him and up to the door, and she knocked thrice.

The door flew open. Amella, bundled in her winter cloak and with a bottle of ale in her hand, beamed down at her. "If it isn't my favorite healer! Come on in, have a drink with me."

Corrin stepped inside. Amella ushered her to her hearth, and Corrin gratefully absorbed the warmth emanating from Amella's hearth-fire, which was well fed and crackling merrily. She savored her drink, too, and felt a different warmth blooming in her chest and spreading to her toes. It was winter ale, brewed strong to chase away the cold.

"I have meat, too," said Amella happily. "Caught two snowshoe hares yesterday. I could make us a stew, tell you a couple of stories."

"Can't," said Corrin with genuine regret, "I need to go see Bathilda in a bit. But there is something I want to talk to you about."

"Oh?"

Corrin withdrew Tenno's letter and passed it to Amella. She watched as Amella's eyes roved over the scroll and as her brows rose higher and higher, until at last Amella handed it back, a grin spreading across her face. Her eyes sparked, warm and bright as her hearth-fire. Corrin's heart leapt. "So," Corrin said. "What do you think of another adventure?"

Acknowledgements

Firstly, a tremendous thank-you to all my friends and family who have supported and encouraged me along the way. My life is better with you in it, and I love you all dearly. Additionally, special thanks of those of you who beta read one or more versions of *Into the Gloamwood*: Manuel Badillo, Scott Bennett-Jeffreys, Phil Chodrow, Alexis Gomez, Agnes Kamasi, Michael A. Luna, Laura Matthews, Dawn Matthews, Joseph Matthews, and Steven Presser. This story is better and stronger because of your feedback.

Thank you again to Laura for feedback on the cover art. You're an amazing artist and ecologist, and I treasure your insights into both those fields.

I'd like to thank, with all my heart, my fiction professors from the undergraduate creative writing program at Northwestern University, Chris Abani and Juan Martinez. I wouldn't be the writer I am today without the mentorship, feedback, and encouragement you gave me. Fun fact: the seed of this novel was planted in a short story I wrote for the introductory fiction class! Obviously much has changed since then, but that story harbors the first glimmerings of this novel's premise and heart.

Thank you to Sarah Nicolas as well. I may have foregone the traditional publishing route, but your feedback on my synopsis, query, and sample pages, as well as your insight into the publishing process, was still valuable and greatly appreciated. Additionally, thank you for Writing Wednesdays—and thanks to Bess Carnan and everyone else there as well. Those sessions always help me get stuff done, and some of those nights went to edits for *Gloamwood.*

Thank you to my friend Emmett Stelter for doing writing sprints and productivity nights with me; those, too, often went to *Gloamwood.*

And thank you to the folks from Boston Writers' Meetup, who helped me continue my writing habit in 2017-2023.

Thank you to my friend and fellow writer Preety Sidhu for helping me connect to other writers, providing insight into the literary landscape, and listening to me ramble about *Gloamwood*. And thank you for encouraging me to get out of my apartment and have adventures around the city together!

Thank you to Sally Kiebdaj, who kindly pointed me to multiple resources and answered several of my questions when I was editing and revising the e-book for accessibility.

Lastly, I'd like to thank my readers. Thank you for picking up this novel and engaging with this story. I appreciate all of you, and I wish you all the best.

About the Author

Sarah G. Matthews is a writer and software developer who grew up in the Midwest and lives and works near Boston, where she spins fantastical tales about creatures, friendships, kindness, and occasional mortal peril. Her shorter work has appeared in *Daily Science Fiction* and in the Boston branch of Grown-Up Story Time (GUST), a local storytelling event.

She studied English writing and physics at Northwestern University, where she completed her BA with an honors thesis (fiction) in 2016. She also co-organized a writer's group called Boston Writers' Meetup from 2019-2023.

In addition to writing, she practices aikido and has made some amazingly kind friends by throwing them (with permission!). She also draws on occasion and has covered her corkboard with Post-it note doodles, which is definitely what Post-it notes are for.

A list of her works is available at www.sarahgmatthews.com.

Appendix: Troll-Tongue Glossary

While many words in troll-tongue are the same as their Staltish counterparts or can be intuited, some are entirely foreign and incomprehensible to the average Staltian. The most common of these from Corrin's adventure are listed below.

Asuk = ask
Bairn = baby, child
Bibbinhead = fool, especially of the stubborn or reckless variety
Bidum = friend, ally
Bodin = body (alive or dead)
Cheng = change
Danku = thanks
Det = but; however
Dono = title for a local leader
Eyen = eye
Fikah = fine, okay, acceptable
Grek = think
Grekka = understand/know
Grok = talk, say
Gruk = remember
Har = hard, difficult
Harth = home
Harahket = call for attention
Hassark = hassle
Hingheket = greetings
Hrr = (thinking/musing/skeptical noise)
Iffen = if
Ikik = disease

Ikres = rescue
Impurrent = important
Inreska = to spare
Inresting = interesting
Ken = can
Krr = troll
Krrkin = trollkind, or adopted friend of the trolls
Lif = life
Namae = name
Nur = dark, night, or twilight
Punik = music
Punula = deity of the dream world
Purf = prove
Purfararg = challenge; call to prove oneself in a duel or fight
Raar = noise of general exasperation
Rahrg = fight
Serdra = snake
Snargak = snack; food
Tarth = teeth
Tintur = tease, pester, bully
Und = and
Watchet = watch
Wid = with
Wis = wise

Wyddscatch = Literally, adulting catch. Idiomatically, adulthood questing ceremony in which a barely-grown troll ventures out to catch or discover something really impressive. Also refers to the thing that they hunt and catch.

Wykrr = adult troll
Wyrman = human
Yus = Yes

www.ingramcontent.com/pod-product-compliance
Lightning Source LLC
LaVergne TN
LVHW100515110826
845146LV00002B/653
* 9 7 9 8 9 9 4 8 5 4 8 1 5 *